2/03

WITHDRAWN

OFFICIALLY NOTED

Stain and Cover cs 6/13

Death at
Glamis Castle

Death at
Glamis Castle

ROBIN PAIGE

BERKLEY PRIME CRIME, NEW YORK

DEATH AT GLAMIS CASTLE

A Berkley Prime Crime Book
Published by The Berkley Publishing Group,
a division of Penguin Putnam Inc.,
375 Hudson Street, New York, New York 10014.

Please visit the authors' website at
www.mysterypartners.com

First edition: March 2003

Library of Congress Cataloging-in-Publication Data

Paige, Robin.
Death at Glamis Castle / Robin Paige.— 1st ed.
p.   cm.
ISBN 0-425-18847-7 (alk. paper)
1. Sheridan, Kate (Fictitious character)—Fiction.   2. Sheridan, Charles
(Fictitious character)—Fiction.   3. Glamis Castle (Scotland)—Fiction.
4. Glamis (Scotland)—Fiction.   5. Women novelists—Fiction.

PS3566.A3396 D45 2003
813'.6—dc21
2002038553

PRINTED IN THE UNITED STATES OF AMERICA

10   9   8   7   6   5   4   3   2   1

TO THE READER

We occasionally (and deliberately) leave plot elements unresolved in our books, with the intention of taking them up later. *Death at Glamis Castle* is a continuation of two previous books: *Death at Whitechapel*, which dealt with Prince Albert Victor, Duke of Clarence and Avondale, eldest son of Bertie and Alexandra, and heir presumptive to the throne of Great Britain; and *Death at Rottingdean*, in which a German agent, Ludwig von Hauptmann, attempts to smuggle arms into England in preparation for an invasion. In this book, we continue the story of the unfortunate prince for whom the crown was a curse that he could not escape, and his unwitting role in the Great Game.

Robin Paige
Bill and Susan Albert
Bertram, Texas
December 2001

This book is dedicated to the memory of
Charles P. Albert
1908–1999

CAST OF CHARACTERS
* Indicates historical persons

Glamis Castle: Visitors, Residents, Staff

Charles, Lord Sheridan, Baron Somersworth

Lady Kathryn Ardleigh Sheridan, Baroness Somersworth, aka Beryl Bardwell

*Prince Albert Victor Christian Edward (Eddy), aka Lord Osborne, Duke of Clarence and Avondale, eldest son of King Edward VII and Queen Alexandra

*Princess Victoria (Toria), daughter of King Edward VII and Queen Alexandra

*Lady Glamis (Cecilia Bowes-Lyon), wife of Lord Glamis, eldest son of Claude Bowes-Lyon, thirteenth Earl of Strathmore

*Lady Elizabeth Bowes-Lyon, youngest daughter of Lord and Lady Glamis, afterward wife of King George V and mother of Queen Elizabeth II, beloved as the Queen Mother

Angus Duff, Glamis estate factor

Simpson, house steward

Hilda Memsdorff MacDonald, housemaid (deceased)

Flora MacDonald, housemaid, daughter of Hilda MacDonald

Gladys, housemaid

Mrs. Leslie, housekeeper

Mrs. Thompson, cook

Mrs. Wollie, laundress

Sally, kitchenmaid

Douglas Hamilton, assistant gamekeeper

Glamis Village, Residents and Visitors

Doctor Henry Ogilvy, village physician and the King's Coroner

Oliver Graham, village constable

Herman Memsdorff, visitor from Edinburgh, nephew of Hilda MacDonald

Alan Donovan, visiting collector of Scottish ballads

Taiso, itinerant gypsy tinker

Military and Diplomatic Personnel

Colonel John Paddington, Coldstream Guards

Captain Andrew Kirk-Smythe, British Intelligence

*Friedrich von Holstein, First Counselor, Political Department, German Foreign Ministry

Count Ludwig von Hauptmann, German Intelligence

Speed, bonnie boat, like a bird on the wing,
   "Onward," the sailors cry;
Carry the lad that's born to be king
   Over the sea to Skye.

"Skye Boat Song"

Glamis thou art, and Cawdor; and shalt be
What thou art promised.

Macbeth
William Shakespeare

PROLOGUE

Huddled in the back of the cold, damp cave, under a heap of loose straw, the man woke with a start. His hands were bound behind him and he was gagged, nor was this the full extent of his discomforts. He couldn't remember when he had last eaten a full meal, or worn dry clothing, or slept in a dry bed. All he could remember was the cold, wet, unending slog through wild and desolate glens and dismal forests, where he stumbled often, his clothes wet through from falling into rippling burns, his arms and legs scraped and bruised from tumbling down rocky banks. It seemed as if he had been wandering for centuries; his past life, whatever that may once have been, was now utterly obliterated, and he recalled only that he had been shut up somewhere in a castle, was mindful only that he must reach the Isle of Skye, where there was refuge and safety and a ship that would take him to France.

He closed his eyes, wishing that his head did not hurt, that he could think more clearly, that he knew what day it was. He had been dragged from the castle in the evening—one or two evenings ago?—and had been brought to this cave, and bound and gagged and hidden under the straw. From time to time, when both of the men were there, they'd let him loose to answer the call of nature. Then they'd given him a piece of dry bread and a cup of tea, and tied him up again, heaping straw over him to hide him.

He groaned despairingly. His men, those faithful Highlanders who had rallied to the Stuart flag of Bonnie Prince Charlie—where were they now? Lost in the forest? Dead on the bloody field at Culloden? Or just as likely waylaid and murdered by Cumberland's bloody British troops, who had for the past months pursued him through the Highlands like a wounded stag. And it was not only him they were after, but all those who had given him their trust, killing and plundering and burning, even among the peaceful clans who had not joined the Forty-five Rebellion.

And where was Flora, the young woman who had served him so long and so devotedly? If only she were here, all would be well, for she had the strength he seemed now to lack, courage and strength and common sense. If Flora were with him, she would see him to Skye, and safety, and the ship to France.

Even if he could manage to free himself, he knew he would never reach Skye without Flora's help.

Without Flora, he was lost.

CHAPTER ONE

Wednesday, 14 August 1901
Housesteads, Northumberland

*We now enter Housesteads, this city of the dead. All is silent;
but dead indeed to all human sympathies must the soul of that
man be who, in each broken column, each turf-covered mound,
each deserted hall, does not recognize a voice telling him,
trumpet-tongued, of the rise and fall of empires, of the doom
and ultimate destiny of man.*

The Handbook of the Roman Wall, 1885
J. Collingwood Bruce

Finding a comfortable spot among the basalt outcrop-
pings, Kate Sheridan set down her camera, dropped her
canvas pack, and took several long breaths. Climbing to the
top of the craggy peak had not been easy, but her perch
afforded a stunning view of the rugged north country.

Below and to the east, she could see the remains of the
old Roman Wall erected at the command of the Emperor
Hadrian, snaking across the green hills of Northumberland,
its spiny ridge lost at last in the late-summer haze and clouds
along the distant horizon. Nearer at hand lay what was left
of the stone walls of Housesteads, the fortified Roman camp
where her husband, Lord Charles Sheridan, was helping to
complete the excavation of the main street, the *via princi-*

palis, in the company of five or six members of the Newcastle Society of Antiquaries, and where Kate had been taking photographs. Earlier in the day, she had walked through the ancient fort with something like awe, treading on the stones that had been worn by the feet of Roman soldiers, tracing with her fingers the Latin words dedicating a stone altar to Jupiter, reflecting on the rise and fall of that long-ago empire and its gods, now all but forgotten in the crusade to build a new British Empire.

Kate picked up her camera—a compact twin-lens model—and looked through the viewfinder. This was a fine vantage point from which to take photographs, and she snapped several, intending to develop them that evening in her new portable developing tent. As she turned to take another, she noticed her husband, who was seated far beneath her on the stones of Hadrian's Wall, gazing contemplatively over what had once been the home of the fierce and barbaric Picts. Not far away, their Panhard was parked at a precarious angle on the slope beneath Housesteads—the very first automobile, according to the Newcastle group, ever to have jolted its bone-jarring way to this section of the Wall.

When Kate finished taking pictures, she sat down and opened her pack, pulling out the packet of letters she had received that morning at the Princess Lodge in Haydon Bridge, where she and Charles had stayed the night before. The first smelled faintly of lemon furniture polish and was from her housekeeper Amelia, letting her know of the goings-on at Bishop's Keep, where Kate and Charles lived for much of the year: the cozy, domestic details of kitchen and garden, of household staff and the nearby village of Dedham, that made home seem suddenly sweet and precious to her. They had been away for a fortnight on this trip, and now that autumn was almost upon them, she was anxious to be back in East Anglia.

The second letter, informative but smelling of Indian cigars, was from Mr. Crombie, the master of Kate's School for the Useful Arts. The school admitted a dozen women, most of whom came daily from the neighboring villages to study horticulture, dairying, bee-keeping, and orchard management. This ambitious project had been Kate's dream for several years. If it succeeded, it would give its graduates the skills which would enable them to earn an independent living in rural areas, without the necessity of moving to a city to find work in some factory or sweatshop.

The third letter, much briefer and smelling of typewriter ink, came from her editor, thanking her for the manuscript of *Death on the Moor*, which she had submitted just before she and Charles had come away on holiday, and promising its publication in the early spring. This was indeed good news, but she had saved the very best letter until last. Chatty and casually affectionate, it was from Patrick, the fifteen-year-old boy whom she and Charles had taken as their own and who was now at Newmarket as an apprentice to George Lambton, one of the country's leading horse trainers. Newmarket was near enough to Bishop's Keep for Patrick to come home on the weekends, and she was looking forward with pleasure to seeing him again.

Kate replaced the letters in her pack and took out a fountain pen and notebook. Under the pseudonym of Beryl Bardwell, she had been a published writer for seven or eight years, first in her native New York (where she lived in a garret and composed penny dreadfuls for a sensation-hungry public), and after '94 in England, where she had enjoyed a gratifying success as a novelist. *Death on the Moor* was a gothic sort of thing, set on the wild, wind-swept reaches of Dartmoor and inspired by an adventure that she and Charles and Conan Doyle had shared earlier in the year. For her next effort, Beryl was thinking of an historical novel in the style of Sir Walter Scott, whose Waverly novels Kate was rereading with great delight. Unfortunately, historical fictions were not quite the thing in these modern days; with the death of the old Queen, the advent of a new King, and the coming of the twentieth century, everyone seemed to want to look into the future, not the past. But the estate bequeathed Kate by her aunts allowed Beryl to write whatever she pleased, and she had been further freed by her marriage to Charles, a landed peer—although his dutiful attendance in the House of Lords took her to London for longer periods than she liked and required her to perform tedious social obligations which she abhorred.

Kate gazed out across the landscape. For a time, she and Beryl had toyed with the idea of writing a novel set during the Roman occupation of Britain, but while they had enjoyed their visit to the Wall and had been impressed no end by the ancient fortifications, they hadn't been inspired. In fact, Beryl's well of inspiration seemed to have run entirely dry, and she couldn't seem to find anything that enticed her. Now, after making a few notes about the landscape, just in case Beryl changed her mind about Roman Britain, Kate put the notebook away and picked up her camera again, thinking to take a photograph of Charles, who was still sitting on the Wall, gazing northward in the direction of Scotland. He did not seem aware that he was being approached from the rear by a man on horseback, in a very great hurry. The hair on the back of Kate's neck prickled as she recognized the man as the local constable, whom they had met the week before. She watched for a moment as the constable dismounted from his horse, ran up to Charles, and handed him an envelope.

With a small sigh, she stood up and reached for her pack. She had the feeling that their leisurely holiday was about to be interrupted.

CHAPTER TWO

TO LORD CHARLES SHERIDAN HAYDON BRIDGE NORTHUMBER-
LAND.

REQUEST YOU MEET SPECIAL TRAIN ARRIVING HAYDON BRIDGE
SHORTLY STOP OUR MUTUAL FRIEND E.R. REQUIRES ASSISTANCE
IN MATTER OF GRAVEST IMPORTANCE FOR WHICH YOU ARE
UNIQUELY QUALIFIED STOP YR SERVANT ANDREW KIRK-SMYTHE
STOP

As he sat on Hadrian's Wall, facing north, Charles was gazing out across Caledonia, the wild land that lay beyond this northernmost border of the Roman Empire. In his imagination, he was seeing the shadowy ghosts of the legions of Roman soldiers and enslaved Britons who, some two millenia before, had labored tirelessly to construct the ancient fortification on which he now sat, block by quarried block. They worked at the order of the Emperor Hadrian, who had conceived the great engineering scheme as much to keep his Roman troops in as to keep the barbarian Picts out. Sensing that his vast territories had reached a size at which their governance was becoming unwieldy and fearing the expansionist passions of his generals, Hadrian had intended the Wall—which ultimately stretched from Wall-send on the Tyne to Bowness on the Solway—as the edge of empire, the boundary beyond which there would be no more territorial enlargement, no more subjugation of native peoples. For the Romans, this was to be the end of their world.

From somewhere behind and below him, Charles half-heard the sound of hoofbeats, and he shifted his position, still lost in thought. With Britain's possessions now flung across a quarter of the globe (that the sun never set on the British Empire was not just a figure of speech), Hadrian's Wall offered a lesson from which the government and the British people might well profit. Whether they would, of course, was doubtful, for the temptation to Empire was as strong at the beginning of this new century as it must have been in Hadrian's distant day. What would the Romans make of the land they had so arduously occupied, as it had been altered by time and technology, transformed into a world they would scarcely recognize? And what would they say of the British Empire, with its jingoistic fervor, its ir-repressible confidence in its own economic and technical superiority, its seemingly-incurable blindness to its many intractable social problems?

"Halloo, m'lord! Halloo!"

The shout shattered the noon-time silence and jarred Charles from his thoughts. He turned as the hail came again, from the village constable whom he and Kate had met when they arrived the week before at Haydon Bridge, where he had joined several members of the Newcastle Society to un-dertake another excavation at Housesteads and Kate had taken to photographing the ruins and tramping the ancient hills in search of inspiration for another of Beryl Bardwell's books.

"Beggin' yer lordship's pardon," the constable said breathlessly, as he dismounted from his horse. "I've been instructed t' locate ye and deliver this telegram." Reaching into the pocket of his blue tunic, he produced an envelope. "I'm also t' escort ye to the train."

"The train?" Charles took the envelope. "What train? Why?"

The constable straightened his shoulders, obviously feeling the gravity of his mission. "A special train, waitin' fer ye down below, sir." He puffed out his cheeks and added importantly, "The biggest engine I ever did see. They've cleared traffic fer it all th' way from Newcastle to Carlisle."

Charles slit the envelope with his pocket knife and scanned the telegram. It had been sent by Andrew Kirk-Smythe, whom he had met half a dozen years before at a house party given by Lady Warwick, where the young man was acting as bodyguard to the Prince of Wales. Charles had quite liked the young lieutenant and knew that he had done well for himself, continuing in the Royal service. The Prince of Wales was now King Edward VII, the "E.R." of Kirk-Smythe's telegram, the one man in the British Empire with the temerity to intrude upon Charles's holiday and expect his instant acquiescence.

Charles frowned. But what was this "matter of gravest importance"? And why all the secrecy? Obviously there was something here that Kirk-Smythe felt he could not trust to the discretion of the local telegraphist. With a sigh, Charles folded the telegram, thinking that it was a good thing that they had packed their baggage into the motorcar that morning. The prospect of returning to the soot and grime of London, only a fortnight after Parliament's adjournment, did not fill him with enthusiasm. Still, there was nothing for it but to find Kate, tell her the news, and board the train.

The constable was already mounting his horse. "Beg pardon, m'lord, but they're waitin' fer ye." He picked up the reins. "If I may be so bold as t' ask, sir, wot's so important that they're willin' to block th' line?"

Charles swung his legs off the wall. "I haven't the foggiest," he said.

A half-hour later, Kate piloting their Panhard through a wretchedly rutted lane, they bounced over a ridge and saw the train waiting for them on the North Eastern Railway line. Charles, still expecting only a rather ordinary locomotive and tender with a single coach, was startled to see a new Big Atlantic, the monster locomotive that was being operated experimentally by the North Eastern line. Its outsized boiler and firebox dwarfed those of ordinary locomotives, and it hissed steam through the exhaust vents of the piston cylinders like a leaky dragon, impatient to be about its business. To this massive engine and its formidable tender were coupled, not the single passenger coach that Charles had expected, but a Royal Mail coach, two baggage cars, and three large passenger coaches. A motley group of men lounged about the idling train, smoking and talking.

"My goodness," Kate gasped in dismay. "They've sent that behemoth for *us?* Where in the name of heaven is it taking us, Charles?"

"Not to London," Charles replied, "unless the engineer plans to run to Newcastle in reverse. The train's headed west, toward Carlisle."

"But what about our automobile?" Kate asked uneasily. "We're not going to leave it here, I hope."

As she pulled on the brake and brought the motorcar to a stop, a dapper, mustached gentleman in an ulster and felt hat, stick tucked under one arm, stepped smartly forward and stopped, snapping his heels together, his spine straight as a ramrod. Charles expected him to offer a salute, but after a second's hesitation, the mustached man extended his hand.

"Lord Sheridan," he said in clipped tones, "Paddington here. Apologize for the inconvenience. Good of you to break off your holiday and join our little expedition."

Charles climbed out and shook Paddington's hand. On the other side of the car, Kate was being helped out by several of the men. They were dressed, Charles saw, in civilian clothing, some of it ill-fitting and worn, although the men themselves were clean-shaven and well-groomed and carried themselves with a wary alertness. At the train windows sat others, similarly attired. Despite their efforts at disguise, they had the look of the military about them. But all available military men of this caliber had long ago been dispatched to fight the Boers, and there were virtually none left in England. None, that is, except—

Charles looked once more at the lounging men. "Household Guards?"

Paddington regarded him with a rueful smile. "Found us out, have you? Coldstream, First Battalion. Colonel Paddington, at your service." He executed a flourish with his stick.

"I see," Charles said crossly, not seeing at all. "What the dickens is this all about, Paddington?"

"Afraid I haven't a clue, sir," the colonel replied in a brisk, cheerful tone. "Happy to put you in the picture with what little I know, though, once we're under way. If you'll board—"

Charles put a hand on the motorcar. "Lady Sheridan is coming with me, of course," he said. "And the Panhard."

"Ah," the colonel said, less cheerfully. He glanced at

Kate and the motorcar. "Afraid my instructions didn't mention—" He managed a tactful cough. "That you were accompanied."

Kate raised the veil of her motoring hat and bestowed her most dazzling smile on Paddington. "The Panhard doesn't take up a great deal of space, Colonel, nor do I. Surely you have room enough for all three of us and our baggage."

Paddington visibly melted under her charm. "Right you are, your ladyship." He turned to one of the men. "Jenkins, be a good chap and clear some room among the kit so the motorcar can be loaded. And see to her ladyship's luggage."

At Jenkins's command, the lounging men dropped their cigarettes and sprang into action. The door of one of the baggage cars slid open, and several men leapt in. Bundles, boxes, and bags were shifted out of the way, and in a moment, four stout wooden poles were handed out and slid under the Panhard's chassis. One man stationed himself at the end of each pole.

"Make ready, men," Jenkins barked. "On three, now. One, two, three!" The Panhard was raised to shoulder height. "For'ard!"

The eight men stepped forward, and the vehicle was neatly maneuvered into the baggage compartment. When it was inside and secured, the men busied themselves repacking the boxes and bundles around it. The door slid shut, and without a word, they formed a file and climbed into the nearest passenger coach, just as the engine's huge brass whistle gave a deafening blast and steam hissed from the massive pistons. The dragon was anxious to get under way.

Colonel Paddington escorted Kate and Charles to the last car, a first-class carriage, and they took their seats. A moment later, a second whistle blast echoed down the green valley. The car clanked and knocked as the couplings took up the slack, and they were off to points unknown, abandoning the ghosts of Housesteads to the dim and distant past.

CHAPTER THREE

Near Kirriemuir, Forfarshire, Scotland

I wish I lived in a caravan,
With a horse to drive, like the pedlar-man!
Where he comes from, nobody knows,
Or where he goes to, but on he goes!

William Brighty Rands
1823–1882

Feri ando payi sitsholpe te nauyas.
It is in the water that one learns to swim.

Romany saying

The small gypsy camp at Roundyhill, on the road between Glamis and Kirriemuir, was a hubbub of activity.
A half-dozen raggle-taggle families prepared their dinners
over fires on the ground near their tents or compact traveling
wagons. Laughing children played among the dogs and cats
and ponies, kicking stones, tossing balls, chanting favorite
songs. Handsome women in bright-colored dresses and knit-
ted scarves stirred soups and bubbling stews in iron kettles,
and the air was rich with the scent of paprika-spiced stews
made of rabbit and pheasant, taken from the fields of nearby

estates. Swarthy-skinned men sat on their haunches around the fires, their dark eyes and white teeth and gold earrings flashing. As dinner was handed round by wives and sisters and mothers, they laid aside the odd bits of work that occupied them during the early evening: the mending of pots and pans; the weaving of baskets and repairing of bellows and harness; the whittling of wooden objects. For a little while after dinner, there would be music and lively dancing and stories around the fires, as a velvety darkness fell over the valley and the moon rose above the hills to the east. And then there would be quiet, as everyone retired to beds or blankets on the ground, and a nighttime's slumber.

The caravan had been at this encampment for several weeks, and all had settled into their routine of work and play. The young men were employed at their usual itinerant labors among the estates and farms in the Strathmore Valley, where their services were in much demand as farmers began the late-summer harvest of grains and vegetables. Old men whittled clothes pegs and skewers from wood gathered by the children, while the young women went into the neighboring villages and hamlets to hawk the hot pies and sweet tarts they baked, and the oldest women, bent and gnarled and wise-looking, told fortunes along the roads. A few of the bolder and more enterprising men did not work in the fields but rather prowled the neighborhood, looking for the odd pony or loose chicken or laundry left on the clothesline. Failing these, there were always rabbits and pheasants to poach, for the manor fields were rich in game, and the game-keepers were not able to watch every corner.

These particular gypsies were regular visitors to this area of Scotland, usually appearing in late summer and lingering through the harvest, then moving south as winter approached. They had traveled together for years, most of them, although there were a few new additions to the group: a family of knife grinders from Surrey, driving a small cart ingeniously fitted up with a forge; and a ragged tinker with raven-black hair who had joined the group just a few days ago, coming from Arbroath, a small fishing town on the coast.

The tinker, who went by the name of Taiso, was new to gypsy life and had acquired his fitted-out wagon, pony, and tin tinker's pig from an old man who could no longer make use of it. Now, his simple meal of rabbit stew simmering in a pot slung over the fire, Taiso sat smoking his pipe on the top step of his caravan, surveying the camp. His hair was dark and rough-cut, like the others, although his skin was several shades lighter, his eyes an almost glacial blue, and his nose patrician, in a narrow, aristocratic face. His features did not surprise the gypsies, for many of them counted middle-European nobility among their ancestors, and his proficiency in Romany was a passport to easy acceptance. They were an hospitable lot and accustomed to welcoming other gypsies without asking where they came from or who they might be, requiring only that they do their share of the communal work and not interfere with the camp's usual activities.

This lack of curiosity suited Taiso very well. Even had he wished, he might not have been able to answer their questions truthfully, having very nearly forgotten who he was and what part of Europe he called home. Over the twenty-five years he had moved from country to country in pursuit of his profession, he had perfected the useful art of submerging himself in his current identity, to the point where he always became the man he pretended to be. Like an actor, he had developed an enormous repertoire of roles and moved so easily and skillfully from one to another that he felt perfectly confident in his ability to become anyone he wished. *Si khohaimo may pachivalo sar o chachimo.* There are lies more believable than truth, it was said among the gypsies, and Taiso knew precisely how to create them.

But the fact that his past lives were a tissue of lies was of no particular concern to Taiso, for his attention was now fully focussed on his present mission and the scheme to which he and Firefly had agreed some months before. This plan was very much in his mind as Taiso leaned back, drawing on his pipe and considering the events of the day. They had not developed satisfactorily, for Firefly had reported an unexpected and unwelcome difficulty in carrying out the agreed-upon tasks according to schedule. Taiso did not like this at all, for he was the kind of man who preferred to control circumstances, rather than be forced to develop an unplanned response to an unpredictable event.

But it is in the water that one learns to swim, as the gypsies say, and Taiso was an eminently resourceful man who could respond quickly when necessary to shape events toward the desired outcome. Having received Firefly's report, Taiso had seen immediately what must be done. The plan had been prematurely executed, and the ship he was expecting would not arrive off the coast at Arbroath until the end of the week. They would leave their charge in safekeeping for the time being, maintaining a close guard over him, while they waited to see what would develop.

But this was a barely-acceptable alternative, Taiso felt, and his instincts, honed over the course of a great many other dangerous operations, told him that all was not as well as might be. He was puzzled, although not particularly alarmed, by the unexpected appearance of a man along the road, just above Wester Logie, who had stopped him and questioned him pointedly before allowing him to proceed.

Of course, his business was perfectly evident from the charcoal brazier on his back and the tinker's pig—outfitted with hammers and tongs, tin snips and vises and soldering irons, solder and rivets—over his shoulder. The man who stopped him, a forester from the estate of Lord Strathmore, had been more than happy to send him on his way. If it were not for the traveling tinker, who would plug the family's leaky basin, or put a new handle on the old dipper, or recast the broken pewter spoons?

But the traveling tinker had other business to attend to, important, secret business that could not be educed from the gear he carried, and there had been no basins or dippers or spoons mended in Glamis Village that day. Now, as Taiso dipped rabbit stew out of the pot and into an enamel dish, another thought came to him, another piece of a plan. He entertained it as he ate and washed the few dishes and utensils he had used. Then he climbed the steps to his wagon and went inside, drawing the hopsacking curtain over the door behind him. A change of clothing—another identity, as it were—hung in the cupboard. When dark began to fall and the gypsies took to their beds, he would change and go into Glamis Village, to the hotel pub. A gypsy would not be welcomed there, but a gentleman would, and Taiso knew how to play a gentleman.

Si khohaimo may pachivalo sar o chachimo. There are lies more believable than truth.

CHAPTER FOUR

Whither away, my bonnie, bonnie May
So late an' so far in the gloamin'?
The mist gathers gray o'er muirland an' brae.
Oh! whither alane art thou roamin'?

"Loch Lomond"
Traditional Scottish ballad

Kate took off her hat and settled back in her seat, look-ing out the window as the train rattled along, contin-uing its gentle climb up the valley of the Tyne between the grassy slopes of the Cheviot Hills and the high, bare ranges of the Pennines. The engine gave a blast as they passed Halt-whistle, which was distinguished by a splendid water tower supported on an arcaded red-brick foundation. Where were they going? Kate wondered, bemused. Why?

"Sorry to keep you waiting, Lord Sheridan," Colonel Pad-dington said crisply, returning to his seat opposite them. "There were one or two things I needed to see to." He opened a leather document case and took out an official-looking envelope, sealed. "Before I fill you in on what I know, sir, you should have a look at this." He cast a pointed glance at Kate. "P'raps Lady Sheridan would prefer to with-draw to another compartment. Rather boring business, this."

Kate, who resented nothing more than being told to leave when something interesting was about to happen, opened her mouth to object. Charles, however, was quicker.

"Thank you, no," he said definitively. "I'm sure that Lady Sheridan will not be at all bored." As Kate wondered with some asperity whether it was worse to be dismissed or to be spoken of in the third person, he opened the sealed envelope and removed two sheets of paper, scanning the first quickly and studying the second. After a moment, he handed both to Kate, with a dry smile. "Read these pages, my dear, and see what you can make of them." Of Paddington, he asked, "Were you informed of the contents, Colonel?"

"I was given to understand, sir, that it is a commission and your orders." Paddington's eyes, distressed, were on the papers in Kate's gloved hand. He did not, apparently, think that a lady should be permitted to read something that a colonel had not.

Kate read both pages, her pulse quickening. The first, signed by King Edward, appointed Charles, Lord Sheridan, Baron of Somersworth, to serve at His Majesty's pleasure at the rank of brigadier. The second specified that Brigadier Lord Sheridan, at the expressed wish of His Royal Majesty, was to take command of a detachment of the Coldstream Guard and "exercise his discretion in resolving such matters as may threaten the peace and security of the British Realm, including the declaration of martial law where necessary to accomplish this end." It bore the signature of C. T. Ritchie, Home Secretary.

" 'Given to understand?' " Charles repeated in some ir-ritation. "That's all? You don't have an idea of what threatening 'matters' I am to use my discretion in resolving?"

"Afraid not, sir," the colonel growled, not yet resigned to Kate's continuing presence.

Kate folded the orders and handed them back to Charles, suppressing a sigh. "It seems," she said, "that you are under royal command."

It wouldn't be the first time, of course. Charles had handled the occasional royal odd job while Edward was still Bertie, the Prince of Wales.* The difficulty was that when the Crown was involved, everything else—all personal intentions, wishes, and plans—had to be laid aside.

Charles thrust the papers into his pocket. "Where is Kirk-Smythe?" he demanded. At the colonel's blank expression, he added, "The man who telegraphed me to meet the train."

"Afraid I don't know, sir," the colonel replied apologetically. "P'rhaps he'll meet us at our destination. Wherever *that* is."

Charles's eyes narrowed. "So you've no idea where we're headed?"

"None at all," the colonel replied uncomfortably. "Since we left London, the lines ahead of us have been cleared of all rail traffic. When we reach a junction, the switches are already thrown." He managed a tight smile. "Invisible hand, as it were."

Kate shivered. She did not at all like the idea that Charles had been involuntarily commissioned, and was frightened by the notion that they were now under the command of an unseen influence with complete control over their destinies.

---

*The record of Lord Sheridan's work for the Prince may be found in *Death at Daisy's Folly, Death at Rottingdean*, and *Death at Epsom Downs*.

For all she knew, Charles might be on his way to South Africa. At the thought, her shiver became a shudder, for she had long feared that he would feel it necessary to volunteer his services, even though he did not support the war against the Boers. But surely the King had better uses for Charles than to send him out to—

"What are *your* orders, Colonel?" Charles reached into his pocket and pulled out his pipe. "What were you told about the mission?"

The colonel cast one last look at Kate, hesitated for the space of two breaths, and offered his unconditional surrender. "I received urgent, written instructions from King Edward to hand-pick a detachment. I was not to take a single unit, but to individually select the cleverest of the lot, men who could be relied upon to remember what was required of them and forget when they were told to. They were to be placed on official leave and attired in the sort of civilian dress that would not attract attention." His brow furrowed as he rehearsed what was clearly an unusual order. "The men were to drift in small groups to certain railway stations north of London, to be collected a few at a time by this train. Quartermaster duties must have been assigned elsewhere, for the mail coach and baggage cars were already loaded with gear when I boarded at Euston Station."

Charles fished in another pocket, found his tobacco pouch, and began to pack tobacco into his pipe. "What sort of gear?"

The colonel gave a short laugh. "Someone must have cleaned out a supply depot. Full field kit and tents, rations for a fortnight. And crates and crates of—" His tone became deeply puzzled. "Bicycles."

"Bicycles?" Charles asked. He struck a match on the sole

of his boot and held it to his pipe. "Dursley Pedersens, I assume. The folding military model?"

The colonel frowned "B'lieve so, sir, although I myself am not much of a bicycle man."

Kate bit her lip. She had read recently of the military deployment of bicycles in South Africa, where they were used for messenger and scout duty. Some infantry troops had been equipped with them, but they had found them a nuisance and often abandoned them by the side of the road. She was frightened by the thought that these bicycles—and Charles—might be bound for the war.

"The official word," the colonel continued, "is to be that we're on maneuvers to explore the feasibility of using bicycles for mounted reconnaissance." He cleared his throat. "I am further instructed to be prepared to cordon an area of some hundred square miles. Upon arrival at our destination, the men are to change to field uniforms without unit insignia."

"Our destination." Charles leaned forward, elbows on knees, pulling on his pipe. "When we reach Carlisle, we should have a clue as to that, at least. If the train turns south, we're probably headed for Liverpool and an ocean voyage."

"Agreed," the colonel said.

Kate, her hands clenched into fists, gave voice to the thought that was tormenting her. "Charles, surely you aren't being sent to South Africa. Please tell me that *can't* be the case."

The colonel spoke first, with confidence and pride. "No need for your ladyship to worry. War's almost done. Kitchener's built eight thousand blockhouses right across the veldt and connected them with barbed wire. Cleared all the farms and removed the civilians to internment camps." He gave a scornful harrumph. "Damn Boers are completely defeated—they're just too stubborn to admit it."

Kate flinched, thinking of the newspaper reports of the Boer women and children who, their farms burned and animals driven away, had been herded together into hastily-constructed camps. Poorly fed, inadequately housed, with no provision for sanitation, the interned civilians were dying of disease and starvation. This appalling treatment of the innocent had aroused a storm of protest not just in Britain but all over the world, and Charles had joined Sir Henry Campbell-Bannerman, leader of the Liberal Party, in public denouncements of Kitchener's barbaric methods. In fact, Charles and Sir Henry were widely viewed as treasonous troublemakers, defaming the British Army and standing in defense of the Boers' rebellion. If he were sent to the front, he would certainly not be a popular officer.

Charles's grave face showed that he understood Kate's concern, and he reached for her hand. "It's unlikely, my dear," he said quietly, "that such an irregular force would be dispatched on a conventional military operation. It wouldn't make any sense."

"I certainly agree to that," the colonel said, "although, so far, nothing about this operation makes sense." He smiled. "However, my lord, I have it on the highest authority that you are uniquely qualified to lead this operation—which, I might add, I find reassuring. I've been privileged to know His Majesty for a number of years as our colonel-in-chief, and have never known him to misjudge someone." A slight frown appeared between his eyes. "Although I doubt there's another man in the King's service who, offered a Victoria Cross, would refuse it and resign his commission instead other than your lordship."

"Refuse the Victoria Cross?" Kate asked, not sure that she had heard the colonel correctly. She looked at Charles.

For the briefest second, his eyes met hers, and then his glance slid away and he turned to look out the window. In that instant she saw an expression she had never seen before. And in the turn of the head, the unwillingness to look her in the eye, she thought she glimpsed something that suggested . . . guilt, was it? Shame?

The colonel bit his lip, mumbled something apologetic, and turned away. Still not sure she had understood, Kate did not want to pursue a question that was obviously embarrassing to both men. She also turned to look out the window, her thoughts going back to their wedding night, when she had seen the ugly scars crisscrossing Charles's chest and back like relics of some ancient battle. But he had never spoken of them and she had not liked to ask, sensing that the scars concealed a painful, tragic experience that still troubled him deeply.

An hour later, as the train reached the outskirts of Carlisle, she had an answer to at least one of her questions. The sun, which had lain before them and was now dropping below the horizon, began to cast its fading light through the window on the left-hand side of the railroad car. The train was turning north toward Edinburgh, along what was called the Waverly Route.

"It seems that we're on our way to Scotland," Charles said quietly, and Kate felt such a wave of enormous relief sweep over her that it almost turned her giddy.

"Thank God," she whispered, and reached for Charles's hand. Wherever they were bound, whatever Charles had been commissioned to do, it wasn't South Africa.

Stretching out his legs, the colonel began to whistle the refrain of "Loch Lomond."

CHAPTER FIVE

Wilhelmstrasse, Berlin

For sixteen years, from the fall of Bismarck in 1890 to his own forced retirement in 1906, Fredrich von Holstein played a principal role in making German foreign policy. Working beneath the surface at the Wilhelmstrasse, he was known as the "Eminence Grise (the Gray Eminence)," the "Empire Jesuit," and the "Monster of the Labyrinth."

Dreadnought
Robert K. Massie

The day had been a pleasant one, and Friedrich von Holstein had allowed the window of his office to be opened. Now, the clock on the tower across the Wilhelmstrasse began to strike nine, each metallic chime sounding deeper into his awareness, until he permitted himself to withdraw his attention from the report he was drafting and raise his head. He had been so deeply engrossed in his work that he had scarcely noticed that the sun had set and that one of his clerks had lit his red-shaded desk lamp. The hour was much later than he had thought, and it was time to end another long day of service to the Fatherland. He would reward himself with his usual leisurely dinner and fine wine in a private room at the Restaurant Borchardt at No. 48 Franzosischstrasse before retiring to the three small rooms in which he chose to live alone.

As Holstein gathered his papers and stacked them neatly on the desk in front of him, he reflected wryly that the Fatherland was still more of an ideal than an historic tradition. Crafted out of a loose federation of competitive states by his patron, Otto von Bismarck, the German Empire as it existed today had been a political entity for just over twenty years. Now sixty-four, Holstein had played a major but covert role in the growth and development of this empire, working in his own quiet corner of the Foreign Ministry while political parties rose and fell in the Bundesrat and Reichstag, imperial chancellors came and went, and foreign ministers and state secretaries assumed their posts and lost them. And since Bismarck's own forced departure from public service a decade ago, Friedrich von Holstein's was the invisible hand that steered Germany's course through the maelstrom of easy animosities and uneasy alliances that marked the European community.

Holstein picked up the neat stack of papers and placed them in the top right-hand desk drawer, closing and locking it. The report was routine but necessary, only one in an endless stream of memoranda, dispatches, and letters that crossed his desk on their way to the desks of ministers and embassy officials across Europe and to Germany's friends around the world. This one, however, was bound for no more distant destination than the large oak filing case in the corner of the room, where he kept the most secret documents.

Holstein sat back in his leather-upholstered desk chair, stroking his mustache and short white beard and considering, for the hundredth time, the progress of the plan and its implications and ramifications. It might be only one in a vast, spidery network of plans and schemes in which he was involved, but it had a very great international significance. By now it should be well in motion, and all that remained was to await von Hautpmann's report of its successful conclusion.

Holstein frowned, reviewing his decision not to inform the Boy of the plan and concluding once again that he was acting correctly. Kaiser Wilhelm II—whose unpredictable immaturity and volatile childish passions had earned him the nickname of the Boy—might well have approved the scheme. It contained just the blend of conspiracy and stealthy intrigue and secrecy that the Kaiser relished, and it threatened King Edward with a deeply embarrassing revelation that might well topple the monarchy. Given the Boy's growing animosity toward the British Empire, ruled for most of the preceding century by his grandmama Victoria, he would most likely seize upon it gleefully.

But Holstein did not consider Wilhelm reliable enough to be entrusted with the details of such a potentially explosive plot. After all, the new King of England—who had so recently succeeded to the throne that he had not yet been crowned—was visiting Berlin and Hamburg just now, following the funeral of his sister and the Kaiser's mother, the Dowager Empress Friedrich. The Boy, who from time to time glowed with a sudden family sentiment, might in a moment of emotional weakness or in an effort to ingratiate himself disclose the plan to his royal uncle. It did not do, Holstein felt, to give Wilhelm any more information than was absolutely necessary to accomplish one's ends, whether they had to do with politics, the military, or espionage. The Kaiser was best managed as one would handle a poisonous snake: as long as one understood the creature's limitations, anticipated its actions, and did not provoke it, one was relatively safe to go about one's business in its vicinity. And if the plan went wrong, Hauptmann had taken great care that the business could not be traced back to Germany and the Foreign Office. If Hauptmann failed, the Kaiser would never hear of it. If Hauptmann succeeded, there would be ample time to determine what should be done with their prize, and when and how the Kaiser should be told.

Holstein smiled into his mustache. Ah, yes, Hauptmann. He was a good man, reliable, resourceful, and fearless. In connection with his espionage work for Gustav Steinhauer, the former Pinkerton private detective who was now in charge of German Intelligence, Hauptmann had enjoyed a great many successes in the past several years—more than enough, certainly, to blot out any lingering embarrassment he might have felt after the disappointing failure of his weapons-smuggling scheme in Rottingdean in '97. Holstein, who often found much fault in the work of subordinates, could find none in Hauptmann or his smuggling plan, for it had been splendidly conceived and skillfully executed, to the very end. That it had failed was due neither to negligence nor poor planning, but to the intervention of a single man.*

Holstein stood and began to button his rusty black frock coat. As was his custom when one of his subordinates failed, he had required Hauptmann to provide him with a full written report documenting the circumstances—in this case, including a dossier of the man who had so adroitly cheated Hauptmann of success. He glanced again at the wooden cabinet, which held (among other secrets) the report Hauptmann had prepared after the operation's unfortunate

*For this tale of espionage and counterespionage, see *Death at Rottingdean*.

conclusion. There was no need to consult either the dossier or supporting documents to refresh his memory, for Holstein could picture its contents as he could mentally picture and recite from each document in every file in his office, a faculty that both awed and terrified his clerks.

CHARLES, LORD SHERIDAN, BARON SOMERSWORTH

Born 1861, second son of fifth Baron of Somersworth. Father, mother dead. No living siblings.

Education: Eton, Royal Military Academy at Woolwich, Royal School of Engineering at Chatham. Later took degree at Oxford in preparation for diplomatic career.

Military service: 1883–85, served with distinction in the Sudan, recommended for Victoria Cross. Refused V.C. and resigned commission, 1885.

Occupation: Succeeded to Peerage upon death of older brother. Active Liberal in the House of Lords. Administers family estates at Somersworth and elsewhere.

Married: 1896, to Kathyrn Ardleigh, Irish-American, writer of popular fictions under pseudonym of Beryl Bardwell. No natural children.

Residences: Sibley House, Mayfair, London; wife's estate (Bishop's Keep) in East Anglia.

Notes: Pursues interests in natural sciences, archaeology, photography, and criminal investigation, and is reported to have been involved with the Yard in setting up fingerprint files. Has close but unofficial connections with Royal Family.

The recollection of the last line of the file gave Holstein a twinge of concern, but it was only fleeting. There was no need to worry. Lord Sheridan was a most interesting man, one whom he might like one day to meet, but in the final analysis, his lordship was nothing more than an amateur and a dilettante, one of those British aristocrats who gadded hither and thither in pursuit of his own precious interests. And lightning did not strike twice in the same place. Hauptmann would return soon with his prize, and they could decide what to do with it.

Holstein finished buttoning his coat, put on his hat, and went to the door, locking it behind him, closing away Hauptmann's defeat and the rest of that unpleasant affair at Rottingdean. The thought of Lord Charles Sheridan would not disturb his dinner.

CHAPTER SIX

Glamis Village, Forfarshire, Scotland

She is a winsome wee thing,
She is a handsome wee thing,
She is a lovesome wee thing,
This dear wee wife o' mine.

I never saw a fairer,
I never loved a dearer,
And nigh my heart I'll wear her
This dear sweet jewel mine.

Traditional Scottish ballad

Constable Oliver Graham was a usually cheerful young man, so far as any Scotsman may be deemed cheerful, for he was satisfied with his life and his work to a degree that most people of his acquaintance were not. Glamis Village and its environs—the constable's precinct stretched almost to Kirriemuir to the north, Forfar to the east, and equal distances to the west and south—were both beautiful and peaceful, with only the occasional drunken farmer or quarrelsome neighbor or vagrant cow with which to contend.

Besides this, Oliver Graham had been born and lived all of his twenty-three years in this place, and he knew every man and his land and all his beasts, every woman and all her children (or as many as could reasonably be known, given the evident fertility of those in his district), and every bend and turn of the footpaths and the roads, which he patrolled regularly on his bicycle. He possessed the confidence of his superior (Chief Superintendent Douglas Mc-Naughton, who was headquartered in Forfar), the respect of the citizens of the district, and a cozy cottage with a sound thatch, inherited from his father and mother, who were old and lived for their comfort with his sister in Dundee.

Indeed, it was no wonder that Oliver Graham's heart was warmed with a genial proprietary glow when he thought of his precinct and all it meant to him. Given the many successes he had achieved at a relatively young age, the constable might perhaps be pardoned for the smugness with which he contemplated the satisfactions of his work and his life.

However, Oliver Graham did not have quite all that he desired, and in one vital area felt himself to be sadly deficient. The constable was in want of a wife, a lack which he had only recently begun to feel strongly and which he hoped to remedy as soon as might be. He had fastened his expectations and hopes upon a young woman whom he had known from childhood, with whom he had played in the streets of Glamis Village and in the woods and fields around the great castle. Indeed, Oliver Graham and Flora MacDonald had in their youth been childhood sweethearts, trading innocent kisses and love-tokens in the shadows of the tall pines, hiding love notes under a rock near St. Fergus Well.

Unfortunately, occupied as he was in establishing himself in his career, Oliver had not had the time in the past two years to pay the proper attention to Flora. Now that he felt comfortable in his position and was sure that he could earn enough to support a growing family, however, he was ready to resume their loving friendship, to make her, in short, his wife.

But while Oliver was furthering his professional ambitions and making a name for himself in the district, Flora had herself grown and changed, from girl-child to young woman. She worked with her mother at the castle, as housemaid and attendant to an invalid resident there, some friend of the Strathmore family. And Oliver now saw, to his great delight, that his Flora had become more winsome and lovesome than ever, with her soft brown hair and steady gray eyes, her skin of roses and cream, her buxom figure. He was more than ready to offer himself, heart and soul and body, to this dear, sweet creature, whom he now admitted had never lost her place in his heart.

Flora, however, did not seem quite so ready to accept as Oliver was to offer. She had rejected his first proposal some weeks ago, but so gently and sweetly that his hopes were not in the least discouraged. After all, it was scarcely immodest of him to believe that Flora MacDonald could find no better husband in all Glamis (in all the Strathmore Vale, come to that), no finer a man in appearance and health nor richer in both present possession and future prospect. And for her part, sweet, shy Flora was not likely to stray far from the village, nor entertain the attentions of a stranger from another district. No, his sweetheart might put him off and protest that she was not ready to marry, but he was confident that she would come round in the course of events—the sooner, of course, the better—and agree to be his dear wife.

However, something terrible had recently happened, something that was likely to affect his relations with Flora, and it was for this reason that Constable Graham's customarily self-satisfied countenance had turned dark and forbidding. Flora had suffered a grave harm a few days ago, and it was the constable's responsibility to see that the perpetrator was brought to justice as quickly as possible. Her mother, Hilda MacDonald, had been viciously murdered—her throat slit from ear to ear, a quick and ugly death—and poor Flora herself had discovered the body on the path between Glamis Castle and the village, early on Monday morning. It was now Wednesday evening, the inquest was scheduled for the following day, and Constable Graham had not yet discovered the murderer, nor uncovered even a single clue to his identity. It was a failure he felt keenly, both professionally and personally. He had failed not only his duty, but Flora as well—Flora, who trusted him to bring her mother's killer to justice; Flora, who would soon, pray God, consent to be his wife.

The constable strode around the corner, past John Buchanan's tobacconist shop, and into the pub room of the Glamis Inn, a gray-stone two-story building with a green-slate roof and chimneys at either end. As usual, the low-ceilinged, smoky room was crowded with village men enjoying a pint and a pipe and discussing the events of the day with their friends, while a generous fire blazed on the brick hearth. The loud buzz of voices that filled the air was silenced when the constable entered, however, and he felt the bitter stab of pitying looks, like poisoned darts digging under his skin. Everyone in the room, including Herman Memsdorff, Flora's cousin, knew he had failed so far to discover the identity of Hilda MacDonald's killer—the first and most significant failure in the two years he had served as their constable—and all felt sorry for him.

Oliver glanced at Memsdorff, to whom he planned to talk. But the man, who came frequently from Edinburgh to visit his aunt and cousin, was engaged in close conversation with Douglas Hamilton, the assistant gamekeeper up at the castle. Hamilton was a cocky, hot-headed little fellow who smoked stinking cigars and was always bragging about his exploits, and the constable had no use for him. Anyway, conversation with Memsdorff could wait until Oliver had fortified himself with a pint in hand.

He pushed his way to the pub's bar, its smoky mirror decorated with two large framed photographs: Queen Victoria's on one side, hung with dusty crape, King Edward's on the other. The difference between the two was evident to any viewer. The Queen wore the gloomy face and mourning she had put on at her husband's death some four decades earlier, while a smiling King Edward was pictured with his last-year's Derby winner, Diamond Jubilee. Behind the bar, Thomas Collpit gave him a sympathetic nod. "The usu'l, Oliver?"

"Aye," Oliver replied gruffly.

Dr. Ogilvy was standing at the bar, surveying the room through his narrow, gold-rimmed glasses. "Good evenin', Oliver," he said in a genial voice. "Wha hae ye found, m'lad?"

Oliver took the pint that the dour Mrs. Collpit pulled for him from a wooden keg. "I've nothing for ye, I'm sorry tae say," he growled. "Ye shall hae t' render an open verdict."

The doctor, a short, stout little man with a round face, bald head, and gold-rimmed glasses, was also the district's coroner, and would preside tomorrow at the inquest into Hilda MacDonald's murder. Oliver had wanted badly to present the killer to the coroner's jury, but although he had pursued his investigation vigorously—interviewing those who discovered the body, going from house to house in the village, questioning the gypsies camped at Roundyhill (who had of course been his first suspects)—he had come up with nothing. There were no witnesses, no weapon, no evidence, no clues, not even a motive for the especially vicious killing. He would have to report to Chief Superintendent McNaughton, with great regret and not a little chagrin, that there was nothing to report.

"Run against a stone wall, hae ye, now?" the doctor inquired gently. He pursed his lips. "Well, I dinna wonder ye ha'n't turned up the villain yet, Oliver. It takes a long spoon tae sup wi' such a de'il as killed our Hilda. How's Flora?" he added sympathetically, for he knew the constable's feelings. There was little about Glamis Village that Dr. Henry Ogilvy did not know, Oliver supposed, privvy as he was to all of the secrets in the neighborhood: the secret births, the secret marriages, the secret dreams and fears and hates. This intimacy made him a perfect coroner, for he knew very well when someone was tempted to testify falsely.

"Canna say, as to Flora," Oliver replied, glum. "Ha'n't seen her this day. She's nowt tae hame, for I called there just now. S'pose she's workin' late at the castle." To tell the truth, he suspected that Flora was deliberately keeping herself out of his way, for he had perhaps been a bit overzealous in pressing his romantic intentions upon her on the Sunday evening before her mother's body was discovered. And now—

There was a stir at the door, and Oliver turned to see a stranger enter the crowded room, an elderly, gray-haired gentleman dressed in clothing suited to tramping the countryside: thick woolen jacket and gray knickers, stout leather boots, a brown felt hat with the brim pulled over his forehead, a canvas pack on his back, a fiddle case strung over his shoulder, and a stout oak walking stick in his hand.

Limping badly, the old gentleman made his way to the bar and ordered a whiskey and water. "But dinna drown the miller," he cautioned, and Thomas Collpits, with a ready laugh, splashed no more than a drop of water in the glass he pushed across the rough plank.

The men in the room visibly relaxed, for here was no stranger but a venerable fellow Scotsman, although perhaps an eccentric one, out on holiday. The constable, however, leaned forward, feeling it his duty to know the identity of every man in his district, particularly now, with a murder investigation under way.

"Good evenin', sir," he said. He frowned, showing his suspicions. "And where'boots be ye frae, may I ask?"

"Glasgow," the man said in broad Scots. "I'm called Alan Donovan. I coom i' search o' ballads and auld stories, for a collection I hae i' the makin'."

The constable was about to inquire of Alan Donovan where in the district he was staying, but his question was forestalled.

"If ye know an auld ballad I dinna know aboot, I'd be pleased t' write it doon," the elderly gentleman said to the room at large. And then, in a tuneful baritone, his pale blue eyes dancing merrily, he broke into the first verse of "The Bonny Earl of Murray":

> *Ye Highlands and ye Lawlands,*
> *Oh where hae ye been?*
> *They hae slain the Earl of Murray,*
> *And layd him on the green.*

"Ah, yes," said a dark-haired, slender man, turning from his conversation with the butcher. Robert Heriot was the village schoolmaster, and the resident expert on the ballads of Strathmore Vale, on the whole history of Scotland, for that matter. Heriot struck a pose and offered up the second verse:

He was a braw gallant,
And he rid at the ring;
And the bonnie Earl of Murray,
Oh he might hae been a king!

"Ye do say so, do ye? Might hae been a king?" The old man smiled genially. Unstrapping his fiddle case and tucking the instrument under his chin, he answered with a third verse:

He was a braw gallant,
And he playd at the glove;
And the bonnie Earl of Murray,
Oh he was the Queen's love!

The air was filled with the plaintive cry of the fiddle as the two men traded the interminable verses of "The Earl of Murray." Then the village butcher, fat Henry Arrat, whistled the refrain of "Broomfield Hill," and the three of them took up that ballad, in harmony. That finished at last, the rest of the room joined in on "The Shepherd's Dochter." The villagers were accustomed to singing hymns at St. Fergus Kirk on Sunday, but they did not often have the privilege of raising their voices to the old ballads, and especially with the accompaniment of such an accomplished fiddler. They laid into the familiar music with grateful hearts and a fervor fueled by yet another round of pints, generously contributed by the ballad collector.

As the men sang, Oliver turned his attention to the crowd, thinking again of the terrible crime that someone— one of them?—had committed this week. Some of the men worked at the castle, or on the castle farms and fields; others plied their trades or vocation in the village, such as the baker, Alex Ross, and Peter Chasehope, the joiner, and the Reverend Cecil Calderwood, the convivial vicar, who enjoyed his pint of ale just like the rest. The station clerk was there, too, and with him one of the signalmen, laughing together with the young clerk at the Royal Bank of Scotland.

Oliver frowned. It was impossible to see any of these men as the man he sought, for they were almost all very well-known to him, and to Hilda, who was held in high regard throughout the village. Theirs was a close-knit, interrelated, and self-sufficient community, in which each man and woman depended on the work and the trade of the others. They worshipped together, attended school together, and danced at each other's weddings, mourned at each other's funerals. The constable could not imagine that any of these men could have killed her.

He did, however, have one suspect in mind. He leaned close to the doctor, lowering his voice so that he could be heard under the by-now raucous singing.

"Hilda once told me that her job at the castle, and Flora's too, was tae take care o' some invalid gentleman who lives in retirement there. Lord Osborne, his name is. Ye havena heard awt o' him?"

"Lord Osborne? Lord Osborne?" The doctor, his brow furrowed, took off his glasses and polished them on his handkerchief. "Canna say, Oliver. Why d'ye ask?"

The constable shrugged, frustrated. "Well, somebody killed Hilda MacDonald," he growled, "and the killer surely isn'a one o' us. I think I shall hae a wee bit o' talk wi' Simpson tomorrow mornin', and ask tae see this Lord Osborne."

"Ye mun do as ye mun do." Behind his glasses, the doctor's usually-sprightly glance was troubled. "Ye spoke wi' the gypsies up by Roundyhill?"

"At the very first," the constable answered grimly. "None had awt tae say, o' course, and with nae evidence tae speak of—" He shrugged again and looked around, his eyes searching the crowd for a tall man with dark hair and eyes bright and black as the eyes of a crow, and a jagged scar across his jaw.

"Herman Memsdorff must hae gone hoom a'ready," he said disgustedly. "I wanted tae talk wi' him." He had thought to inquire about Flora's health and state of mind, hoping that her cousin might know how she was feeling. He hated to think of the girl having to give evidence at the inquest the next day, as low in mind and spirit as she must surely be, poor thing.

"Memsdorff? Aye, I saw him leave just after ye coom in," the doctor said. "Strange chap, that." He put his pipe in one pocket, tugged his watch out of another, and glanced at it. "Well, I must be off tae hoom, afore Mrs. Ogilvy cooms tae fetch me. I shall see ye at the inquest tomorrow, Oliver." He pulled a long face. "Sad business, this, verra sad. I shall be glad when Hilda's laid tae rest."

Oliver nodded. He lingered in the pub for an hour after the doctor departed, listening to the singing and hoping that Memsdorff might return. But Flora's cousin did not reappear, and finally, his ears ringing with the sound of the old man's fiddle and the lilting tune of "Loch Lomond," the constable made his own way home, to his solidly thatched but lonely cottage.

It would be several days before he would learn that he had seen the last of Herman Memsdorff.

CHAPTER SEVEN

Thursday, 15 August 1901
Glamis, Forfarshire, Scotland

*Glamis is, indeed, one of the finest old built Palaces in Scotland,
and by far the largest; and this makes me speak of it here,
because I am naming the Pretender and his Affairs. . . . When
you see it at a Distance it is so full of Turrets and lofty Build-
ings, Spires and Towers, some plain, others shining with gilded
Tops, that it looks not like a Town, but a City; and the noble
Appearance seen through the long Vistas of the Park are so
differing that it does not seem like the same Place any two
Ways together.*

  A Tour Thro the Whole Island of Great Britain, 1724–1727
  Daniel Defoe

The train was traveling up the Valley of Strathmore on
the Caledonian Railway, while Kate watched the dawn
come up in a slate-gray sky. Late on the previous night, a
fault had developed in one of the locomotive's steam valves,
and the engineer had been required to reduce the speed.
Having arrived at Perth, they had lain by for several hours
while midnight repairs were organized, and Kate, snuggled
in blankets against the chill, tried to sleep in the uncomfortable seat. Now they were once again heading north, past
Scone and Balbeggie, with the brown pillows of the Sidlaw

Hills visible to the east in the metallic gray light of a drizzly dawn. The highest of the hills, at a thousand feet, Charles told her, was Dunsinane, where a ruined fort called Macbeth's Castle was the traditional site of Macbeth's final defeat.

" 'Fear not,' " he reminded Kate, " 'till Birnam wood do come to Dunsinane.' *Macbeth*, Act Five, Scene Five."

"I'm not in the least afraid," Kate replied, "although I will confess to being more than a little glad when *we* have come to Dunsinane, or wherever it is we are meant to be." She stretched wearily, her eyes grainy with sleep. "Do you have any idea where we are, or where we are bound?"

"As a matter of fact, I can tell you where we are," Charles replied, "although where we are bound, I haven't a clue. We're north of the Firth of Tay, traveling through the Strathmore Valley, not far from Glamis Castle." He pronounced the word *Glamis* as one syllable, so that it rhymed with the word *palms.*

"Glamis Castle?" Kate exclaimed. "Oh, I should love to see it, Charles. I've heard that it is a beautiful place, and haunted."

"Beautiful it certainly is," Charles said, "although I'm afraid I'm not up on the hauntings. Glamis is the home of Lord and Lady Strathmore," he added. "I visited there several times some years ago, as the guest of their son, Patrick Bowes-Lyon."

"Do you think we're going to Glamis?"

Charles shrugged. "I'm afraid we'll just have to wait and see." He spoke philosophically, but there was an undertone of excitement in his voice.

Kate regarded him thoughtfully. He was the same Charles she loved, his face so familiar to her now that it was

almost commonplace. But behind what she always saw—
the sincere and resolute strength, the mature deliberation,
the steadfast moral courage that led him to support unpop-
ular Liberal causes in the House of Lords—she now
glimpsed something different. A certain boyishness, perhaps, that was intrigued by this summons from his sover-
eign. A strength that might reach to obstinance, a courage
that might be tempted to recklessness if there were a need
for defiant action. These were glimpses of a different
Charles—perhaps the Charles of his military career, about
which she knew almost nothing—and they made her wonder. She thought again about the Victoria Cross, which she
knew was awarded only for the greatest acts of valor, and
the resigned commission. She leaned forward, thinking to
ask Charles what was behind Colonel Paddington's earlier
remark, but he had turned away to consult with one of the
men, and the opportunity was lost. It would have to wait
for a more private moment.

Within the quarter hour, the train began to slow. The
valley had broadened and was filled with fields of golden
grain and grazing cattle. Shortly after they crossed a broad,
clear river—the Dene Water, Charles said it was called—
Kate heard the screech of brakes.

"Glamis Station, I believe," Charles said with satisfaction,
rising from his seat. "The castle is not far away. It seems
that you will be able to see it, after all."

"But *why,* for heaven's sake," Kate asked, as she gathered
her things. "Why would King Edward send you here? What
could threaten the peace and security of the realm in such
an out-of-the-way place as this?"

Charles picked up her portmanteau. "Perhaps Lord
Strathmore will be able to tell us. Do you recall meeting
him and his wife at Marlborough House several years ago?"

"Oh, yes," Kate said, remembering the dinner that then-Princess Alexandra had given. Lord Strathmore was a hawk-nosed, stern-faced elderly gentleman, Lady Strathmore sweet and motherly. She should be glad to see them both—although why she and Charles and a trainful of troops and bicycles should have been sent to Glamis Castle, she couldn't possibly imagine.

A few minutes later, Kate was alighting from the train into the chilly morning mist that shrouded the tall, red-trunked Scotch pines. She shivered with a sudden chill, despite her warm motoring coat. The Glamis station consisted of a mossy and damp-stained brick platform along either side of the double tracks, with a depot on one side and the stationmaster's house on the other, the whole overhung with gloomy pines. A little distance beyond the end of the train, a stone bridge arched over the tracks, carrying the road.

A fair-haired young gentleman sporting a neat blond mustache and wearing a wool cap and a tan mackintosh detached himself from a small group of men and wagons at the rear of the platform and came quickly toward them.

"Lord Sheridan," he said with a tight smile, offering his hand. "Welcome to Glamis. I was beginning to fear that something had happened to you."

"It's good to see you, Andrew," Charles said. He set down the portmanteau and shook the man's hand. "There was some sort of difficulty with a steam valve. It delayed us in Perth for several hours."

"It's no matter, now that you're here. I was sorry to interrupt your holiday, but pleased that we managed to locate you." The man—Andrew Kirk-Smythe, who had sent the mysterious telegram summoning Charles—caught sight of Kate and hurriedly lifted his hat. "My dear Lady Sheridan, a pleasure, as always."

"Hello, Andrew," Kate said, offering her hand with a smile. She probed his face for an answer to the mystery of their summons but could read nothing there.

"Her ladyship was with me when I received your telegram," Charles said. "I trust that her coming along presents no special difficulty." He smiled and said in a lighter tone, "You know our Kate, Andrew. She would not have allowed me to send her back home, even had I wished it."

"Of course there's no difficulty," Kirk-Smythe replied. "I anticipated her coming, so I arranged for you both to be accommodated at Glamis Castle. Lord and Lady Strathmore are traveling abroad, but Lord Strathmore telegraphed their regards from Calcutta. They are delighted to have you as their guests."

Glamis Castle! Kate suppressed a little shiver of pleasure. She would not only see the most historic castle in Scotland, she would actually *stay* there—she and Beryl Bardwell, who was looking for inspiration for the next book. The opportunity seemed heaven-sent.

Colonel Paddington came up, and Kirk-Smythe drew himself to attention. "Captain Andrew Kirk-Smythe," he said, introducing himself. "Welcome to Glamis, Colonel."

So Andrew was a captain now, Kate thought approvingly. Since he had been a mere lieutenant at their first meeting, he had done well.

"I realize that you weren't given much time, Colonel Paddington," Kirk-Smythe was saying in a deferential, apologetic tone, "but you've obviously succeeded in assembling your detachment in quite good order." He nodded toward the baggage cars. "Your special equipment was loaded properly?"

"Seems to've been," the colonel replied, "although there hasn't been time to check the manifest." Like his troops, whom Kate could see peering through the windows of the train, he had changed into a khaki field uniform. "Your man in London had it loaded before I boarded."

"Very good." Kirk-Smythe motioned, and a fleshy, heavy-faced man with vigorous side-whiskers and a heavy mustache stepped forward. He was dressed in a yeoman's thick green tweed jacket and heavy trousers. "This is Angus Duff, Lord Strathmore's estate factor. He has been of great assistance since I arrived from London yesterday, and has offered his help in getting things under way."

Duff took off his green wool cap and addressed Kate in a musical Scots baritone. "Lord and Lady Strathmore'll be that sorry they werena at the castle tae receive ye, m'lady. Lady Glamis is expectin' ye, however. And sin' ye sart'nly willna wish tae bide here i' the wet, one o' our gamekeepers—Hamilton's his name—is waitin' wi' a pony cart tae take ye an' yer bags t' the castle."

Kate hesitated, torn between her wish to see the famous Scottish castle and her eagerness to learn why the King had summoned Charles to this remote corner of Scotland. The castle could wait, of course, although she did not like to embarrass her husband by making what might be considered an unladylike protest against her exile, especially since Colonel Paddington, apparently heartened now that he was back in uniform, was giving her a severe look.

Kirk-Smythe cleared his throat. "If you will forgive me, Lady Sheridan," he said tactfully, "I'm afraid that there is a great deal of rather tedious work to be done just now: unloading the men and gear and setting things in motion."

Charles put his arm around her shoulder and his lips close to her ear. "Go along with Hamilton, my dear. I'll join you when I can."

Kate frowned. She disliked being excluded from the action, but she knew that Charles would share as much information with her as he could, as soon as he could. And while it might still be August, this was Scotland, and the platform was damp and chilly. Inside her boots, she realized, her feet were awfully cold.

"Of course, dear," she said sweetly, giving Charles a look under her lashes to remind him that he now owed her a favor.

In a moment, she was being handed into the cart by a slender, fair-haired Scotsman in a gray knit sweater, a long woolen scarf wound round his throat, and heavy trousers tucked into leather boots. His clothing reeked of whiskey and those wretched Indian cigars that her schoolmaster Crombie favored, and his bloodshot, puffy eyes gave him the look of a man who was suffering the effects of too much drink the previous night. He loaded the bags, then climbed into the cart and clucked to the pony.

"It's very pretty here," Kate said, venturing conversation.

"Aye, 'tis," Hamilton agreed sourly. After a long silence, he gave her a sidelong look. "Yer ladyship's first visit tae Glamis?"

"Yes," Kate replied, "although my husband has been here several times before."

"His lordship seems tae hae brought a great many soldiers wi' him," Hamilton remarked in a tone that bordered on brash. He forced a smile. "More'n we're like tae see in our wee corner o' Scotland. Wha's it all aboot?"

"I'm sure I don't know," Kate said, remembering that the business with the soldiers, whatever it was, was supposed to be secret. "You shall have to ask Lord Sheridan."

"Aye, that I shall," Hamilton said, and chirruped to the pony.

The road, with a forest on the left and open fields on the

right, crossed over a rippling burn and up a gentle hill toward the village, which was built on both sides of a road
junction outside the castle wall. Within fifteen minutes they
were driving through a massive stone archway adorned with
figures of medieval beasts carved from stone. Whether it was
the ominous sky, the overhanging dark trees, or the grotesque animal shapes, Kate was suddenly seized by a shiver.
The memory of Macbeth's three sinister witches leapt to her
mind, and the opening lines from the play that had im-
mortalized the Thane of Glamis.

> *When shall we three meet again,*
> *in thunder, lightning, or in rain?*
> *When the hurlyburly's done,*
> *when the battle's lost and won.*

"What interesting carvings," Kate said, pushing the lines
out of her mind. "I suppose the gate has a history."

"It be the De'il's Gate," Hamilton replied shortly.

Kate frowned. "That's an odd name for a gate to a great
estate."

"Ye wilna think it odd when ye ken wha gaes on i' the
castle," he replied, tucking his chin into his woollen scarf.

Kate gave a little laugh. "And what goes on in the castle?"

Hamilton turned to gaze at her. "Ye've nae heard tell of
th' Monster o' Glamis?"

"Actually, I have," Kate replied. She had heard the story
from Lord Halifax, who had a passion for collecting ghost
stories and telling them to friends after dinner. As she recalled, there was something about a secret room, an ancestral
mystery, and a poor, deformed creature—some member of
the Strathmore family who was deemed unfit to carry on the

family name and was shut away from the world for his entire lifetime.

"I would certainly love to hear more," she added, thinking that the Monster, or his ghost, might be an interesting character for Beryl's new project. "I like nothing better than a good ghost story."

"There's nae such thing as a guid ghost," Hamilton replied. In a darkly insolent tone, he added, "Yer ladyship had best keep tae yer room i' the castle, partic'larly when night cooms." And then he shut his mouth firmly, as if he had not another word to say on the subject.

But Kate would not have paid the proper attention to the story even if Hamilton had been willing to tell it, for at that moment, the narrow lane became a grand, tree-lined avenue, and the vista opened onto a sweeping carpet of grassy park grazed by white sheep and shaggy brown Highland cattle. Some little distance away, the castle rose out of the low, silvery fog like the legendary Camelot, wreathed in the ethereal mists of Avalon.

At this first glimpse of Glamis, Kate pulled in her breath, scarcely believing what she saw. A towering central keep, splendid with a fanfare of conical spires, pepper-pot turrets, and a rippling flag, rose magnificently above the crenellated parapets of the wings flung out on either side. The castle was entirely constructed of a warm reddish-gray stone, glistening softly with damp, and its many casements reflected the pale morning light like glittering diamonds set into the stone. It rested in the lap of the soft, green meadow, behind it rising the far-off peaks of the Grampian Mountains, their ridges dusted with an early snow. Even on such a gray and gloomy day as this, Glamis was a fairy jewel in a setting of otherworldly beauty.

Speechless for the remainder of the drive, Kate did not

recover her voice until she alighted from the cart at the castle entry in the great tower, which was crowned by a large clock and the Royal Arms of Scotland. The door itself seemed quite small for such a grand house, but it had obviously been constructed at a time when a castle doorway might require an armed defense, and was guarded by an iron yett, or gate.

As Kate alighted from the pony cart, the door opened, and out came a handsome woman in her late thirties, dressed in a traveling suit of green serge, with a ruffle of dark hair about her face, under a green felt hat. Behind her were a frock-coated manservant and a woman in the dark dress of a servant.

The lady stepped forward and said, with dignified grace, "Good morning, Lady Sheridan. I am Cecilia Bowes-Lyon, Lady Glamis. My mother- and father-in-law—Lord and Lady Strathmore—are abroad, I regret to say, but perhaps Mr. Duff mentioned that."

"Yes, he did," Kate said. "I'm so sorry that they will not be here, Lady Glamis." She took the woman's outstretched hand. "It is kind of you to welcome me. Lord Sheridan will be along later, I believe."

Lady Glamis gestured in the direction of a wagon, which was loaded with trunks and wicker baskets and other traveling gear. "I am also sorry to tell you that the children and I are leaving this morning for our home in Hertfordshire. Simpson, the house steward, will do his best to look after you and Lord Sheridan." With a small smile, the steward inclined his head. "And this is Flora."

Lady Glamis motioned to the servant, a pale young woman entirely dressed in black, her brown hair brushed back from her wide forehead, the ringlets caught by a black ribbon.

"She will show you to your room," Lady Glamis was continuing. "Since Mr. Kirk-Smythe said it was doubtful that you had brought a maid, I have asked her to put herself at your disposal whilst you are here. She can begin by taking you around the castle, if you wish, since she knows it quite well and enjoys showing it off. Most visitors want to see the crypt, which seems to have become quite famous." She paused and looked distractedly at the watch on her lapel. "I do hope you'll excuse me so that I may see to the rest of the packing."

"Thank you, my lady," Kate said warmly. "I apologize for interrupting your departure. You see—"

She hesitated, wishing she had a reason to offer for the uninvited visit. But at that moment, the conversation was interrupted by a young boy in kilts, who raced precipitously around the corner at the helm of a wooden wheelbarrow, its passenger, a rosy, round-cheeked little girl squealing with laughter.

"Mickie!" Lady Glamis exclaimed in a horrified tone, apprehending the boy and removing the baby from the barrow. "Elizabeth is much too young for such rough games."

"But she *wanted* to!" Mickie exclaimed.

"No doubt she did," Lady Glamis replied, as Mickie dashed off with the wheelbarrow. The little girl wriggling in her arms, she turned apologetically to Kate. "My youngest daughter," she said with a rueful smile. "A hoyden already, and she has scarcely passed her first birthday. We call her Merry Mischief."

"She is precious," Kate said, taking the dimpled pink hand in hers and feeling, as she always did with babies, the pang of sharp regret. That she was not able to bear children was an enormous sorrow to her, but she often admitted, and truthfully, that her childlessness had its advantages. If the nursery at Bishop's Keep had been full of boys and little girls as appealing as Merry Mischief, she would certainly be at home with them instead of sharing Charles's adventures. She raised the baby's hand to her lips and kissed it gently.

"Little princess," she murmured. "Princess Elizabeth."

Lady Glamis gave her a startled look. "My goodness," she said. "You, too?" At Kate's questioning glance, she added, "I was walking with the children in the Kirriemuir Road yesterday, when we encountered a band of traveling gypsies. One of the Romany women offered to tell the children's fortunes. She seemed quite definite about Elizabeth's. 'You will live to be a queen,' she said, 'and the mother of a queen.' " She laughed self-consciously. "You will think me superstitious, but the old woman had me half-believing."

"Not a bit of it." Kate smiled. "Queen Elizabeth, then," she said gently, and touched the baby's petal-soft cheek.

CHAPTER EIGHT

Prince Eddy resembled no one so much as his Hanoverian fore-bears. Like them, he could never be trusted to behave quite like other people . . . for he was dissolute and essentially trivial, in racing language "not quite up to the weight". What was to be done with this unsatisfactory young man?

Queen Alexandra
Georgina Battiscombe

As Kate was being handed into the pony cart, Kirk-Smythe turned to Charles and Colonel Paddington. "A word in private, if you please, gentlemen. Shall we go to the end of the platform?"

When they were well out of earshot of the other men, Charles stopped. "Well, now, Andrew. What's this all about?"

Kirk-Smythe put his hands into the pocket of his mack-intosh. "I'm sure you're aware that King Edward is in Germany, attending the funeral of his sister, the Dowager Empress. He has directed me to deliver his instructions ver-bally, since they are highly confidential." He cleared his throat. "Brigadier Lord Sheridan is of course in command here. However, in the interest of time and with his permission, I should like to put you both in the picture on certain key facts. As you no doubt already know, we are at Glamis, some fifteen miles to the north of Dundee. The Caledonian Railway—"

"Perhaps," Charles interrupted gently, "you have a map?"

Kirk-Smythe colored. "Oh, right. Sorry." From his pocket, he withdrew an Ordnance Survey map of the county of Forfarshire, and unfolded it on a nearby wooden bench. He pointed to a dashed line running diagonally across the lower right-hand corner of the map. "This is the Caledonian Railway, and here is the railway station. The road at the other end of this platform—here, on the map—runs north to Kirriemuir about three and a half miles, and south to the village of Glamis, just over a mile. To the east of the road lies the estate of Glamis Castle. Its immediate policies are approximately two miles long and a mile wide, appearing as this shaded area, here. That's where your troops are to bivouac, Colonel. Mr. Duff can help you find a suitable location. He has made available enough wagons to move your baggage and kit and is willing to provide anything you need in the way of food and supplies."

"Colonel Paddington was told to prepare to establish a cordon," Charles said. "Around what area?"

"This entire vicinity," Kirk-Smythe replied, outlining a wide circle around the estate and the village.

"Have the roads been sealed?" the colonel asked.

"I have stationed men from the estate to watch the road at Jericho, here, to the east." Kirk-Smythe put his finger on the map. "Also at Hatton to the south, and at Ewnie and at the old Manse rail crossing to the west. To the north, there's a man at the road junction south of Wester Logie." He straightened. "I respectfully suggest, Colonel, that troops be immediately dispatched to reinforce these checkpoints and that traffic be restricted. If questioned, your men are to say that they are on military maneuvers, testing the use of bicycles for reconnaissance."

Charles bent over to study the map, the colonel looking over his shoulder. Kirk-Smythe's plan would close the main roads leading to Glamis, but the surrounding countryside was a labyrinth of secondary roads, lanes, and footpaths—and no doubt the local folk were well acquainted with many other byways invisible to the map surveyors. It would be the devil of a job to seal off the area. Likely, it couldn't be done successfully, but that didn't mean that they shouldn't try.

"I take it that we are searching for someone or something." Charles straightened. "The object of our search?"

Kirk-Smythe produced a photograph of a serious-looking, mustached young man seated on a stone wall, wearing a tweed hunting suit, a tweed cap, and a high white collar. "This man," he said quietly. "Here at Glamis, he goes under the name of Lord Osborne."

The colonel stared at the photograph blankly for a moment; then, as recognition dawned, so did disbelief. "But he's . . . he's *dead!*" he sputtered incomprehendingly. "Died years ago. And his name isn't Osborne! It's—"

"You're correct on both counts, Colonel Paddington," Kirk-Smythe interrupted, returning the photograph to his pocket. "He died on January 14, 1892, to be precise. I have been instructed by His Royal Majesty that the fiction of this man's death be protected at all costs." He paused, giving his words special weight, and repeated: *"At all costs, gentlemen."*

"I'll be damned." The colonel sucked in his breath. "I'm shocked. Shocked, I tell you."

But for Charles, the information that the man was still

alive was less a shocking surprise than the confirmation of a long-held suspicion. The photograph was one that he himself, in his role as a friend and photographer of the Royal Family, had taken on a holiday visit to Sandringham in 1890. Its subject was Prince Albert Victor, Duke of Clarence and Avondale, known to his family and friends as Eddy. The eldest son of the then–Prince and Princess of Wales, Prince Eddy was heir presumptive to the throne and stood next in the line of succession after his father, who was now King Edward.

But the prince had led a wayward life, and by the age of twenty-five, his reputation as a notorious playboy was the cause of much headshaking and public rebuke. Charles himself, in his investigation into a blackmail plot against young Winston Churchill and his mother Jennie, had uncovered the details of Eddy's illegal marriage to a Roman Catholic commoner named Annie Crook, who was still living, and the birth of a daughter, now under the care of the artist, Walter Sickert. Worse, during the dreadful days of the Ripper killings, there had been endless rumors that the Prince— who was derisively known as Collars and Cuffs to the newspapers—was involved in the murders, and that he might even have been the Ripper himself.

And then, as if that wasn't bad enough, the Prince had been caught up in a terrible scandal in a male brothel on Cleveland Street, involving a group of young boys, postal employees, and several of Eddy's close friends. The Prince of Wales himself had taken charge of concealing his son's criminal and immoral acts, with the help of the Prime Minister, Lord Salisbury. Eddy's father managed to keep his son out of the dock, packing him off to India, where his frivolities were less likely to make the London papers.

Given all this, it was widely felt that the Prince was

utterly unfit to be King, and there were those in the Court who were convinced that if Eddy remained in the line of succession, the monarchy would surely fall. So when news came in early 1892 of the Prince's sudden and completely unexpected death, most were vastly relieved, feeling that the Crown itself had been saved. Some, however, believed that his death, which had taken place in the privacy of Sandringham, was far too convenient. Many said openly that it wasn't illness that had felled him, and a few even said that he must have been murdered—poisoned, perhaps. Others had whispered that perhaps the Prince had not died at all but had been shut away somewhere, so that his younger brother George, a more acceptable and better-behaved heir, could step into his place.

But all this had happened a full decade ago. Prince Albert Victor was a distant and distasteful memory that was awakened only by the Royal Family's annual pilgrimage to his ornate marble tomb and occasional Royal references to "poor darling, departed Eddy." If word got out that his death had been a sham, the revelation would have an incalculable impact upon the general public—especially now that the old Queen Victoria was dead, the new King Edward had ascended the throne, and a living Prince Eddy would stand just behind his father in the succession. An announcement that the Prince was alive would certainly cause enormous embarrassment and perhaps even the fall of the monarchy. The new King hadn't been crowned yet, the Government held a precarious position because of protests against the war, and the whole situation was uncomfortably volatile. No wonder His Royal Majesty commanded secrecy.

The colonel cleared his throat, attempting to regain his composure. "This . . . Lord Osborne. He's the man we're looking for, Captain?"

"That's right." Kirk-Smythe's face tightened. "Lord Osborne's likeness may be recognized, unfortunately, so we can't put the picture out without giving away the game. In the event, he is rather changed, according to Angus Duff. His hair has grown quite gray, and he has gained a stone or more. I suggest that we rely upon a description which I have prepared and had copied for your use, Colonel Paddington. Anyone fitting Lord Osborne's general description should be brought in for identification."

Recollecting his duty, the colonel put away his disbelief. "Thank you, Captain," he said in a formal tone. "Is there anything else?"

Kirk-Smythe paused, selecting his words carefully. "Only this, Colonel. Should your men encounter anyone speaking in a foreign accent or seeming to be a stranger to the district, he should be conveyed immediately to Brigadier Lord Sheridan for questioning. Until we get this sorted out, no one from the outside should be allowed in and no one from the inside should go out. The local men already at the observation posts can help your men identify residents of the area." He cleared his throat. "Now, if you don't object, I should like to have a further word with Brigadier Lord Sheridan."

"There will no doubt be additional orders shortly, Colonel Paddington," Charles said tactfully, "as the situation becomes somewhat clearer. Perhaps you could deploy your troops now."

Deployment, at least, was something the colonel understood. He stepped back, snapped a salute to Charles, nodded to Kirk-Smythe, and strode down the platform. "Sergeant-Major!" he bawled. "Get the men out. Empty the train!"

CHAPTER NINE

(The "monster" of Glamis died some time before 1876) but the story was deliberately continued and extended in order to camouflage the latest secret: that Prince Albert Victor, Eddy, the man who should have been king, was still alive and locked away in the castle, perhaps in the very same secret parts that had once housed the so-called monster.

The Ripper & the Royals
Melvyn Fairclough

The men in Germany who at the turn of the century were organising their Secret Service on a war basis had concentrated their attention on spying against Britain and by doing so had stolen an advantage in the espionage game.

A History of the British Secret Service
Richard Deacon

Charles turned back to Kirk-Smythe. "So Prince Eddy has been sequestered here at Glamis for the past ten years?"

"It's true, m'lord, incredible as it may seem."

Charles put his hand on the younger man's arm. "Sheridan, please, Andrew. There's no need for formality between us."

Kirk-Smythe tried not to look flattered. "Right, then. Well, as you probably know, Lord Strathmore is a close friend of the King's, and his lordship's son Patrick was a classmate of Eddy's at Cambridge. I suppose it was natural for them to offer Glamis as a place of safe-keeping."

"I know Lord Strathmore quite well," Charles said, "and Patrick and I were once friends, although we haven't seen one another recently. I've visited Glamis Castle on several occasions—the last time around ninety-four, I think." He paused, recalling that Prince George, Eddy's younger brother, had been one of the party, as well. "That would have been two years after the so-called death. Was Eddy here then?"

Kirk-Smythe nodded. "Immediately after his death was staged, the Prince was brought here, under the name of Lord Osborne. Since you've been in the castle, you know that there's ample room for someone to live in complete privacy." His grin was wry. "An entire cricket squad, come to that. Biggest damn castle in Scotland. Hundreds of places to hide a fellow—like that 'monster' who's said to have been locked up in some secret place."

"But Eddy's not hiding there now," Charles said gravely.

Kirk-Smythe gave him a wry look. "He was discovered missing on Monday morning." He paused uncomfortably. "But that's not the whole of it, I'm afraid. That same morning, the body of one of the women who attended to Eddy, a long-time employee of the Strathmore family, was discovered in the park. Her throat was slit ear-to-ear, in the manner of the Ripper."

"Uh-oh," Charles said in a low voice, seeing the difficulty at once. "Bad business."

"Very bad business indeed," Kirk-Smythe said. "Angus Duff telegraphed word of the escape and the murder to Whitehall, and the Prime Minister relayed it to King Edward, who devised the plan that I've communicated to you. He has instructed me to tell you that the woman's murder must be resolved expeditiously, for obvious reasons. I'm speaking of the similarity to the Ripper's method, of course."

Charles could only imagine the Royal reaction to this horrifying tangle of events. "But Prince Eddy wasn't responsible for the Whitechapel killings," he said. At least not directly, he added to himself, although it had been the Prince's illicit marriage to Annie Crook that set the stage for the Ripper murders.*

"That may be true," Kirk-Smythe replied. "But the King is concerned that this murder be solved as quickly and quietly as possible. If word gets to the Edinburgh newspapers, a great deal of unwelcome attention will be focussed on Glamis, and another safe haven will have to be arranged for the Prince—when he is found."

Charles shook his head. "My God," he said softly. "This *is* an unholy mess."

Kirk-Smythe made a rueful face. "I'm afraid it's likely to get even messier. For some time, we've been aware of a German agent—his code name is Firefly—who is operating in and around Edinburgh. One of Gustav Steinhauer's men, perhaps. He has recently been seen in this district. I'm attempting to obtain a photograph from our archives, so that

---

*The story of these events is related in *Death at Whitechapel*.

we can keep a lookout for him." He paused and added reluctantly, "I fear that we must face the possibility that the Germans are somehow responsible for Prince Eddy's disappearance."

Charles let out his breath slowly. "You're suggesting that the Prince did not simply escape? That he was *kidnapped?*" The thought left him cold, for he knew very well that the Kaiser wouldn't hesitate to use Prince Eddy to embarrass the British Crown, even to the extent of endangering the monarchy.

"It's a likelihood that we must consider," Kirk-Smythe replied gravely, "although I should hope we won't have to reveal the possibility to Colonel Paddington. The fewer people who know about this, the better." He looked out toward the Grampians, rising to the west, and added reflectively, "If they've already got him away, he could be anywhere. There, in the mountains, which are nothing but rugged crag and cranny, blanketed with forest." He grimaced. "That's where Bonnie Prince Charlie eluded Cumberland's capture for nearly half a year, you know, during the Forty-five Rebellion. Eddy could be hidden in those mountains, or he could be halfway to Germany. We have a few agents watching the major ports, but it's a thin net, with far too many holes."

Charles shook his head bleakly, feeling that he was faced with an impossible task. "You mentioned an agent named Firefly. What was he up to in Edinburgh?"

"The same thing we're up to ourselves, here and there, I should imagine. Keeping track of arms production, estimating naval capabilities, identifying disaffected indigenous groups who might be useful in certain circumstances." Kirk-Smythe gave a little shrug. "That sort of thing."

That sort of thing. Charles knew that the Military Intelligence branch had come to new life during the war in South Africa, but British intelligence still lagged far behind that of France and Russia—and particularly Germany. Downing Street rarely saw intelligence reports, and the War Office regarded MI as rather like a reference library, able to provide useful background information but not good for much else. The thought that foreign espionage agents might be responsible for Prince Eddy's disappearance from Glamis made him desperately uneasy, for the Lord knew that this business was already complicated enough, and the prospects for success were not encouraging. He silently entertained the wish that he could return to Housesteads and the long-dead Romans, where the puzzles were more easily resolved. But he was under the King's instructions. There was nothing for it but to carry on.

Aloud, he said, "How did you manage to get yourself involved in this, Andrew?"

Kirk-Smythe spoke with dry humor. "How did I manage to get mixed up in this wretched mess, do you mean? The group to which I am attached works with codes and ciphers, and I was seconded as cryptographer for the King's trip to Germany. I was with him and the German Court in Hamburg—that's another interesting story, believe me—when we received the coded dispatch from Whitehall, relaying Duff's message that Prince Eddy was gone, and there was a murder to hand. It was at first hoped that Eddy had simply got lost and might wander back to the castle before the lot of you arrived. In that case, the mission would have been aborted, the train would have returned to London, and no one would have been the wiser." He sighed. "Nothing has been seen or heard of the Prince since Monday, however. I've done my best to get things under control since I arrived here, but the resources have been entirely inadequate. And as far as the murder is concerned—well, I must tell you frankly that this is out of my league. The King insists that the killer's identity be established beyond question. A tall order, it seems to me."

Charles chewed on his lower lip. He had nothing of what would be required for even a minimal criminal investigation, and he was doubtful about finding a chemist's shop in a village as tiny as Glamis. "I'm afraid we are in the same boat, Andrew. My holiday was not a photographic expedition. Kate has her camera and developing equipment with her, but I do not, much less—"

Kirk-Smythe broke into a broad grin. "Not to worry, Sheridan. I made a quick visit to one of your friends at the Yard. He's sent what you need to take fingerprints, and more besides."

Charles wished fleetingly that Kirk-Smythe had not been so thorough in his preparations. It left him no excuses. But he refrained from saying so, merely nodding and asking instead, "What else has been done besides putting out the observation posts?"

"Some searching, but not terribly systematic, I'm afraid. Duff went round to several possible hiding places—I've marked them on the map—but we haven't had the time nor the men for a comprehensive manhunt. I've also had Duff prepare a roster of the household staff—twenty or so." He took out a paper and handed it to Charles, who unfolded it and glanced at the handwritten list of names.

"The four marked with asterisks?" he asked.

"They had regular contact with the Prince, bringing his meals, taking care of his personal needs, and so on. Hilda MacDonald, who's first on the list, was the murder victim. Flora MacDonald is her daughter; it was she who found her mother's body on the path to the village. Both of them had daily responsibilities for Prince Eddy's care, Hilda for the entire time of his stay, Flora for the past four or five years. You've already met Angus Duff, the factor. He was in overall charge. Simpson is the house steward."

Charles pocketed the list. "You've spoken to them?"

"To all but Hilda," Kirk-Smythe replied dryly. "Whatever she knew goes to the grave with her. None of the other three admit to any knowledge of the Prince's disappearance. They didn't seem entirely comfortable with my questions, but in the circumstance . . ." He shrugged. "I told them that you would be conducting more extensive interviews."

"What is known in the village about this affair?"

"The village is an extension of the estate, to all intents and purposes. Most of the villagers are either on the Strathmore staff or related to an employee. On the one hand, this has the disadvantage of encouraging the spread of rumor—especially with regard to the murder of Hilda MacDonald. On the other, it has the advantage of encouraging the villagers' cooperation." He paused. "Declaring martial law would have been damned awkward, if we'd had to do it. It would have attracted attention."

"To say the least." Charles turned to watch a squad of men unloading the military bicycles. "The idea of using a bicycle reconnaissance maneuver to explain the presence of the Guards—it was masterful. Yours?"

Kirk-Smythe nodded briefly. "Thanks. It was the best I could think of."

Charles thought back to what he knew of Prince Eddy, whom he had last seen only a few months before his so-called death, ten years before. Then, his behavior had been noticeably irrational. "What does Duff say about the Prince's behavior and mental state in the past few weeks?"

"At times, he apparently seemed almost normal, whilst

at other times . . ." Kirk-Smythe pursed his lips. "Apparently he suffers from intermittent delusions of some sort, rather serious, I take it. Duff was vague, but the coroner, Dr. Henry Ogilvy, is a Strathmore family confidante and has treated the Prince from time to time. His name is on your list. He will no doubt be able to give you better information."

"Ah, the coroner," Charles said, feeling on more familiar ground. "Has he held the inquest into Hilda MacDonald's murder?"

"It's been called for this afternoon, but he could probably be persuaded to postpone it, if you think best. The body is in his care. At my request, the constable showed me the murder scene on the path to the village. Couldn't make much of it, but I posted a guard with orders that it not be disturbed." He paused. "I'm afraid that the constable—a youngish fellow—may be a bit of a problem. Glamis is his territory, and he doesn't like interference."

"I don't suppose one can blame him for that. Anything else?"

Kirk-Smythe turned up his collar against a spit of rain. "I haven't inspected the Prince's quarters in the castle. I locked the rooms, Charles, thinking to leave that to you."

Charles hunched his shoulders. "Well, then," he said, "that seems like the place to begin." He looked up at the gray, blowing clouds. "At least it will take us indoors, out of the weather. Let's get on with it, shall we?"

CHAPTER TEN

I must own that when I heard door after door shut, after my conductor had retired, I began to consider myself as too far from the living, and somewhat too near the dead.

Sir Walter Scott
on a visit to Glamis Castle, 1793

Flora took up a paraffin lamp from a hallway table and lit it. Kate's bags were being taken upstairs, and she was about to be given her promised tour of the castle.

"If ye'll come this way, m'lady," Flora said in a low voice, "I'll show ye the aulder parts o' the castle first."

Picking up her skirts, Kate followed the young woman down the circular stone staircase into the depths of the Great Tower, which had been built, according to Flora, between 1435 and 1459. A moment later, Flora took a key off a peg set high in the wall and opened a heavy wooden door, stepping aside to let Kate enter.

They were standing just inside the crypt, a stone-walled, vaulted room said to be the place where Macbeth treacherously slew King Duncan. Flora pointed out, however, that the story of Duncan's murder could scarcely be true, since he had actually died in 1040, some four hundred years before even the oldest part of the castle was begun.

But Flora's matter-of-fact recital took away none of the room's sinister, shadowy mystery. Kate shivered as she looked around, imagining the echo of tramping feet and angry shouts, the clang of swords, the final despairing cry.

"Ghosts," she whispered, thinking that this was exactly the place Beryl Bardwell had been looking for.

"Aye," Flora said in a low, uneasy voice. "There be many restless spirits who walk o' nights in this place." She bit her lip and might have said more, but seemed to think better of it.

Kate caught the flicker of a shadow out of the corner of her eye and turned. "This must be where the Monster of Glamis was imprisoned," she said eagerly. "Lord Halifax told me that when he visited the castle, he heard that someone had been shut up in a secret room just off the crypt, within the wall itself. He said—"

"Lord Strathmore has forbidden us tae say awt about the matter," Flora interrupted. She raised her lamp and went toward the door.

Kate wanted to ask her to wait so she could explore the crypt more thoroughly, but since she did not want to be left in the dark, she followed obediently.

Once on the stairway again, the key safely on its peg, Flora seemed easier. "There be ghosts aplenty in th' castle, if ghosts're what ye've coom seeking." Her voice lightened. "Ye might look out for th' Gray Lady who cooms intae the chapel tae say her prayers. Or the little servant boy who sits on th' bench outside one of th' bedrooms. Or Earl Beardie, who gambles and carouses with th' devil in one of the towers, makin' no end o' racket. Many say they've heard him, rantin' an' ravin'.'" She smiled with a dry irony. "Oh, there be a great plenty o' ghosts here at Glamis."

"Yes, of course," Kate murmured, feeling that she had inadvertently stumbled upon a most interesting subject and making a mental note to dig a little deeper into the mystery of the crypt and the Monster of Glamis, about whom the servants were forbidden to speak. But now they were going up the stairs again to a grand dining room sumptuously decorated with a splendid plaster ceiling, an elaborate fireplace with a tall oak armorial mantel, and impressive full-length portraits of various members of the Strathmore family—a dining room fit for royalty, certainly. From the dining room, they went to the vaulted drawing room, the former Great Hall where Mary, Queen of Scots held court during her visit in August 1562. Kate drew in her breath, imagining the tragic Queen, now over three hundred years dead, sitting with her ladies-in-waiting in royal splendor in this very room. Everywhere she turned at Glamis, some chapter of its ancient story was opened up, as if the castle were a book filled with six hundred years of human history—nearly a thousand, if one turned all the way back to the tale of King Duncan and the faithless Thane of Glamis. Her fingers itched for her notebook and camera, to record some of these fascinating scenes.

At last, they stopped at the open door to a bedroom, where, Flora told her, the young Sir Walter Scott had spent an uneasy night in 1793, disturbed by the unhappy spirit of the defeated Bonnie Prince Charlie. The bed was still covered with the Scott tartan, Flora pointed out, adding that Scottish visitors to Glamis always slept beneath their own plaid.

"Sir Walter used part o' the story o' Glamis in his novel

The Antiquary," she added. "He gave it th' name o' Glenallan House."

Kate smiled, looking around the small room and reflecting happily that Glamis was the ideal setting for a book— Beryl's *next* book. Lady Macbeth might be the main character, perhaps. Or Mary, Queen of Scots. Or—

"Didn't Bonnie Prince Charlie also visit Glamis?" she asked excitedly. Now, *that* would be a marvelous story, full of romance, mystery, and bloody intrigue. The tale of the Young Pretender to the throne of England, forced to hide out in the Highlands, then fleeing for his life to the islands off the west coast of Scotland.

"The Bonnie Prince slept here for sev'ral nights after the battle at Falkirk," Flora replied, "in January of 1746. But his stay was a great secret, for his cause was already lost, y'see. Lord Thomas Strathmore, his host, feared that if 'twere known he had harbored the Prince, the English'd seize the estate. Shortly after," she added, "Lord Strathmore was forced to accommodate the e'il Duke o' Cumberland, who was hot on the trail of Prince Charlie, burning and looting and plundering."

Kate listened with interest, for this was a chapter in the history of Scotland that had always fascinated her. Bonnie Prince Charlie was one of the most famous of Scottish heroes, although he was not a true Scot at all but an Englishman born in exile, into the Stuart line. Prince Charlie's Catholic grandfather, James II, who ruled England from 1685 to 1689, had been deposed by William of Orange, a Dutch Protestant who aimed to make the country proof against Popery. Charlie's father, James III (often called the Old Pretender), came to Scotland in 1715 in an unsuccessful effort to regain the English throne. That was what came to be called the First Jacobite Rebellion. Prince Charlie—the Young Pretender—was born after his father's flight to France, and in 1745 made another bid to recover the throne for the Stuarts, the brutal campaign of the Forty-five, the Last Jacobite Rebellion. When the charismatic young leader raised his father's Stuart standard at Glenfinnan in August of 1745, the Catholic clans rallied to him. Within the month, he held control of nearly all of Scotland and began to move south into England, defeating the troops of George II at several points along the way.

By January, the Prince had reached Derby, 127 miles from London, but the promised French support did not materialize, and the English Catholics, fearing reprisals, failed to join the rebellion. It was clear that the Stuart cause was lost, and Charlie and his men turned back northward. Their ragged retreat became a rout after the Battle of Culloden, the bloodiest battle in Scottish history. By April 1746, the Prince, who had fired the imagination and raised the hopes of so many, was a hunted fugitive with thirty thousand English pounds on his head. While the English general, Lord Cumberland (the Bloody Duke, he was called), leveled reprisals against the Scots, Bonnie Prince Charlie spent the next five months hiding in the Highlands. At last, disguised as the maid of a loyal Scotswoman, he escaped to the Isle of Skye and thence to France.

"There's so much history in this place," Kate said softly. "So many stories in these stones." She added, in a lighter tone, "You know, I wouldn't be a bit surprised to meet Prince Charlie's ghost tonight."

Flora's luminous gray eyes rested on her. Kate saw that they were filled with sadness, and that there were lines of strain around her mouth. She put out her hand to ask if there was some trouble, but the young woman seemed to pull away, and Kate dropped her hand.

Several staircases and passageways later, Kate found herself installed in a spacious suite of guest rooms: a large bedroom, a sitting room, and even a modern bathroom, all decorated in a cheerful yellow. The diamond-paned casements looked out onto a pretty garden, beyond which Kate could see the wagon into which the baggage of Lady Glamis had been loaded. Lady Glamis herself was being handed into a waiting carriage. As Kate watched, another woman—the nanny, probably—appeared with little Elizabeth, the antic Mickie, and two older children. They got into the carriage, and a moment later, were gone.

Taking off her hat and gloves, Kate went to put them on the bed, noticing that the bags had arrived and were sitting beside the door, along with the large wooden box that contained her portable darkroom equipment. As she turned, she saw Flora standing at the other window, a wrenching sadness on her face and tears pooling in her gray eyes.

"Why, whatever is the matter, my dear?" Kate exclaimed. And then, belatedly grasping the significance of the black ribbon in the young woman's hair, added, "You're in mourning, aren't you, Flora?"

Flora nodded, making an effort to compose herself. But when Kate stepped forward and took her in her arms, she gave in and began to weep. At last, she stepped back, scrubbing the tears from her cheek with the back of her hand. "Please forgive me, m'lady. I shouldn't hae distressed ye."

"I'm only distressed for your sake," Kate said, taking her hand and leading her to a sofa, then sitting beside her. She took out a handkerchief and handed it to Flora. "You've lost someone dear to you?"

"My mother, Hilda MacDonald," Flora whispered. "I found her on Monday mornin', on th' path tae th' village. Ye can almost see the spot frae the window."

"Oh, I'm so sorry!" Kate exclaimed. She was suddenly seized by a guilty thought. "But surely the Strathmores could have spared you for a few days. If you've been pressed into service because Lord Sheridan and I have come, I shall be glad to tell Simpson that we can look after ourselves. We are accustomed to traveling without servants." This was very true, for Kate could not accustom herself to being dressed and undressed as if she had no strength of her own, and she wore her hair simply enough that she did not require someone to manage it.

"Nae, truly, m'lady," Flora replied, beginning to recover herself. "I could hae had th' time, had I asked. But I prefer tae be here, at work. I need tae be doin' ordin'ry things, so I willna hae time tae think aboot it." She swallowed. "But I fear I mun be absent this afternoon, tae attend th' coroner's inquest. My mother was . . . she was murdered, y'see."

"Murdered!" Kate took the young woman's cold hands in her own. "Oh, how dreadful, Flora! Have the police apprehended the killer?"

Flora shook her head dumbly, her mouth trembling. "Nae," she whispered.

Feeling a deep pity, Kate squeezed her hands and let them go. "Perhaps you'd feel better if you talked about it."

"There's nowt tae say." Flora dropped her head. "Mother and me, we live in Glamis Village. Sometimes she stayed here all th' night, though, so I didn't worry o'ermuch when she didn't coom home on th' Sunday evenin'. I found her th' next mornin,' on my way tae the castle, dead. It was . . . a dreadful sight tae see."

A dreadful sight—of course, it must have been, for a young daughter to have found her mother dead. Kate swallowed hard. It was all well and good for novelists to write about violent death—she had certainly written enough about it when Beryl Bardwell was composing those sensational penny dreadfuls for her American audience. But the awful horror of real violence was often beyond belief, not a fit subject for fiction.

Flora straightened her shoulders, and her voice steadied. "I'm quite all right now, m'lady. I'm sorry tae've burdened you wi' my misfortune." She stood, pulling herself erect. "I'll see tae yer unpackin', and if ye've any pressin' tae be done, I'll take care of it. But p'rhaps ye'd like a tea tray first?"

Kate stood, too, shaking her head. "A tea tray won't be necessary, Flora. And I can manage the unpacking myself, thank you."

Flora gave her a surprised look. "Ye're sure, m'lady?" When Kate nodded, she indicated a bell-button on the wall. "Well, then, please ring if ye need me. Luncheon is us'lly served at twelve-thirty. Ye're free t' walk i' the garden, if ye like. It looks tae be rainin' now, but it'll likely clear afore long, and th' roses are verra pretty just now."

When Flora had gone, Kate went to the window and stood, gazing out across the emerald-green park to the fringe of dark trees and the wilder wood beyond. The misting rain did nothing to diminish the beauty of the landscape, and murder here seemed grotesquely out of place. Who would have killed a servant on her innocent way home from a day's hard work? She frowned a little. Might the woman's death have something to do with Charles's summons to Scotland?

But surely not, she decided. Flora must feel her mother's loss very deeply, but it was hardly the sort of event that would prompt King Edward to call up a company of Household Guards.

And however sad or tragic, one more death could be of little consequence to Glamis Castle, where death had been so frequently in residence for nearly five centuries.

CHAPTER ELEVEN

What of the ghastly Glamis secret? About a century or more ago, the legend says, a monster was born into the Strathmore family. He was the heir—a creature fearful to behold. It was impossible to allow this deformed caricature of humanity to be seen—even by their friends. . . . But, however warped and twisted his body, the child had to be reared to manhood—in secret. But where? Glamis, with its sixteen-feet-thick walls, had many answers.

The Queen Mother's Family Story
James Wentworth Day

It took some time to pry Angus Duff away from his consultation with Colonel Paddington, and even then, he seemed oddly reluctant to lead Charles and Kirk-Smythe to the Prince's quarters. After listening to several lame excuses, Charles at last insisted that they must not delay any longer. The Panhard had by that time been unloaded from the train, and at Duff's direction, Charles drove the motorcar across muddy fields and through a damp wood to the back of the castle where the stables, smithy, and kitchen gardens were located.

If Charles had thought that they might be going to a

secret dungeon prison, hidden away in the thick stone walls of the castle, he was quickly disabused of the notion. Passing through a small, low door, they climbed several twisting flights of stairs to a remote wing of the massive building, where Duff took two iron keys from a peg in the wall and unlocked a door onto an empty corridor, then another to a private apartment.

While Kirk-Smythe stood near the door and Duff looked on, chewing nervously on his mustache, Charles surveyed the suite of rooms where Prince Albert Victor had lived. It was large and elegantly appointed, more like a suite in an exclusive hotel than a place of imprisonment. True, there were no windows, but skylights admitted plenty of light, and the gray-stone walls were brightened by paintings, tapestry hangings, and bookshelves full of leather-bound volumes—a quite respectable library, he thought, glancing at the titles. All of Sir Walter Scott's work, Dickens, Tennyson, Shakespeare, along with Conan Doyle, Winston Churchill, Robert Louis Stevenson, Rudyard Kipling, even two of Beryl Bardwell's novels. The Prince evidently spent a great deal of time reading—a fact that was perhaps a little surprising, since the Royal Family, like most aristocrats of Charles's acquaintance, seemed to regard bookishness as an impediment to good sense. Perhaps, ironically, Eddy's imprisonment had freed him to choose art and literature over the pursuit of other, more unsavory pleasures.

Charles turned around, taking in other details of the place. A door in one wall led to a comfortably-appointed bedroom, the bed neatly made. The sitting room, where they were, was furnished with upholstered chairs, a sofa, and a small dining table. A fire had burned to ashes in the fireplace.

The other end of the room, under a skylight, had been used as a painter's studio. Oils and watercolors were stacked against the wall, and there was an easel with a tall stool in front of it. On the easel sat an unfinished portrait of Queen Alexandra, apparently painted from a photograph, which was propped on a nearby table. Charles stood in front of the portrait for a moment or two, studying it with a growing sense of sadness. If he had needed any more proof to convince him that Prince Eddy had indeed lived in these rooms, this portrait of the Queen would have done so.

Charles came back to the center of the room and turned to the factor. "I understand that you have been responsible for Prince Eddy's care, for . . ." He paused, wanting to draw the man into conversation, rather than hammer at him with questions. "For how long, now? Seven or eight years?"

Duff hesitated. Charles sensed that long, loyal service had made the safeguarding of the Strathmore family secrets a kind of second nature with the man. He would not be able to give them up easily to a stranger, even to one who possessed a royal commission.

"Glamis is certainly an ideal place to get away from the world of the Court," Charles went on reminiscently. "I've been here myself on several occasions, the last time with Patrick and Prince George in ninety-four. I'm not much of a gun, but I remember a rare day when Patrick, George, Lord Strathmore, and I bagged over three hundred wild pheasants. We got all sorts—Chinese, black-necks, ring-necks, Mongolians. Walked them up in the wet bogs." He shook his head. "Odd to think that Eddy might've been in residence here at the time, and I had no notion of it."

Duff visibly relaxed. "Ninety-four? Aye, Prince Eddy was here right enough, m'lord. He's been here just on ten years and a few months." He looked around. "It isna Buckingham Palace, o'course, and it's a bit nippy i' the winter, when the wind whips across the Grampians and doon Strathmore

Vale." He paused and added thoughtfully, "But he's been happy here, I b'lieve. He seems tae like the quiet, p'rhaps on account of his deafness. Loud noises distress him, y'see. He doesna like tae hunt for that reason, although I'm told he was a good 'un with a gun, in his youth."

His deafness. Charles looked again at the portrait of Queen Alexandra, painted by a loving hand, with great tenderness and regard. Their shared deafness—a family trait that the Queen had inherited from her mother and passed on to her son—had always been one of the powerful bonds of affinity between Eddy and his mother. As a young boy, his tutor and subsequent instructors had thought him slow, even mentally deficient, and no one except Alexandra had ever seemed to connect the Prince's learning difficulty with his hearing difficulty. The Queen's own deafness was quite obviously progressive, worsening in the past few years to the point where she no longer tried to listen and only half-pretended to hear and understand. Like his mother, Eddy must by now be nearly stone deaf, which meant that no amount of hailing by searchers was likely to gain a response.

He doesn't like to hunt, Duff had said. Charles turned back to the factor. "The Prince is allowed out of the castle, then?"

Duff nodded. "Lord Strathmore instructed that he's tae hae the freedom o' the policies frae ten tae three every day, when there are nae guests in the house. He might gae further, if he's escorted."

"Escorted by whom?"

"By mysel'," Duff replied, "or by Simpson, or Hilda or Flora MacDonald. He fancies a bit of a walk in the woods on fine days with Flora."

"How many of the staff know he's here, or who he is?"

Duff spoke cautiously. "Simpson and I knew who he is o' course, and Dr. Ogilvy, who is a friend of Lord Strathmore. The rest of the staff, includin' the MacDonald mother and daughter—they were all told that his name is Lord Osborne, a Strathmore fam'ly friend confined for reasons o' health tae this private wing. Naebody but the MacDonalds are tae hae any contact with him. If they should come upon him in the grounds, they are tae gi'e him a wide berth and in no circumstance are tae speak with him." He grunted. "Willna do them much good tae try, if I may say, so deaf the poor fellow has become."

"I see," Charles said quietly. "Besides walking, what does he do with his time?"

"He likes tae read, o'course." Duff gestured toward the crowded bookshelves. "And paint. Often takes his gear and an easel intae the garden or up in the hills. And he writes poetry. He's always scribblin' verse. Seems tae keep himself busy and fit. And his family visits from time tae time— brother and sisters, I should say." He pulled a long face. "Never his mother or father."

Charles nodded. He himself had witnessed the strained relationship between the then–Prince of Wales and his eldest son. He could easily understand why the father would not find it personally comfortable to visit—not to mention the possibility that a visit might lead to discovery. Alexandra would have wanted to see her eldest son, of course, but had probably been forbidden to do so.

He turned, his eye caught by a book that had fallen on the floor beside the chair nearest the fireplace. He went to it and picked it up, noticing that it was a first edition of Sir Walter Scott's *From Montrose to Culloden*, signed by the author and inscribed, "To my darling Eddy, from his loving Grandmama, Victoria R." And yet this valuable book was lying open and facedown on the floor, and some of the pages were bent over. He glanced at the table beside the chair, taking in the various items: a bottle of cognac and an empty glass, an ashtray overfull of stubbed-out cigarettes, a gold cigarette case, a Delft plate with two oranges, the peel from a third lying haphazardly on the table. Charles guessed that the Prince had been interrupted, perhaps violently, while he was reading, and that his book had fallen unnoticed to the floor.

"He was discovered missing early on Monday morning?" Charles asked, placing the book on the table and picking up the gold cigarette case. He wrapped it carefully in his handkerchief and pocketed it. At Duff's nod, he said, "Tell me what you know of his activities on Sunday."

Duff shifted from one foot to the other, uneasily, Charles thought. "O' course, I wasn't here, it bein' the Sabbath and me and mine at the kirk for services. But he prob'ly slept late, as was his custom. Hilda would've brought his breakfast. I know for a fact that he went for a walk, because I saw him in the park, late in the afternoon. May've worked on his painting. Hilda would've brought him his supper, then checked tae see what he needed 'fore she went home tae the village that night."

"But Hilda did not reach her home, as I understand it," Charles said. He looked up, catching the tightening around the factor's mouth, the flush that crept up his jaw.

Duff nodded. "Flora—her daughter—found her, on her way tae the castle early on Monday morning. On the path near the castle gate, where the poor woman had her throat slit." He looked down at the rug. "When Simpson and I checked these rooms, they were empty. I sent the men out tae look, o' course, but they found not a trace. Prince Eddy'd just vanished."

Charles followed Duff's glance at the floor, then raised

his eyes to the man's face. "His health? How did the Prince seem in the days before his disappearance?"

"No diff'rent than usual, m'lord. He'd got an odd notion intae his head, though." He looked embarrassed. "Thought he was Bonnie Prince Charlie, y'see. Not all the time, o'course. Came and went with him, the idea did. Dr. Ogilvy said it'd be best tae humor him. Said it couldna harm him tae think he was the Bonnie Prince, coom back tae th' Highland."

Bonnie Prince Charlie, who hid in the Highlands whilst Cumberland searched. Who eventually escaped over the sea to Skye, and France. "So you and the others fell in with his idea, then?"

Duff nodded. " 'Twas a game, I s'pose ye'd say. 'Specially for Flora. Flora MacDonald," he added gravely, making sure that Charles caught the significance.

"Ah," Charles said, understanding. "She of the famous name." The legendary Flora MacDonald was the brave Scotswoman who dressed Prince Charlie as her servant girl and got him safely to the Isle of Skye, under the nose of Cumberland's men. The name was revered, and by now, every MacDonald family in Scotland had its Flora. If Eddy had conceived the notion that he was the Bonnie Prince, Flora's presence would likely have fortified it.

Duff's mouth curled up at the corners. "Aye, Flora MacDonald. A bright girl, like her namesake. It was a game she played with the Prince, y'see—her bein' Flora herself. He seemed t'take it real, though. He was always talkin' aboot goin' o'er the sea tae Skye."

Charles thought that he should have to have a serious talk with Flora MacDonald, who might be able to tell him more about Eddy than anyone else. But for now, he had something else in mind.

"Thank you, Duff," he said. "I think that will be all, at

least for now. May I have the keys?" As Duff handed them over, he added, "I'll keep them, if you don't mind. Are there others?"

Duff shook his head. "Just these. Will that be all, m'lord?"

"For the moment, although I would appreciate it if you would wait with the motorcar. After I'm finished here, we have an errand, you and I."

When the door had closed, Charles beckoned to Kirk-Smythe and pointed to a waist-high spray of brown spots on the stone wall to the left of the door. "Dried blood, unless I miss my guess," he said. He crouched down, leaning closer to the wall, and found several smears and a large stained area. "Most of it has been washed away, but the traces are unmistakeable, wouldn't you say?"

Kirk-Smythe bent over to look. "It appears to be blood," he said doubtfully, "but—"

"And look at this rug." Charles went to the spot where Duff had been standing, on the red-figured rug near the door. "Notice this sun-faded area. It couldn't have been faded at this spot in the room, for there's no direct light here. I'd guess that this rug has been moved here from somewhere else. Give me a hand with it, Andrew, and we'll have a look at the floor beneath."

Together, they rolled the heavy carpet back. A large area of the dark wooden floor had been scoured hard enough to lighten its color. Charles took out his pocket knife, got to his knees, and began to dig at a joint between the floor boards. He lifted his knife, with thick brown residue on the tip.

"Blood here, too," he said, "although there's been a valiant effort to clean it up."

Kirk-Smythe frowned. "But how can you be sure it's

blood, Charles? Perhaps it's something else. Hot chocolate spilled from a pot, for instance. Or animal blood—leaving aside the question of how an animal might have come to be killed in this room, of course."

"I can't be absolutely sure, of course," Charles replied. "It's a pity that Professor Uhlenhuth isn't on the scene, with a beaker of that new serum of his. He could tell us whether it's blood, and if so, whether it's human blood."

Paul Uhlenhuth was a German professor who had recently developed a serum that—quite remarkably—could distinguish among the proteins of different blood residues, animal and human, regardless of the age or size of the sample. His pioneering work answered a question that forensic medicine had long, and sometimes desperately, asked: whether spots or stains found at the scene of a crime or on the property or person of a suspect were indeed bloodstains. And, just as important, Dr. Karl Landsteiner, a Viennese scientist, had the preceding March published a paper asserting that human blood could be identified according to a particular type, which he referred to as Types A, B, O, and AB. If true, this was indeed exciting, for it suggested that scientists might at some future time be able to distinguish the blood of one person from that of another.

"Uhlenhuth?" Kirk-Smythe looked thoughtful. "Now that you've mentioned it, I recall reading a newspaper report of a crime whilst I was in Germany, which Uhlenhuth appears to have solved. Happened on an island in the Baltic, as I recall. Two boys were murdered, and the police apprehended a man named Tessnow, who had been seen talking to them on the day of their deaths. He claimed that the stains on his clothing weren't blood but a certain dark-red wood stain that he used in his carpentry work. The clothing was sent to Professor Uhlenhuth, who found numerous evidences of human blood. I don't know that the accused has been tried yet, but the evidence against him seems quite strong."* He paused. "Are you considering the testing of this—whatever it is?"

"Perhaps that won't be necessary," Charles said, standing up. "We may be able to convince Duff to tell us what he knows about it."

Kirk-Smythe gave him a searching look. "So you think he's lying?"

Charles thought of the factor's glance at the rug—the telltale glance that had pulled his own attention to it. "I certainly think he knows about the bloodstains on the floor."

Kirk-Smythe was frowning. "Well, then, shouldn't we arrest the man?"

"Not yet," Charles said. "For the time being, we'll lock up the room and leave it as we found it. I'll come back later to take fingerprints. I'd especially like to have those of the Prince."

They arranged the rug as before, and Charles dusted his hands. "As to the factor, we'll leave him alone, too, for the time being. If he believes we've been taken in by his story, he may make a mistake. And we don't yet know who, if anyone, was killed here. It might be the woman whose body was found on the path, or—"

"But if she died in this room, that suggests that the Prince could have killed her," Kirk-Smythe exclaimed.

"It's something we must consider," Charles said. "However, I very much doubt that the Prince could have managed this very thorough clean-up. And the man I knew was not

---

*Ludwig Tessnow was tried, convicted, and finally executed in Griefswald Prison in 1904. Uhlenhuth's serum immediately became a vital tool in the forensic investigative process.

terribly strong. If Eddy killed Hilda MacDonald, someone else must have disposed of the body on the path where it was found. But there's another possibility, you know."

Kirk-Smythe stared at him. "That the blood is that of Prince Eddy himself?"

"Yes." Charles reflected that if Eddy had died here, King Edward might think it for the best—or might even have been involved, heaven help them. Charles certainly did not like the idea that he himself might have become a pawn in yet another royal deception involving the hapless Eddy. But he felt that King Edward knew him well enough to understand that he would follow the truth, wherever it took him. And the deployment of a trainload of Household Guards would be too much theater for even the King's theatrical tastes.

Kirk-Smythe groaned. "Well, if he's dead, I should hate to be the one to carry the news to the King."

"Let's hope that won't be necessary," Charles said, with feeling. "Let Paddington know that Duff and his men can't be trusted, and that there's a chance that the man we're searching for may be injured or dead. If he hasn't deployed the bicycles yet, have them sent out straightaway. It would also be good to send out small parties of men—no more than two or three—to search the barns and sheds on the estate's outlying farms. Oh, and if it hasn't been done, we'll need a guard at the castle gates."

"I'm on my way." Kirk-Smythe went to the door. "And you? Where are you off to?"

"I'll ask Duff to show me where Flora MacDonald found her mother's body, and then I'm bound for the village, to have a talk with Dr. Ogilvy."

It wasn't long before Charles was back in the Panhard, several lengths behind Duff and his skittish horse, which

seemed not to know what to make of the motorcar that
chugged noisily along behind him. They were headed down
the lane, in the direction of the place where Hilda Mac-
Donald's body had been discovered.

CHAPTER TWELVE

Tea . . . that newly invented luxury for ladies, so indispensable for their happiness, and so ruinous for their health—a forenoon tea.

The Victorian Kitchen
Jennifer Davies

Flora left Lady Sheridan to do her own unpacking with a little shake of her head, for most of the ladies who came to stay at the castle would never have thought of unpacking their own dresses, and would certainly never have turned down the offer of tea. But Flora understood from her speech that Lady Sheridan was an American, and she'd had enough experience with American guests to know that they were more independent than English ladies. More, Lady Sheridan's many questions about the castle's history had suggested both a deep curiosity and a wide intelligence, and her sympathy had been very warm and welcome—so warm, indeed, that it had encouraged Flora to say much more than she should have about her mother's death.

At the thought of her mother, Flora pressed her lips together. It was no good giving in to sadness, when she had something very important to do—and time to do it, since Lady Sheridan had so opportunely dismissed her. She hurried down the servants' stair to the lowest level of the castle, where the kitchen, pantries, larders, sculleries, and laundry rooms were located, along with the various closets and nooks where houseboys sharpened knives, cleaned shoes, and performed required valet services. If she made haste, she could have the task completed within the half hour.

When the Strathmores' children were growing up, the castle's permanent indoor staff had been quite large, forty or more, in the old days. But the children had moved away and returned only now and again for their holidays, as Lady Glamis and her brood had done. Lord and Lady Strathmore rarely gave large entertainments, so it was only the two of them to care for—and Lord Osborne, of course, who had been in residence for ten years or so. But a sizable staff still lived in, and various other people, including Flora and her mother, had their own homes in the nearby village and walked to and from the castle in the early mornings and late evenings.

At the door to the tea pantry, Flora cast a quick glance in both directions before going in and closing the door behind her. The tea pantry was out-of-bounds to the staff between early morning and afternoon tea, but Flora felt relatively safe. To judge from the rich odor of boiled chicken coming from the direction of the kitchen, Mrs. Thompson was already engaged in luncheon preparations, and the scullery and kitchenmaids were helping. The houseboys were out, the footman was elsewhere, the housekeeper, Mrs. Leslie, would be busy, and Simpson was nowhere to be seen. The pantry was as deserted now as it was likely to be all day.

Flora poked up the fire in the small stove that stood in

the corner and lifted the kettle that always sat on top to be sure that it contained enough hot water. Then she took down the largest tea tray she could find and began swiftly to collect what was needed: a large china pot and cup, with sugar and a pitcher of milk; several apples, a pear, a large chunk of cheese, and a knife; and a dozen of Lord Osborne's favorite ginger biscuits from the tin that stood full on the shelf. She did not want to risk discovery by venturing into the kitchen to see what might have been left from breakfast, but there was a plate of Sally Lunns and a few oatcakes on the shelf, and she took as many of these as she thought might not be missed when afternoon tea was prepared. Then, as an afterthought, she added half a loaf of bread and a pot of marmalade.

The kettle was boiling by the time the tray was full, and Flora was just filling the teapot when the door opened and Gladys Bruce came in with a wooden box of polished silver. Flora gave a guilty gasp, and Gladys jumped, spilling the box.

"I'm sorry," Flora said penitently, for Gladys was her friend. "Here, let me help ye pick it up."

"I should hope so," Gladys replied in an exasperated tone, as the two of them bent to gather the knives, spoons, and forks. "Ye'd scare a body tae death!" She pushed back the corkscrews of curly red hair that escaped from her white, lace-trimmed cap. "What're ye doin' in the tea pantry, Flora? Ye're s'posed tae be waitin' on the new lady guest this mornin'."

Flora pulled in her breath. She liked Gladys, and they had shared many confidences about their lives and loves as they changed bed linens, aired blankets, and dusted the family's rooms—all this before Flora had gone to work in Lord Osborne's suite. Moreover, Flora's mother had brought her up to regard a lie, even a minor one, as a dark and dangerous sin. But she had been caught proper, and since she could not tell Gladys the truth, she had no choice but to lie.

"I *am* waitin' on the new lady," she said. She spoke with as much dignity as she could muster, seeing that she was on her knees. She fished the last fork out of the corner and handed it to Gladys. "See there?" She pointed to the laden tea tray. "Lady Sheridan asked for a forenoon tea."

Gladys's eyes grew large. "All that for one lady?" she exclaimed, getting to her feet. "My goodness, Flora, she must hae an enormous appetite. Most ladies couldna eat that much in a week o' teas." She frowned. "An' she isna that large, either. I caught a glimpse o' her when she and Hamilton drove up, an' she seemed delicate enough. Who'd hae thought she'd eat like a bothy lad?"

Flora flushed, feeling herself not quite up to another, more elaborate lie. "She hadna breakfast," she said shortly, and changed the subject. "I mun gae along tae the inquest this afternoon, Gladys. I've Mr. Simpson's permission, and I've told Lady Sheridan that I mun be oot. Would ye mind lookin' in on her durin' the afternoon late, tae see if she needs awt afore I coom back?"

"Aye, o' course," Gladys said. She gave Flora an inquiring look. "Heard anything aboot Lord Osborne? Has he been found yet?"

"Gladys!" Flora gasped. "Ye're nae s'posed tae talk aboot Lord Osborne!"

"Ah, bosh, Flora," Gladys said, with a careless wave of her hand. "Ye can't keep folks frae talkin', here in the house and b'yond. Everybody knows the poor man's gone, and the soldiers hae coom tae look for him."

"The . . . soldiers?" Flora asked faintly.

"Aye," Gladys said. "Dinna ye hear of it?" She leaned

forward, her voice eager, her green eyes sparkling. "A whole trainload of soldiers, early this mornin'. Fine lookin' fellows, they are, with bicycles and guns. They're settin' up posts in all the roads, tae make sure that he doesna get clean away."

"How do ye *know* all this?" Flora asked, aghast. Mr. Simpson and Mr. Duff had dinned into her, time and again, that she was not under any circumstances to speak about Lord Osborne with any of the other servants, not even one whom she knew as well as she knew Gladys. Flora, a cooperative young woman, had obeyed, in part because she felt that it was a privilege to be allowed to wait on poor Lord Osborne, who bore all his trials with such patient fortitude. Of course, the other servants knew that an invalid friend of the family lived quietly to himself in a private suite on an upper floor of the west wing, and she supposed that from time to time they gossiped about him. But no one but she and her mother—and Mr. Simpson and Mr. Duff, of course—were ever permitted to be in his company, and no one had ever mentioned his name to her until now.

Gladys's freckled face became serious, and she put out her hand. "P'raps ye don't know what's bein' said, Flora. Aboot Lord Osborne, I mean. And what he did tae yer poor mother."

Flora stared at her. "What Lord Osborne did . . . Gladys, what *are* ye talkin' aboot?"

"Why, I'm tellin' ye what others are sayin'," Gladys replied. Her forehead creased. "But mayhap it's nae so guid tae talk about it just now, wi' the inquest and—"

Flora became fierce. "What are they sayin'?" she demanded, and when the other did not immediately speak, she seized her hand. "If ye're my friend, Gladys, ye'll tell me."

Gladys bit her lip, her green eyes dark with sympathy. "They're sayin' that he's the one who killed her," she replied, retrieving her hand. "But nae on the path, where ye found her. In his rooms, it were, and Mr. Simpson and Mr. Duff carried her oot, tae save him from bein' accused. And then he ran away, and has hid himself out in the forest. That's why the soldiers are here, ye see. They've coom tae arrest him fer murderin' your poor mother."

"But it's not true!" Flora exclaimed, horrified. "Lord Osborne couldna hae killed my mother. I know it! He's a guid man, and verra kind and sweet. He'd never—"

"Pooh, now, Flora," Gladys chided. She put out a hand and stroked her friend's cheek. "Ye know he's a strange one, nowt quite right in his mind. Ye canna know what he mighta done. Everybody's saying that it's only guid luck that he dinna kill you, too."

Flora dashed the hand aside and whirled to snatch up the heavy tray. "Everybody's wrong," she snapped. "And ye're wrong too, Gladys. Dinna stand in my way. I've work tae do." And with that, she shouldered the door open and marched out of the room.

Puzzled and hurt, Gladys went to the door and watched her friend as she walked toward the end of the hall. But instead of turning left to climb the stairs to the guest suites, where the new lady guest had been installed, Flora went straight ahead, in the direction of the oldest part of the castle.

Growing more puzzled by the moment, Gladys cocked her head and frowned, watching Flora out of sight.

CHAPTER THIRTEEN

On entering Glamis from the west on the left hand side is the Royal Bank of Scotland opened in 1865. Moving along is a row of cottages for workers. There are two thatched cottages, one of which was a bakers shop with a Bake House to the rear and behind the cottages there was a small hall where the Gardeners Society held their meetings and beside that was the local jail. Next is the Inn attached to which is a small farm with a pair of horses, two milk cows and some cattle. Next to this is the Post Office where all letters are stamped Glamis before being sent on. . . .

Glamis: A Village History
edited by A. R. Nicoll and D. Quigley

The misting rain had stopped, the skies were beginning to clear, and a pale sun shone, but the little village of Glamis—three dozen houses, a handful of shops, the Post Office, a smithy, and an austere church—remained gloomy, for it was built mostly of dark-gray stone that was stained even darker by the damp. This small village was huddled close against the park wall, as if claiming the protection of the lord whose castle was concealed beyond the trees.

Having just inspected the spot where the murdered

woman's body was found, Charles drove the Panhard along the narrow main street of the village. Passing a tobacconist's shop, the inn, and the Post Office, he kept well behind Duff's horse, which was still noticeably dismayed by the occasional pop and bang of the car's engine. As he drove, he saw surprised faces appearing at the mullioned windows of the one- and two-story houses which were set near the street, their steep tiled roofs topped with brick chimneys and clay chimney pots. At street level, a few windows sported window boxes, bright with geraniums and trailing ivy, and the street itself was cleanly swept. Between some of the houses Charles could glimpse green back-gardens filled with flowers and lines heavy with fresh laundry.

A pair of women in dark dresses, white aprons, and woolen shawls pressed themselves against a wall as he passed, clutching their market baskets and staring. Charles had the feeling that the attention was not due to the novelty of the motorcar, for the village was only fifteen miles from Dundee, and motorists must have already begun frequenting the roads. It was more likely the strange events of the morning that had them wondering, for gossiping tongues had no doubt spread word of the arrival of the soldiers, and the villagers must be curious about what was going on at Glamis estate. Paddington was already deploying his men across the countryside, and people were bound to be talking about the unusual sight of uniformed troops pedaling up and down the roads. He could only hope that the villagers had no idea of their real reason for being here—but he could not be sure even of that. Hilda MacDonald's murder had complicated everything.

As they reached the south end of the street, Duff reined in his horse and pointed to the red-painted door of a stone house, rather larger than most, befitting the station of a man who was the village doctor, the King's coroner, and a confidante of Lord Strathmore.

Charles pulled the Panhard as close to the wall as possible and cut the motor, waving as Duff turned his horse and rode, as he had been directed, back toward the castle. He had not wanted the factor, who was quite obviously withholding important information about Hilda MacDonald's murder—and quite possibly the disappearance of Prince Eddy—to be present during his interview with the doctor.

A shy little servant, barely into her teens, answered Charles's knock, and a moment later, showed him down the hall to a small consulting room at the back of the house. It was furnished with several chairs and a desk littered with papers and medical journals, a square table on which sat a compound microscope and several trays of glass slides, a dark oak bookcase crowded with leather-bound books, and a row of grinning skulls displayed on a shelf. Narrow windows looked out on a garden full of neatly-kept roses, and a small fire blazed in the grate of a brick fireplace. A closed door led, Charles suspected, to the surgery.

A stout man in a dark frock coat, nearly bald, rose from the chair in front of the fire where he had been reading, peering owlishly at Charles through thick, gold-rimmed glasses.

"Doctor Henry Ogilvy?" Charles asked.

The little man—standing, he came to no more than Charles's shoulder—inclined his bald head. "I am, my guid sir, at yer service." His Scots accent was thick and burry.

"I'm Charles Sheridan," Charles said. He added, a little self-consciously, for he was not accustomed to the rank, "Brigadier Lord Sheridan."

"Ah, yes," the doctor said briskly. "Ye're the man who's responsible for a' the commotion at the railway station this mornin'. Well, well, sit ye doon, my guid sir, sit ye doon." He pushed a stack of books off a chair and moved it nearer his own. "Maud will fetch us some tea—be off wi' ye, lassie—and when ye've warmed yer innards, ye shall tell me what brings ye tae Glamis."

Charles accepted the upholstered leather chair that the doctor offered, and they exchanged the usual pleasantries about the weather until Maud reappeared, quite soon, with a tray containing a cozied teapot, cups, sugar and milk, and a plate of hot scones. The doctor himself, his round face wreathed in smiles, poured tea.

"Now, then," he said invitingly, handing Charles a cup. "Will ye begin?"

Charles cleared his throat and spoke somewhat more formally than he had intended. "I have been authorized by the Home Secretary to take such actions as are necessary to resolve a delicate situation at the castle. I must ask you to treat what passes between us as a professional confidence."

"My guidness," Dr. Ogilvy said mildly. He leaned back in his chair, stretching his feet to the fire. "In other words, my lips are t'be sealed." He gave Charles a frown of exaggerated reproach. "Although, if I may say so, m'lord, ye need hardly hae mentioned it. One canna be a village doctor an' fail tae keep confidences."

Charles relaxed. "Yes, of course, thank you." He paused. "Perhaps we might begin with your observations—both as doctor and as coroner—regarding the murder of Hilda Mac-Donald."

"Ah, our poor Hilda." The doctor sighed gustily. "A terr'ble, terr'ble end. What d'ye wish tae know of it, sir?"

"I understand that you did not view the body where it was found—on the path, that is."

"Right. I knew naething of the murder until Constable Graham brought the body here. Flora, Hilda's daughter, discovered her mother on her way tae the castle early on Monday mornin'." He rubbed his hand across the top of his bald head. "Flora took it hard, o'course, an' the constable—who has a soft spot in his heart for the lass—dinna feel guid aboot leavin' poor Hilda on the wet ground."

"Rigor mortis had set in?"

"Already well advanced, I'd say."

"And what time was the body brought here?"

"A wee bit after sev'n in the mornin'."

Charles reflected. "So you would agree that Mrs. Mac-Donald must have been killed before midnight?"

"Aye, I would." The doctor peered through his glasses. "Ye're a doctor, m'lord?"

"I'm familiar with the conduct of postmortem examinations," Charles replied. "You might say that it is a hobby of mine. The body is still here, I assume? May I have a look at it?"

Without a word Dr. Ogilvy put down his teacup, hoisted himself out of his chair, and led the way into the surgery, then through an outside door and down a path to a small, vine-covered building, where the remains of Hilda Mac-Donald lay on a stone slab, covered with a white sheet.

Charles lifted the sheet and gazed at the naked body, pity welling up in him. She had been a handsome woman, with soft brown hair just faintly frosted with gray and a generous mouth that looked as if it were given to smiling. The gaping wound that slashed across the pretty throat was crusted with dried blood.

"The left carotid artery was severed," the doctor said quietly. " 'Twas most likely done from behind by a right-handed person wieldin' a sharp blade. The blessing is that death came quickly."

Charles studied the woman's upper torso, noting the pallor of the skin. Turning her gently to one side, he saw that her back was blue and mottled, where the blood that remained in the body had pooled. He lowered the body.

"Did Duff or the constable tell you in what position she was found?"

"I don't believe they did," the doctor said. "But from the mottling, I should think she was lying on her back."

Charles nodded. "I agree with your assessment," he said, taking out the small fingerprint kit that had been made up for him at the Yard. "But it seems to pose a problem. A short while ago, when Duff took me to the spot on the path where Flora found her mother, he said that the victim was discovered lying facedown."

The doctor's mouth tightened. "Ah," he said regretfully.

"And when I examined the soil of the path, I could find only a few small spots of blood, nothing like the larger quantity that must have been spilled had the victim's throat been cut there." Gently, Charles grasped the dead woman's hands and began to ink the tips of her fingers, in preparation for taking her prints.

"It would seem she must hae been killed elsewhere, then," the doctor said, his eyes fixed on what Charles was doing. "And brought tae the place where Flora found her."

Charles nodded. He felt it quite likely that Hilda Mac-Donald had been killed in Prince Eddy's apartment. And judging from Duff's demeanor, at the same time antagonistic and abashed, he was quite sure that the man possessed a guilty knowledge of the crime. Charles was not yet ready to share that information with the coroner, however, and went about his work in silence.

The doctor, observing, frowned. "I hae read about the uses of fingerprints," he said. "Collectin' them is one o' yer hobbies, too, I take it."

"Yes," Charles said. "I've been helping to set up a project designed to obtain fingerprints from every prisoner incarcerated in English prisons."

"I take it that the pris'ners aren't permitted tae object," the doctor remarked. With a dry *harumph*, he added, "Calipers measurin' our skulls, X rays peerin' into our bones, microscopes lookin' into our bluid—it won't be long before there willna be naethin' secret. Science will hae discovered everything."

"Everything?" Charles shook his head. "We're some distance from that. Although I must confess to being glad that science has given us a few tools that may help us solve crimes like this one." He finished the job, wiped the ink from the woman's fingertips, and covered the body again. "I think that will be all for the moment," he said, and he and the doctor returned to the consulting room, where the cheerful fire felt especially welcome.

Seated in his chair and holding out his cup for more tea, Charles opened a new subject. "I understand that you have had occasion to treat Lord Osborne, at Glamis Castle."

"Lord Osborne?" the doctor asked in a startled tone, splashing tea on Charles's hand. He looked up, the light glinting on his gold-rimmed glasses. "Sorry," he muttered. He handed Charles a napkin. "Hope I havena burned ye."

"I'll survive," Charles said, wiping his hand. He added a sugar cube to his cup and stirred. "Perhaps I should have mentioned," he went on, not looking up, "that I am also here at the request of King Edward. He is deeply concerned for Lord Osborne's health and safety—as you might imagine."

"Aye, and well he might be," the doctor said without inflection. "He might indeed." He gave a long sigh. "Well, then. What can I tell yer lordship of the gentleman in question?" His voice became dry and ironic. "The gentleman who is so dear tae the heart of the King."

Charles regarded him thoughtfully. "I take it that you were told that Lord Osborne disappeared about the time of Hilda MacDonald's murder?"

"Aye, Angus Duff told me," the doctor replied, refreshing his own cup. "And sorry I was tae hear it, I must say. I have been summoned quite frequently tae treat the poor chap. His health is not robust, as ye may know. Throat ailments, lung troubles, a bout or two with pneumonia. Had he been my son and in need of private care, I would hae sent him off tae the south of France, rather than tae a drafty castle in Scotland." A smile tugging at his lips, he added, "He's remarkably well, though, for a man who's been dead nigh on a decade."

"I daresay," Charles agreed, hiding a smile.

The doctor gave him a sidelong look and grew serious. "But it isna jokin' matter, of course. Lord Osborne isna strong. If he's out there somewhere in the rain and cold, he shall most certainly fall ill."

"I understand that Lord Osborne suffers from a hearing loss." When the doctor nodded, Charles asked, "And his mental state?"

"Nearly as perilous as his physical health, I'm afraid." The doctor pursed his round mouth and his eyes glittered. "He suffers from the delusion that he is our Bonnie Prince Charlie, and that he has come tae Scotland in pursuit of the

Stuart throne, stolen by those Hanover thieves."

Not an altogether unreasonable presumption, Charles thought ironically, *since Prince Eddy himself has been removed from the succession and the throne denied him.* Aloud, he murmured the words of "The Skye Boat Song."

> *Speed, bonnie boat, like a bird on the wing,*
> *"Onward," the sailors cry;*
> *Carry the lad that's born to be king*
> *Over the sea to Skye.*

"O'er the sea tae Skye," the doctor replied softly. "I have heard Lord Osborne sing the song again and again, with Flora playin' the fiddle."

Charles raised his eyebrows. "He is able to sing, in spite of his deafness?"

"I shouldna be surprised," the doctor said dryly, "if Lord Osborne's deafness be half-pretense, a means of escape from social interchange. In the event, he has guid pitch, and he and Flora often sing together."

"This delusion," Charles said. "It's persisted for some time?"

"Two years or more, I should say, though it waxes and wanes. Of recent weeks, it's been quite strong and persistent. He has spoken often of goin' tae Skye."

"You would not describe it as an insanity?"

"Not insanity, since he frequently comes back tae himself." The doctor gave Charles a rueful look. "I hope I am not tae blame in this. Lord Osborne is quite nervous and excitable, y'see. When I first began tae witness his delusion, it seemed tae me that he was rather more calm when under its influence. I encouraged Hilda and Flora tae go along with his odd notion." He smiled. "The girl rather enjoyed it, I should say, playing Flora tae her Prince. She and Lord Osborne hae spent a deal o' time readin' the great Sir Walter Scott together." The smile became ironic. "Particularly, I fear, *From Montrose to Culloden*."

Charles frowned. He himself had read and reread Scott's four-volume history of Scotland, reveling in the heroic tales of the battle at Culloden Moor and Prince Charlie's flight to the Isle of Skye. If Eddy had immersed himself in Scott's powerful tale of the Forty-Five uprising, no wonder he'd fallen into the notion that he was the Bonnie Prince.

"The two MacDonalds, mother and daughter," he said, after a moment's silence. "Duff says they were not told Lord Osborne's real identity."

"Aye. But Hilda may hae guessed it frae the many photographs of King Edward and Queen Alexandra in Lord Osborne's apartments—although I'm sure you'll find photographs of the Royal Family in every home in the countryside. She never mentioned a suspicion tae me, though, and I'm sure she didna share it wi' her daughter. She'd been in service with Lord and Lady Strathmore for most of her life, y'see, and was utterly loyal. Flora herself grew up at the castle, playin' as her mother worked. She would've been a child when she first met Lord Osborne."

"His mental state," Charles said carefully. "Might it have led him, do you think, to violence?"

The doctor rubbed his upper lip for a moment, considering, then shook his head. "I shouldna hae thought so. He is a verra gentle man, kind and thoughtful, especially tae Hilda and Flora." He frowned. "If ye're suggestin' that Lord Osborne might hae slit Hilda's throat, m'lord, I should disagree most vehemently. He regarded her with the deepest love and affection, as if she were a mother tae him, and Flora his sister. I canna believe that he would harm either in any way."

"And if it was discovered that the victim was killed in his apartment? What would you say then?"

The doctor's round eyes narrowed. "Then I should say that whoever killed her also made off with him," he said firmly. "I couldna entertain any other explanation."

"Thank you, Doctor." Charles sat for a moment, gazing thoughtfully at the fire, then roused himself. "I suppose, in the circumstance, you might be willing to postpone the inquest for a day or two? By that time, we may be able to identify the killer." He did not speak with any great conviction. It was beginning to seem to him that the solution to Hilda MacDonald's murder might come about only through some stroke of great good luck.

"If that is your wish," the doctor said heavily, "although I remind you that the condition of the body—" He cleared his throat. "And Flora's feelings mun be considered. I'm sure she wishes tae bury her mother soon as may be."

"No doubt," Charles said. He finished his tea and put down the cup. "Only a few more questions, if you don't mind. The constable, Oliver Graham. What sort of fellow is he?"

The doctor shrugged. "Local man, a good sort, although rather too serious about his position at times. Occasionally a wee bit officious, although that is most likely due tae his youth and inexperience. He's a verra young man."

"Has he spoken to you about possible suspects he might have turned up?"

"Only to say that he hasna found anything." The doctor gave Charles a slantwise look. "However, he told me last night that he thought he should walk up tae the castle and have a go at Lord Osborne, tae see if that gentleman had anything tae do with Hilda's murder. He's empty-handed and frustrated, I'm afraid. It might be easy for him tae latch onto Lord Osborne as a chief suspect, especially if he should learn of his lordship's disappearance."

"I see," Charles said, hoping that the house steward at the castle would have the wisdom to turn the constable away without providing any additional information, and certainly without telling him that Lord Osborne had gone missing. That would only fuel whatever speculations the frustrated constable might be inclined to entertain.

The doctor sighed. "We dinna see many murders here, o' course, and Oliver's not experienced in such matters. I should like tae hae viewed Hilda's body where it was found, for instance. Had I seen it, I should hae deduced for myself that she had been moved."

Charles set down his cup. "Does Graham have any connection with the castle?"

"Relations who work there, you mean?" The doctor's eyes twinkled. "Nae, but he has a bit of an interest in Flora. As well he might," he added. "She's a verra pretty girl, although a deep one. 'Tis hard tae know what's in her heart." He cleared his throat, not quite meeting Charles's eyes. "She might, for instance, fancy Lord Osborne."

Charles sighed. If that were true, it was not a romance that promised a happy ending. It would, however, add another twist to this already bizarre plot. How many complications were there to be in this case? He was about to ask the doctor for more details, but he was interrupted by a light tap at the door. Maud put her head through.

" 'Tis Constable Graham tae see ye, Doctor Ogilvy." She glanced nervously over her shoulder. "He says tae tell ye it's urgent. He seems a wee bit disturbed in his mind."

"Disturbed, is he?" The doctor looked at Charles, and at his brief nod, turned back to the servant. "Well, then, show the guid constable in, my lassie. And bring us another pot of tea." He sighed heavily. "I fear we shall need it."

CHAPTER FOURTEEN

Stone walls do not a prison make,
Nor iron bars a cage;
Minds innocent and quiet take
That for an hermitage;
If I have freedom in my life,
And in my soul am free,
Angels alone that soar above,
Enjoy such liberty.

"To Althea, From Prison"
Richard Lovelace, 1618–1657

This might not be the comfortable quarters in which he had spent the previous months of his exile, the Prince thought as he looked around his stone-walled, stone-floored cell. But at least he was no longer bound and gagged in the cave—the ice house, as one of his captors had called it—or wandering in the cold, wet woods, as he had until Flora had found him.

He wrapped the plaid blanket closer around his shoulders, trembling at the thought of those deceitful, dangerous betrayers who had promised their loyalty and allegiance to the man they called their Bonnie Prince, and then had viciously turned on him, revealing themselves for the pitiless mercenaries they were, willing to deliver him for the price that was on his head. He had managed to escape only when one had fallen into a drunken slumber.

Cold to the bone and trembling at the confused memory of all that had happened to him since he had left the safety of Glamis Castle, the prince pulled his knees to his chin and leaned back against the stone wall of his cell. He had just roused from another snatch of fitful sleep and had no idea what time it was, but he could tell from the light shining through the tiny aperature close to the stone ceiling that it was day. Morning? Afternoon? And was it still summer, or was autumn already upon them?

He could not say, nor could he tell how many days had passed since he had last known where he was or been in touch with his own *true* men, those who had pledged to help him evade Cumberland's searching armies. For the prince, the passage of time had become a dream-like procession of long-ago events, intruding like dim and shadowy ghosts into a present in which they did not belong.

How long since the march into England, where they had come so close to London—and would have triumphed, but for the perfidy of the French and the cowardice of the English who called themselves his friends?

How long since the slaughter at Culloden Moor, where upwards of a thousand of the best and the bravest of Highlanders were lost, and he himself had been covered with the filth flung up by the English cannon balls?

How long since he had sought refuge, first with Lord Lovat at Gortuleg, and then, when that gentleman offered him neither counsel nor aid, with the Laird of Glengarry? By that time, he had totally renounced his efforts to regain the Stuart throne from the Hanoverian usurpers, his sanguine hopes extinguished like flickering candles in the black despair of his defeat.

But when was that, and when was *now?* He could not tell, only that there had been a stay of some weeks, perhaps a comfortable month or two, in seclusion at Glamis Castle, under the protection of the Earl of Strathmore. A pleasant time, when he had been surrounded by things in which he could take pleasure: books and art and music, and walks about the land.

The Prince sighed and looked with distaste around the dim, musty-smelling room. Other than the two straw mattresses stacked together on which he was sitting, there was only a tipsy chair, a wobbly stool, and a table on which stood an ancient wine bottle decorated with the waxen rivulets of long-ago candles, into which Flora MacDonald had stuck a taper the night before.

Flora. He half-smiled as he thought about her gray eyes and graceful movements, and the lines from the poet Lovelace which she had recited to him last night, after she had found him in the dark woods and brought him here. *"Stone walls do not a prison make, nor iron bars a cage; Minds innocent and quiet take that for an hermitage."* Well, his mind was neither innocent nor quiet, and he could hardly take this damp cell for an hermitage.

But he appreciated Flora's efforts to hearten and soothe him, and when they reached Skye and safety, he would see her amply rewarded for all that she had suffered for his sake. He might even do more than that, for he was beginning to acknowledge to himself (although not yet to her) that he felt a tender affection for the girl, so sweetly innocent, so careful of his person and comfort—and beautiful, too. He might take her to France with him. He might marry her and make her a princess, the wife of the Stuart king-to-be, the mother of Stuart princes.

The Prince stirred, stretched, and frowned. Now that he was awake, he was also hungry, and he hoped that Flora would not forget where he was or fail to bring him something to eat—and especially that she would not allow herself to be taken captive by the King's men who were pursuing them both.

But his apprehension was short-lived, for there was a noise at the door. It opened with a heavy groan, and Flora appeared with a large tea tray.

"I've brought you something to eat, m'lord," she said, smiling.

He understood her easily, in part because his hearing was not as impaired as he liked to pretend, in part because she was careful to say her words distinctly and to speak directly to him, so that he could watch her lips.

He smiled and threw off the blanket. "What a feast!" he exclaimed, seeing that not only had she brought him a large pot of tea, but fruit and cheese and oatcakes and his favorite ginger biscuits. "I shan't go hungry. Thank you, my dear."

"Guid." She returned his smile. "If ye'll be only a little patient, sir, and make nae noise at all, ye'll be perfectly safe here."

His brow clouded, and he frowned petulantly. "But I thought we were going to Skye," he muttered, going to the table. "I am more than ready, now that I'm free from those dreadful men. The French ships may already be waiting at Skye, Flora, so we should not delay much longer."

"We *are* going tae Skye, sir," Flora replied, pouring his tea. "Just as soon as it may be arranged. But I do hope that ye'll restrain yer eagerness, and that ye'll trust me."

He pulled up the tipsy chair. "I shall try, Flora." He gave her a small smile. "And I must trust you, mustn't I? My life is in your hands."

CHAPTER FIFTEEN

From a purely practical point of view, Philip Magnus (biographer of Edward VII) is right when he states: "The promotion of Prince George to the position of heir presumptive was a merciful act of providence. Prince George, who possessed a strong and exemplary character as well as a robust constitution, had early given promise of becoming the embodiment of all those domestic and public virtues which the British peoples cherish." There was even a rumour current for many years that Prince Eddy had been the victim of a judicial killing; that . . . he had to die, to make way for one better suited to be King and Emperor.

Clarence
Michael Harrison

Kate looked down at the gold watch pinned to her dress. Seeing that it was nearly lunchtime, she turned back toward the castle, hoping that Charles might finish his tasks and arrive in time to join her and tell her what was going on. At a distance, she had caught several glimpses of men and wagons moving through the park, and a bivouac area had been set up in a large field at the rear of the castle. Obviously, Colonel Paddington's men were going about their business, although what that business was, she hadn't a clue.

The morning mist was brightening, the pale sun shining behind it like a silver coin. Her camera on a strap around her neck, Kate was strolling through the garden at the south-east corner of the castle, enjoying the colorful begonias and pelargoniums, the gay scarlet salvias and glowing golden chrysanthemums, their colors the brighter against the gray of the day. Clematis and roses made a lovely pastel display against a rosy brick wall, and several varieties of hydrangea were heavy with bloom, the heavier for being damp still with the morning's chilly mist. She had nearly reached the main entrance of the castle when she heard hurrying hoofbeats and turned to see a hired carriage coming fast along the lane. Glamis Castle, it seemed, was about to receive another guest.

The carriage pulled up in a shower of gravel, and a liveried man seated beside the coachman jumped down to open the carriage door and give his hand to an alighting woman. She wore black and was heavily veiled, and it was not until she lifted her veil that Kate realized, with some surprise, that the woman was Princess Victoria, daughter of King Edward and Queen Alexandra.

Kate had first met the Princess during the year after she and Charles married. They made occasion to see one another when they were both in London, and since Victoria—or Toria, as she was called by her family and friends—was a loyal reader of Beryl Bardwell's novels, Kate always inscribed a first-edition copy of each book to her. Toria, now in her early thirties, was Queen Alexandra's only unmarried daughter. She served as her mother's companion and personal secretary, rarely venturing far from the Queen's side.

An encounter with her here, in this remote corner of Scotland, was startling, to say the very least.

Kate stepped forward. "Welcome to Glamis, Your Highness," she said and dipped a practiced curtsy.

"Hello, Kate," the Princess said with no surprise in her voice. She held out both her hands eagerly, and Kate rose. "I have been hoping that you would come to Glamis with Lord Sheridan. It's been far too long since we've seen each other. Do you remember that wonderful day last winter when we stole away and went shopping at the new Woolland in Knightsbridge? I certainly do—and I treasure the tea gown I bought there, even though Motherdear objects to my wearing it."

Kate went to the Princess and took her offered hands, and they exchanged affectionate kisses. "You thought I might be here?" She gave a chiding little laugh. "Well, then, you certainly know more than I, Toria. Perhaps you'll let me in on the secret."

The Princess did not answer, for behind them, the coachman lifted the reins, and the carriage moved off. At the same moment, the castle door opened, and the house steward, Simpson, came out onto the steps. At the expression that came and went on his face, Kate judged that he recognized the Princess, was surprised to see her, but also understood why she had come—which was certainly more than Kate could fathom. It was true that Balmoral, the royal Scottish retreat, was no more than a day's journey by coach, and that the Duchess of Fife, Toria's older sister, lived not far away. But Glamis was rather out of the way and certainly not on the usual route of travel.

Simpson made a deep bow. "Your Highness," he said with aplomb. "Welcome to Glamis. I regret to say that Lord and Lady Strathmore are not in residence at the moment, and that Lady Glamis has just this morning departed. But the staff and I shall certainly do all in our power to make you comfortable during your stay." It was the only speech Kate had heard from him, and there was not a trace of Scots in it. The man was obviously a Londoner.

"Thank you, Simpson," Toria said. "I'm sure I shall be quite all right. Might it be possible for me to have the Rose Room? I should also very much like some luncheon, the sooner the better." She began to strip off her gloves. "And immediately after lunch, I should like to have a talk with you and Duff about my—" She paused, with a quick glance at the man who had helped her down from the carriage, who was now standing beside her trunk. "About Lord Osborne."

"Very good, Your Highness," Simpson said. "The Rose Room, Thomas," he added to a footman, who went to help the waiting manservant with the trunk. As a gong sounded somewhere inside, Simpson bowed again to the Princess. "As to luncheon, ma'am, it is just now being served in the family dining room. Of course, if Your Highness would like to freshen up first—"

"Luncheon," the Princess said decidedly, "is of the highest priority. I've come from Denmark, and it was not convenient to stop for breakfast."

Kate, too, was hungry, her own breakfast having consisted of bread and butter and coffee procured on the railway platform in Perth, and had spent the last hour repenting of her decision not to let Flora bring a tea tray. But only a few minutes later, she and Toria were in the pleasant and informal Strathmore family dining room, with pots of ferns at the window and pastel watercolor landscapes on the walls, an agreeable change from the forbidding portraits of ancestors that hung everywhere else.

Kate unfolded her napkin across her lap. "I was very sorry

to hear of your aunt's death," she said. "Please accept my condolences." The news of the long-expected death of the Dowager Empress Friedrich had been in all the newspapers, along with reports of the Royal Family's trip to Germany to attend the funeral. "You were in Berlin with your mother and father?"

"In Hamburg and Potsdam," Toria replied, "where the ceremonies for Aunt Vicky took place. Papa has stayed on for a planned state visit with Cousin Willie." She made a little face, and Kate was reminded that none of Queen Victoria's English grandchildren had any admiration for their German cousin, who was now the Kaiser. "And Motherdear has gone on to Denmark," Toria added, "for her usual visit with Grandmama and Grandpapa. I left her in Bernstorff." *Motherdear* was her children's name for the beautiful Queen Alexandra. The Queen's parents were the rulers of Denmark, and she always spent a few late-summer weeks with them.

"And you have come to Glamis," Kate remarked thoughtfully, as a footman set steaming bowls of giblet soup before them. "I should rather have expected you to stay in Denmark with Her Majesty."

What Kate did not say was that she was deeply surprised that Queen Alexandra had permitted her daughter to leave the Danish court and come to Scotland. Over the fifteen years or so since Toria had come of marriageable age, many in Court circles had expressed concern that the Princess had not been permitted to find a husband. It was even whispered that Queen Alexandra had refused at least one match—a love match, sadly—and intended to keep her daughter by her side, unmarried, as her life-long companion. If this was true, Kate thought, it was a very unfortunate thing. There was no shortage of ladies-in-waiting anxious to serve the

Queen, and Toria ought to have the right to do as she wished.

Of course, it would have been one thing if Toria herself had chosen not to marry and if she were happy to be constantly with her mother. But as Kate well knew from earlier conversations with the Princess, neither was the case. Now, looking at her friend, she thought the Princess looked even more unhappy than she had when they took their clandestine shopping expedition the previous winter. She was thinner and more pale, her eyes bleak, her mouth pinched. It looked as if she were increasingly frustrated by the narrow limits imposed upon her life by a compulsively possessive mother.

Toria picked up a roll and began to butter it. "Motherdear *did* expect me to stay with her, but she finally allowed me to be excused when I told her that I felt very ill." After a moment, she added, with a carefully restrained bitterness, "It is the one reason Motherdear will accept when I want to be apart from her. She supposes me to have returned to Sandringham for a week of resting in bed." Her face lightened. "Of course, Papa knows that I am here and encouraged me to practice my little deception. It was he who instructed me to come." Roll in hand, she began to eat her soup.

King Edward had sent his daughter to Glamis? Feeling rather confused, Kate took up her soup spoon. "Why, if I may ask?"

"Why, for the same reason he dispatched Lord Sheridan and the men from London." Toria's dark eyes rested quizzically upon Kate. "Papa believes that one family member must be here, to make sure that things are done properly. He needs Georgie with him for the talks with the Kaiser, although I'm not sure why, since nothing is ever decided. They just talk and talk, and then the Kaiser struts off and does exactly as he pleases." Her voice softened. "But I was the logical one for Papa to send. After all, Eddy and I have always been very close. We understand one another, whilst the others . . ." She shrugged. "And of course I'm very glad that Papa feels he can count on me in an emergency like this."

Eddy. Nothing about this was making sense. More confused than ever, Kate sipped soup from her spoon. "You obviously know more than I about the reason Lord Sheridan was sent here," she said ruefully. "Perhaps you can tell me."

Startled, Toria met her eyes. "You mean, you don't *know?* Lord Sheridan didn't tell you what happened here?"

"He couldn't," Kate replied. "He didn't know either—at least, not until we arrived early this morning, at which point I was immediately whisked off to the castle. No doubt he has been told what is going on, but I haven't seen him."

Toria was silent for a moment. "Well, then," she said at last, "we shall have to have a frank talk." To the footman, she said, "I would be glad if you could put the serving dishes on the table so that her ladyship and I may help ourselves. And please see that we're not disturbed."

A few moments later, they were alone. Toria leaned forward and spoke in a low voice. "You must keep what I'm about to tell you in the strictest confidence, Kate. As Papa says, it is a state secret."

A state secret? "Of course," Kate said, startled. "But I don't understand what—"

"My brother Eddy lives here at Glamis Castle."

"Your brother—" Kate stared at her, only half-comprehending. "Prince Albert Victor? But I thought . . . I lived in America then, but the story was in all the newspapers. About his death, I mean. It was—how long ago? A decade, surely."

"Well, that's just the thing, you see," Toria said matter-of-factly, pushing her soup bowl away and beginning to fill her plate with sandwiches and salad. "Eddy's death was only a pretense, a necessary pretense. Papa and Mama arranged it in order to permit him to live quietly here, and allow Georgie to take his place as Papa's heir. Perhaps you don't know, because you were in America during those years, but the rumors and gossip—most of them lies, of course—made it utterly impossible for dear Eddy to ascend to the throne. Georgie has made a much more suitable heir. Eddy himself says so."

Kate checked her first feelings of amazed incredulity. The British people were quite aware that the Royal Family held many closely guarded secrets, in particular those involving the scandalous behavior of Prince Eddy in the late 1880s. But she and Charles had come to know rather more than most people about the Prince's secret life, since Charles's investigation of a blackmail scheme involving Jennie and Winston Churchill had led to the discovery that Prince Eddy had entered into a secret marriage to a Roman Catholic commoner, and that he had fathered a child by the woman. Then there was all that wild talk about his being involved with the Ripper killings, which had no more died down than the papers began trumpeting the notorious scandal at the male brothel on Cleveland Street. There was little doubt that Prince Eddy was involved in the sordid business, since his best friend, Sir Arthur Somerset, fled the country to escape being brought to trial and forced to name Royal names. The whole thing was quashed quick as you please, the one journalist who dared to write of it being hustled off to jail. Eddy himself was dispatched to India to protect him from further public scandal.

Meanwhile, however, it was also well-known that Queen

Victoria was seeking a wife for her erratic grandson. After her advances were rejected by two more promising princesses, she fastened her attention upon the unpromising Princess May, spinster daughter of a penniless aristocratic cousin, who dutifully agreed to marry the Prince in return, it was said, for the settling of the family's debts. The engagement was announced with the usual fanfare. Eddy's parents professed themselves satisfied, and a posed photograph of the Royal couple appeared in the newspapers, May wearing an ironic smile, Eddy gloomy and remote, his expression as stiff as his neatly-waxed mustaches.

All seemed well, or as well as could be expected, since this was an engagement arranged by royal decree. But a mere month before the wedding, at the family home at Sandringham, Eddy had died, suddenly, unexpectedly, inexplicably. His tragic death had transfigured him from the butt of jokes in the press to a romantic hero of Byronic proportions, and he was entombed in the Memorial Chapel at Windsor Castle amidst an outpouring of national sympathy for the bereaved family.

And now, Eddy's sister, in a brisk, matter-of-fact tone that rang with absolute truth, was saying that her dead brother was still alive, and living at Glamis Castle.

"I . . . see," Kate said quietly. "It was your brother's choice, then? He preferred exile?"

Kate could hear a world of hurt in Toria's deep sigh, and in the words that came very slowly and painfully, as if they were being carved out of her heart. "To tell the truth, Kate, it was difficult to know just what Eddy would have preferred. He was then—is still, unhappily—quite muddled in his mind."

Muddled in his mind? "You mean," Kate asked, concealing her pity, "that he was—is—deranged?"

"Not that, exactly, I don't think," Toria replied, not looking at her. "Perhaps 'unbalanced' is a better word, or 'troubled.' Eddy's behavior was always erratic and impulsive, and when Grandmama and Papa ordered him to marry May, he seemed to . . . well, to snap. He actually set a fire at Sandringham that nearly destroyed—" She stopped, biting her lip as if she was afraid she had said too much. After a moment, she took a breath and went on, in a steadier voice. "To answer your question, Kate, yes—Eddy chose not to be King. And the time it became clear that something had to be done, the whole family could see that it was impossible for him to ever inherit the throne. He was far too unstable for that."

"How dreadful for him—for all of you!" Kate exclaimed, thinking that mental instability was difficult enough in an ordinary family. In the Royal Family, whose every member had many public duties to perform, it must be agonizing. And when an heir to the throne was unbalanced—

Toria nodded. "Papa and Motherdear were devastated, of course. Papa tried to persuade Eddy in all the usual ways to do his duty, but nothing succeeded. Perhaps, if Grandmama hadn't been so absolutely dead set on Eddy's marrying May, something might have been worked out. There was even some talk of sending him to an asylum, but that was felt to be too horribly public and embarrassing. In the end, Papa and two or three of his closest advisors conceived the pretended death and carried it all out—with Eddy's consent, of course. Motherdear was aghast at the idea, as were Georgie and I, but we were finally forced to agree that it was the only way out of the dilemma. Grandmama never knew. Like everyone else in the kingdom, she thought Eddy had died."

Kate felt as if all the dirty Royal laundry of the past decade was being washed right in her lap. "It must have been very difficult for your brother George, who had to take Prince Eddy's place as heir," she murmured, trying not to show how moved she was by the tragedy of all this. "But especially for poor Prince Eddy."

"Oh, my dear, *yes!*" Toria exclaimed passionately. "Of course, George has been a brick through it all. But Eddy . . . You know, Kate, all those terrible things the newspapers wrote about him, none of them were true." She paused. "Well, almost none. Eddy was—he *is*—such a gentle person, but quite naive and malleable. I'm afraid that for most of his growing-up years, he felt like a fraud, as if he was born into royalty but somehow didn't deserve it."

A fraud, Kate thought. She could understand why the Prince might have felt that way. Royal birth must have seemed a burden that he was not equipped to carry.

"And he was often misled," the Princess was going on, "by wicked men who took advantage of his trusting nature and his deafness. I honestly believe that if Eddy could have heard everything that was said to him, he would have been a different person."

"Deafness?" Kate asked, in surprise. "Like the Queen?"

"Exactly." Toria's expression was inexpressibly sad. "Another of our family traits, I'm afraid, passed down from Motherdear's side. Poor Eddy. He didn't ask to be born into the Royal Family—none of us did, and it certainly hasn't made any of us very happy." Her eyes lightened. "But things have turned out for the best, I suppose. Eddy has been content here at Glamis. George is far better suited to public life, and he and May do their duties without a fuss. They even seem, amazingly, to love one another."

Kate knew that part of the story, anyway, since it was a matter of public record, a romance that had caught the public fancy. After Eddy was dead—or exiled, as it now seemed—Prince George took his older brother's place in the line of succession. Eighteen months later, he also took his brother's place at the altar, and he and May were married. Now the Prince and Princess of Wales, the pair had quickly performed their most important Royal responsibility, producing, to date, three healthy sons and one daughter, thereby ensuring that the succession would continue.*

From the well-filled tray on the table, Kate took a slice of cold jellied ham and a serving of chicken salad garnished with slices of hard-boiled egg and cucumber, neatly contained in a lettuce cup.

"So Prince Eddy has lived privately here at Glamis for the past ten years, then," she said in a musing tone. She didn't doubt that he could have done so in complete secrecy, given the monumental size and complexity of Glamis Castle. He would require only a few trusted servants to meet his needs, and perhaps occasional visits from his family, to cheer him up and bring him news of the outer world. "I suppose you've come to spend some time with your brother," she said, "but what has brought my husband here, and all those soldiers on the train?"

The Princess tried to mask her anxiety with a casual tone, but Kate could see the worry in her eyes. "It appears that Eddy—Lord Osborne, as he is known here at Glamis—has disappeared. Angus Duff, the estate manager, wired Whitehall with the news, and Lord Salisbury wired Papa, in Hamburg. Some men from the Household Guard were sent to

---

*The eldest son became King Edward VIII, who in 1936 abdicated the throne to marry an American divorcée, Wallis Warfield Simpson. As the Duke of Windsor, he left England to live in permanent exile until his death in 1972. Edward's younger brother Albert, who in 1923 married Elizabeth Boyes-Lyon of Glamis (the little Lady Elizabeth Kate meets in Chapter Seven), succeeded Edward as King George V, father of the present Queen Elizabeth II.

search for him, and Papa sent Lord Sheridan, to make sure that the job was done right." She paused, managing a smile. "And I have come as Papa's emissary, to report back to him personally when Eddy is found."

"I see," Kate said, and then looked up. "I'm so sorry, Toria. This must be very difficult for you."

The Princess looked down at her plate, and something like anguish came into her voice. "I have been afraid for years of something like this, Kate, terribly afraid. Eddy must be found and returned to the castle just as quickly as possible. It would not do for anyone to discover who he is."

"No," Kate said softly, understanding the enormous public embarrassment that would be caused by a dead prince who was discovered to be alive and living in exile in Scotland. "It would not do at all."

Poor Toria, she thought with a sudden sympathy, *living day to miserable day with the awful fear that her dead brother might somehow be discovered to be alive, and his death revealed as a fraud and a sham. It would bring down the monarchy.*

Toria pulled in her breath, steadying herself. "I'm glad I've told you, Kate. And I'm very glad you're here, because you can help me get to the bottom of this. I am quite sure that dear Eddy, confused as he is, would never have left this place on his own account. He must have been coerced into leaving, or even taken by force. After lunch, I intend to question Angus Duff and the house steward, Simpson. They may be in possession of some facts they don't understand, or they may know something they have not yet revealed." Her expression darkened, and her voice took on an imperious ring. "But they shall reveal it to me, or we will know the reason why."

CHAPTER SIXTEEN

*If I had not taken things for granted, if I had approached every-
thing with care which I should have shown had we approached
the case* de novo *and had no cut-and-dried story to warp my
mind, should I not have found something more definite to go
upon?*

Sherlock Holmes, in
"The Adventure of the Abbey Grange"
Sir Arthur Conan Doyle

Oliver Graham was in a state of high dudgeon. Dis-
mounting from his bicycle and leaning it against the
front wall of Dr. Ogilvy's house, he glared at the motorcar,
with its opulent leather seats, ostentatious headlamps, and
gleaming brass fittings. He had been at the railway station
that morning when the Panhard was unloaded from the
train, and he knew very well to whom the bloody thing
belonged: to Lord Charles Sheridan, the gentleman in command of the mounted troops who were even now barreling
along the local roads on their green bicycles, heedless of the
rights of pedestrians and other vehicles. In fact, the constable, pedaling back to the village from the hamlet of New-
town, had been forced to fling himself and his bicycle

ignominiously onto the weedy verge when a half-dozen men came flying around a bend without even so much as a halloo or a warning jingle of their bicycle bells. Not to mention that these military maneuvers were taking place at a damned inconvenient time. Here he was, in the midst of a most important murder investigation, with suspects to interview and an inquest scheduled for that afternoon, and he had to put up with the interference of men playing war, under the command of the very man whose whacking great motorcar was blocking the road.

Oliver stepped forward, raised his fist, and pounded on the doctor's door. When Maud appeared, her eyes widening at the sight of his blue serge uniform and brass buttons, he barked, "I've coom tae see the doctor. Tell him it's urgent."

"But he has a visitor just now," Maud said in a trembling tone. "Couldna ye coom back later, Constable?"

"Don't gie me that saucy talk, girl," the constable growled. "Tell the doctor I'm here tae see him. Tae see both him *and* his visitor."

A moment later, Oliver was being ushered into the doctor's consulting room, his blue constable's helmet under his arm. He had been here many times, boy and man, for his father and the doctor had been friends, and Oliver had often sat on the hearth, watching the flames while the two men discussed politics over their tea. But he had never come in such a passion as seized him now.

"Doctor," he growled, "I've coom tae instruct yer guest tae move his machine, which is blockin' the street."

"Well, well, Oliver!" The doctor's eyes twinkled genially behind his glasses. "Welcome, lad. Sit ye doon an' hae a cup o' tea. Maudie is bringin' a fresh pot." He turned to the gentleman seated across from him, a man of medium height, with a neat brown beard, dressed in a brown tweed suit and wearing polished brown boots. "Brigadier Lord Sheridan, I should like you tae meet our constable, Oliver Graham."

"Good morning, Constable," Lord Sheridan said in a deep voice with the cultured accents of the aristocracy. His brown eyes rested upon Oliver with a disconcerting steadiness. "I understand that you are conducting the investigation into Mrs. MacDonald's murder."

"*Attemptin'* tae conduct the investigation," Oliver retorted. He did not take the proffered chair, preferring to do battle on his feet, where he had the advantage of height, at least, over the seated man. "I was barred frae makin' a visit tae the castle tae interview Lord Osborne—at yer instructions, so I was told. I've coom tae demand that ye permit me tae enter the castle and speak tae the gentleman. *And* that ye move yer motorcar," he added hastily.

"You were barred from the castle?" Lord Sheridan raised his eyebrows, seeming pleased. "Just now?"

"Aye. There was a soldier posted at the gate, who said that the estate was bein' used for military maneuvers, at yer orders." He paused, and added cuttingly, "Sir."

Lord Sheridan's gaze sharpened, and his mouth tightened imperceptibly, but his voice remained soft. "And why was it that you wished to gain access to the castle, Constable?"

"Tae talk tae Lord Osborne," the constable repeated sourly, attempting to ignore the uneasiness that was beginning to stir inside him. The man's gaze was uncomfortably penetrating, and he did not seem to want to let the subject go.

"Talk to him for what purpose?"

"Tae hear what he has tae say about Mrs. MacDonald's death," the constable replied in a louder voice. "Lord Osborne is the only one close tae the victim who hasna yet been questioned." He turned to the doctor. "And if I canna get into the castle tae question Lord Osborne, I suggest that ye subpoena him tae the inquest, Doctor, and let him answer the questions under oath. P'raps Brigadier Lord Sheridan," he added scathingly, "would be sae guid as tae serve the subpoena on his elusive lordship, since he has placed the castle out-of-bounds tae us ordin'ry folk."

With a remonstrating look, the doctor said, "There won't be any need for a subpoena today, Oliver. The inquest has been postponed."

"Postponed!" Oliver exclaimed, feeling that control of this important case was being rapidly and inexplicably wrenched out of his hands. "But why? Tae be sure, I dinna yet hae the guilty man, but ye can render an open verdict and—"

"The inquest is being postponed," Lord Sheridan said quietly, "because it does not appear that your investigation has yielded accurate information about the murder itself."

"Doesna appear that—!" Oliver felt his mouth gape open, and he snapped it shut. "What's wrong wi' the information the investigation has yielded? And who th' de'il are *ye,* sir, tae interfere wi' a duly-appointed police officer who is carryin' out his duties?"

The doctor cleared his throat. "Brigadier Lord Sheridan is here," he said in a politic tone, "on an urgent matter for the Crown. It appears that our Hilda's death is somehow involved—how, it isna quite clear yet—with the matter he has coom tae look into. O' course, ye may wish to ask for special instructions from Chief Superintendent McNaughton. But speakin' as the King's coroner, I urge ye tae cooperate wi' his lordship."

The Crown! Oliver swallowed, cursing his rotten luck. It was bad enough that he was required to solve the murder of the mother of the woman he wished to wed, without the Crown somehow getting tangled up in it. But there was no point in complicating the matter by involving Chief Superintendent McNaughton, who—if official attention were called to the situation—would probably only take him to task for not yet having found the guilty man. The doctor was right. He should have to cooperate, like it or not.

"Aye," he growled. "Aye, I'll gae along wi' ye."

"Very well, then." Lord Sheridan leaned back in his chair and gave him a long, probing look that seemed to reach into the depths of his mind and turn it inside out. "Perhaps you will be so good as to reconstruct the crime for me?"

That was easy enough, for there was only one construction that could be put upon the hideous event. "Mrs. MacDonald was walkin' home frae the castle the night afore she was found, which would be Sunday night," Oliver said, striving for an authoritative tone. "The killer coom up behind her with a knife, sudden and quiet-like, and slit the poor woman's throat. She died without so much as a struggle."

"I see," Lord Sheridan said gravely. "And why did you allow Mrs. MacDonald's body to be moved from the place of its discovery before the coroner was given the opportunity to examine it?"

"Tae be moved—" Oliver swallowed uneasily, feeling himself placed upon the defensive. He had known that it was not good police procedure to move a body before the coroner could see it, and under other circumstances, he would not have allowed it. But the site seemed to present so little useful evidence and the cause of the poor woman's death was so grievously apparent, that he—

Lord Sheridan's tone grew sharper. "Did Angus Duff say or do anything to persuade you to remove the body?"

This was entirely unexpected. "Angus?" Oliver blinked. "Why, no, unless—" Angus had agreed with him that moving Mrs. MacDonald was of no consequence, but it had not been his suggestion.

"Unless what?" Lord Sheridan prompted. He frowned. "Come on, constable. Let's get to the bottom of this."

Oliver took a deep breath, feeling his face redden. If this was what his lordship was determined to know, there was no point in prolonging the inquisition any longer than necessary. He might as well confess and get the bloody business over with.

"The decision tae move the body was entirely mine, m'lord," he said. "I moved it because . . ." He flicked his tongue across his dry lips and spoke again, in rather more of a rush than he intended. "Because it was rainin' something fierce, and I hated tae see Flora's poor mother lyin' facedown in the rain, wi' her daughter weepin' her heart out beside her. And since there was so little tae be seen on the path—no blood tae speak of, no signs o' struggle . . ." He fought the impulse to swallow, and stiffened his spine. "I felt it was right tae move the body, m'lord."

"I see," Lord Sheridan said quietly. A look of something like compassion came and went in his eyes, and his mouth relaxed. "If there was no blood to speak of and no indications of a struggle on the path, then perhaps you would be inclined to agree that the victim was likely killed elsewhere and her body transported to the place where she was found?"

Oliver stared blankly, feeling himself suddenly cut adrift from his hasty assumptions. *Yes, of course that was what had happened. No signs of struggle, no evidence of blood, although such a gaping wound would surely have spouted blood like a—* He sucked in his breath. What a blockhead he had been!

"I . . . I wud agree, m'lord," he managed, miserably. He

pulled himself together, mentally revising the report that lay on his desk, waiting to be forwarded to Chief Superintendent McNaughton. "Yes, sir, I'd say so, sir."

"Very good," Lord Sheridan said, with satisfaction. "Another question, if you don't mind. I understand that Miss MacDonald came upon the body of her mother as she was taking her accustomed path to the castle, around six in the morning. But how was it that Angus Duff came to be there, too, at such an early hour? As I understand it, Duff lives quite some distance from the place where the body was discovered. What was his business in the area?"

Oliver frowned, reviewing in his mind the sequence of events of that terrible morning. "I can't say, m'lord. Angus told me that he came upon Flora just after she happened on the body, and stayed tae comfort her for a moment or twa before comin' along tae fetch me." He let out an incredulous breath. "You're not suggestin', sir, that Angus Duff *knew* the body was there, and was waitin' for Flora tae stumble on her mother?"

"I suppose that's one possible interpretation," Lord Sheridan said, "but I am not confident of it." He stood. "As to an interview with Lord Osborne, constable, I'm afraid you shall have to leave that to me. However, I do commend you for having the wisdom to see that his lordship might be able to offer some insight into what has happened." With what almost looked like a twinkle, he added, "And I am glad that you are willing to revise your first impressions regarding the events of the murder. I might add that concern for the family of the victim is a praiseworthy thing, but one should not allow it to overcome one's rational assessment of the situation. And it is better if one does not take things for granted, or approaches a case with a cut-and-dried story already in one's mind."

"Aye, sir," Oliver said, feeling that he had been justly and fairly rebuked, and with rather less severity than his carelessness deserved.

"Well, then," Lord Sheridan said briskly. "I should be grateful if you would tell Miss MacDonald, should you see her, that I wish to interview her as soon as possible. She may have some vital information that she has so far kept to herself. And do let me know at once if you come upon possible clues, or if you should discover strangers in your district, particularly foreign-speaking strangers. You've looked into all the possible suspects, I suppose."

Oliver was deeply disturbed to hear that his lordship had it in mind to interview Flora, who in his estimation had no vital information and should, in any case, be treated with the deference due to a grieving daughter. But having made himself enough of a fool, he only said, "I've spoken tae the gypsies at Roundyhill, which was my first thought, o' course. Gypsies're an e'il lot o' thieves and beggars, gen'rally speakin'. But news o' the murder seemed tae be a surprise tae them. They had nae motive, either, as far as I could see. The victim wasna wearin' jewelry and dinna carry a purse nor money. As for other strangers in Glamis Village, we've had none, save for an elderly gentleman ballad collector. And yer own troops, o' course." He paused. "Military maneuvers, I was told. Reconnaissance?"

"Yes," his lordship said. The clock on the mantel whirred and began to strike half-past eleven, as he rose from his chair and reached for his hat. "Thank you, Constable Graham. Doctor, I'm grateful for the tea. No doubt we shall see one another again before this is over." He went to the door. "Good-bye, gentlemen."

CHAPTER SEVENTEEN

Ae fond kiss, and then we sever,
Ae fareweel, and then forever!
Deep in heart-wrung tears I'll pledge thee,
Warring signs and groans I'll wage thee.
Who shall say that Fortune grieves him,
While the star of hope she leaves him?
Me, nae cheerfu' twinkle lights me;
Dark despair around benights me.

"Ae Fond Kiss"
Robert Burns, 1792

Two minutes later, Oliver let himself out the front door. The motorcar was gone, leaving behind only the objectionable odor of oily smoke. He was still standing there, ruefully contemplating his exchange with Lord Sheridan and feeling not nearly so confident as he had upon entering the house, when he saw Flora coming along the street, wearing a black dress and shawl and a neat black bonnet, and carrying a wrapped parcel.

Snatching off his helmet, Oliver stepped forward to greet her, a rush of tender ardor suffusing him. "Hullo, Flora," he said gruffly. "Ye're well?"

"As well as may be, thank ye, Oliver," Flora replied, pulling her shawl around her. She was pale and drawn, and did not quite meet his eyes.

Oliver flushed, remembering the sweet gentleness with which she had rejected his advances on the previous Sunday evening and hoping to renew his suit, although of course it would not be right to take advantage of the sadness she must feel regarding the death of her mother. But he reminded himself that she was now quite alone in the world, her cousin her only kinsman and not a resident of Glamis nor able to offer her protection and security. Like any other young woman in such a solitary situation, she must be anxious to have things settled and would no doubt welcome the renewal of his suit. He took heart.

"I thought I might call on ye this evenin' after supper, Flora," he said. And then, recollecting that if her cousin was not at home they would be unchaperoned, added, "Perhaps we might walk i' the kirk yard."

She did not hesitate. "Thank ye, Oliver," she said in a low voice that seemed to him tense and heavy with fatigue, "but that wud not be . . . wise."

He felt a sharp disappointment. "Later, then," he said, lowering his voice so that he might not be overheard by Mrs. Lovel, who had come out to sweep her stoop across the way, and was watching them curiously. His words came out in an unpracticed, unrehearsed rush. "Ye must be verra concerned for th' future, Flora, and I want ye tae know that my hand an' my heart are yours an' forever will be. I can offer ye a fine cottage an'—"

"But I told ye on Sunday night," Flora interrupted, "that I dinna be ready tae wed, Oliver. An' now that I've lost Mother, I'm even less ready than 'fore." She bit her lip. "I've . . . other business tae tend, afore I even think on weddin'."

Oliver heard an invitation in her words, although he did not like the tone of her voice. It was agitated and anxious, not the voice of the Flora he knew, who was unfailingly calm in spirit and composed in outward demeanor.

"I understand," he said, and added, in an effort to comfort her, "I shall be glad tae wait 'til th' grief has 'bated a bit an' ye're ready tae consider yer situation in the world. 'Til then, please know that I love ye wi' a' my heart, dear."

She raised her eyes, which were filled with a wild pain. "But I don't *want* ye tae wait for me, Oliver!" she cried, a quite unexpected passion trembling in her voice. "I hae things tae do, an' when they be done, ye may—" She turned abruptly away, and when she spoke again, her voice was controlled once more, flat and hard, almost a man's voice. "When they be done, ye're likely tae repent o' yer offer."

Repent? Oliver stared at her, suspicion rising like an ominous cloud in his mind. *What could she possibly mean? Was she about to do something terrible, something that might make her an outcast, place her beyond the pale?* But as the questions arose, he suppressed them, for he could not imagine his pure, dear Flora doing anything that would bring shame to herself or discredit to the memory of her mother, nor could he think how best to refute her words. But for her sweet sake, and not less for his own, he had to try.

He held out his hand. "Repent?" He forced a chuckle. "Nae, ne'er, my own Flora. Ye canna do anything tae change my mind or my heart. Ye are and mun always be th' sweetest, purest—"

"Nae, Oliver." She ignored his hand, drawing away from him and gathering her shawl closer around her. "Ye mustna be so sure o' yer feelings, for feelings change. And ye mustna be sure of me, for ye scarcely know me, as ye'll nae doubt realize, when ye think more on't." She made as if to step on, then paused, her voice softening somewhat. "I shall see ye at the inquest this afternoon, o' course. And we must gae on as friends, nae matter what happens, for a friend I shall always be tae ye, Oliver, for the sake of the auld days." She gave him a glance in which he could read real gratitude. "And I shall always be thankful that ye carried Mother out of the wet on Monday mornin'."

"The inquest has been postponed, I'm afraid," Oliver said gruffly. There was something in Flora's voice that dismayed him, but he could only blame himself. He had spoken much too soon and far too ardently. Of course she had business to tend to—any daughter whose mother had met such an untimely death would have a great many things to do. He made an effort to gain control of himself. "I've just coom frae seein' the doctor, and he's told me. There'sna word yet as tae when it will be held. I'm sorry, Flora. I'm sure ye wanted tae hae it o'er."

"Postponed?" She lifted her head and looked at him doubtfully. "But why?"

He gave a little shrug, not wanting to worry her. "Th' doctor didna say. I'm sure 'twill be soon, tomorrow or th' day after, mayhap." He cleared his throat and added reluctantly, "I' th' meantime, the gentleman in charge o' th' soldiers has asked me tae tell ye that he would like tae talk tae ye. Lord Sheridan, his name is. He's the one who's told th' doctor tae postpone the inquest. He has, it seems, a commission frae the Crown—although what the Crown has tae do with yer mother's murder is beyond me."

Flora seemed to grow quite still and hard, but when she spoke, her tone was mild. "Lord Sheridan wishes tae talk tae *me?* Why, whatever for, Oliver?"

"I canna say," Oliver replied, not wanting to tell her that His Lordship appeared to feel that she might be withholding information about her mother's murder. "He was urgent aboot it, though, Flora."

Flora let out her breath in a little puff. "Well, then," she said, seeming calmer now, and resigned, "I suppose I shall hae tae talk wi' his lordship." She hesitated, frowning again, and changed the subject. "I wonder, Oliver, if ye've seen my cousin Herman. He's been keepin' with Mother and me for th' past few weeks, but he dinna coom home last night. It's nae like him tae go awae wi'out sayin' good-bye, especially now."

"I saw him i' the pub," Oliver replied, "but he left early, afore I could talk wi' him. Flora—"

Flora pressed her lips together. "Fareweel, Oliver," she said, in a tone of finality, and hurried on, in the direction of the small cottage that she and her mother had shared.

The constable stood, watching her go, trying to dispel the awful feeling that he was seeing the last of the woman he loved. Across the way, Mrs. Lovel finished brushing her stoop and gave him a sympathetic look.

"Take heart, Oliver," she called. "She's bound to coom round 'fore long. It's all just too much for th' dear girl just now."

Oliver scowled. "Nosy auld body," he muttered to himself, going to his bicycle. He mounted and rode back in the direction of the Glamis Inn, where he usually purchased his lunch, at first slowly and disconsolately, then with a quicker motion and the beginnings of a whistle on his lips. Flora may have rebuffed him again, but Mrs. Lovel, he felt, must be right. After the pain of her mother's death had faded and the reality of her uncertain position in the world had begun to be clear, Flora would no doubt begin to see how much she needed him and to value all he had to offer. She was anxious now, that was all, and who could blame her? He would wait. Oh, yes, he would wait.

The whistle grew louder as he thought of the grateful glance she had given him. That glance had been well worth the dressing-down he'd received in the doctor's consulting room. If he had it to do over again, he'd move Hilda's body just the same, and Brigadier Lord Charles Sheridan be damned.

CHAPTER EIGHTEEN

There were three gypsies a-come to my door,
And downstairs ran my lady-o.
One sang high and another sang low
And the other sang bonny bonny Biscay, O!
Then she pulled off her silken gown,
And put on hose of leather-o
And a bright red gown and a ragged apron
And she's gone with the wraggle-taggle gypies O!

"The Wraggle Taggle Gypsies"
Scottish ballad

Flora picked up her skirts and hurried along the street, lifting her hand to Mrs. Johnstone, who was coming out of the butcher's with a plucked chicken in her basket. But Mrs. Johnstone, a tall woman, thin as a leather strap, put her nose into the air with an audible "Hmmpff" and pointedly failed to return the greeting. She had been offended some months before when Hilda MacDonald had rebuked her for gossiping about the vicar's wife—Mrs. Johnstone was known around the village for her vicious tale-telling—and since had refused to speak to either Flora or her mother.

"Think they're too good for ordin'ry folks, they do," she'd huffed.

With a sigh, Flora turned her back on Mrs. Johnstone and turned down the unpaved alley opposite the joiner's shop. At the end, half-hidden behind a large birch tree, sat the white-painted, tile-roofed cottage where Flora had lived with her mother, all to itself in its small patch of garden. Sadness weighed on Flora's shoulders like a heavy load as she went along the path between the roses her mother had planted, sweet with a late-summer fragrance that mingled with the spicy scent of the mauve Michaelmas daisies. Flora hated to disappoint Oliver Graham, and the sight of his crestfallen expression had been almost more than she could bear. Once upon a time, she had thought that marriage to Oliver would bring the greatest happiness into her life, for she knew him to be a good and true man who would strive above all else to make a home for her and their children. Now, she knew that this could not be, for what had happened and might be about to happen would change everything, including Oliver's feelings for her.

But Flora, who had a practical turn of mind and a bolder heart than Oliver Graham might have imagined, could not be prevented from doing what she must, either by grief for what once was and was gone or by fear of what might be but was not yet. She knew that her mother would not wish her to linger in the past but to move on to what must be done, especially where Lord Osborne was concerned. And that was exactly what she meant to do, just as soon as the inquest was over—which, pray God, would be very soon— and she could see her mother laid to rest beside her dear father. Malcolm MacDonald had been waiting for over ten years for his wife to join him under his granite headstone in the village graveyard. He had died a young man, with a young wife and daughter, and the thought that the two would be united at last was some consolation to Flora.

No villagers locked their doors, and the MacDonalds were no exception. Flora went up the stone steps and pushed open the plank door, which her father had painted blue a great many years before, and on which her mother had hung a simple straw wreath, tucked full of dried flowers and herbs.

"Herman," she called hopefully, "Herman, are ye here, dear?"

But her question echoed in an empty house. Flora took off her bonnet and gloves and set her parcel on the table, then climbed the wooden ladder to the low loft under the roof, thinking perhaps that her cousin might be having a nap. But although his brown woolen coat still hung on the peg beside the window and his carpet bag sat open on the floor, there was no Herman sleeping on the bed. She could not imagine that he had left without saying good-bye, and especially without seeing his Aunt Hilda buried. But if he had, he'd left bag and baggage behind.

Mystified, worried, and feeling an urgent need to talk with her cousin about the vexatious postponement of the inquest, Flora descended the ladder, poked up the fire in the iron stove, and put on the kettle. Going to the cupboard, she took down a loaf of bread, fresh yesterday from the baker's ovens. She carried it to the table, where she opened her parcel, revealing a chunk of fresh cheese she had brought from the castle dairy. Deep in thought, she sliced off enough bread and cheese for her meal. When the kettle began to steam, she brewed a pot of tea and took her simple luncheon to the table.

It was difficult to sit down to a meal alone in an empty

house, for this was the time Flora missed her mother most, missed the laughter and the shared confidences, missed her mother's good advice and practical observations. The cottage was full of reminders, of course: the red-checked curtains at the casement windows; the rag rug on the brick floor, braided from Flora's childhood pinafores and dresses; the framed photographs of her mother and father, her MacDonald grandparents, and her cousin Herman crowding the mantle; the dishes in the oaken sideboard, especially the fragile Bavarian porcelain cups from her mother's family, the Memsdorffs; the handmade quilt on the bed in the adjoining room, which she and her mother had shared since her father died. But dear as these family possessions were to Flora, these were only *things,* and she would willingly give all of them up, and more beside, if she could have just one more hour with her mother, who would surely know what she should do to help Lord Osborne.

But her mother could not help her now. Flora had tried very hard not to show her fear, but she had been shaken by Oliver Graham's report that Lord Sheridan—the man who had brought the soldiers to Glamis—intended to question her. That could mean only one thing: that his lordship suspected her of hiding something. And while Lady Sheridan had already proved herself both gentle and sympathetic, Flora was under no illusions about the sort of man her husband might be. Lord Sheridan had brought that large contingent of soldiers to Glamis for only one reason, and Flora knew exactly what it was. They had come to find Lord Osborne—although what they intended to do with him once they'd laid hands on him was a dark mystery.

She wrapped her hands around her cup, absorbing its comforting warmth, and tried to think through her dilemma. If Herman were here, she knew he would help her. Like her mother, his aunt, he came from Bavaria, and he was resourceful, inventive, and daring, afraid of nothing and no one. Herman would know what she ought to do, and she was desperate to talk with him.

Apart from her cousin, though, there was no one else. She longed to turn for help to those she had known since girlhood as her friends: Mr. Duff and Mr. Simpson, who had always been amiable toward her; or Lord and Lady Strathmore, who were kindness itself. But their lordships were in India or somewhere equally remote. And she now knew, with a paralyzing fear, that she could trust neither Angus Duff, who had surely known of her mother's murder before she stumbled onto the body, nor Mr. Simpson, who unfailingly took his direction from the estate factor. The thought turned her weak and sick, but she had to face the possibility that one or even both of these men, whom she had known and respected since she was a little girl, might have killed her mother and made off with Lord Osborne.

For strength, she took a gulp of tea. If only *he* could tell her what had happened—could identify whoever had entered his rooms and taken him against his will. But he could not or would not speak of the violence of that night, no matter how much she questioned him. She could only conclude that the memory of it was locked away in his mind, as the memory of his real identity had been locked away and replaced with the delusion that he was Bonnie Prince Charlie, living in the year 1746. Her heart quailed at the thought of the enemies that surrounded her and threatened him, and she had no idea how long she could keep him hidden from them.

Flora set down her empty cup and picked up the pot to

pour another. What about Dr. Ogilvy? She had known him, like the others, since girlhood, and he had proved himself a trustworthy friend both to her mother and to Lord Osborne. He enjoyed Lord Strathmore's confidence and had come often to the castle to treat Lord Osborne for various illnesses, always behaving toward him with friendship and courtesy. It had been Dr. Ogilvy's suggestion that they humor his lordship in his odd fancies about Bonnie Prince Charlie, and that Flora should play-act the role of Flora MacDonald, the loyal Scotswoman who had helped Prince Charlie flee to Skye. Under other circumstances, Flora would turn immediately to him.

But the doctor had allowed Lord Sheridan to persuade him to postpone the inquest and had no doubt answered his lordship's questions about Lord Osborne's disappearance. She did not know what sort of relationship there might be between them, and, not knowing, felt she could not trust even Dr. Ogilvy, who might, if he knew where she had hidden Lord Osborne, feel compelled to yield him up to Lord Sheridan and the soldiers.

Bleakly, Flora finished the last crumb of cheese and licked her fingers. The problem was that *so many* people seemed desperate to get their hands on Lord Osborne, and she did not know which of them she could trust, or whether she could trust any of them. To be sure, his lordship was safe enough for the moment, hidden in a place where no one was likely to look and where she could easily provide him with food and drink. But the hiding place was cold and dank and certainly unwholesome. How long would he be willing to remain concealed there? Lord Osborne was the tenderest, the gentlest, the sweetest of men—she could not serve him so wholeheartedly otherwise—but his temperament was unpredictable, especially when he was left alone for a long period of time. His spirit, never strong, might falter. He might believe that she had abandoned him, and, losing heart, might try to escape or go searching for help.

Flora stood up and began to pace back and forth across the brick floor, trying to think what should be done. So far, all was as well as might be expected. Lord Osborne had managed to escape from his captors and make his way to the spot where he always liked to take his easel and paints. She had found him there yesterday evening, wet and shivering, and had led him to safety. But while his refuge was secure, it could only be temporary. Clearly, she had to find the means to get both of them away from Glamis, to a place of permanent safety.

But that destination was no great puzzle, thankfully. Flora's father was descended from Sir Alexander MacDonald, chief of the MacDonalds of Sleat and Skye. The MacDonald tartan, woven into a beautiful red-and-black plaid wool shawl, had been the family's proud wedding gift to the young Hilda. And when Flora was a girl, her father had taken her and her mother back to his home for a visit. They had traveled by rail from Glamis to Glasgow and then by boat from Glasgow to Skye, where they had been warmly welcomed by a large and hospitable group of MacDonalds. Flora knew that if she and Lord Osborne could somehow reach the family stronghold on the Isle of Skye, they would be given sanctuary for as long as they wished to stay.

Flora paused in her pacing. Worried as she was, she couldn't suppress a small smile. It was amazingly ironic that Lord Osborne should be seized by a fancy that, wild and absurd as it was, pointed straight to Skye and their only hope of safe harbor.

But a moment later, Flora was pacing again. The safety of the Isle might as well be the safety of the moon, for it was very nearly impossible to reach. If she took all her mother's savings from under the brick in the corner, there was enough for a pair of railway tickets and boat passage, and a little more beside. But the station at Glamis was sure to be watched, so they could not leave from there. A horse and private carriage to the train station at Dundee or Perth would be much safer, but that was equally impossible, for she could not hire a carriage in this small village, where everyone's business was known to everyone else.

Flora paused again. No, the only thing she could do was to keep Lord Osborne safely hidden, hoping that someone— Herman, perhaps—would offer another alternative. And to do that, she had at all costs to avoid Lord Sheridan and his questions, for she wasn't sure she could trust herself, if severely pressed, not to give away some hint of Lord Osborne's hiding place. That meant that she could not appear at the inquest, whenever it was held, for she was certain to have to answer questions under oath. It also meant that she must leave this house at once, for this was the first place Lord Sheridan would look for her.

Flora turned and started toward the room where she and her mother had slept. She had only the vaguest of plans, but she knew what she needed, in case she managed to find a way to fund their secret journey. A change of clothing, warm boots, a cloak, and—

There was a knock at the half-open door, and Flora turned, her heart leaping into her mouth. Dear God, was it too late to escape? Had Lord Sheridan found her already?

But the man at the door was no lord. He was a tinker, to judge from the tinker's pig slung over his shoulder, a tall man, darkly handsome, with a bold smile, ragged black hair, and blue eyes, like the palest of blue flax blossoms. He wore ragged trousers and a stained leather jerkin and dirty red neckerchief, and his wide-brimmed felt hat, decorated with colored beads and a feather, was cocked at a rakish angle.

"Pots t' mend, missy?" he asked, and raised his hat. "Brok'n spoons?" He swung his pig off his shoulder and dropped it, stepping just inside the open door, smiling the while. "All kinds o' tin work, expertly done." And then, gaily, as if to soothe the concern that must be written on her face, "Your cousin suggested I stop an' ask."

Flora shook her head, discomfited by the man's bold entrance into the cottage and by the almost mesmerizing glance he rested on her. She recognized most men of the gypsy clan that had camped at Roundyhill in the late summer for as long as she could remember, but this man was a stranger.

"I'm sorry," she said, trying not to show her uneasiness, "I dinna hae work for ye today." Pulling herself away from his penetrating gaze, she turned to the table and picked up her bonnet and gloves, making as if to leave. "I'deed, I'm just on my way out. I'm expected at th' castle."

"But Herman Memsdorff suggested that I stop here," the tinker persisted. "He said he was sure that Miss Flora would have some work for me. Ye're Miss Flora?" At her nod, he looked around, his sharp eyes searching the two lower rooms, noticing the ladder to the loft. "Is Memsdorff here?"

Flora shook her head. Putting her bonnet and gloves back on the table, she asked, "You've seen Herman today, then?"

"Yesterday," the tinker replied. "He insisted I come as soon as may be, since he'd heard that the band is to move on soon. We're friends, y'see." His eyes came to her face, his gaze intent and searching. "If he isn't here, do ye know where t' find him?"

"I dinna know, I'm sorry tae say," Flora replied quite truthfully. She pursed her lips and regarded the tinker with a frown, for she had just been struck by an intriguing thought, one that under ordinary circumstances she would not have dared to consider. But these were not ordinary circumstances, and after all, this man was an acquaintance of her cousin's. Screwing up her courage, she ventured, "The gypsy clan—it's leavin' soon? Which direction will ye gae?"

The man took out a cigarette and, striking a match against the whitewashed plaster of the wall, lit it. "South to Scone, then Perth." He eyed her obliquely, his voice becoming almost impudent. "And why d'ye ask, missy Flora?" His handsome mouth curved in a half-mocking smile. "Are ye ready to run away with the gypsies-o?" And he whistled a bar of the old ballad.

Over his whistling, Flora spoke all in a rush, and boldly, before she could lose heart.

"Oh, no, not to run away, not at all! But a . . . my uncle and I were thinkin' tae gae along tae Perth for a few days, and I wondered if p'rhaps there might be room in one o' the caravans. We can pay." She remembered that enough would have to be saved out for the rail trip to Glasgow and the boat to Skye, and added hastily, "as long as it's not too much, o' course."

"Ah, well." The man pulled on his cigarette and blew out the smoke, which wreathed around his head like a ghostly halo. There was a moment of silence. His eyes were slitted now, and she had the odd feeling that he was reappraising her, revising his estimation, his assumptions. "Your . . . uncle, eh?" An oddly speculative note had come into his voice. "And what would be his name, pray tell?"

"Uncle Angus," Flora said hastily, speaking the first name that came into her head. She forced herself to slow, and smile. "My dear auntie died last year, ye see. The three o' us used tae gae often tae Perth, an' I thought . . . well, I thought Uncle Angus might fancy a bit of a holiday."

"Folks goin' on holiday usu'lly take the train," the tinker remarked. Before she could frame a response, he added, with a little shrug, "But no matter. P'raps ye and yer uncle might come to Roundyhill this evenin' an' have a look at my caravan. It's red and green, tidy and private, and there's plenty o' room for an uncle and a niece on their way to Perth." He paused, pulling on his cigarette again and eyeing her through the smoke. "What about yer cousin? Won't Herman be comin' wi' ye on this grand adventure?"

Flora made herself speak lightly. "Herman? Oh, I dinna think so. He's his own business tae tend. When d'ye say the clan is leavin' for Perth?"

The tinker shrugged, fixing her with a searching look. "If there's money in it, there's no need to wait for the clan. I can go whenever ye're ready—tonight, if ye'd like to leave right away. Ye'll bring yer uncle?"

"Oh, tonight'd be too soon," Flora said, now half-frightened by her own boldness and feeling the need to pause and think things through. There was something about this man that warned her off, some aura of danger, some scent of peril, that made her feel she could not trust him. But she already knew she could trust no one, and hiring this man, while risky and reckless, might be her only means of spiriting Lord Osborne away. "In the mornin', early," she said breathlessly. "We could coom then." She'd have to find clothing for his lordship—perhaps something from the closet belowstairs at the castle, where old jackets and working trousers were kept.

"Very well, then," the man said, turning to toss his cigarette onto the path outside the door. "Look for the red-and-green caravan or ask for Taiso the tinker, and someone will point the way." He paused. "And if ye see Herman, ye'll tell him that Taiso was here t' talk to him, won't ye?"

"I shall," Flora said.

"Until morning, then," he said, and dropped a mock bow. "Yer ladyship's carriage'll be waitin'. Bring yer uncle and the three of us'll be off straightaway."

Flora did not answer. When he had gone, she sat down limply at the table and dropped her face into her hands. It would be grand if she could snatch Lord Osborne out from under the noses of Lord Sheridan's soldiers, and the tinker's willingness to take them to Perth seemed almost heaven-sent. From there, they could take the railway to Glasgow, and find a boat to Skye, and safety. But she was more than half-afraid of the mocking fellow, and leaving Glamis Village now meant abandoning two pieces of sadly unfinished business: the inquest into her mother's murder, now postponed; and her mother's burial, which could not be arranged until after the inquest. How could she go away, with two such important tasks undone?

But even as the question echoed in her mind, the answer came with it, in her mother's calm, loving voice. "Do as ye mun do, my verra dear, and dinna worry aboot me. I'm wi' yer father now, an' all is well wi' the both o' us."

Flora dropped her hands. Yes, of course. Whatever might be said and done at the inquest, whatever words the vicar might speak over the grave—nothing would change the ir-revocable fact of her mother's murder nor the blessed truth of her union, at last, with Flora's father, whose love she had held in her heart through all the long, lonely years. And it was certainly best not to talk to Lord Sheridan or risk her own appearance at the inquest, where she might be forced to reveal what she knew. So what should she do? Where could she go?

Flora sat for a few moments in silence, debating with herself. Then she stood and went toward the bedroom, her mouth set in a determined line. She had a clearer idea what she must do, and the journey she must take. What she couldn't know was how it would all come out in the end.

CHAPTER NINETEEN

Still it cried "Sleep no more!" to all the house:
"Glamis hath murder'd sleep, and therefore Cawdor
Shall sleep no more; Macbeth shall sleep no more."

Macbeth, II, ii
William Shakespeare

As soon as they had both finished lunch, Kate followed
Princess Victoria to the Strathmore family sitting
room, a large, pleasant room on the second floor of a
recently-renovated wing, with rosy-pink walls, tall windows, and a vaulted ceiling with intricate plaster-work.
Toria seated herself in an ornate gilded chair and Kate on a
rose-damask divan to the left of the chair. A moment later,
two men were shown into the room: the estate factor, whom
Kate had met that morning, still wearing his rough outdoor
clothes and leather boots; and Simpson, the house steward,
in the customary black morning coat. Both men seemed
extremely nervous as they bowed themselves into the Royal
presence. Their agitation escalated, Kate felt, when they saw
her, and she tried to excuse herself.

But Toria made an authoritative gesture. "I prefer you to

stay, Kate," she said firmly. "There may be something you can do to help."

Kate couldn't think what help she might offer, especially since Charles had so many men searching the area. But it didn't do to disagree with the Princess when she spoke in that tone, so she only nodded and resumed her seat on the divan.

The Princess turned first to the factor. "I understand, Mr. Duff, that it was you who discovered that my brother had run away. I should be grateful if you would tell me the circumstances."

Twisting his wool cap in his hands, Angus Duff cleared his throat. Now that she had a closer look at him, he seemed, Kate thought, perfectly wretched, as if he had not slept in several days. "Yer Royal Highness," he began in a faltering tone, "the message I telegraphed tae Whitehall wasna altogether accurate, I'm afraid." He swallowed. "Not in every respect, that is, ma'am. Not entirely."

"Not accurate?" Toria frowned. "Well, then, I suppose we should clear up these small inaccuracies. What are they?"

"Well . . . that is . . ." He looked down at his boots. "I mean tae say—"

But whatever it was that Angus Duff meant to say was interrupted when the door opened and a footman announced, in stately tones, "Brigadier Lord Sheridan."

Angus Duff and Simpson turned, surprise and consternation registering on their faces, as Charles came in. He turned and said something that Kate couldn't hear to the footman, and then the door closed behind him, and he came forward.

"Your Royal Highness," he said, and made the requisite bow. He nodded to Kate. "Lady Sheridan."

If Charles were surprised to see the Princess at Glamis, Kate thought, or his wife in her company, he didn't show it. But she had learnt long ago that he was adept at keeping emotion from showing on his face, a capability that she did not always admire. He was a candid man who could be relied on to speak the truth, but there were times when he wrapped himself in a kind of grave and unrevealing reserve, and this was one of them.

"Lord Sheridan!" Toria exclaimed, smiling. "How good of you to interrupt your tasks and come to see me. Or perhaps you have news?" She leaned forward eagerly. "You and your men have already found my brother? He is safe?"

"I'm sorry to say, Your Highness, that he has not yet been found," Charles replied, unsmiling. "We are, of course, continuing to search, and have sealed off all the roads. If he is in the area, I'm confident that he will be found."

Toria, Kate knew, was nobody's fool, and she understood Charles's implication immediately. "If he is in the area?" she asked, frowning. "How can he have got *out* of the area? He knows no one outside of the castle. He has no friends, no means of transportation." Her frown became sterner. "Or does he? I hope you're not suggesting that someone may have—"

"We're continuing to search, ma'am," Charles replied, forestalling a difficult question. From the way he had broken into Toria's sentence, Kate had the feeling that he suspected that friends of Prince Eddy might have taken him away, but could not reveal his suspicions, especially in front of the listening men. "I'll be able to make a more full report to-night," he added. He gestured at Duff and Simpson. "I've come to the castle, actually, to interview these two men, and a servant who waited on the Prince. I would like to learn more of the details of his disappearance."

"Then you've come at just the right time," Toria replied dryly, "for Mr. Duff was just about to correct certain inaccuracies that apparently crept into his telegram to Whitehall, and hence were forwarded to His Majesty the King."

"Inaccuracies?" Charles did not seat himself, and Kate was aware of the tension in his stance and the guarded sharpness in his voice.

"Indeed." Toria fixed her gaze on Duff, and her voice hardened. "I am confident, however, that Mr. Duff will be able to make things clear. Isn't that true?"

Kate had almost forgotten how perceptive the Princess was, and how quick and discerning. Like her Royal father, Toria was an excellent judge of character, and here, a safe distance from her mother, she had assumed a definite air of command.

All this was too much for Angus Duff, however, who was clearly terrified by the combined force of a Royal Princess and Brigadier Lord Sheridan. His mouth opened and shut without a sound. After a moment, he managed to blurt out a few husky words, his voice thickened by fright.

"Well, then, ma'am, the Prince was found tae be missin' on Monday mornin', and I telegraphed Whitehall as quick as I—"

Charles shook his head. "That won't do, Duff," he said, in an admonitory tone. "We must have the *whole* truth." When the factor did not immediately answer, he turned to the Princess. "May I, Your Highness? I do have a few specific questions, based on several facts I have uncovered since I arrived."

"Yes, of course," she replied hesitantly, "although I cannot see—" She frowned slightly. "Duff, you are to answer his lordship truthfully. Do you understand?"

"Yes, Yer Highness," Duff said, so low that Kate could barely hear him.

"Then tell me whose blood it was that was cleaned up in Prince Eddy's apartment," Charles commanded. "It was not entirely removed, of course. There was far too much for that."

At the word *blood,* Toria had gasped, her hand going to her mouth, her eyes opening wide. "There was *blood* in Eddy's rooms?" she whispered.

Suddenly chilled to the bone, as if by an icy winter blast, Kate stared at Charles. She was thinking of Flora, who had told her of discovering her mother's body early on Monday morning, her throat cut. A horrible murder like that must have produced a vast quantity of gushing blood. But the body had been found on the path to the village, and not in the castle, unless—

"Did you clean it up?" Charles asked gravely, his eyes holding Duff's. When Duff didn't answer, he turned to the butler. "Simpson, was it you who scrubbed that floor to remove the stains, and then put down the rug to cover the spots that could not be washed away?"

"Out, damned spot, out I say!" Kate thought wildly of the words of Lady Macbeth, ceaselessly washing. *"What, will these hands ne'er be clean?"*

"Yes, m'lord," Simpson answered, low. "It was the two of us, m'lord, and nobody else." He looked down at his hands with loathing, as if he was afraid that he would see the horror of blood yet on them. "We didn't want anyone else on the staff to guess what had happened, you see, sir. What we had found in the Prince's—in Lord Osborne's rooms."

"Here's the smell of the blood still," Kate thought. *"All the perfumes of Arabia—"*

"And whose blood was it?" Charles asked sharply.

Duff raised his head, squared his shoulders, and met Charles's eyes straight on. "T'was Hilda MacDonald's blood, sir," he said, finding his voice at last. There was a shudder of revulsion in it.

Toria shut her eyes and sat still, as if she were paralyzed, but Kate's eyes were wide open, and her thoughts were racing. So Flora's mother had been killed in the castle, and not on the path, where her body was found. Her own earlier question echoed again in her mind. What kind of horrible person could have slit a servant's throat, as if she were an animal brought to the slaughter? An answer came, again in words from *Macbeth*: "*Unnatural deeds do breed unnatural troubles; infected minds—*"

Infected minds. Kate shuddered violently. *Could Eddy have murdered Flora's mother? Prince Eddy, unnaturally exiled from his rightful place in the succession. Prince Eddy, whose mind was unbalanced, his sister had said, perhaps even completely deranged. Were they dealing with a madman?*

"Hilda MacDonald's blood," Charles repeated, more softly. Oddly, something in him seemed to relax, and Kate guessed that he had been half-afraid that the blood might have belonged to someone else—to the prince, perhaps? He smiled thinly. "Now that we have established this much, perhaps you will tell us the rest of your own accord."

Duff took a deep breath. His face looked utterly haggard, as if the truth would drain all the life out of him. "On Sunday night about eleven, m'lord, Simpson heard scuffling on the stair near th' kitchen."

"The stair that goes to the wing where the Prince lived?" Charles asked.

"Yes, m'lord," Duff replied. "There was naebody on the stairs when he went tae look, so he went upstairs tae th'

Prince's apartments. He found Hilda, dead on the floor just inside th' door. There was blood—" He swallowed again, painfully. "There was blood all o'er the place."

"Hilda?" the Princess asked faintly. "Who *is* this Hilda?"

"A servant here at the castle, Your Highness," Simpson said. "She looked after Prince Eddy from the day he arrived. In recent years, she was helped by her daughter, Flora. Hilda was much-loved by us all."

"Oh, dear," Toria said, her face twisting. "I remember her now. Oh, I'm so sorry for her death." She looked from Simpson to Duff with sympathy. "And how awful for you, to have discovered her as she was. Do go on, please."

"Yes, Yer Highness," Duff said, his eyes averted, as if her compassion were painful to him. "When Simpson found Hilda, he sent for me, an' we debated what tae do. We felt it would raise too many questions if the body were tae be found in Lord Osborne's rooms. So we rolled her up in a rug an' carried her tae a spot on the path, near the castle gates. But first we cleaned up the blood as well as we could." His jaw muscles clenched. "There was quite a deal of it, as ye might imagine—her throat cut an' all. It was a . . . a gruesome sight. I haen't slept sin' I saw it. To speak God's truth, I dinna know if I'll ever sleep again."

"Her throat was . . . cut?" the Princess whispered. Kate put out her hand, and the Princess seized it as if she were drowning.

"Yes, Your Highness," Duff muttered. "I'm afraid so, ma'am."

Her throat was cut. Kate could not help thinking of the Ripper victims, all with their throats cut. She looked at Charles. Was this why he was here? Because the King was afraid that someone would connect this crime to the Ripper's awful murders? And then connect Prince Eddy to—

"What about the Prince?" Charles asked, turning to Simpson. "Was he in the apartment when you arrived?"

"He was already gone, m'lord. I thought p'rhaps—" He stopped.

"You thought what?" Charles prompted.

Simpson seemed to steel himself, and when he spoke, the words came out in a rush. "I thought that p'rhaps the Prince had killed her in a fit of passion and then gone off, to escape discovery. Duff doesn't agree with me, but I . . ." Biting his lip, he glanced at the Princess. "Well, it seemed a possibility. The Prince hasn't been himself lately, I'm afraid."

"No," Charles said in a tone of reflective irony. "I don't suppose he *has* been himself, if we are to take the term literally. He believes himself to be Bonnie Prince Charlie, as I understand it."

"Bonnie Prince Charlie?" Toria asked in a choked voice, grasping Kate's hand the harder.

"It is a delusion that he has suffered from, intermittently, for two years or so," Charles said. "Dr. Ogilvy tells me that it became quite pronounced in the past few weeks. Prince Eddy seemed anxious to get to Skye."

Bonnie Prince Charlie! Kate stared at him, searching his face for more of this surprising truth. But was it unforeseen that the Prince should suffer delusions? Toria had said that Prince Eddy experienced a serious mental instability some ten years ago. And living in this place, which Prince Charlie may have visited, would certainly influence his thinking. Was it so unlikely, then, if he wished to escape and a servant tried to detain him, that he might have killed her?

"Oh, dear God," Toria murmured. Kate could sense the chaotic feelings that must be sweeping through the Princess, and she felt the pity rising up in her own throat. Toria had tried to put the best face on everything that had happened, but it must have been frightful to live for a decade with the constant apprehension that Prince Eddy might somehow be discovered, her family blamed and discredited for lying to the public, and the monarchy threatened. And now, to learn that her brother might be a killer! It must seem to Toria that her world had tilted on its axis.

Charles's question to Duff intruded on Kate's inner tumult, his voice amazingly calm and level, as if he were inquiring about the weather or the latest crop yields. "Did you see or remove any evidence that someone else had been in the Prince's apartment?"

"No, m'lord," Duff said. "Everything was in place." He wiped his brow with the back of his hand. "I don't s'pose it'ud do any good tae say we're sorry," he went on wretchedly. "Simpson and me, we didn't mean tae cause trouble— we just felt we had tae get th' body out of th' apartment, that's all. How Hilda came tae be dead, well, we just couldn't think it. It was too awful."

"You can't really believe that my brother killed this servant, Lord Sheridan," Toria said tautly. She dropped Kate's hand and sat up straight in her chair, assuming a regal posture. "I assure you that such a thing would be utterly impossible. Eddy is a mild, gentle man, with a sweet and caring nature. He could not have injured an animal, much less have killed a woman who looked after him."

"We have no indication that he did, Your Highness," Charles replied impassively. "All that we know is that his servant is dead, and he has disappeared. There are several possible explanations for—"

There was a light tap at the door, and the footman entered. Going to Charles, he said something in a low voice. Charles thanked and dismissed him. When the servant was gone, he turned to the Princess.

"I asked that Flora MacDonald be located and brought here, so that I might question her. She is the dead woman's daughter, and also a servant to the Prince. She may be able to give us a clue to his whereabouts." He turned to Simpson. "But I've just been told that she seems to be nowhere in the castle. Do you know where she might be found?"

"Yes, m'lord," Simpson replied promptly. "She's attending the inquest into her mother's death. Should you want to question her immediately, you might go to the village hall, where the inquest is being held. Or you can find her back here directly after."

"The inquest has been postponed for a day or two," Charles said. "Perhaps she is at home?"

Simpson looked startled at the news of the postponement. "Yes, perhaps. She and her mother lived together, alone, in a cottage in the village. Flora's father died some years ago."

Kate sat forward and spoke for the first time. "If you're going to interview the girl, Charles, I should like to go with you."

"Oh?" He raised his eyebrows at her.

"I met Flora earlier today," she said. "She told me about her mother's murder, and my heart went out to her." She added, tactfully, "I think she might be more comfortable if I were present."

"Less threatened, you mean," he said evenly. "Yes, of course, my dear, that is very wise. You must come with me." To the Princess, he said, "You will excuse us to go to the village, Your Highness? I think this had better be seen to at once."

"Of course," Toria replied. She turned to Duff and Simpson. "I appreciate your candor. I believe that you concealed the truth out of concern for my brother, and for that, I thank you." In a sterner voice, she added, "Your falsehoods have complicated Brigadier Lord Sheridan's work, however, and you shall have to answer to him on that score."

The two men could only exchange gloomy glances.

CHAPTER TWENTY

By the pricking of my thumbs,
Something wicked this way comes.
Open, locks,
Whoever knocks!

Macbeth, IV, i
William Shakespeare

Angus Duff had given them directions to Flora Mac-
Donald's cottage, and Charles had decided that it was
best that he and Kate walk, since the village wasn't far. The
motorcar had attracted attention on his earlier visit, and he
did not want Flora's neighbors to know that she was being
singled out for attention.

It wasn't a pleasant afternoon for a walk, however. Pewter
clouds hung low over the Grampians, and the morning fog
had returned, turning the afternoon chill and damp, an early
taste of autumn. The silver birches stood out of the misty
woodland like a troop of disheveled dancers, and the rich
scent of decaying woodlands, of damp fern and bracken and
meadowsweet, rose up around their feet. If Charles had had
more time, he would have enjoyed foraging for mushrooms,

for a great many grew in the leaf-litter under the birches: fungi of all sizes, from tiny pearl-button mushrooms to those as large as a football, in shades of white, black, cream, purple, yellow, scarlet. He noticed several chunky *Boletus edulis,* or penny-buns, which were tasty when they were sliced and cooked quickly in butter, and some saffron milkcaps, aptly named *Lactarius deliciosus.* One could collect enough for a fine meal within just a few minutes. The most numerous of all, however, were the handsome *Amanita muscaria,* the wicked fly agaric, which always reminded him of a shiny, egg-brushed Christmas bread studded with rich flecks of almond. But its sturdy beauty was deceptive and sinister, for while not always fatal, this *Amanita* would certainly make one very ill.

Kate had put her arm through his, and as they walked, in some excitement, she confided what the Princess had told her at lunch about the charade of Prince Eddy's sham death. She ended her tale with a question. "Did you know this before we came, Charles? That the Prince was still alive, I mean."

"Not before we came," Charles replied. "Kirk-Smythe told me some of it this morning, but he did not have as many insights into the Prince's mental condition as Toria has given you." He patted the neatly-gloved hand on his arm, thinking that his wife had learned in a few minutes of conversation what he might never have discovered, search as he might.

"Andrew certainly didn't know all of the reasons behind Eddy's exile," he added. "Queen Victoria's determination that he should marry May, for instance, which seems to have brought Eddy to the breaking point." He shook his head. The business of arranged marriages among royalty was a tragedy for the individuals involved, and almost never served their countries well.

And in this case, there was an even greater tragedy, for Eddy had been legally, if not wisely, married, and his Roman Catholic commoner wife, Annie Crook, had been still living at the time of the Prince's forced engagement to Princess May. If Eddy had married May, he would have been forced to become a bigamist, their children illegitimate. And the irony was perhaps as great as the tragedy, for his earlier marriage, while legal in civil law, excluded him from the succession. All this was yet another—and an even more compelling—reason for his exile: the man who would be King could not legally marry, which meant that he could not produce a dynastic heir, and his father and mother surely knew it.

Charles looked down at its wife, at her neat costume of white blouse, green silk tie, gray woolen skirt, and close-fitting jacket; at the shining circlet of russet hair pinned beneath her narrow-brimmed straw boater, trimmed with a green silk ribbon; at her firm-featured face, not beautiful, but strikingly individual and infinitely dear. It deeply saddened him to think that other men did not find the same love in marriage that he had found, a love so rare and precious that—

"Yes," Kate said, interrupting his thoughts. "The Princess said that when Queen Victoria—'Grandmama,' Toria calls her—ordered Eddy to marry May, he simply went to pieces. 'Snapped' was the word she used." She looked up at him wonderingly. "She said he set fire to Sandringham, Charles. Do you think that could possibly be true?"

Startled, Charles frowned. "I heard about a fire there," he said, "although I had no notion that Eddy had anything to do with it. It began in a bedroom on the nursery floor, as I remember, and destroyed the entire top floor and the roof. It was said that the cause was accidental."

He paused, wondering how many other violent acts Eddy had committed and how many people had schemed and lied to cover them up. Someone who had grown up without ever being held accountable for his actions, no matter how harmful or hazardous they might be, might very well believe that he could commit murder and get away with it. No matter what his sister or the doctor said, Prince Eddy might very well have killed Hilda MacDonald.

"Thank you, Kate," he added with a sigh. "What you've told me is very helpful. I'm grateful."

Kate pulled a yellowing leaf from an overhanging hazel and turned it in her gloved fingers. "Well, I must say that I was utterly amazed, Charles. To think that King Edward would connive to remove his own son from the succession! It sounds more like the plot of one of Beryl's fictions than the real truth. But what I don't understand," she added, frowning, "is why Eddy had to 'die.' Why couldn't he simply say he didn't want to be King, and let that be the end of it?"

"Because," Charles said, "a King can't abdicate until he is actually King. And even if that had been possible, it wouldn't have solved his problem with Princess May, or the Royal Family's embarrassment over his reckless behavior." They passed under a twisted oak, a mossy boulder half-hidden in fern at its feet. Somewhere nearby, he could hear the musical chatter of a burn, its clear water spilling over mossy rocks. "In the circumstance, exile at Glamis might have seemed the best alternative, to Eddy and everyone else."

"I'm also amazed that they were able to bring it off," Kate went on. "You'd think that somebody would have spilled the beans, as we say in America."

Charles smiled "In America, perhaps, but not here in England. The Royal Family commands enormous loyalty. All they have to do is snap their fingers, and people say what they're told to say, or shut their mouths, as necessary."

"You're right, you know." Kate tapped the leaf on his sleeve. "Something like this would never have happened in America. We have a far better arrangement than your hereditary monarchy. It's called a *president*. If the fellow doesn't do what he promised, he's simply voted out of office, and somebody else is voted in. There's none of this silly business of exile and mock funerals and sons and grandsons standing in line for the job." She frowned. "Of course, women don't yet have the right to vote. But that's coming."

Charles couldn't help laughing. "I suppose you're right, Kate. And we English are certainly far less skeptical than you Americans, especially the press. Your American newspapers would have gone poking into the details of Eddy's so-called illness and might well have found the whole scheme out. However, I suspect that the English press and the people were actually glad to accept the story of his death, as sudden and improbable as it might have seemed."

"Glad?" Kate asked, startled. "Why on earth should they have been glad at his death?"

"Why, don't you see? It put the problem behind them. Toria is right; Prince George is much more acceptable. He says and does all the right things, and no one can ever complain that he is lazy. Just look at all the fine little Princes he and May have produced since their marriage." He chuckled again, wryly. "Give the country an heir and a spare or two, and everyone is supremely content."

The joking words were no sooner out of his mouth, however, than Charles was cursing his insensitivity. Kate could not have children, and his wretched thoughtlessness must have hurt her. He tried to think of something that would soothe the pain he had caused, but he could not. When would he learn not to say such things?

At that moment, they came to the spot in the path where Hilda's body had been found, and he filled the awkward silence by pointing it out to Kate.

"As you can see," he added, "there are no traces of blood, nor of a scuffle. It's very clear that she was not killed at this place."

Still, Charles could not help thinking that there was an aura of murder here—no scent of spilled blood or corrupted flesh, or the victim's lingering horror. But something like an emanation of evil hung around the place where Hilda MacDonald's body had lain, or at least it seemed so to him. Murder was always wicked.

Kate studied the ground, her face sad. After a moment, she broke the silence with a question. "Do you think Prince Eddy could have cut the poor woman's throat, Charles?"

He answered slowly. "He certainly had the opportunity, and possibly a motive—if he had determined to escape, for instance, and she tried to hinder him." He frowned. "Although, when I viewed the dead woman, I saw no evidence of a struggle—no bruises, no scratches. And her throat was slit from behind. Not the sort of thing one would expect if she had attempted to prevent his escape. There are other possibilities that seem equally likely to me. Someone may have killed her in order to abduct him, for instance."

"But why?" Kate asked, as they began to walk again. "For ransom?" She frowned. "But there's been no ransom note, has there?"

"No." He hesitated, and then, because he trusted Kate so completely, he confided what Kirk-Smythe had told him that morning. "You must keep this secret, Kate, even from the Princess. In fact, *especially* from the Princess." When she nodded, he said, "It's possible that some sort of an international conspiracy is involved."

"An international conspiracy!" Kate exclaimed, a note of suppressed excitement in her voice. "Oh, tell me, Charles!"

Charles tried not to smile. Above all else, Kate loved intrigue. In fact, her favorite photograph was one she had taken on the beach at Rottingdean, of a German spy who had been attempting to set up a base for the invasion of Southern England.

"Andrew reports that a German agent who goes by the code name of Firefly has been seen in this area," he replied. "We're speculating, of course, but it's possible that Firefly somehow got onto Eddy and told his German masters that the Prince was alive and living in Scotland. You can see what a prize he would be."

"No," Kate said, "not exactly." She looked at him with a puzzled frown. "I'm afraid you'll have to explain to me why any foreign government would be interested in such a tragic figure with so little power."

They came to the main road, then, just as a trio of bicycle-riding soldiers pedaled by, dressed in field uniforms. They paused and then crossed, making for the village's main street.

"The German government," Charles went on in a lower voice, "and especially the Kaiser, would love to do something, *anything,* to humiliate the British." He spoke seriously, because this was a very serious business. "The times are changing, Kate. Britain must abandon its policy of 'splendid isolation' and look for friends and allies. Lord Lansdowne is talking seriously with Baron Hayashi about an alliance with the Japanese, and the King hopes to strike up some kind of Anglo-French entente. The German government would very much like to scuttle these efforts. They would discredit us in any way they could, especially with the French, so that if war comes, we would be forced to stand alone, without friends. It would mean a very great deal to them to get their hands on Prince Eddy."

"But what on earth would they do with him, once they had him?" Kate asked, as they walked past the tobacconist's shop. "It all seems very—"

"Tell yer fortune, m'lady?" A gnarled old Romany woman, a dirty red kerchief tied round her head and golden earrings dangling from her ears, had stepped around the corner and accosted them, holding out one thin brown hand. "I'll tell it true, that I will, and no lie." Her wheedling voice was low and gritty, like rusty nails rattling in a can.

"Thank you, no," Kate said. She smiled. "I think I'd rather go into the future without knowing what's waiting for me."

Charles expected the old woman to renew her appeal— most fortune-tellers did not give up easily—but to his surprise, she stepped back, looking from Kate to him, and back again. Something like fright came into her eyes, and she immediately cast them down, muttering something he could not quite catch.

"I'm sorry," he said, leaning forward. "What did you say?"

She looked up, pulling her red fringed shawl around her shoulders. "I said beware," she replied, in her cracked voice. "Beware, the both o' ye. Something wicked comes this way."

"Something wicked?" Kate asked, in a startled tone. "What—"

"Beware," the old lady repeated. And with a rustle of skirts, she strode up the street.

Kate turned and watched her go, a bemused look on her

face. " 'By the pricking of my thumbs,' " she murmured, " 'Something wicked this way comes.' "

Charles shook his head. "I hope you don't put any credence in that sort of thing," he said lightly. "No doubt, if you'd offered her a coin, the old woman would have told you a much more favorable fortune."

"I'm sure you're right." Kate tucked her arm in his again. "Actually, I was wondering whether she was the same gypsy who predicted that baby Elizabeth—Lady Glamis's little girl—would someday be Queen. Now, there's a favorable future for you—although I'd put no more credence in little Elizabeth's fortune than in mine." As they began to walk on, she paused and added, "You were about to tell me, Charles, what the Germans would do if Eddy fell into their hands."

"What would they do?" Charles grimaced. "Why, the Kaiser would hand him back to the King, straight away, with a great public show of puzzlement." He raised his fist in a mock salute. " 'We thought the heir to the British throne was dead, but now it appears, quite magically, that he is alive. We are returning him to the bosom of his family, with our very best wishes for a long and healthy life. Long live Prince Eddy!' "

"Oh, dear," Kate said, distressed. "The King and Queen would be mortally embarrassed."

"And the monarchy would be fatally wounded," Charles replied grimly. "The country would lose faith in the King and the Government. And the revolution—which is coming, whether we like it or not—would be immediately upon us."

"Well, then," Kate said in a practical tone, "there is nothing for it but to find him as quickly as possible. Do you think Flora MacDonald will have an idea where he is?"

"I certainly hope so," Charles replied, reaching into his pocket for the map of the village that Simpson had sketched for him, giving directions to the MacDonald cottage. "What kind of young woman is she, Kate?"

Kate hesitated. "She's in her early twenties, and pleasant, with an air of self-sufficiency that makes her seem older than her years. She was quite disturbed about her mother's death, of course. She said nothing about the Prince."

"According to Dr. Ogilvy, who has treated Eddy from time to time, she isn't aware of his real identity. She knows him as Lord Osborne. Her mother, however, may have known who he was, so perhaps—" He broke off and looked down at the map. "Here we are, I believe. There is the joiner's shop, and the butcher's shop." He pointed. "The cottage is at the end of that alley."

CHAPTER TWENTY-ONE

What makes you leave your house and land?
What makes you leave your money, O?
What makes you leave your loving friends,
To follow the wraggle-taggle gypsies, O?

What care I for my house and land?
What care I for my money, O?
What care I for my loving friends?
I'm off with the wraggle-taggle gypsies, O!

Variation on a Scottish Ballad

It was a well-kept little cottage, Kate thought, as they went down the walk between blooming rose bushes. The dooryard was brushed clean, a wreath of dried herbs and flowers hung on the blue-painted door, and red geraniums bloomed spiritedly in a window box. An old wooden bench sat under a neglected apple tree. The air was filled with the rich sweetness of rotting windfall apples, and tipsy wasps and butterflies lolled among the fallen fruit.

Charles stepped up to the door and knocked loudly. After a moment he knocked again, and when there was no answer, put his hand to the door and pushed. "People in these small villages don't lock their doors," he said to Kate. He put his head in and called, "Miss MacDonald? Is anyone at home?"

When no answer came, he opened the door wider and stepped inside.

"Charles," Kate said, with a little anxiety, "don't you think we should wait until Flora comes back?"

"I think we should take this opportunity to look around," Charles replied firmly. "We might not have another chance." And Kate, who did not like to stand on the step by herself, followed him in and pushed the door shut behind her.

The small cottage was made up of two adjoining brick-floored rooms, with a wooden ladder to the loft. In the larger room there was a fireplace, a wooden dresser filled with china plates and cups, a wooden sink under a window, a scarred table with three wooden stools, and a rocking chair beside the fireplace. The braided rug on the floor, the plants bloom-ing in the window, and the framed family photographs on the mantel all gave the place a homey look—making up, although only a little, for the damp-stained walls from which patches of plaster had fallen, the empty coal bucket beside the hearth, the broken bricks in the floor, and the window frames and sashes stuffed with rags to keep out the cold wind. The cottage might look like a romantic retreat, with its tumbling roses and red geraniums, but there was near-poverty here, and cold, and damp, and it made Kate shiver to think of Hilda and Flora living out their lives in this place.

Charles was standing in the doorway of the adjacent bed-room. "Why don't you take a quick look in the loft?" He turned to give Kate an encouraging smile. "Well, go on, dear. Beryl Bardwell never hesitates to snoop, does she?"

She couldn't argue with that, for Beryl Bardwell, in the

name of research, often did things that Kate wouldn't ordinarily do herself, such as scanning the addresses on envelopes, or eavesdropping on a conversation. Now, smothering her guilt, she gathered her skirts and climbed the steep ladder to the dusty loft. It was empty except for a broken chair and a narrow rope bed which was covered by two thin mattresses, a coarsely-woven sheet, and a scratchy woolen blanket. With some surprise, she noticed a man's brown woolen coat hanging on a peg beside the window, and a scuffed leather satchel open beside the bed. Hadn't Simpson said that Flora and her mother lived alone, and that her father was dead? Then whose was the coat and the satchel? Some relative's, perhaps, who had come to stay with Flora after the death of her mother?

Suppressing her dislike for the task, Kate went to the coat and quickly searched the outside pockets, finding nothing but a tin of tobacco and a small leather purse with a shilling, a wooden match, and a button in it. Inside the torn lining of an inner breast pocket, however, she found a piece of lined notepaper, folded, with several columns of minuscule numbers written in blue ink. The coat itself, which smelled of tobacco and whiskey and was worn nearly through at the elbows, bore the label of an Edinburgh tailor.

The unlined satchel proved to contain a pair of gray wool trousers, a neatly-folded blue shirt, darned black woolen stockings, and several handkerchiefs. Kate took the clothing out and laid it on the bed, then from the bottom of the bag pulled two books: a small New Testament printed in German, and a thin-leaved leather-bound copy of Sir Walter Scott's volume of Scottish history, *From Montrose to Culloden*. Quickly, she riffled through the pages, but there were no loose papers tucked into either book. On the fly-leaf of the New Testament, however, she found a name—Herman

Memsdorff—neatly written in the same blue ink as that of the list of numbers.

A quick glance under the mattress, under the bed, and around the loft revealed that there was nothing more to be seen, so Kate replaced the clothing in the satchel and, tucking her finds under her arm, went back down the ladder to the main room.

Charles was standing in front of the fireplace, holding a framed photo in his hand. "The young woman in the middle would be Flora, I take it," he said, handing her the photo. "I recognize the woman on the right as her mother," he added reflectively. "Hilda Memsdorff MacDonald. I've no idea who the man might be."

Kate studied the photo, which appeared to have been taken in front of the cottage. "Yes, that's Flora," she said. The two women looked enough alike to be sisters, both with the same pleasant smiles, the same firm jaw, the same dark hair curling about their faces. The man, in his mid-thirties and also dark, with very dark eyes, had something of a similar look, she thought, although the set of his jaw was partially disguised by a jagged scar. She looked up. "Memsdorff, did you say? Is that Hilda's maiden name?"

He nodded. "I found it on a framed marriage certificate, on the wall in the bedroom. She was born in Bavaria, it would seem. She and Malcolm MacDonald were married in Glasgow."

"Then these things," Kate said, putting the books on the table and handing the folded piece of paper to Charles, "must belong to her brother or to a cousin. Some male relative, at any rate. The name Herman Memsdorff is written inside the New Testament." She replaced the photograph on the mantel, and as she did, it fell out of the frame. "A man's coat with an Edinburgh tailor's label is hanging beside the window," she added, as she bent to pick it up. "I found the paper in a breast pocket, inside the lining. The man would seem to be visiting, for there's a satchel with a few clean garments in it, as well. I found the books in the satchel."

"Well done, Kate," Charles said, looking down at the paper she had handed him.

Kate straightened, turning the photograph over. There was a date on the back, June 1900, and three names, written in a flowing script: Herman, Flora, Hilda. "Charles," she said, placing the picture on the table, "this man in the photo—he's Herman Memsdorff, the same man who's sleeping upstairs. His name is on the back."

"Ah," Charles said absently. He sat down at the table, still studying the list of numbers. After a moment, he pulled the two books toward him and began to turn the pages as if he were looking for something. As Kate watched, he began to work from the list, first to one book, then the other, a frown growing between his eyes. Finally, he laid the list aside and reached for the photograph.

"Herman Memsdorff, eh?" he said, examining it closely. "Kate, we may have found Firefly."

"Firefly!" Kate exclaimed, staring at him disbelievingly. "Andrew's German spy? Here, in the MacDonald house?" Her skin began to prickle. If the spy was indeed related to Hilda MacDonald—her brother, say—the murdered woman might have been an accomplice in Prince Eddy's disappearance. She might even have been a spy as well. But what about Flora? How much did she know about what had happened? Was she—

"There's no point in speculating about any of this," Charles said, "until Andrew has a chance to look at what you've found. But I'm virtually certain that the list of numbers you found is some sort of cipher code." He took a small notebook from his pocket, tore out a page, and scribbled a note on it, asking Flora MacDonald to come to the castle immediately for an interview. He folded the paper, wrote the words EXTREMELY URGENT on the outside in block letters, and propped it against a salt shaker.

"In the circumstance," he went on, rising from the table, "I think the coat and the satchel had better come with us. If they turn out to be innocent, we can easily return them." He climbed the ladder and came down a moment later with the satchel in his hand. He gathered the photograph, the list, and the books, and put them in it.

"Come on, Kate," he said, taking the satchel and starting for the door. "We have another call to make."

"Oh?" Kate asked, hurrying after him. "Where are we going?"

"To find Constable Graham," he replied.

Kate and Charles were partway down the walk when they were stopped in their tracks by a woman's high, shrill voice, sounding half-exultant and perhaps a little mad.

"Lookin' fer our Flora, are ye? Well, ye willna find her here. She's gone."

Startled, Kate turned. The voice belonged to a thin woman sitting on a stool in the dooryard of a cottage that fronted on the alley, her dirty white apron full of beans, which she was shelling into a basket at her feet. Her iron-gray hair was twisted into a black chenille net at the back of her head. Her face was twisted, too, with a look of righteous wrath.

"You're right," Kate said with a pleasant smile, speaking up before Charles could say anything. "Flora doesn't seem to be at home, unfortunately. We'd be very grateful if you could tell us where we might find her." At Charles's nudge, she added, "And Mr. Memsdorff as well."

The woman stuck her long nose up into the air. "As tae Memsdorff, I canna say, sin' I haen't seen him for a day or twa. But Flora, now . . ." She shook her head scornfully. "Flora's gone, an' by my reckonin', she willna be back. Runnin' after the gypsies, she is."

"Running after the gypsies?" Kate asked, puzzled.

"Aye." The woman snorted and threw a handful of bean pods onto the ground. A chicken darted out of the weeds, picked up a pod in its beak, and scuttled off. "Nae better'n she needs tae be, is our Flora, for all her flouncy airs. A bonnie kettle o'fish, it is! Her poor mother murdered an' not yet in her grave, and Flora's awae wi' th' first man who cooms knockin'."

Charles stepped forward. "What man? It's important that we find Miss MacDonald. If you know where she's gone—"

"Where?" The woman tossed her head. "Who can tell? Packed her clothes in a valise, an' off she's gone. Once these young women run off wi' the gypsies, ye mun give 'em up for lost, for lost they be."

"How do you know," Kate asked, "that Flora's run off with the gypsies?"

"Because I saw her with these awn twa eyes!" the woman replied triumphantly. "That handsome tinker wi' his pig on his back coom an' knocked bold as brass on her door an' she let him in an' closed it b'hind him. And her a lone woman!" She rolled her eyes, obviously relishing the thought of what had gone on behind the closed door.

"And then what happened?" Kate prompted.

"He was in there for a long time afore he left. But he hadna been gone five minutes when she was out o' the house after him, valise in her hand an' her hair tumblin' all wild an' loose around her ears, hussy-like."

"A valise?" Charles asked.

"A valise," the woman asserted. "But did she coom down th' path tae the street like a guid Christian girl wi' naething tae hide? Nae, o'course not. She crept round the back o' the cottage tae the path tae the auld flax mill. Runnin' off, she was. Her voice rose victoriously. "Off with the raggle-taggle gypsies."

Somewhere in the weeds, a chicken cackled.

CHAPTER TWENTY-TWO

Such is the fate of artless maid,
Sweet flow'ret of the rural shade!
By love's simplicity betray'd
   And guileless trust,
Till she, like thee, all soil'd, is laid
   Low i' the dust.

"To a Mountain Daisy"
Robert Burns, 1786

For the better part of the last hour, Oliver Graham had been sitting at the small wooden table which he used as a desk, in the tiny anteroom that was his office in the Glamis Village jail. Before him on a greasy paper lay the malodorous remnants of the lunch which he had obtained from Mrs. Collpit at the Glamis Inn pub: hot fish pie, buttered bread, a scrap of briny pickle, and a baked potato, scorched on the bottom. Usually, Oliver ate in the pub, at a table facing onto the street. In that way, he could see what went on outside, and he could be seen keeping watch, as it were. But today, feeling impertinent eyes on his back and fearing that Mrs. Lovell might not be the only nosy body who had over-heard his conversation with Flora, he had asked for his lunch to be wrapped so that he could take it to the privacy of the jail to eat, along with a bottle of ale.

But the pie and potato had proved rather hard going, for the confidence that had soared in Oliver's heart after the encounter with Flora had plunged again, as he reviewed the conversation that ran like a refrain in his mind.

"We must gae on as friends," Flora had said with finality, "for a friend I shall always be tae ye, for the sake of the auld days."

With sad reflection, Oliver thought that her words did not hold out a promise that a lover could fasten his hopes to. Friendship for the sake of old times was not what he wanted, no, not at all! What he wanted, with an almost frightening passion, was Flora as mistress of his heart and his hearth, as the mother of his children. What he wanted was to wrap his arms around that slender waist and hold her tight against him, and he feared that her proffer of friendship was a repudiation of his greater passion.

But as he reflected further on their conversation, a greater fear began to grow within him, as he remembered the wildness in Flora's voice when she said, "I hae things tae do, and when they are done, ye are likely tae repent o' yer offer." The venomous cloud of doubt and suspicion began to darken his thoughts once again. What might she do that could cause him to reject her? What could she have done that—

The office door opened and a neatly-dressed lady came in, a straw boater perched on coils of russet hair. Lord Sheridan followed on her heels, carrying a badly-scuffed leather satchel—not at all the sort of satchel that belonged to a gentleman, Oliver thought. He set it down just inside the door, and stepped forward.

"Good afternoon, Constable." Lord Sheridan turned to

the lady, who was watching Oliver with a penetrating gaze that seemed to reach deep into his concealed thoughts. "Lady Sheridan, I should like you to meet Constable Graham. Constable, this is my wife."

Evading Lady Sheridan's probing gaze, Oliver rose hastily from his seat. "Yer ladyship," he said, with what he hoped was the right sort of bow. Hastily, he bundled what was left of his lunch in the paper and thrust it into the small iron stove in the corner behind him, where to his chagrin it sizzled fiercely, with the smell of frying fish. Turning back, he asked, "What can I do for ye, m'lord?" He spoke somewhat humbly, chastened by the recollection of his earlier encounter with this man.

"We urgently need to speak with Miss MacDonald," Lord Sheridan said without preamble, "but we have not been able to find her. She is not at the castle, and not at her cottage. Do you know where else she might have gone?"

"Flora?" Oliver blinked, taken aback by the directness of the question and the urgency in his lordship's voice. "I saw her directly after ye left the doctor's, and told her that the inquest was postponed. I also said ye wanted tae see her." He glanced at the clock. "That would've been a couple of hours ago. But—"

"And when she left you, where did she seem to be heading?"

"Why, tae her cottage." He frowned. "You're sure she isna there?"

"No," Lady Sheridan said in a low, rich voice, "she's not there." Her smile warmed her glance, and Oliver's apprehension diminished somewhat. "Is there someone whom she might visit? Or a special friend with whom she might stay, in the village or elsewhere?"

"Nae," Oliver said, considering. "She an' her mother always kept tae themselves, an' she works all day at the castle. Her friends'd be among th' servants there." He looked from one of his visitors to the other, the cloud of doubt that had risen in his mind now seeming to fog his vision. "Why're ye askin'? What's Flora done that ye hae tae find her?"

Lord Sheridan did not answer his question. Instead, he said, "Since you seem to know Miss MacDonald quite well, perhaps you can give us some information. Are you acquainted with a man named Herman Memsdorff?"

"Yes," Oliver said slowly. The question puzzled him for a moment. What did Herman Memsdorff have to do with any of this? "Memsdorff is Flora's cousin," he said, and paused, frowning. "Hilda's nephew, actually. Amounts tae th' same thing."

"Memsdorff lives with the MacDonalds?"

"Nae, nae." The constable shook his head. What *was* all this about? "He cooms tae visit 'em, once in a while. He's been here for a week or twa this time."

"Comes from where?"

"Edinburgh, where he lives. Though he's German, from th' sound of him." Memsdorff's accent had already raised suspicion among the men at the pub. Like many Lowland country people, they feared that the European powers might take advantage of the British Army's unfortunate preoccupation with the Boers, which left the homeland vulnerable to attack by the German fleet, berthed just on the other side of the North Sea—the German Sea, some called it.

"And where would I find Herr Memsdorff?" Lord Sheridan asked.

Oliver shrugged. "I canna tell ye. I was lookin' for him meself. Flora was, too, for that matter," he added, remembering that she had asked after her cousin. "The last I saw him was in the pub, yesterday evenin'. I wanted tae speak wi' him, but he was talkin' tae Hamilton, one o' the game-keepers. He made off afore I could catch him."

Lady Sheridan put a gloved hand on her husband's arm. "Hamilton is the man who drove me to the castle this morning," she told him, in that low, vibrant voice of hers.

His lordship looked at Oliver. "This man Hamilton—is he a friend of Memsdorff's?"

"I canna say," Oliver replied, wishing fervently that he had paid more attention to Memsdorff's comings and go-ings, and to his friends among the villagers. But why should he have done? After all, the man was Flora's cousin, not some stranger. "Why are ye askin' about Herman? What's he done?"

Lord Sheridan did not answer his question. "If you see Memsdorff, Constable, I would like you to detain him." He glanced over the constable's shoulder, where the iron bars of the jail's single cell were clearly visible through an open door. "That cell would be adequate."

In the jail, as if he were a criminal? Now, Oliver was fully alarmed. "But ye canna think that Herman had anything tae do wi' Hilda's murder! Why, she was his awn aunt!"

"I'm afraid I can't say," Lord Sheridan replied in a level tone. He paused and added, almost casually, "Oh, by the way, this morning you mentioned a wish to interview Lord Osborne. I think I should advise you that the gentleman has gone missing, as well, wandered away from the castle, it would seem. If you should happen to hear—"

"Gone missin'!" Oliver felt the skin prickle at the back of his neck. "When?" he demanded hoarsely.

Lord Sheridan hesitated, as if determining how much to tell him. "On Sunday night, it would seem," he said, rather carelessly. He picked up the satchel. "As I was saying, Constable, if you should happen on a trace of him, or of Flora or her cousin, I'd be glad if you'd send a message to me through the soldier who is posted at the castle gate. He'll see that I get it quickly."

"But . . . but if Lord Osborne's gone," Oliver stammered, "what's tae say that he didn't murder Hilda afore he went off? What's tae say that he—" He couldn't finish his sentence, for another thought, even more horrible, had struck him like a sudden, sharp blow, and he couldn't bring himself to give voice to it.

"Murder Hilda?" Lord Sheridan said in a dismissive tone. He smiled. "I shouldn't think it likely. However, if you should hear of his whereabouts, I'd be glad to know."

Lady Sheridan leaned forward, and now there was a look of genuine concern in her eyes. "There is one more thing, Constable. One of Flora's neighbors saw a gypsy tinker enter her house this afternoon, and shortly afterward, Flora went out. She went around the cottage and took the path to the old mill. The neighbor thinks she might have gone somewhere with the man. Is that likely, do you think?"

"A tinker?" he whispered. Oliver felt as if he had been hit by not just one blow, but by a second, equally savage. With a great effort, he pulled himself together. "Ye've been talkin' to auld Mrs. Johnstone, haen't ye?" he demanded scornfully. "That woman is th' wretchedest telltale in th' whole district. Ye canna b'lieve a word the auld witch says."

"You're sure of that, Constable?" Lady Sheridan asked, watching him with what seemed like compassion. "She claims to have seen—"

And at that, Oliver lost all control. "Nae! Never!" he shouted, slamming his fist on the table. "I *know* her! I've known her from a child. Flora MacDonald wudna do such a thing!"

But when the Sheridans had left Oliver alone to wrestle

with the devil of his mounting despair, he had to admit that
Flora had been right when she'd said that he didn't know
her. To be sure, they had been together constantly as children, but she had worked at the castle for the past few years,
and there was no telling what evil influences she might have
succumbed to there, surrounded by the ostentatious wealth
and gaudy finery and low morals of the castle folk. Who
could say how far she might have been tempted into the
paths of wickedness, or to what depths she might have
fallen, or by what awful arts she had been seduced, or by
whom?

And then Flora's voice came back to him once again. *"I
hae things tae do,"* she had said in a voice as low and harsh
as any man's, *"and when they're done, ye're likely tae repent o'
yer offer."*

With a low moan, Oliver put his hands over his ears,
trying to shut out the words. Had his Flora, once so sweet
and pure, become the kind of woman who could be soiled
and then betrayed by some wealthy, unprincipled, corrupt
lord—by Lord Osborne, say—who might have plied her
with pretty words and baubles? Her purity tarnished, she
would be deathly afraid that she could never be a wife to
any good man, so she had—

And then, with an awful, sickening clarity, Oliver Graham understood what Flora had done.

CHAPTER TWENTY-THREE

Twas on a Monday morning,
Right early in the year,
That Charlie came to our town,
The young Chevalier.
An' Charlie he's my darling,
My darling, my darling
The Young Chevalier!

> "Charlie He's My Darling"
> Robert Burns

Kate's thoughts on her way back to the castle were filled with pity for Constable Oliver Graham. While it had not seemed to occur to Charles that the constable was in love with Flora, Kate knew that it was so. Whether it was her feminine intuition or simply her habit of close observation, she had understood the look of horror that dawned in the constable's eyes as he grappled with the possibility that the woman he loved might have gone off with the tinker, and she sympathized with the young man's distress. Kate, however, did not think for a moment that Flora was the sort of young woman who would embark on an adventure whose outcome she could not foresee. Whatever the relationship between Flora and the gypsy, it was not what the forlorn Oliver Graham, groping blindly amidst the rubble of his innocent ideals, had immediately feared.

"Kate, you are a marvel," Charles said, smiling in his beard when she had told him what she knew. "All of that went right past me, I must confess. I hadn't a clue that Graham was in love with her, although, come to think of it, Dr. Ogilvy did mention something of the sort when I spoke to him this morning. I suppose that's why Graham so quickly rejected the idea that she had gone off with the tinker."

"Perhaps," Kate said, although she doubted that poor Oliver Graham had rejected the idea as thoroughly as he hoped they would do. "I'm afraid I can't so easily discount what Flora's neighbor told us, though. The woman may be a malicious gossip, but her story certainly had the ring of truth." Kate glanced sideways at Charles and added, "The constable said that if Flora had any special friends, they'd be among the servants at the castle. Perhaps it would be a good idea to see what can be learnt below-stairs. Would you mind if I made a few inquiries?"

"Mind?" With a laugh, Charles slipped his arm around her shoulders. "Of course I won't mind, Kate. You may be able to find out something very useful, not only about Flora, but about Prince Eddy's disappearance. So inquire away, and let me know if you find out anything of immediate importance."

"I shall," Kate replied, feeling a growing excitement. Their hasty trip to Glamis may have interrupted Charles's excavation project, but she and Beryl Bardwell had certainly found far more of interest here than among the ruins of the old Roman wall. She looked up as they approached the castle, its splendid pepper-pot turrets gleaming in the afternoon sunlight. With its long and illustrious past, its well-known ghosts and apparitions, its association with Shakespeare's famous play, Glamis would make an ideal setting for Beryl's next book.

But it wasn't just the setting that fired Kate's imagination, it was the real people she had met since she'd arrived, who were far more intriguing than any fictional characters she and Beryl might have conjured up. A faithful attendant—or perhaps she was really a German spy!—had been hideously murdered, her body left for her daughter to find. An exiled Prince, half-deaf and half-mad, was about to fall into the clutches of the German Kaiser, who would use him to embarrass King Edward. The Prince's pretty young servant had been seen running after a handsome gypsy tinker. The village constable was in love with the pretty servant and fearful that she had betrayed him.

And around and among all these fascinating people were the ghosts who inhabited the castle: the sad Monster of Glamis, shut up for life in a secret cell; the Gray Lady saying her prayers in the chapel; Earl Beardie gambling with the Devil; Bonnie Prince Charlie hiding from his pursuers. There was material here for a half-dozen different novels. All she and Beryl had to do was decide which one they wanted to write.

As they came up to the castle entrance, the clock on the tower chimed three. "I'm afraid you'll have to excuse me, Kate," Charles said, checking his watch against the tower clock. "I'm off to see what progress Andrew and Colonel Paddington have made with the search."

"Don't forget to tell them," Kate reminded him in a wifely tone, "that they're invited to have dinner here at the castle at nine tonight. It's formal, I'm afraid."

Charles made a wry face. "This is a military operation, not a dress parade. But of course I shall tell them." He dropped an absent kiss on her forehead and went off.

Kate went straight up to her sitting room and rang for Simpson. When the house steward came, she inquired whether Flora had returned to the castle, and when he shook his head, asked for the names of the servants who worked most closely with Flora. Only four were offered, because, Simpson explained, "Flora and her mother were really Lord Osborne's servants. Hilda was his personal maid, and Flora was something of a companion as well. They rarely took meals in the servant hall, and they lived in the village." He frowned. "As well, they were a bit aloof, which may not have sat well with the others, I suspect. Hilda was German, you see, and still had quite the accent." His face was tight. "While the staff don't dislike Germans, a certain amount of hostility is probably natural." He added quickly, in case Kate had got the wrong idea, "It's the stand the German papers took on the Boer War, m'lady. We're not that isolated that we don't get news from the Continent."

Kate looked at the list she'd jotted down, which consisted of the cook, the laundress, the housekeeper, and an upstairs maid. "Well, then, since there are only four, my inquiries shouldn't take long."

Simpson bowed. "I'll have each of them sent up."

"Oh, no," Kate said hastily. "I'll go find them myself, where they work—that is, if you have no objection."

Simpson coughed. "Of course, if your ladyship wishes," he replied delicately, forebearing to point out that this might be considered an invasion of staff privacy. But Kate was experienced enough with her own servants to know that they were more forthcoming if she met them on their turf, if only because she surprised the information out of them.

"One more question," she said, looking down once again at the list. "What do these women know of Lord Osborne?"

Simpson pursed his lips. "All four are aware that an invalid gentleman by that name lives in the west wing. They are not supposed to know anything other than that, although——" He stopped.

"Although one of them may in fact have discovered his real identity?" Kate pursed her lips. If so, that information might not be so closely-held as the Royal Family would like to think. Prince Eddy's identity could be known all over the village, and perhaps beyond—which meant that a clever German agent might have easily got wind of it.

Simpson looked uncomfortable. "It's possible," he conceded warily. "As your ladyship undoubtedly knows, it is very difficult to keep secrets from servants."

Kate regarded Simpson with a small frown. Of course, *he* had been in on the secret, presumably from the beginning, as had Duff. Perhaps one of them had revealed the Prince's identity. Oh, it was all so complicated! Just the sort of mystery that Beryl loved to unravel.

Some moments later, Kate found herself in the castle's vast flagstone-floored kitchens, seated beside a cheerful fire with a cup of fragrant tea. Across from her sat the astonished cook, Mrs. Thompson, whose face was as round and ruddy as a Christmas pudding. Over her shoulder, Kate could see a high tripod with metal shelves holding burnished copper saucepans, and a huge black kitchen range that occupied half of one whole wall, the usual equipment in a country-house kitchen. A sullen kitchenmaid in a blue cotton dress and white apron was wielding a large, sharp knife, chopping vegetables for that night's dinner at the long wooden table in the middle of the room, and making quite a bit of noise about it. On the table sat a large china plate of sandwiches, covered with a damp towel. Beside it was a bowl of grapes.

Mrs. Thompson was a homely soul, who—once past her surprise at her ladyship's visit—was more than willing to answer her questions about the MacDonalds, mother and daughter.

Shaking her head, she said sadly, "They're gude folks, both of 'em, an' loyal workers who never shirked a day. Hilda was a'ready here when I came, five years agon. 'Tis a great wickedness wha' was done tae her. My heart gaes out tae Flora, poor thing."

Kate set her teacup in its saucer. "If Flora were to go away somewhere," she asked carefully, "where might she go?" At the table, the kitchenmaid stopped chopping.

"Gae awae?" Mrs. Thompson asked doubtfully. "I'm sure I canna say, m'lady. P'raps tae that cousin o' hers, who lives in Edinburgh. Or tae Bavaria, where Hilda's people live." She frowned. "But why should Flora gae anywhere, wi' her poor dear dead mother still lyin' 'bove ground? An' her with a gude place and a cottage an' all? Why, she's much better off here than in Edinburgh." She sniffed. "Or Germany, sart'nly."

As to Lord Osborne, Mrs. Thompson could report only a few salient facts. "He's partial tae fish," she said, "an' stuffed partridge, an' rice puddin' wi' nutmeg." She smiled, showing a missing tooth. "An' my gooseberry fool, which he told Hilda is th' best he's tasted in this world." Her smile faded and she leaned forward, dropping her voice. "Is't true that he's dead? He's been ill so long, poor wretch, an' we've sent up nae meals sin' Sunday." Becoming aware of the silence in the room, she planted her thick hands on her knees and turned around to glare at the kitchenmaid. "Get back tae work, Sally me girl, or ye'll find yerself in th' scullery!"

Mrs. Thompson's feelings about Flora were shared by

Mrs. Wollie, the laundress, a large-framed, muscular woman with a pock-marked face. Her cotton skirts were tucked up out of the damp and her sleeves rolled to the elbows, exposing forearms that would have done credit to a blacksmith. Mrs. Wollie was loose-tongued and not as deferential as Mrs. Thompson.

"Gae awae?" she repeated incredulously, turning from the clothesline in her basement empire where she was pegging freshly-washed sheets. "Flora wudna gae without seein' her mother put intae the graveyard. It wudna be Christian, now, would it?" Questioned further, she became vague. "Anyways, where wud she gae, poor thing, and she wi' naebody left i' this world save a cousin who cooms an' goes now an' then?"

Mrs. Wollie seemed to know little about Lord Osborne's person, although she knew a great deal about his laundry. On Wednesdays, Flora had charge of washing the clothing—shirts and collars and smallclothes and such—of an invalid gentleman who contributed no more than two sheets and two pillowcases to the household laundry each week, as well as one or two tablecloths, seven linen napkins, and three towels and a facecloth.

"No bother 't all, is he," she added approvingly. "Nowt like Lady Glamis, wi' all those children spillin' chocolate an' wipin' jelly fingers on th' nursery nappikins an' tablecloths." She snapped a pillowcase violently. "Thank th' gude Lord *they've* gone!"

To Kate's inquiry about gypsies and tinkers in the neighborhood, Mrs. Wollie offered a more informative response. "O'course there be gypsies," she said, as if Kate had asked a foolish question. "They're camped at Roundyhill, where they always stop, th' whole lot o' em. One o' th' men, Awld Pietro, carves new pegs for me every year, tae replace th' ones that break. They dinna last forever, ye know." In evidence, she held out a broken clothes peg. "As for tinkers, ye mun ask Mr. Fewell, th' third footman. He's responsible for seein' tae th' mendin' o' pots an' pitchers an' basins an' such. He'd know if th' tinker's been round yet." When asked if Flora might have been inclined to go off with any of the gypsies, Mrs. Wollie's response was equally definitive and scornful.

"Flora? A gypsy? Dinna be daft! Flora's a *gude* girl! She hasna even had a sweetheart, though there be sev'ral who fancy her—like th' young constable, who wears his heart on his sleeve. Anyways, she's devoted tae th' invalid gentleman." She sighed gustily. "Ye should see the pair of 'em walkin' in the grounds in the afternoon, their heads close together. Like innocent lovers, they are." She pushed up her sleeves. "Now,'f ye'll pardon me, I've got starch cookin' on th' fire for Mr. Simpson's collars."

Kate had just left the room and turned into the hall, pondering the ambiguities of "innocent lovers," when Sally the kitchenmaid stepped out of the shadows near the laundry-room door, startling her.

"I heard ye askin' Cook aboot th' invalid gentleman," she said. She leaned closer, speaking in a hurried whisper. "Mrs. Thompson dinna ken naething aboot him an' her—Flora, I mean. But *I* do."

Kate took an involuntary step backward. The girl's breath smelled of onions and garlic and rotten teeth, and her hair had not been washed for some time. "What do you know, Sally?"

"Needs tae be somethin' in it for me," Sally said sourly. "I has tae work for a livin'. Got six brothers 'n' sisters an' a sick mother, haen't I?"

The girl was far too thin to be pretty, with knobby wrists

and sallow skin and unnatural spots of color in her cheeks that told of consumption, and Kate felt a sharp sympathy. Service was a hard life for young women, even when they had a relatively secure place. Kate reached into the pocket of her skirt and pulled out a sixpence.

"It's all I have," she said apologetically.

"Then it'll hae tae do, won't it?" the girl replied, snatching the coin out of her hand and thrusting it into her dirty bodice. She glanced over her shoulder to assure herself that they were alone in the hall.

"Flora thought she was sae smart," she said sourly. "Struttin' round th' grounds wi' that rich gentl'man o' hers, recitin' poetry, puttin' on airs, like she was a real lady." Her laugh was short and sardonic. "Fawn o'er him, she did, like she really thought he'd marry her an' make her an honest woman. And her nae better'n me!"

It was impossible to tell whether the girl was speaking the truth or something close to it, or fabricating a complete lie out of jealousy and resentment. Kate moved a little closer.

"Do you think," she asked quietly, "that they might have been lovers?"

Sally's eyes glittered. If the question shocked her, she didn't show it. Her scornful reply came without hesitation. "I'm sure of 't, more fool she. These rich gentl'men, they can't wait tae get yer skirts o'er yer head. But once they do, it's done wi' ye, they are, an' on tae the next." Her thin face twisted. "It happened tae me sister, who went out an' hung herself in th' gentl'man's barn for th' shame of it. An' now it's happened tae Flora."

Hung herself? Kate pulled in her breath, feeling herself grow cold. But it should not be a shock. She understood too well the risks that were run daily by young women in service, easy prey to men of birth and education who ought to know better than to wrong those who were without defense. And while the men were rarely, if ever, called to account, the women, ill-used and desperate and pregnant, had no alternative but shame and the workhouse—or death.

"I'm very sorry for your sister," Kate managed, feeling an infinite sadness, undergirded with anger. "But how do you know that the same thing has happened to Flora? Did she *tell* you so?" If Prince Eddy had taken advantage of Flora, Kate vowed fiercely to herself, she would see justice done, if she had to take the matter directly to Queen Alexandra. She leaned forward, her hands clenched at her sides. "How do you know?"

"B'cause he's gone, isna he?" The girl laughed mirthlessly, showing rotten teeth. "He's gone, an' Hilda got her throat slit when she tried tae stop him, an' lit'le Miss High-and-Mighty's run off with a gypsy. Ye said so yerself. An' who but a harlot wud do such a low thing?" And with that parting remark, she turned and went down the hall toward the kitchen, swinging her hips in an exaggerated flounce.

Chagrined, Kate stared after the girl, realizing that Sally had overheard the question she had put to Mrs. Wollie about Flora and the gypsy and would now spread the gossip as if it were gospel to all her friends. Unless Kate missed her guess, both Sally and the constable were all too ready to conclude the worst about Flora, and perhaps from not dissimilar motives. Jealousy was a stern and powerful shaper of perception. Was the conclusion a valid one? Perhaps, perhaps not. Who could tell?

Kate waited a few moments for her feelings to subside before she went to seek out her next interview, with the housekeeper. Their conversation took place in the tea pantry, where Mrs. Leslie was setting out the afternoon tea on a large silver tray sitting on a tray stand in the center of the room. This interview yielded somewhat more real information than the others, for Mrs. Leslie, a genial little black-garbed woman with a horsehair bun on the top of her head, only partially disguised by her own hair, had a longer acquaintance with the MacDonalds. It turned out that she had known Flora's father Malcolm as well, who had died some ten years earlier.

"Malcolm was a MacDonald of Skye," Mrs. Leslie said. She took down a tin of ginger biscuits and carefully counted out a dozen, placing them on a crystal plate. She peered into the tin with a puzzled look, as if expecting to have found more. "Such a fine man, Malcolm," she added. " 'Twas quite a love match, him and Hilda. 'Tis a great pity he didna live tae see his daughter grown up, and sae beautiful. Hilda always hoped tae take her back tae Skye again, tae visit Flora's grandparents."

"Flora has family there, then?" Kate asked.

"Oh, yes, indeed," Mrs. Leslie replied, taking down a box of almond confections. "Malcolm took the family tae visit there when Flora was a young girl." She opened the box and frowned down into it. "Really," she said, in an accusatory tone, "I must speak tae Simpson. Someone has been stealin' from the tea supplies."

"Do you think," Kate asked, "that Flora might undertake such a journey for herself?"

"Oh, I'm sure she will," Mrs. Leslie replied, arranging candies on a small silver tray. "When her mother's taken care of proper, that is. I've heard her humming the song."

"The song?"

"Why, the 'Skye Boat Song.' Aboot Bonnie Prince Charlie. Ye've heard it, I'm sure." She looked up, blue eyes twinkling, and sang a catchy tune, half-under her breath: "Speed, bonnie boat, like a bird on the wing, 'Onward,' the sailors cry; Carry the lad that's born to be king Over the sea to Skye."

Hearing the melody, Kate remembered the song. It had been written some twenty years before and had been so popular that it was often sung at musical performances. It told the romantic story of the escape of Bonnie Prince Charlie, "the lad that's born to be king," to the Isle of Skye, disguised as the servant of the famous Flora MacDonald. If she remembered correctly, there was even a verse that mentioned Flora:

> *Though the waves leap, soft shall ye sleep,*
> *Ocean's a royal bed,*
> *Rocked in the deep Flora will keep*
> *Watch by your weary head.*

At the recollection, an idea began to take shape in Kate's mind—an idea with a certain novelistic twist. Prince Eddy was possessed of the notion that he was Bonnie Prince Charlie. Perhaps he and Flora had planned to take a romantic journey to Skye. Perhaps Hilda had discovered the scheme, resisted it, and Eddy had killed her! Perhaps—

"Ah, there ye are, Gladys," Mrs. Leslie said crossly, as a pretty, red-haired servant came into the tea pantry, clad in a trim black dress and lacy white apron. "Tell me, now, what d'ye know aboot this?" She thrust the now-empty tin of ginger biscuits at the young woman.

Gladys put both hands behind her back and assumed an expression of virtuous innocence. "I dinna know anythin' aboot it, Mrs. Leslie, truly." Her green eyes went to Kate, widened, and then seemed to grow merry.

"But this tin was full yesterday afternoon, when I prepared the tea tray for Lady Glamis," Mrs. Leslie protested. "And you, my girl, were the last tae take tea upstairs."

"Nae, Mrs. Leslie," Gladys replied, shaking her head energetically, her red curls bobbing. "Flora took tea tae her ladyship's rooms this mornin'." She smiled and dropped a quick curtsy to Kate. "Quite a substantial tea,'twas. I imagine that's where th' ginger biscuits went."

Mrs. Leslie looked chagrined. "Oh, my, yes, of course," she said in a fluttery tone. She bowed her head in Kate's direction. "I should hae remembered that your ladyship would've wanted a forenoon tea—"

"Oh, that's perfectly all right," Kate said quickly, even though it wasn't. Wherever Flora had taken the tea, it hadn't been to her suite. "Please don't give it another thought, Mrs. Leslie."

At that moment, a bell rang in the hallway. "Dear, dear, that'll be Mr. Simpson." Mrs. Leslie was, by now, entirely flustered. "What in the world can he want, at this hour of the afternoon? I'm afraid I must gae and see. If I've answered your ladyship's questions . . ."

"Oh, yes, thank you," Kate said, smiling. "You've been very helpful."

Mrs. Leslie turned to the servant and said, in a more business-like tone, "Well, then, Gladys, you'll hae tae be responsible for assembling the sitting-room tea. Her Royal Highness'll want the iced fruit cake, as always. You'll find a plate of sandwiches and a bowl of fresh fruit in the kitchen. Make up the tray, and I'll check it over after I've seen what Mr. Simpson wants."

"Aye, Mrs. Leslie," Gladys said demurely. The housekeeper bustled out, her keys jingling at the waist of her black dress.

"Now, Gladys," Kate said sternly, when they were alone.

"What's all this business about Flora making a tea for me this morning? She asked if I wanted something, but I told her no."

"But I *saw* her, m'lady," Gladys protested, in a tone that spoke an undeniable truth. "She was puttin' taegether an enormous tea." She opened her arms wide to indicate a huge tray. "T'was enough tae feed a whole fam'ly o' workin' folk, 'twas, honest! I'd seen yer ladyship, o' course, when ye arrived, an' I told Flora I didn't think ye was th' sort tae eat like a bothy lad." She clapped her hand over her mouth, her green eyes growing large. "Oh, I'm sorry, m'lady," she said in a rush, through her fingers. "I didn't mean tae be disrespectful."

"Don't apologize, Gladys," Kate said. "It's quite all right." She eyed the sprightly young woman, who clearly thrived on intrigue. "I wonder . . . might you have happened to notice whether Flora took the tea to the guest wing where I'm staying, or . . ." She left her sentence unfinished.

"As a matter of fact," Gladys said in a conspiratorial tone, "I did just happen tae notice." She glanced behind her, saw that the door was open, and tiptoed over to shut it. "Y'see, after I said that it was by way o' bein' quite a large tea for a lady, Flora coom o'er all huffy an' flounced out with th' tray. I went into the hallway and watched tae see where she'd take it. But she *didn't* gae t'ward the guest wing. Oh, nae!" Gladys leaned forward, her eyes sparkling with her secret. "She took th' tray in th' direction of th' *auld* part o' th' castle."

"The old part of the castle?" Kate repeated, her curiosity now definitely aroused. "But why? What on earth could she possibly—"

Gladys straightened. "Oh, I'm sure *I* dinna know, m'lady." She shivered. "That part o' the castle is haunted.

I'd never gae there meself, even if somebody paid me."

Kate nodded, thinking that this was probably true. "I wonder," she ventured, "if you've seen the soldiers."

"Oh, aye!" Gladys said eagerly. "They're here for poor Lord Osborne. He's gone off, ye see, an' th' troops are here tae search for him." A small frown appeared between her brows, and she half-turned away, as if she were conscious of having said too much.

Kate became stern. "I am asking these questions, Gladys, because my husband, Lord Sheridan, is in charge of the troops. He has asked me to learn what is being said among the servants about Lord Osborne. What do you know about this business?"

Gladys turned back, her green eyes startled, her look apprehensive. "Oh, naething, m'lady," she said quickly. "Naething at all! Only that his lordship is a poor half-mad creature who's been hidden away in th' west wing for e'er so long. Thirty or forty years, some say."

"I see," Kate replied in a friendlier tone. "Well, then, perhaps you can tell me what else is being said about him. And please don't be afraid, Gladys. None of the other staff will know what you've told me."

Gladys seemed relieved by the warmer note in Kate's voice, and became confidential. "Well, tae tell the awful truth, m'lady, they're sayin' that he murdered poor Hilda in his rooms an' then ran off." She took a deep breath. "An' that Mr. Duff an' Mr. Simpson carried Hilda out an' put her on the path, so naebody'd suspect that his lordship did it."

"Oh, dear!" Kate exclaimed weakly. One should never underestimate the servants' abilities to find out what had gone on and create their own explanations for it, true or untrue. "They're saying all *that* about Lord Osborne?"

"Oh, aye!" Gladys was now fully drawn into the excitement of revealing what she knew. "An' more, m'lady! They're sayin' that th' soldiers hae coom tae find his lordship an' arrest him for murderin' poor Hilda!" She pursed her lips judiciously. "Which I'm sure makes Flora verra unhappy."

"Flora?" Kate pretended a puzzled surprise. "Why? If he killed her mother, I should imagine that she would be glad to—"

"Why, because!" Gladys exclaimed, half-closing her eyes and clasping her hands over her shapely bosom. "Because Flora *loves* th' poor man, that's why! Nae matter that he's auld 'nough tae be her father, she's given him her hand an' her heart an' pledged herself tae him, forever and ever!"

"How do you know this, Gladys?" Kate asked, now genuinely surprised. "Has she told you this herself, or—"

But Kate was not to have her question answered, for the door opened and Mrs. Leslie sailed in. Kate and Gladys jumped guiltily apart, as Mrs. Leslie's glance went to the large silver tray, sitting just as she had left it in the center of the room.

"Gladys!" she exclaimed irritably. "What hae ye been doing, girl? Gae an' get those sandwiches an' fruit immediately! Her Royal Highness'll be verra cross if she has tae wait for her tea."

As Gladys fled, her apron ties flapping, Kate said penitently, "I'm very sorry, Mrs. Leslie. I had a few questions to ask Gladys, and I'm afraid I kept her from doing her work. Please don't blame her."

"Yes, m'lady," Mrs. Leslie said, as if she were surprised by Kate's apologies, and added, "I hope the girl was helpful tae ye." Her doubtful tone did not express confidence that Gladys could have been of any assistance at all.

"Oh, yes," Kate said quickly. "She was very helpful. As you have been, as well."

"There's one more thing," Mrs. Leslie said hesitantly. "I thought of it just as I left you. It's aboot Skye—although I dinna know if it's at all important." She leaned forward. "Early last week, Hilda got a letter from th' MacDonalds of Skye. I know, because she mentioned it tae me. She said she was goin' tae write back."

"Oh?" Kate asked in a casual tone. "Do you know why the MacDonalds wrote her?"

"I've nae idea, I'm afraid." She turned to the tea tray, frowning. "Now, where did I put those napkins?"

CHAPTER TWENTY-FOUR

Ye trusted in your highland men,
They trusted ye, dear Charlie.
They sheltered ye safely in the glen
Death and exile braving.

Will ye no coom back again?
Will ye no coom back again?
Better loved ye canna be.
Will ye no coom back again?

"Will Ye No Come Back Again?"
Scottish ballad

The constable had spent the entire afternoon in a state of inner turmoil, but he had at least put the time to good service. He had gone to every place he could think of: to the various shops along the main street of Glamis Village; the graveyard where her father was buried; St. Fergus Kirk, cool and dim as a cave within, and the old well behind the kirk, where he and Flora, as children, had spent so many carefree hours; and finally, and with a sense of leaden despair, to the pond above the old flax mill, where some two years before, a wretched young girl, wronged by a local lord, had ended her life.

But Flora was nowhere to be found, and neither the shop-keepers nor the Reverend Calderwood, whom Oliver en-countered on his way out of the kirk, could give him any news of her. From the millpond, he mounted his bicycle and rode out to Roundyhill, where he should have gone in the first place. At the encampment there, he questioned the gypsy women about the tinker, who, it appeared, had only recently joined the band.

"Ah, it's Taiso ye're lookin' for," an old Romany woman said knowingly. She motioned with her head, which was tied in a dirty red kerchief, and her gold earrings glinted. "That's his caravan, over there."

"So he hasna left th' band, then?" the constable asked, feeling, to his chagrin, a great relief.

"Nah," the old woman said. "We'll all be goin' off in a few days, though." She squinted suspiciously. "What's Taiso done?"

The constable didn't answer. "Has anyone coom lookin' fer him? A woman, p'rhaps?"

"A woman?" she asked, with an oblique glance. "Young, was she?"

The constable bit his lip. "Young, and pretty."

The old woman's black eyes glinted shrewdly. "Well, she didn't say her name, but I might be able to recall what she wanted." She held out a brown claw and added, in a whee-dling tone, "If me pore old mem'ry was prompted just a bit."

But the constable was already certain that he knew who the woman was and what she wanted. Deeply offended at the old woman's audacity, he snapped, "Don't beg frae me, auld hag. Tell that tinker he's wanted by th' constable. He's not tae leave this place without talkin' tae me first."

Taking some pleasure in the surprise on her face, he stalked to his bicycle and rode like the very devil was on his back—as indeed it was. A menacing devil of doubt and jealousy, of fear and anger, even of remorse. If he had not been so caught up in forwarding his prospering career, if he had paid the right sort of attention to Flora, he might have saved her. If . . . if . . . if . . .

The constable went home to his comfortable cottage, but he had no appetite for either tea nor supper, and by evening, his grim mood had darkened. He was certain now that Flora had gone to the gypsy camp to meet the tinker, and just as certain that she was lost to him forever, for only a woman of easy virtue could bring herself to consider such a loathsome liaison.

But if Flora had sinned, he knew that she could not be the worst sinner. No, that blame belonged, he thought bitterly, to the high-born wretch who had brought her so low. To Lord Osborne, who had corrupted his sweet Flora and who, according to Lord Sheridan, had now disappeared—had been driven away, no doubt, by his own fierce shame and guilt.

As evening began to fall in the village, the constable made his usual way to the pub at the Glamis Inn. Several horses were tied up in front, a few bicycles leaned against the building, and the low-ceilinged room was full of men, the air flavored with tobacco smoke and woodsmoke and the fragrance of hot pies and frying chips. When he entered, the men, quieting, parted so that he could make his way to the bar. The constable, feeling wretchedly wounded and angry, could not doubt that every man in the room knew of every place he had visited that afternoon, and why.

"Good evenin' tae ye, Oliver," said Thomas Collpit in a

loud and genial voice, drawing the constable's pint. At his words, as at a signal, the buzz of voices resumed.

"Good evenin' tae ye, Thomas," the constable said, forcing a normal tone. He turned away from the publican to face the room, his narrowed glance taking in the assembled men. Robert Heriot, the schoolmaster, was talking with Peter Chasehope, the joiner, at a small table in the corner. At the larger table under the front window, the one-armed baker, Alex Ross, and the Reverend Cecil Calderwood were sharing a boisterous tale with the old ballad collector, whose fiddle lay on the table beside a bottle of good Scotch whiskey, while Douglas Hamilton, a gamekeeper from the castle, was hunched dourly over an empty glass. As the constable watched, the ballad collector picked up the bottle and refilled it, although Hamilton looked like a man who had already had more than enough of drink. There was nothing unusual about that, however, since Hamilton frequently drank too much.

At the end of the bar, the station clerk, a brash, bearded young man named Gibbie, raised his pint. "So, Constable! Did ye see that train o' bonnie soldiers that coom in this mornin'? Brought in a great lot o' bicycles, too, an' God knows what else. What'd'ye know of 'em, eh?"

Chasehope, the joiner, who fancied himself well informed about everything that went on in the village, glanced up from his pint. "Milit'ry maneuvers is what was told tae me, Gibbie," he replied loudly, his side-whiskers bristling. "Testin' some new-fangled bicycles afore they take 'em tae Africa tae use 'gainst th' filthy Boers."

"Testin' bicycles," harrumped the schoolmaster scornfully. "I tell ye, Peter, I dinna like it. Soldiers cyclin' along th' roads like fiends and bargin' through th' woods an' fields with a' manner o' noise, an' none can say what they're really up tae. Could be mortal mischief."

"Could be they're Germans," said the old ballad collector helpfully. "Over near Glasgow way, at the shipyards, they turned up three German spies yesterweek." He glanced brightly around the table, his gaze birdlike. "Bad folks, those Germans."

"Nae, sir," the joiner disputed him. "The soldiers dinna be German spies, for they speak English." He pulled his brows together with a wise look. "What they're really doin', if ye should like my opinion on th' matter, is *huntin'*."

"Hunting?" asked the ballad collector in surprise. "Hunting for what? Grouse?" He frowned and shook his head. "Nivver did I see sae many a-huntin'. The grouse'll be outnumbered, for sure." He laughed heartily, and Hamilton, the only one who seemed to have got the joke, joined in.

"Hunting for *who,* more like," said the baker sternly, thumping the table with his stump of an arm. "For that laird that's gone missin' from th' castle. Angus Duff sent his men out tae find him early in th' week, but they coom up empty handed, so now thcy've brought in th' soldiers tae search."

"Aye," Hamilton agreed in a sour tone. "They've posted men on a' th' roads. They dinna let folks in or out unless they're sure it isna him." He lifted his whiskey and drained it in a gulp. "A brigadier named Sheridan is in charge o' the show," he added, wiping his mouth. "Lord Sheridan, it is."

The ballad collector leaned forward. "Sheridan, ye say?"

"Aye." Hamilton hiccupped.

The constable stared uncomprehendingly at the men. He knew that rumors flew through the village like fire through dry grass on a windy day, but where had they heard all *this,* which was supposed to be entirely secret?

"Ye're a' daft, ever'one o' ye" The station clerk chuckled into his blond beard. "Lairds don't go missin', that's only for poor men, who've nae other way out o' their debts. Wherever did ye hear such foolery?"

"My cousin's son Tom works in th' stables up at th' castle," the baker replied, lighting his pipe with his one good hand and leaning back in his chair. "He told his mum, an' his mum told me when she coom in tae get a fresh loaf. Said he heard th' soldiers talkin' about this laird they're 'sposed tae find. An' since there's only one laird lost, it must be him."

"A lost laird," the ballad collector chortled, refreshing the baker's glass. He picked up his fiddle and bow and began to saw at the strings. "His lairdship he went a huntin', and nivver was seen again," he warbled.

The schoolmaster, who had perhaps had more ale than was good for him, laughed heartily. "I shouldna wonder that Laird Osborne wandered awae an' got lost. From a' I hear of th' fellow, he's tot'lly daft."

"Deaf, rather'n daft," said the joiner darkly. He reached for the whiskey bottle, but the old ballad collector forestalled him, putting down his fiddle and filling the joiner's glass with a flourish. "Can't hear a word said tae him. My niece Mabel told me all about it. An invalid gentl'man, third son of a duke or somethin'. Has lived hidden away at th' castle for nigh on fifty years. Gaes naewhere, only paints pictures an' walks in th' woods." He seemed about to say more, but pulled down his mouth, muttering, "Wretched fellow."

"Deaf, eh," said the ballad collector, shaking his head sympathetically. "Poor chap." He glanced at Hamilton, sprawled in the chair next to him. "You work at the castle, eh? Have you met his lordship?"

Hamilton tipped up his glass and drank. "Oh, aye," he said sourly. "I've met the fellow, an' it's true. Deaf as a post, an' daft as well." His chuckle was bitter. "Thinks he's the Bonnie Prince, he does."

The constable was dumbfounded at this unexpected fragment of information. The Bonnie Prince? Lord Osborne must be as mad as a hatter! Then another thought came, and he shivered. If Lord Osborne imagined himself to be Prince Charles Stuart, perhaps he fancied Flora as the Flora MacDonald of legend, who had ferried the Young Pretender to the Isle of—

"The Bonnie Prince, is it?" exclaimed the ballad collector. "Now, there's an admirable chap. Would that he were wi' us again!" And he swung into a soul-stirring rendition of the first verse of "Will He No Come Back Again?"

> *Royal Charlie's now awae,*
> *Safely o'er the friendly main;*
> *Many a heart will break in twae*
> *Should he ne'er coom back again.*
>
> *Will ye no coom back again?*
> *Will ye no coom back again?*
> *Better loved ye canna be,*
> *And will ye no coom back again?*

At the familiar refrain, "Will ye no come back again?" the whole room joined in with good heart and harmony and much stamping of feet, until the old black rafters rang with the men's voices. Pleased with themselves, they sang the song again, and at the conclusion, several of the thirsty fellows elbowed their way to the bar to have their glasses refilled.

Reverend Calderwood, however, was frowning. "I don't see," he said sternly, "that 'tis anything tae celebrate. A poor deaf man who's daft enough tae think he's our Royal Charlie . . ." He shook his head mournfully. "Christ tells us that we should rather pity such wretched folk, than heap scorn on them."

"Ye wouldna pity th' fellow, Reverend," said the joiner darkly, "if ye knew what th' castle folk are sayin' he's done."

"Whatever he's done," Reverend Calderwood replied in a pious tone, "Our Lord will forgive him. God is gracious tae forgive our sins, no matter how low we have—"

"What's he done?" asked the ballad collector, putting down his fiddle and cocking his head to the side. "What's he done, this poor, deaf Royal Charlie?"

"What's he done?" The joiner pushed back his chair with a loud scraping sound. "They say it's him who murdered Hilda."

A quiet descended on the room. Behind the bar, Thomas Collpit's wife dropped a plate, shattering the silence with a great crash of crockery. Pale and shaking, she bent to pick up the pieces.

"Murdered Hilda?" the reverend whispered. "May God hae mercy on his wretched soul!"

"Murdered Hilda?" gasped the station clerk in great excitement. "Ye don't say!"

"A *laird* murdered our Hilda?" cried the baker.

"Aye. And what's more," the joiner continued, in a low and deliberate voice, " 'tis said that Angus Duff an' Simpson the house steward found her dead in th' laird's rooms an' carried her poor body tae th' spot where Flora found it."

The constable felt himself gaping. "How do ye know that, Peter Chasehope?" he asked, finding his voice at last. "Can ye swear to it?"

The joiner gave the constable a stony look. "I can only swear to what my wife's niece Mabel said. She's a maidservant at the castle, ye know. She told me and her aunt at tea this evenin' that it was th' deaf laird who cut Hilda's throat." His hard glance softened. "She says he did it for th' sake o' Flora. She says a' th' castle folk think so."

At this mention of Flora's name, all eyes went to the constable, who felt his throat gone dry. The scaly red devil that had ridden on his back all the way from the gypsy camp to the village now crouched on his shoulder, grinning hideously and shaking his barbed tail with a dry rattle.

"Flora?" Oliver whispered. "What does this laird hae tae do wi' Flora?"

The joiner shifted uncomfortably. "Well—" He stopped.

The constable pulled in his breath. "Well, what, Peter Chasehope?" he demanded hoarsely. The devil jumped from his shoulder to the floor, then leapt up and grasped his throat in its two gnarled hands, as hot as if they'd just been struck from an anvil. "Speak up, man!" he croaked, as the grip tightened on his throat. "What're ye sayin' aboot Flora?"

"I'm sayin'," the joiner said in a low voice, "that this laird an' Flora made it up b'tween 'em tae leave, an' Hilda got in th' way, an' he killed her." He cleared his throat. "At least," he amended, "that's what Mabel says they're sayin' at th' castle." He cast a half-defiant look around him. "O' course, it may be a lie, for aught I know. Ye can't always b'lieve them castle folk. No morals, most of 'em. 'Cept for Mabel, o' course."

The constable tried to speak, but the devil grasped him so tightly by the throat that he could not say a word, could scarcely breathe. Flora's pale face, once so pure and blameless, seemed to swim before his darkening gaze, suffused with shame and guilt.

"There's a judgment preparin'," said Reverend Calderwood ominously. He raised his voice, declaiming. "This is th' work of the de'il, of th' foul fiend who dwells among th' high an' mighty an' wreaks great harm on th' poor and th' lowly." He clasped his hands and cast his eyes upward. "Oh God, deliver us from th' devils of lust and avarice and murder. In Laird Jesus's name, amen."

"Amen," several of the men echoed, while the station clerk raised his glass and cried "Hear! hear!" and one or two stamped their feet.

Hamilton cleared his throat loudly. "O' course, it may be a lie," he said, agreeing with the joiner, "but I heard th' same thing said 'mongst the stable staff. 'Twas his lairdship who murdered Hilda." His words slurred and he stopped to get command of his voice. "But Osborne isna the laird's real name. He's somebody else a'together."

"Somebody else?" asked the ballad collector, goggling at him in amazement. "A duke in disguise, mayhap? The ballads are full o' dukes in disguise."

"A duke or a son of a duke," said Hamilton with a wise look. "He's somebody high up, for sartin."

"Douglas," the joiner said, "ye've drunk too much again."

The ballad collector eyed Hamilton. "How d'ye know he's not who he says?"

Hamilton shrugged. "There's them that's seen his quarters. Pictures of the Royal Family a' around." He tossed off the rest of his whiskey and stood up. "Time tae go home," he said thickly. He swayed.

"I'm off as well," said the baker. He put his hand under Hamilton's elbow to keep him straight on his feet.

"And I," said the ballad collector, picking up his fiddle and packing it into its case. "Enough good times for one evenin'."

The constable turned back to the bar. "Pull me another pint, Thomas," he said sourly. Beside him, the devil leapt up onto the bar and squatted there, giggling and scratching and making fiendish faces, as Oliver drained his glass and called for another.

CHAPTER TWENTY-FIVE

English bribes were all in vain
Though poor and poorer we may be,
Silver canna buy the heart
That aye beats warm for thine and thee.

Will ye no coom back again?
Will ye no coom back again?
Better loved ye canna be.
Will ye no coom back again?

"Will Ye No Come Back Again?"
Scottish ballad

Outside, Hamilton pushed the baker away, steadied himself, and stumbled down the street. He knew he'd drunk too much whiskey again, and feared he'd gone too far when he mentioned the pictures of the Royal Family. But among all the bloody events of the past few days, he thought incoherently, it was those bloody pictures that plagued him the most, that stayed in his mind and wouldn't go away. Who the bloody hell *was* this bloody Lord Osborne, and why should he have so many photographs—such recent ones, too—of the King and Queen and the rest of the bloody lot?

"Hold up, Hamilton," a cheerful voice said, and a firm hand grasped his left elbow. "I'll walk a distance with you."

Hamilton glanced up in surprise at the speaker, who seemed to loom over him, almost a full head taller. It was the old ballad collector, but he was no longer stooped, and his cane and fiddle case were tucked under his arm.

"No need tae gae wi' me," Hamilton said, willing himself to speak without slurring. "I dinna want tae take ye out o' yer way." He tried to free his elbow, but the old man's grasp was surprisingly powerful, and he could not pull away from it, no matter how hard he tried.

They were almost at the end of the street now, just passing the joiner's shop. Neither Hamilton nor the other had a light, and their way was lit only by the moon, its pale face veiled with gauzy clouds. To Hamilton, whose eyes seemed to be playing tricks on him, the shadows under his feet suddenly became a nest of black, entangling vines, alive as snakes, writhing up to snare him. He stretched out his right hand for the stone wall, once again muttering, "I dinna want tae take ye out o' yer way."

"It's not out of my way at all," the old man said. His grip was a vise, his voice as cold and brittle as glass, without a trace of Scots. "By the by, Hamilton, what's become of your friend Herman Memsdorff? I've been looking for him all day."

Memsdorff. Hamilton was seized by a terror so cold that it seemed to chill him to the bone. "Memsdorff?" His lips were taut and dry, like old leather, and he suddenly felt light-headed and giddy. He reached for the wall again, to brace himself. "I haen't seen Memsdorff since—" *Since the night before, when the two of them had left the pub with the bottle of whiskey and gone to the ice house, where—* He shivered, scarcely able to keep his teeth from chattering.

"Memsdorff was to meet me this morning," the old man said. He turned to look full at Hamilton, his eyes even colder than his voice, and empty. "With the merchandise."

Hamilton stopped, frozen. A sudden knowledge flew across his mind, like the clouds across the moon. But it could not be true. He must be mistaken, for he was certainly drunk. He shook his head.

"The merchandise?" he replied. "What merchandise? I dinna—"

And then suddenly he was grabbed by the hair and his head was slammed backward, hard, against the wall. In the same movement, the old man's bent forearm, strong and unyielding as an iron pipe, pressed against his throat, cutting off his breathing. Hamilton hung there for what seemed an endless time, the arm pinning him breathless and gasping against the wall's cold stone, his fingers scrabbling ineffectually at the old man's prickly woolen sleeve, his knees weakening, vision blurring, red flashes exploding in fountains of fire behind his eyes, ears roaring as if he were fathoms underwater, drowning, dying.

The old man pushed his face within inches of Hamilton's. "Where is Memsdorff?" he snarled. "Where are you keeping the merchandise?"

And then, as suddenly as he had been seized, Hamilton was released. He fell to his knees in the dust, dragging in great, gasping, painful lungfuls of air, gagging and choking and retching. Just then, the joiner and the baker went past, down the middle of the street. Dimly, through the tumult in his ears, he heard them asking if they could be of any help; dimly, he heard the old man replying in a merry voice that his companion had only had a drop too much whiskey and would be fine as soon as he'd puked it all up.

When they were gone, the old man reached down and hauled him up by the collar, propping him against the wall. "Where's Memsdorff?" he repeated, his voice steely and flat, without merriment, without inflection. "What have you done with the merchandise?"

And now, Hamilton could no longer deny what he knew to be true. This was no old man. This ballad collector was the man with whom Herman Memsdorff had been dealing for the past several weeks, with whom he had made the arrangements for delivery and payment. And now Memsdorff was—

"Memsdorff's bloody gone," Hamilton choked out. He put both hands to his throat. "Ye've smashed my windpipe." He sagged against the wall, gagging for air. "I can't breathe."

The man, his empty eyes the color of moonlight, towered fiercely over him. "Gone where?"

"I canna say." Hamilton turned his head aside from those infernal eyes. "Back . . . back tae Edinburg, most like."

The man's laugh was ugly, implacable. "Not bloody likely." With his left hand, he gathered the lapels of Hamilton's jacket, yanking him close so that he could not turn away. "Where's the merchandise, Hamilton? Tell me, or so help me God, I'll break your worthless neck." He raised his bent right forearm again, like a deadly weapon.

Helplessly, Hamilton yielded. "It . . . it got away from us," he blurted, and added hastily, "Only temporarily, o' course. It's safe now. I locked it up for safe-keeping."

He looked up to see the man's eyes fixed on him like daggers, impaling him with a savage contempt. The face was no longer old, but not young, either. It was ageless, with clean, diamond-cut lines and the terrible coldness of a skilled and clever killer.

"It's true," Hamilton cried, panicked, his voice rising. And then, sobbing in desperation and fear, heard himself say, "It's in a safe place. I'll take you there." His heart quailed as he spoke, for he had only staved off the final terror, not canceled it.

Slowly, the man dropped his arm and straightened, staring at Hamilton all the while. Then, surprisingly, he laughed, with a bitter, self-deprecating humor.

"Well, then, that's all right. Although I must say that this is a hell of a mess." He took a step backward and stood for a moment staring off into the distance, as if he were considering what to do. At last, with a sigh, he shrugged and seemed to relax, the steel going out of him. He reached into his coat pocket and pulled out a crumpled pack of cigarettes. Extracting two, putting them both in his mouth, he lit them from the same match and handed one to Hamilton.

"Sorry about your throat, old chap," he said, his tone lightened by a wry, exasperated amusement. "I'm afraid I was a little rougher just now than I meant to be. But you were very drunk, and I didn't think I'd knock the truth out of you any other way." He cocked his head, a worried frown flickering between his pale eyes. "Sober now, are you? You'll be all right?"

Hamilton hesitated, confused by the shift in the man's demeanor. "I dinna think th' damage is permanent," he said finally. He pulled on the cigarette, the smoke filling his lungs and somewhat clearing his head, although he could hardly say he was sober. He'd prefer one of his own cigars, but he didn't like to refuse. "Aye, I'm sharpenin' up some."

"That's all right, then," the man said amiably. "Shouldn't've liked to cause you any lasting grief."

Down the street, the pub lights had been put out. The village was silent, the only sound that of a distant owl and, somewhat closer, a man snoring sonorously in his bed. Overhead, the clouds had thickened, blotting out the stars and almost entirely extinguishing the moon. As they stood and smoked in silence, the blackness seemed to wrap them in a fraternal cloak.

At last, in a tone of something like regret, the man remarked, "It was a pity about the woman. Which of you had to kill her?"

The smoke turned sour in Hamilton's throat and he coughed. "It was Memsdorff," he said, when he could get his breath. "She . . . we didna expect her tae coom up tae the rooms so late at night."

"So she interrupted you, then?" The man's tone was compassionate, comradely, and his mouth, in the flickering moonlight, seemed to be faintly smiling. "Surprised you, I suppose. Caught you off guard."

Hamilton nodded. "We'd come tae scout out the place. Memsdorff wanted tae make sure we could get in an' upstairs tae get him—tae pick up the merchandise, I mean—a day or twae later, when it was time." He pulled on the cigarette. "We were by the door when she came up an' saw us. She stepped back an' made as if tae scream. Memsdorff grabbed her an' spun her round an' slit her throat, quick as thought." He gulped down the sudden taste of vomit that filled his mouth. "His awn aunt. His awn flesh an' blood."

"Too bad," the man said softly. He put his head to one side and half-closed his eyes. "Thundering bad luck, and a dreadful experience, for the both of you. I'm sorry it had to happen, although of course, you cannot be blamed. It was well that you acted with dispatch, or things might've gone off worse."

"Ye're right, 'twas dreadful." Hamilton pulled himself straighter, fighting off a bit of dizziness. "Blood spoutin' all o'er th' place, her dyin' there on th' floor wi' just a bit of a gurgle."

The only thing good about the business, he reflected to himself, was that they were able to get Lord Osborne. He'd been reading and, nearly deaf, had hardly heard the scuffle, not enough to know what had happened. Hamilton had stripped off his jacket, dropped it over his head, and hurried him off. If they'd waited, of course, and Hilda's body had been discovered, a guard would have been put on the fellow and they'd never have got at him.

"I suppose," the man said in a resigned tone, "that when it was over, poor Memsdorff went to pieces or threatened to go to the constable and confess the whole business." He sighed heavily. "So you had no choice but to kill him, to keep from endangering our mission. Regrettable, but necessary. I commend you."

Hamilton's head jerked up. It hadn't happened that way, of course. The unpleasant truth was that he himself had fallen asleep while guarding the prisoner, and Lord Osborne had managed to slip his bonds and get away. And last night, when Memsdorff had charged him with carelessness, they'd fallen into a quarrel. Memsdorff had pulled out his revolver, they had struggled, the gun had gone off, and by God's mercy, he'd been the one to walk away. Even now, Memsdorff's body was lying in the ice house, heaped over with loose straw.

Apparently taking Hamilton's silence for assent, the man patted his shoulder. "Well, it can't be helped now," he said. "But no harm done, except to Memsdorff and his aunt, of course. Just to clear up our arrangements, I'll take the merchandise with me tonight. Where shall I pick it up?"

Hamilton swallowed. "I dinna b'lieve—" He paused, thinking fast. "It wudna be gude tae fetch it tonight. It's locked up, and tomorrow will do just as well."

"Not tonight?" the man asked, as if he were disappointed. "You're very sure of that?"

Hamilton shook his head. The truth was, of course, that he couldn't come up with Lord Osborne, night or day. The mad wretch had got clean away, and God only knew where he was hiding. Not even the soldiers had been able to find him.

The man eyed him for a moment, as if he were measuring Hamilton with his shrewd glance. "Ah, yes. You must be concerned about payment."

Hamilton smiled thinly. Here was a man he could deal with. "Well, I was thinkin' aboot it," he acknowledged in a careless tone. "Memsdorff did tell me that—"

"Fifty pounds?" the man inquired. He peered into Hamilton's surprised face. "You were expecting more." He sighed. "Seventy-five, then."

Hamilton tried to find his voice and failed.

"You drive a hard bargain, my friend," the man said, resigned. "I'll go a hundred, if you can deliver tonight." He reached into his pocket.

The man's voice was light and comradely, but his eyes were like lances, penetrating to the very soul, and Hamilton looked down in self-defense, fearing to give himself away. He shook his head. "Not tonight."

"Well, then, that's all right," the man said with the air of someone who has just made up his mind. "Here's fifty, to cement our bargain, and the rest tomorrow, when you deliver."

Hamilton nodded wordlessly, and the man counted

money into his hand. Ten fivers. Fifty pounds. Seven months' pay. Swallowing hard, he put it into his pocket.

"Where and when tomorrow shall we say?" the man asked.

After a little thought, Hamilton named a time and a spot and gave directions.

The man nodded. "It's a bloody shame about Memsdorff," he said again, "but I have the feeling that this small task is in competent hands. I shall look forward to seeing you tomorrow—with our merchandise."

"Aye, tomorrow." Hamilton fingered the money in his pocket. His brother had been urging him to come to Montreal and buy a share of a draper's shop. Fifty pounds would see him there and settled, with some to spare. "Now, I think I'd better gae home an' get some sleep."

"Do that," the man said, and smiled.

They parted, the man turning back to the north, Hamilton walking to the south along the road to Dundee, stumbling a little, for his brain was still drink-addled. He lived on the far side of the burn, and to get home he always went across Glamis Dam, a hundred yards above the old flax mill. The fitful moon offered just enough illumination for him to make his way across the narrow stone structure. The water was high, the stones were slippery, and another man, less accustomed to the path or more sober, might have thought twice about crossing it. But Hamilton came this way to and from his work, and knew the path so well that he would have crossed even without a moon.

He put his hand in his pocket for another comforting touch of the money, and began to whistle. Thinking of the new life that awaited him in Montreal, he left the path and stepped out jauntily across the dam. He didn't have much gear in the small room where he slept and it wouldn't take long to pack it up. He wouldn't wait for the morning train, or risk being stopped by those soldiers on the Dundee road. He'd strike off across country straightaway, and be in Petterden by first light. He could catch a ride there—a farmer taking a wagon-load of fresh vegetables into Dundee, perhaps. Then passage to Canada, and Montreal, and—

And on that happy thought, Douglas Hamilton died.

CHAPTER TWENTY-SIX

Truth will come to light. . . .

William Shakespeare
Merchant of Venice

Wearily, Charles sat down in the chair and tugged off one boot. He was wrestling with the second when Kate knelt before him and pulled it off.

"You must be very tired, my dear," she said. "The railway journey last night, all your work today, and that dreadful dinner tonight."

"It was truly dreadful, then," Charles asked with a wry chuckle, "and not just my martyred imagination?" He had not brought dress clothes for the occasion, so he'd had to ask Simpson to find something suitable in Lord Strathmore's closet. The coat and waistcoat were far too tight, and it was a merciful relief to get out of them. And Kate was right. He *was* tired. He was, in fact, exhausted.

"Yes," Kate said. She rose and poked up the fire. "It was frightful." She went to a table, unstoppered a decanter, and poured two small glasses of port. "The Princess was stiff and formal and unable to say what was on her mind, Colonel

Paddington was unbearably full of military exploits, Andrew was anxious and stammering, you were absent-minded, and I was bored." She handed him one glass and took the second to a yellow-upholstered sofa. "Not to mention that the sweetbreads were inedible and the mutton as tough as a piece of boot leather."

Charles chuckled as he stretched out his stockinged feet, wiggled his toes, and glanced appreciatively at his barefoot wife. She was wrapped in a green silk dressing-gown, her russet hair tumbled loose around her shoulders. The front of her gown had fallen open slightly, and he could see the inviting curve of her bare breast.

"Well, it's over at last," he said, "and we can go to bed."

"In a moment." Kate tucked her bare feet under her, pulling her dressing-gown over her knees. "I've dissected the dinner party, and now it's your turn. You must tell me what happened this afternoon after you left me in front of the castle, and why you and Andrew were so preoccupied this evening."

Charles leaned his head far back, watching the light from the flames dancing across the ceiling. "Nothing much happened," he said dejectedly. "Nothing worth telling, anyway." Was it just that he was tired, or was it really true that for all their efforts, he and Andrew had learned nothing very helpful? They had not found the Prince, he had no clue as to Hilda MacDonald's murderer, and while he was now sure that German agents somehow had a hand in the business, he wasn't an inch closer to locating them. *"Truth will come to light,"* Shakespeare had said, but it all seemed very dark to him.

"That's not good enough!" Kate sat up, took aim, and tossed a pillow at him. "You're to tell *all,* Charles Sheridan, no matter how trivial, or I shall march straight down to the camp and wring the information out of Andrew." She looked down at her silk dressing-gown and smiled slightly. "Perhaps I shall *vamp* it out of him."

"Oh, dear," he murmured ironically. "Well, to keep you from throwing your virtue away, I suppose I'd best fill you in."

"Yes, please, m'lord," Kate said, settling back again. "You can start with Memsdorff. Is it true that he is a German agent?"

"It seems so," Charles said. "The list of numbers you found is a simple cipher, and the volume of Scott turned out to be the key. Andrew is clever with such things, and it took him only a few minutes to decode it. The message confirmed that the Germans planned to kidnap Prince Eddy. Wilhelmstrasse—the office of the German Foreign Ministry—was involved, which suggests that the affair was coordinated at a high level, not by Steinhauer, their Intelligence man, but by Friedrich von Holstein himself."

"Oh, dear!" Kate exclaimed. She clasped her hands around her knees, frowning. "But you're speaking in the past tense. Are you suggesting that their plot has failed?"

"We can't be sure, although things definitely did not go as they planned. According to the cipher message, Firefly—Herman Memsdorff—was meant to abduct the Prince tomorrow night. Then he would meet his spy-master, and together they would take Eddy to a fishing village not far from here, where a German freighter would be standing by offshore to pick them up."

"But that's not what happened, is it?" Kate said thoughtfully. "The Prince was kidnapped on Sunday night, at the same time that Hilda MacDonald was killed." Her eyes grew large. "But all this suggests that it was Herman Memsdorff who murdered Hilda—his own aunt!"

"Either he, or the other one," Charles said. "There was someone with him."

Kate frowned. "How do you know?"

"The cipher message indicates that Memsdorff was working with a local man," Charles replied. "Unfortunately, he is not named in the message, and while he may have left fingerprints in the Prince's rooms, they cannot yet be matched. But the worst of it is that we have no idea whether the two of them still have the Prince in their custody."

When he and Kate had parted that afternoon, Charles had first sought out Andrew, to have the message decoded, and then had gone to the Prince's suite to look for any evidence that the kidnappers had left behind. He had found nothing immediately helpful, although he'd collected a number of clear fingerprints: a set that was presumably Eddy's, from the Prince's cigarette case and the silver hairbrush on the dresser; several that matched the prints he himself had taken from Hilda, and several as yet unidentified. In the morning, he would obtain prints from Duff and Simpson, and from Flora, too, as soon as she was located. Presumably, the remaining prints would belong to Memsdorff and his accomplice. Memsdorff's could be verified by taking prints in the cottage loft where Firefly had slept. If a match could be made, the case against Memsdorff would be proven, since he had no business in the Prince's rooms.

"I suppose," Kate remarked quietly, "that Memsdorff would need another man to help him abduct the Prince, even if Eddy wasn't very strong."

"Yes," Charles agreed. "And he'd need someone who knew his way around the castle. Or *her* way," he added.

"Not Hilda," Kate said firmly. Her conviction spoke in the lift of her chin, the flash of her gray eyes. "She would never have betrayed the Prince. She served him too long and faithfully to become part of a plot against him."

"Not knowingly, perhaps," Charles replied, hating to disillusion his wife. "But she may have been the unwitting source of Firefly's intelligence regarding Eddy—who he was, where he was. After all, Memsdorff was Hilda's nephew, and she had no reason to suspect him of deceiving her or harming the Prince. Perhaps he simply asked a few casual questions, and she told him, bit by bit and over a period of several months, without any idea how her information would be put to use."

"Poor Hilda," Kate murmured sadly. "And Flora, too— what a tragedy for both of them." She leaned forward to put her glass on the low table in front of her, and her dressing-gown fell open to her waist. "And nothing has been heard of Flora?"

"Not a thing," Charles said. "Simpson is quite put out, since she was expected back here at the castle before teatime, to serve you." He tossed off his port and stood up. "I'm ready for bed. As you said, it's been a long day." He was less tired now, though. The sight of his wife's bare breast was a powerful restorative, and he found himself wanting to hold her against him.

Kate gave him a frowning glance from under her lashes. "But I haven't told you what *I* found out, Charles."

Sighing, Charles sat back down again and prepared himself, patiently, to listen, thinking that she might have found out one or two interesting bits. But it took several moments for Kate to relay the information she'd obtained from the servants, together with her own speculations. When she was finished, he stared at her, amazed as he always was by her ability to persuade people to tell her things they would never in a hundred years confide to him, or to anyone else, for that matter. If the Germans employed her as a spy, it would be all up with England.

"So the servants believe that Flora and the Prince are romantically involved," he said thoughtfully. "And that they've gone off together—to Skye. I must say, it's an interesting way to explain the fact that they've both disappeared."

Kate nodded. "Of course, we know it's not true. The Prince was kidnapped." She frowned. "Although you seemed to suggest, a moment ago, that the kidnappers might have lost him."

Charles nodded. "But it's Flora's disappearance that bothers me most. She has every reason to go on about her business as usual: to testify at the inquest, bury her mother, remain in her accustomed post at the castle. And yet she's gone, without trace, without explanation. She was aware that I was anxious to question her—perhaps she's attempting to evade my questions, for fear of giving away what she knows." He sat forward in his chair, elbows on his knees, chin in his hands, pondering the flames. Kate's information had opened other possibilities for him to consider. "What if Eddy has given Memsdorff and his cohort the slip," he said, thinking aloud, "and he and Flora are in hiding somewhere, together? If they're romantically involved—"

"I don't think that's likely, Charles," Kate said, shaking her head. "Flora may care for him in a sisterly way—after all, she was only a girl when her mother began taking care of the Prince, and the two have apparently spent a great deal of time together. But she struck me as a practical young woman, not the sort to lose her heart to a man who . . ."

"Who is so much above her station?" Charles asked skeptically. He did not trust the distinctions between the classes, especially where love was concerned. On the other hand, the men he knew who'd had affairs with servant girls had not loved them, only used them for pleasure and discarded them.

"Perhaps," Kate said, frowning, "although I am thinking about his mental state rather than his station, and doubting, somehow, that Flora could find herself loving him, in a romantic way. And he is a great deal older than she—some fifteen years, at least."

"You certainly formed a clear idea of her character on the strength of a few moments' conversation," Charles remarked. And then, fearing he had sounded harsh, added, "But you are so often right, Kate, that I don't doubt you're right in this situation, as well." He paused. "Let's say, though, just for the sake of argument, that the two are together. Do you believe they may be planning to go to Skye? Eddy because he believes himself to be the Bonnie Prince, Flora to get him out of the way of the men who murdered her mother and captured him? After all, you did say that Flora's MacDonald grandparents are there, and that her mother had recently had a letter from them."

Kate gave him a doubtful look, her hair brushing her check. "Well, then, perhaps they're *hoping* to go to Skye. But seriously, Charles, how could Flora manage to get him away, under the noses of your soldiers?" She wrinkled her nose. "They couldn't go by railway, and you've blocked all the roads."

Charles looked at her, loving her seriousness and her passion, loving the way she held her head, the way her hair fell over her shoulder. He stood. "Well, wherever they are, we won't find them tonight. Shall we—"

She shook her head, still caught in her thoughts. "If the Prince managed to break free from his captors, Charles, I think they're both in hiding, somewhere in this neighborhood. Somewhere very near, most likely. Flora has lived here all her life, and she probably knows every nook and cranny. They couldn't have got away, so they must be nearby. And Gladys said that she saw Flora—"

Charles cupped his hand under her chin and raised her face. "Kate," he said softly. He bent to kiss her mouth. "Stop talking and come to bed with me, Kate."

It was a long while before either of them felt like talking again.

Charles held his wife against him, feeling the warmth and softness of her body. In the moonlight that came through the window, her hand was like alabaster. It rested on his bare chest, her fingers gently tracing the stripings of scars. He captured her hand and raised it to his lips, kissing her fingers.

She pulled her hand away and touched his scars again, speaking quietly. "I know you don't want me to ask, Charles, but it's time that you told me what happened in the Sudan. Colonel Paddington mentioned it when we were on the train—the business about your refusing the Victoria Cross, I mean. And resigning your commission."

He was panicked. How could he tell the woman he loved the truth after he had kept it from her for so long? Come to that, what *was* the truth? Therein lay the problem, of course: he had not explained it to her because he had never resolved the matter in his own mind. He knew he wasn't a coward, but he was certainly a fraud. That was what the Army, for its own purposes, had made him. He took a deep breath and spoke.

"Yes, I suppose it's time I told you. You're probably the only person in the kingdom who hasn't heard the tale of my trumped-up triumph, and I'd rather you had it from me—

the truth, that is. The King knows, or thinks he does, and Andrew, and Paddington. It's probably part of the reason I was chosen to command here." He tightened his jaw. "But they're wrong, all of them. They only know what the Army reported, you see. They——"

"Excuse me, love." Kate propped herself on her elbow, her face half-shadowed in the moonlight. "*What* tale haven't I heard? I know that you were a hero in the Sudan; I've caught snatches of that, here and there, and it's made me very proud of you. But what's this about people being wrong? *Who's* wrong?"

He spoke quietly. "The people who think I'm a hero."

"And you're not?"

"That's the Army's version." The words were bitter in his mouth. Would she still be proud of him when she heard what really happened? "The truth is that I got a lot of good men killed for little reason, and was made a hero for it."

"I see," she said gravely. "So that's the end of the story. Where does it begin?"

He pulled himself up, sitting against the pillow. "After I finished my studies at the military academy and the Royal Engineering School, I got myself posted to Cairo. I wanted to study the glories of ancient Egypt, you see: the pyramids, the Sphinx, bones and fossils, all that. It fit into the Army's plan for me very well. I was put in charge of a survey unit, laying out roads and the like. All quite peaceful, and lots of opportunity to pursue my own interests. But about that time, Gladstone sent Gordon to evacuate Khartoum."

"Oh, dear," Kate said. She lay down against him, her warm cheek against his bare chest. He could no longer see her face, and was glad.

"Yes. It was a singularly unwise move. Once there, the bloody fool decided to make a stand, apparently thinking that the British would decide to hold on to the Sudan. But they'd already given it up as a bad show, so he was out there on his own. Eventually, though, the Government realized that he'd have to be rescued, or there'd be a political disaster. So off we went—a motley collection of infantry, artillery, and an improvised camel corps."

"To relieve Gordon?"

He heard the surprise in her tone, and the dismay. He dropped a kiss on her forehead and tangled his hand in her hair. "We almost succeeded. On our way south, we didn't have much contact with the Mahdi, so one morning I left the camp at Abu Fahr with a small detachment, to go out and survey a wadi." He paused and added ruefully, "Of course, it was the fossils I was after. The evening before, we'd passed an interesting outcrop, and I wanted to have a closer look. On the way back, we were joined by a foraging party led by Captain Blake. As we got near the bivouac, we heard fighting, and when we topped the ridge, we saw Dervish troops swarming all over the camp."

Kate took his hand from her hair and kissed it. "How awful, Charles."

"It was, rather," he said bleakly. "To hold them off, the men below had formed into a square. Blake ordered us to open fire from the ridge, but our fire had no effect, for the Dervish force had broken into the square. In desperation, Blake ordered his men to fix bayonets. But he'd no sooner given the order than he took a bullet in the head. He fell, and everyone looked at me. Without much thinking about it, I waved my Webley, shouted something—God only knows what, 'For Queen and country,' or something equally silly—and ran down the slope, straight into the melee. My men followed me, pell-mell, and Blake's men followed them. I fired until my revolver was empty, then picked up a Henry-Martini rifle and got a cartridge into it." The words seemed to burn in his throat, like something corrosive. "There was a Dervish right in front of me with his spear drawn back, ready to fling. I pulled the trigger a split-second too late. The spear point sailed past my left shoulder. The shaft stopped abruptly, almost touching it, and when I turned to see what had happened, I found it was embedded in the chest of my young sergeant. I will never forget the look of surprise on his face." He swallowed hard. "That was the last thing I recall until I woke up in hospital, with everyone making a great fuss over me. They made out that I had personally saved the regiment, managing somehow to drive the attackers off—long enough, anyway, for what was left of the regiment to regroup. But of all the men who followed me down that hill, thirty or forty or so, I was the only one left alive."

"Oh, dear God." Kate raised her head, and he saw tears in her eyes. "Still, if their sacrifice saved the others—"

"The point is," he interrupted roughly, "that I've never been sure of that. All I know is that my men trusted me and died because of it. And in the long run, nothing we did that day made a ha'pworth of difference. An advance party got within sight of Khartoum whilst I was unconscious and discovered that Gordon and the entire garrison had been slaughtered."

"But you *earned* the Victoria Cross," she said, frowning. "Why did you refuse it?"

"Because I couldn't stand the thought of becoming a military institution," he burst out, desperate to make her understand. "The hero of Abu Fahr. That's what they were up to, of course. The Army needed heroes, to distract from the loss of Gordon and his men. But the whole thing made me feel like a fraud, don't you see?"

"Yes," she murmured, "I do see."

"I hoped that refusing the V.C. would put paid to it. But it didn't. I had to resign, as well, and get away. And even that wasn't enough. Bits and pieces of the story got out, and my refusal and the resignation only made the whole thing seem more heroic. In the end, I had to accept a knighthood."

"But that was for the photograph you took of the Queen at her Jubilee," Kate objected. "The one she liked so much."

"Another bit of Royal subterfuge," he said. "You don't know what they're like, those Royals. When Victoria wanted something, she got her way, regardless. And Edward is no different."

"I do know, a little," Kate said in a musing tone, "from listening to Toria. And I think that Prince Eddy might not have been so different from you."

"Eddy?" Charles frowned. "I'm not sure I understand."

"You didn't want to be a hero, he didn't want to be a king. He must have felt that he somehow wasn't worthy, or deserving, or even up to the task. I think his earlier peccadilloes—all that erratic behavior that worried the Royal Family so much—might simply have been a protest against an accident of birth. Given a choice between being a king and going into exile, he chose exile. You say that you felt like a fraud; perhaps he felt like a fraud, too."

"If it's true," Charles said somberly, "I pity him. Born to be king, but knowing he didn't have it in him. And being pushed to do something he couldn't do—"

"Being forced to marry a woman he didn't love," Kate put in. "By the Queen, whose only concern was to preserve the Royal dynasty."

Swept by a powerful surge of feeling, Charles tipped up her face. "Yes, I pity him," he said. "I pity any man who cannot have what he wants. Who cannot have what you and

I share." He paused. He felt better now, much better, but perhaps she wasn't yet satisfied. Suddenly he was overwhelmed by a sense of grave misgiving: how would she feel about him now that she knew his secret, the secret that he had kept from her so long? Half-fearing to hear her reply, he said, "Have I answered your questions, Kate? Is there anything else you'd like to know?"

She touched his lips with her finger and smiled, loving, teasing, playful, a smile that eased and delighted his heart. "Does my hero want me?" she whispered.

And once again, there was no more talking.

CHAPTER TWENTY-SEVEN

Sing me a song of a lad that is gone,
Say, could that lad be I?
Merry of soul he sailed on a day
Over the sea to Skye.

"Songs of Travel and Other Verses"
Robert Louis Stevenson

The darkness was not absolute, for the moon, dim and pale, shone a flickering light through the window, and there was still a glow from the fire that had done little to warm the chilly room. Long after Charles had gone to sleep, his hand gently cupping her bare breast, Kate lay awake, thinking of all he had told her, shivering at the thought of how near he had come to death and wondering at the way he had held his feelings within himself all these years.

She could understand his resentment at being made into a hero when he himself doubted his heroism—doubted, even, the idea of heroism itself, when men like Gordon could sacrifice thousands of soldiers and civilians on the altar of self-aggrandizement and absurd dreams of glory. She could understand, as well, Charles's grief at the loss of his men:

over fifteen years had gone by since Abu Fahr, but the anguish could still be heard in his voice when he spoke of the young sergeant who had been surprised by death. He was not the sort of Army officer to insist on the prerogatives of birth and breeding; he knew that the distinctions between classes were paper-thin, and would never have held himself above his men. No wonder they had followed him so willingly down the hill and into the terror of battle—and no wonder he blamed himself for their loss. But she could not understand why men kept such terrible secrets to themselves and refused to talk of the things that troubled them. A question suddenly occurred to her: would she and Beryl ever dare to put this tale into one of their stories? She had her doubts, but Beryl was incorrigible. Smiling, Kate put her hand over Charles's and held it as she fell asleep.

Kate woke abruptly as the great clock at the top of the tower struck twice, the sounds shivering eerily into silence. She had been dreaming of her conversation in the tea pantry that afternoon with Gladys. In her dream, the girl repeated several times what she had said earlier: that she had seen Flora carrying a large tea tray, heavily laden, going in the direction of the old part of the castle. "That part's haunted," Gladys said, giving her coppery curls a warning shake. "I'd never gae there meself."

Once awake, Kate's dream remained with her, and although she curved herself closer to Charles's warmth and firmly closed her eyes, she could not go back to sleep. For whom had Flora prepared that tea tray? Why had she taken it to the old part of the castle? The questions chased one another through her mind like the castle's fretful ghosts, rattling their chains, jostling her into restlessness.

Kate herself was not inclined to wander through haunted hallways in the dead of night, but the bold and incorrigible

Beryl felt differently about such adventures. As Kate moved closer to Charles and tried to return to sleep, Beryl kept prodding her. Glamis was the oldest inhabited castle in Scotland and certainly the most ghostly, and night was the time when all those ghosts would be out and about. Famous ghosts, like the Gray Lady, Earl Beardie, the tragic Monster of Glamis, perhaps even Bonnie Prince Charlie or Sir Walter Scott. If she and Kate were going to gather ideas and material for the book, there would be no better time than tonight. Beryl grinned invitingly and cuffed her on the shoulder. *Shall we have a go, old girl?*

No, not tonight, Kate replied, as she fitted herself more snugly against Charles and pulled the covers over her head. The past two days had been long and tiring, and she was weary. They could explore the castle tomorrow, she promised Beryl. Tonight, they would sleep.

Suiting the deed to the thought, Kate closed her eyelids. A moment later, however, they were wide open again, and the irrepressible Beryl was poking more questions at her. *Well, if you're not interested in the castle's ghosts, Kate, what about that odd business of Flora and the tea tray? Where was Flora going? Why? Surely we ought to at least go and have a look. What are you afraid of? A few moldy old ghosts?*

At last, wide awake and feeling exasperated with Beryl's relentless upbraiding and her own inability to sleep, Kate slid away from Charles, climbed carefully out of bed, and pushed her feet into her slippers. Charles turned over with a muffled sigh but did not seem to wake, as Kate, shivering in her nakedness, found the white flannel nightgown she had not bothered to put on earlier and dropped it over her head. Then she pulled on her flannel knickers and shrugged into her green dressing-gown, wrapping a thick woolen shawl around her shoulders for extra warmth. It might be

August, but Glamis Castle held the chill of centuries of winters.

Feeling better now that she was dressed and moving about, Kate took the candlestick from the mantel and slipped extra matches into the pocket of her dressing-gown. Out in the pitch-black windowless hall, the door safely shut behind her, she lit the candle. Holding it in her hand, its tiny flame flickering bravely against the dark, she gathered her courage and groped her way toward the stairs.

But Kate had just reached the head of the stair when she put her hand to her mouth, stifling a small scream. A huge, ghostly monster, all in silver, lurched angrily out of a dark corner, wielding a monstrous cleaver, swinging it at her head. But as she stepped back, heart thumping, she realized that the apparition was no monster, and certainly not some fierce ghost. It was just a very large suit of full-body armor, with a very large sword in its mailed fist, propped in a corner at the head of the stair.

Kate stood for a moment, catching her breath, waiting for her heart to stop pounding, and hoping that Beryl's curiosity about ghosts was satisfied at last. She lifted the candle higher, pulled her shawl tighter, and started cautiously down the wide stone stairs. Once, she thought she heard a soft step behind her and whirled, to see a threatening shadow. But she was not daunted. After all, it wasn't the thought of ghosts that had lured her out of bed. It was Flora and her tray full of food—more than enough for one person, Gladys had seemed to suggest, or for more than one meal.

That's right, Beryl said encouragingly. *For more than one meal. Think about it, Kate. Perhaps Flora was taking the food to Eddy, who is hiding right here in the castle.*

Kate stopped still, the candlelight casting uncertain shadows on the stones of the hallway staircase. *In the castle?*

Why, of course! Where else? If German agents were trying to abduct him, Glamis Castle would be the safest place to hide, wouldn't it? There must be dozens of places of concealment within this enormous stone pile, with its many cellars, its secret rooms, its pepper-pot turrets, and probably entire floors where the servants never went. Where the servants refused to go, because they were said to be haunted.

Now you're on the right track, Beryl said approvingly, as Kate went down the stone stairs. *Remember the way Flora acted when she was showing you the old crypt? You asked about the Monster, and she refused to talk about it. She didn't really take you into the room, either, or give you a chance to look around. The two of you stood just inside the door, and she hurried you out as fast as she could. Was it because she was afraid you might see something you shouldn't? The very first place to look for Prince Eddy—Lord Osborne, as she knows him—is the cell where the Monster of Glamis was hidden for so many years. And while you're at it, my girl, keep your eyes peeled for ghosts, too.* Always determined to get the most out of any experience, Beryl pulled out her mental notebook and pencil and began to jot down impressions. The ghostly suit of armor with its massive sword, like a figure of Death. The flickering candle casting grotesque shadows on the stone walls, giving the impression that she was being followed. The ancient clock ticking loudly at the foot of the stair. The massive stones all around her, each one soaked with the secrets of the ages. The heavy air, so thick that it felt almost furry. Chill, musty air that had been breathed by Sir Walter Scott, by the tragic Queen Mary, by Macbeth and Lady Macbeth and—

What rubbish! Kate shook herself impatiently. If Beryl wanted to take mental notes of her observations, she could at least make them accurate. Macbeth had never lived in this castle; that was Shakespeare's mistake. Or his fiction. After all, Shakespeare's plays only seemed to present historical truth. It was all a canny illusion.

She lifted her candle higher. She was in the main keep now, the castle's great central tower, its oldest structure. The silence seemed audibly restless, small creatures scratching in the corners, furry things sidling out of dark hiding places, the candle flame licking and hissing at the wax, her silk dressing-gown rustling, and she winding around and down the circular staircase until she was dizzy.

And now, at last, at the very bottom, she was standing before the heavy wooden door to the crypt. She held up the candle, looking for the key on the peg, but to her surprise it wasn't there. *Of course!* Beryl crowed triumphantly. *Flora's taken the key—which means that she must be in there, with Prince Eddy.* And when Kate hesitated, feeling that the room was somehow forbidden, and quite sensibly aware that danger could lurk within, Beryl said into her ear, quite loudly, *Why, Kate! You're not afraid, are you?*

Of course I'm not afraid, Kate told herself indignantly. *I'm just cautious, that's all.* She put her ear to the door, but it was so thick that she would have heard nothing, even had Earl Beardie and the devil been carousing inside. Carefully, as quietly as she could, she lifted the rusty handle and pushed at the door. When it swung open, she saw that the large room was empty—of people, anyway. Whether there were ghosts here or not, she thought, she would leave it to Beryl to decide.

Closing the door behind her, her pulse hammering, her blood chilly in her veins, Kate stood in the oldest room in the castle, the long, narrow room that must have once been the lord's banqueting room. Her candle was barely sufficient to light the whole space at once, so she received only a confused impression of flickering sights and sensations. The vaulted stone ceiling shimmered with damp, its narrow alcoves were full of moving shadows, and its walls were hung with ancient tapestries, ornate carvings, pieces of armor, and the stuffed heads of great curly-horned sheep, their glass eyes sinister in the candlelight. She stood for a moment, indecisively, not sure what she was looking for. The silence was so profound that all she could hear was the quick sighing of her own breath.

And then it began to seem to Kate that she could hear something else: the melodious murmur of low voices, much muted, as if they came from a very great distance. Lifting her candle higher, she crept toward the far end of the crypt, keeping close to one of the walls. On the left, there was another arched alcove, just wide enough to step into. The rear wall was hung with a heavy tapestry, suspended from a carved wooden rod. But the hanging did not quite extend to the floor, and beneath it Kate saw the faintest ribbon of light. Was there a doorway behind the tapestry? Did it lead to the cell where the Monster had been imprisoned for all those long, sad years?

She stepped closer. The voices ceased, and she stepped back, holding her breath. And then, after a moment, they began again, in harmony, a light female voice and a lower, heavier male voice. They were singing, and Kate could just make out the words.

> *Sing me a song of a lad that is gone,*
> *Say, could that lad be I?*
> *Merry of soul he sailed on a day*
> *Over the sea to Skye.*

CHAPTER TWENTY-EIGHT

Watson: *"How do you know that?"*
Holmes: *"Because the ash had twice dropped from his cigar."*

The Hound of the Baskervilles
Arthur Conan Doyle

"There, sir," Flora said, when they'd finished their last song. "Thank ye for joining in." She looked straight at him and shaped her words distinctly, so that he could read her lips if he did not catch the sounds of her words. She knew, however, that Lord Osborne was not nearly as deaf as he pretended to be, but rather used his deafness as a defense against unwanted annoyances. "D'ye feel better now?" she asked solicitously, extending her hand across the table.

"I do," Lord Osborne replied, draining the last of the wine from his glass and pushing the empty bottle away. He took her hand, held it briefly, and released it. "Our singing always comforts me, Flora MacDonald."

"I'm glad, Yer Highness," Flora said, with the gay little smile she used to remind him that they were only playing— he at being the Bonnie Prince, she at being the Flora who was helping him to escape from the British soldiers who were pursuing him. "Shall we see if we can sleep, sir?"

"Sleep," he said with a sigh. "It seems to me that I have been doing nothing but sleep for the past few days, ever since I came to this place." He made an irritable, impatient sound, and pushed the empty glass across the table. "The danger must be past by now, Flora. When are we going to get away from here?"

"The danger isna past, I fear," Flora replied gently, repeating something she had already told him several times over since she had returned to his cell in the afternoon. "The soldiers are still blockin' th' roads an' searchin' th' woods for Yer Highness, an' th' grassy field tae th' north is filled with tents, where they're bivouacked. But I've found a tinker who's willing tae take us tae Perth in his caravan, an' from there we can take th' train tae Glasgow, and a boat tae Skye. I'm sorry I can't make Yer Highness more comfort'ble tonight," she added. "But afore we leave on th' morrow, I'll creep up tae your rooms an' find Yer Highness's shaving gear an' some clean linen." That part worried her. He needed to be cleanly-shaved in order to defeat recognition, but his rooms might be guarded, and then what would she do?

"It's all right, Flora." Wearily, Lord Osborne rubbed his hands through his gray hair, which seemed to have grown grayer in the past few days, his face more lined, his stoop more pronounced. He was not a good-looking man, for his heavy-lidded eyes were large, his face narrow and horsey, and his neck extraordinarily long, so that his head seemed unnaturally high above his shoulders. His wide collars usually disguised this defect, but he was not wearing a collar now. His gray hair, stubbly gray beard, and sagging shoulders gave him almost the look of an old man, Flora thought, although she knew that he could not yet be forty. She began to reply, but he interrupted her.

"No, I must speak," he said, and when he looked at her, his glance was calmer and more lucid than it had been for some time. "You are a dear, sweet girl to take such good care of me, Flora. But please don't call me Highness." His tone became sadly ironic. "I know who I am, and I promise you, I am no prince."

"As yer lordship wishes," Flora said, her worry lightening. She had been through this—periods of sad derangement alternating with clarity and sound sense—too many times to be hopeful that Lord Osborne's delusions had disappeared. But if they were to travel as far as Perth with the tinker, it would certainly be helpful if she could count on him to take her instructions, or at least follow her lead, and without all that nonsense about his being a prince, and her being his lady.

She spread her cloak and the MacDonald-tartan shawl on one of the straw pallets Lord Osborne had taken from his bed and put in the corner for her, and prepared to lie down. She had at first been reluctant to stay here with him, for fear of how it might look to others. Of course, she hoped that no one would ever discover where they'd been and that they had been together, but if it became known, she would learn to live with it. Her virtue was far more important to her than her reputation, and she knew Lord Osborne to be a true gentleman, sweet and kind and with no lechery in his heart.

And with luck, this would be their only night together in this place. Before dawn, they would steal out of the castle and walk through the woods to Roundyhill, where they would meet the tinker and find safe passage to Perth. The soldiers would almost certainly stop them on the road, but she felt she could count on the tinker to spin a fine tale about where he had been and where he was going, and why. And she and Lord Osborne would be only two raggle-taggle gypsies, not worth a minute's thought or a second look.

"If you're settled, I shall put out the candle," Lord Osborne said, as Flora made herself comfortable.

And with that, he extinguished the flame, and the cell was immediately dark, a blackness so complete that Flora could feel the smothery weight of it pressing against her face, smelling of damp stone and burnt candle-wick. But she was not afraid, for even though this apartment adjacent to the crypt—once the secret residence of the poor creature known as the Monster of Glamis—was said to be haunted by that poor unfortunate's weary spirit, she had never seen any evidence of it when she'd explored here as a child.

The Monster, her mother had told her, was the first son of Lord Strathmore's grandfather Thomas, the eleventh earl. The infant was horribly deformed and judged unfit to take his part in the society to which he was born. His father ordered that the baby be done away with immediately, but he was spared by some sympathetic intervention, perhaps because it was felt that he must soon die of natural causes. But the Monster proved to be surprisingly healthy, despite his evident handicaps. He lived out the span of his life— some forty years—in these small rooms, occasionally allowed the freedom of the park and the pleasures of the woods but permitted no human society other than those who served him. The poor creature had died in the 1860s, but Lord Strathmore was so distressed by the imprisonment of the Monster—who must have been his father's uncle—that he would not allow anyone to speak of it, even to this day.

Lord Osborne's straw mattress rustled as he settled himself upon it. "It's a good thing neither of us is troubled by fears of ghosts," he reflected somberly. "This place is full of them. Ghosts of dead dreams, of forgotten pasts, of lives and loves that once were." His sigh was laced with pain and a heavy regret. "Oh, to go back and do it all over again, Flora, from the beginning. To have another chance." The pain became passion. "I should do it all differently, oh, so differently, knowing what I know of myself now. I would never let Papa and Grandmama force me to give up my wife, and the baby. I would stand by Annie forever—such a dear, good girl, and so loving and devoted." He groaned bitterly. "And lovely little Alice, my sweet Alice. If I could do it again, I would claim them both, and take them to France, and to *hell* with the throne. I would . . ." His voice trailed away, blurred with tears.

To hell with the throne? Flora could not answer to that, for she had no idea what Lord Osborne was talking about, or whether he was speaking of a real or an imagined past. But she had seen in his rooms several photographs of a pretty young woman with a baby in her arms, and while she had never heard of a marriage, it might very well be true. If Lord Osborne had been somehow compelled to give up his wife and baby, therein might lie the cause of his delusional fancies. For who could bear a real life from which the heart's love had been forcibly stripped away?

Flora lay silently on her pallet, her eyes open and staring into the dark, and after a moment her breast began to heave with silent sobs, the tears running down her cheeks and into her hair. It was not Lord Osborne's loss for which she wept, of course, but her own. When the two of them left for Perth in the morning, she would be leaving her mother behind, yet unburied, her killer yet unnamed. To do such a deed went against all Flora had been taught, and her heart ached as if it might burst wide open. The only thing that eased her pain was the knowledge that Hilda MacDonald, who had loved Lord Osborne as if he were her son, would surely approve of what her daughter was doing. She would certainly want Flora to help him get away from this place and find a safe haven, to protect him from any who would harm him, and especially from that wretched Lord Sheridan and his soldiers, who—

Flora's eyes widened and she sat bolt upright, her heart in her mouth and a half-stifled scream on her lips. The door of the cell had opened with a rusty sigh, and in the blackness, a candle flame shimmered. A pale, disembodied face floated behind the flickering flame, its eyes gleaming with reflected light, its teeth showing white and fierce, a mass of loose hair flowing raggedly over its shoulders. *The Monster!* Flora thought, in a panic.

And then, in the next instant, a woman was kneeling beside her mattress, a comforting hand on Flora's shoulder. It was Lady Sheridan, her dressing-gown smelling faintly of lavender, her voice soft and gentle.

"Don't be frightened, please, Flora. I'm not here to hurt anyone."

To his credit, Lord Osborne had been quick to act. Seeing the light, he'd bounded out of bed and snatched the empty wine bottle from the table. Seizing it by the neck, he slammed it hard against the table edge, sending glass shards in all directions. He held the jagged remainder in his hand as if it were a sword.

"Stay bloody well back!" he shouted, brandishing the broken bottle, "or I'll—"

"Eddy," a quiet voice said, "we're here to help you." A slim, brown-bearded man stepped forward, authoritative even in pajamas, robe, and slippers.

"Charles!" Lady Sheridan gasped. "You *followed* me!"

"Forgive me, my dear," the man said apologetically. To Lord Osborne, he said, "I'm Charles Sheridan, and this is my wife." He paused, holding the candle so that it illuminated his face, which bore the unmistakeable stamp of aristocracy, the jaw firm, the nose aquiline. "Charles Sheridan," he repeated, speaking louder, forming his words distinctly. "The last time we met, I think, was in late '91, at Sandringham. Do you remember?"

"Sandringham?" Lord Osborne, uncomprehending, stared at the man's face, then lowered the bottle. "Sheridan? Well, deuced if it isn't! What the devil are *you* doing here?" He frowned. "My father didn't send you, did he?"

As Flora scrambled confusedly to her feet, Lady Sheridan rose, lit the candle on the table by the flame of her own, setting the two side by side. In the brighter light, Flora saw that Lady Sheridan, like her husband, was in her night-clothes, her hair flowing loose around her shoulders.

"As a matter of fact, he did," Lord Sheridan acknowledged. He came a step closer, his hands out, so it could be seen that they were empty. "He sent both me and Toria."

"The devil!" Lord Osborne exclaimed angrily. "My sister's here *too*?"

"She arrived yesterday," Lord Sheridan said. "The King fears for your safety. When you went missing, he ordered me to bring a few troops to look for you. He—"

Lord Osborne snorted contemptuously. "Safety! What a thumping great lie. It's my *security* the King is worried about, Charles. The truth is that he doesn't want me running around loose. He's afraid somebody will tumble to who I am." His voice was bitter. "I'd be made a laughing-stock, and the whole bloody family a butt for ridicule. Papa and Motherdear would be mortified, and the monarchy would be in for another round of drubbing in the press."

The King? Flora looked in amazement from Lord Osborne to Lord Sheridan. What in the world were they talking about? What did any of this have to do with kings and monarchies?

Lord Sheridan shook his head. "The matter is more serious than that, I'm afraid," he said gravely. "As it turns out, the men who kidnapped you and killed Flora's mother are—"

"Killed Hilda?" His face tightening, Lord Osborne stared. "I didn't hear that right, did I?" he whispered. "Tell me I've misheard!"

"You didn't know?" Lord Sheridan asked.

"Know? Know? Of course I didn't know!" Lord Osborne swung around to Flora, his eyes searching her face. "Say it's not true, Flora. Say that your mother isn't—" He stopped when he saw her expression. "It's true, then?" he whispered. "She's dead?"

Fighting back tears, Flora nodded. "Her throat was cut, m'lord. I found her body on the path tae the village, early on Monday mornin'. I didna like tae tell ye, sir, for fear it would upset ye." She began to sob, and Lady Sheridan gathered her into her arms and held her as she wept.

"Oh, dear God." Lord Osborne's voice broke, and tears began to flow unrestrained down his face. After a moment, he wiped his eyes and turned back to Lord Sheridan. "Hilda has been like a mother to me for almost ten years. When was she killed? *Why?*"

Lord Sheridan countered with a question. "You were abducted on Sunday night?"

"I think so," Lord Osborne replied slowly. "Perhaps it was Sunday, or . . ." He passed a hand over his face. "I . . . I have not been well, Charles. The past few days and nights have all blurred together. To tell God's honest truth, sometimes I think I'm losing my mind." He cleared his throat and plunged on, as if he were anxious to get the words out. "It started out as a game, you see, this business of being the Bonnie Prince. A way to pass the time, to amuse myself and keep myself occupied." His voice was rising unsteadily, his words coming faster. "But now I find it hard to distinguish between what's real and what's fancy. It's quite ridiculously mad, of course, but I seem to have lost the ability to—"

"I'm sure everything has been extraordinarily difficult," Lord Sheridan cut in, his voice kindly. He pulled out the broken chair for Lord Osborne, and the stool on the other side of the table for himself. "But perhaps you could tell us how the abduction was managed." From the pocket of his robe, he took a gold cigarette case and a packet of matches. He held the case out.

"That's mine!" Lord Osborne exclaimed. "Where did you—"

"In your rooms," Lord Sheridan replied, handing it to him. "I thought you might want it when you were found." He struck a match and lit the cigarette Lord Osborne took from the case. "Tell us anything you can remember about what happened," he said, putting the matches on the table. "Any scrap of information, no matter how small, may be of use to us."

Lord Osborne pulled on the cigarette, making an effort to get hold of himself. A heavy gold ring glinted on his finger, catching the glimmer of the candle. "It . . . it must have been on Sunday night. Because of no dinner, you see, to give the kitchen a free evening. I always have a cold supper and then Hilda brings me—brought me something quite late, before she went home. I was smoking and reading in my chair. Reading Scott, I think." He paused, and a smile trembled across his mouth. "Yes, Scott. His story of the Second Jacobite Rebellion and Prince Charlie's escape to Skye. One of my favorites."

He paused, seeming lost in memory. Lord Sheridan prompted him. "And then?"

"And then I heard noises in the hall outside my room. Voices, angry voices. But I was deep in my story, and of course I don't hear very well." He stopped, pulling on his cigarette. "Then the door burst open. Before I could get out of my chair, someone grabbed me from behind and dropped a jacket over my head."

Lord Sheridan leaned forward, his eyes glinting. "How many were there?"

"How many?" Lord Osborne chewed on his lip. "Two, although I can't be sure. There may have been more. They bound my arms and gagged me and took me down the stairs. They carried me some distance—how far, I don't know—to an ice house."

"An ice house?" Lord Sheridan asked in surprise.

"At first I thought it was a cave," Lord Osborne said, "but later, one of the men called it an ice house. There were wooden pallets on the floor and it was full of straw."

Flora freed herself from Lady Sheridan's embrace and sat forward on the edge of the bed. "The ice house is dug intae th' bank of th' stream south of the castle," she said, "and lined wi' brick, so as tae keep in th' cold. In winter, men cut ice out o' the pond and store it there, packed in straw, until it's needed in th' kitchen."

Lord Osborne nodded. "There wasn't any ice as far as I could see, but there was a great deal of straw. Anyway, they kept me locked up there. I think it was a couple of days, but I'm not sure. At one point, one of the men was there alone, and freed me to eat something. He had a bottle of whiskey, and before long he fell asleep. I managed to slip away and hide in the woods. Some time later, an hour or so, p'rhaps, I heard a shot."

"Someone was shooting at you?"

Lord Osborne shook his head. "I don't think so. It came from the direction of the ice house, or at least it seemed so. After that, I walked for a while, to a place where I have often gone to paint. Flora had always been with me there, and I thought, if she were searching, that was where she would go. She found me there and brought me to this place." He looked up, frowning, his silvery brows coming together. "Hilda was murdered the night the men came to my rooms?"

"She seems to have caught your kidnappers in the act," Lord Sheridan replied. "She was killed there. Later, her body was carried out and left on the path, where Flora found her the next morning."

Lord Osborne turned to look at Flora. "Oh, Flora," he said, shaking his head sadly. "My poor, poor Flora. Fatherless, and now motherless. I am very sorry, my child, and even sorrier for the part I have played in this tragedy."

Flora leaned forward, holding out her hands. "But it was not yer fault, m'lord!" she burst out. "Ye had naething tae do with—"

Lord Osborne raised his hand to stop her words, and a look of unutterable despair passed over his lined face. "It *is* my fault, Flora, by virtue of who I am. It is a curse I thought I could escape by letting everyone think I was dead. By coming here to Glamis, where I could live away from the world." He shook his head. "But I was wrong, and it's too late to do anything about it. Too late to change anything."

His voice became ragged. "Too late, too late. I should better have died."

He pulled in his breath as if he were reaching for control, and turned back to Lord Sheridan. "What did they want of me, those men? To force the King to pay for my release? He would do it, of course. He would feel obligated, even though he and Motherdear no longer think of me as their son." A note of self-pity came into his voice. "When they bother to think of me at all, which is seldom. I'm better forgotten, you see. Better dead. I'm the one who could always be counted on to do the wrong thing, get involved with the wrong sort of fellows, make the wrong sort of choices. The one shut away for the blackest of all Royal sins: for being an embarrassment."

The image of the Monster, shut away for forty years because he was an embarrassment to his father and mother, rose like a disconsolate ghost in Flora's thoughts. Poor Lord Osborne, whose father and mother never bothered to think of him. And then her mouth was suddenly dry, as she realized that the parents Lord Osborne was speaking of with such sadness must be, could *only* be King Edward and Queen Alexandra! Improbable, impossible as it seemed, it must be the truth. It would account for all the photographs of the Royal Family in his room, for his portrait of the Queen, painted with such loving attention, which she had counted off to one of his many flights of fancy.

Lord Osborne sighed wearily. "So they were after money," he said in a bleak voice. "Poor Hilda died on account of my sins—and someone else's greed."

"Not money, I should think," Lord Sheridan said. "The kidnapping seems to have been your cousin Willie's idea. Or someone close to him in the German high command."

"Cousin Willie?" Incredulous, Lord Osborne squinted at

him, a wreath of cigarette smoke curling around his head. "The Kaiser? Why, that's bloody absurd!" He paused, seeming to reconsider. "On second thought, though, p'rhaps it isn't. Willie's always been a great one for cruel jokes—almost worse than my father, if that's possible. I recall once, when he was visiting Buckingham Palace, he tied a firecracker on the tail of a poor—" He broke off, shaking his head. "But no matter."

Flora stared. Lord Osborne was cousin to the German Kaiser? All of this seemed so inconceivable, even more bizarre than Lord Osborne's fancy that he was the Bonnie Prince.

"The Kaiser may be in the dark on this one," Lord Sheridan said. "Perhaps the planning was done by someone like Holstein, for instance, or even Bülow. More likely, they intended to hold you for a time and bring you out at the most opportune moment. Perhaps they intended to use you to scuttle Chamberlain's proposals for an Anglo-German alliance. Or they may have planned to embarrass the Crown by releasing you in November, when George is due to be named Prince of Wales. Or even next spring, at your father's coronation."

"Embarrass the Crown?" Lord Osborne's laugh was mocking. "If they trotted me out at Georgie's investiture, it would *topple* the Crown, and Papa hasn't even got it on yet. Officially, that is." His voice was corrosive. "It would be a thumping good show, wouldn't it, Charles? The newspapers would make a circus of it. 'Dead prince resurrected after decade buried in Scotland.' " He frowned again, smoking fiercely. "How'd Willie find out? Not from me, by God. I've never wanted anyone to know who I am. As far as I'm concerned, Prince Eddy is dead, and dead he will stay."

Flora felt dazed. This was all too much. She couldn't

understand it. *Lord Osborne had once been a prince, and dead? But how—*

"They seem to have planted a spy," Lord Sheridan replied. He turned to look directly at Flora. "A man who used the code name Firefly was dispatched from Edinburg to have a look around."

"Firefly?" Flora gasped, getting to her feet. But her legs failed her, and she sat back on the bed. Lady Sheridan grasped her hand.

"Yes, Firefly." Lord Sheridan's eyes glinted in the light of the candle. "You know him, then, do you, Flora?"

Lady Sheridan's arm was around her shoulder now, steadying her. Flora took a deep breath, feeling herself tremble. "Firefly is . . . a childhood nickname for my cousin Herman, who comes frae Edinburg tae visit us. He used tae love tae capture fireflies an' carry them around in glass bottles, like a lantern. But he couldn't be—" She stopped, shaking her head, thinking of funny, loving Herman, bringing her little presents from Edinburg, telling her jokes and stories, laughing and carefee. "He couldn't be a *spy*."

"Spies are not usually what they seem, Flora," Lord Sheridan said gently. "That, I fear, is their nature."

Flora stared at him, another denial on her lips. But even as she opened her mouth to speak, she knew that what he said must be true. All those little number games Herman continually played with—weren't spies supposed to send their messages in ciphers? And there was the conversation she had overheard one evening some weeks before. She had already gone to bed, and her mother and Herman were sitting before the fire. Her mother was speaking to Herman about her work with Lord Osborne, telling him—

Flora's hand went to her mouth and her eyes widened, as she remembered. Her mother had told Herman that Lord

Osborne must be somehow related to the Royal Family, for he had photos in his room of the King and Queen, recent photos. And books inscribed by Queen Victoria, as well as—But then she had heard nothing more, for Herman had got up from his chair and closed the bedroom door, so he and her mother could talk in private.

Now Lord Sheridan rose and came over to the bed where she was sitting. "I'm sorry, Flora." His voice was gentle, and he seemed almost to read her mind. "I'm sure that your mother didn't realize that the questions your cousin asked and the answers she gave had any special importance, or would put Lord Osborne in danger. She must have trusted him."

"But if Herman was one o' th' men who took Lord Osborne," Flora whispered urgently, "was he there when my mother was killed?"

"I'm afraid he would have been, yes," Lord Sheridan said regretfully.

"But he didna kill her." Flora's lips felt stiff and cold, and she could hardly manage the words. "He couldna! She was his *aunt!* She took care o' him when he was a boy, ye see, back in Bavaria. His mother was her sister, and—" Her voice broke.

"I wonder," Lord Sheridan said, "if you can tell us anything about your cousin's friends? Did anyone visit him? Did you see him with anyone in the village?"

Mutely, Flora shook her head. "He . . . he went often tae the pub, but I dinna know who he might hae spoke with there." She frowned, thinking. "The tinker knew him, though."

"The tinker?"

She nodded. "Taiso, he's called. He stopped at the cottage today, in the afternoon. He asked after Herman. We talked, an' he—" She stopped, not wanting to go further.

"He what?" Lord Sheridan prompted.

She swallowed. "He offered tae take me tae Perth in th' morning," she said uncomfortably. She was reluctant to give away her secret plan, but Lady Sheridan's warm arm around her shoulders reassured her. "Tae take me an' my uncle, in his caravan." She nodded at Lord Osborne. "I found some old clothes for his lordship tae wear, an' pretend tae be my uncle. When we got tae Perth, I thought we would take th' train tae Glasgow, an' then a boat tae the Isle of Skye. My father's people—the MacDonalds—live there. I knew they would take us in and give us refuge."

"I see," Lord Sheridan said, his tone approving. "You're a very resourceful girl, Flora. I'm sure Lord Osborne is grateful to you for making such a good plan." He went back to his place at the table. "You said you were taken by two men, Eddy. Herman Memsdorff seems to have been one of them. Can you give us any clue to the identity of the other?"

Lord Osborne bent over to stub out his cigarette on the stone floor. "Perhaps," he said, straightening, "although I can't tell you his name. He is one of the gamekeepers here—there are four or five, I believe. It was his cigars that gave the fellow away."

Beside Flora, Lady Sheridan leaned forward. "Cigars?" she asked sharply. "A gamekeeper?"

Lord Osborne nodded. "The man smokes some sort of vile Indian cigars. I smelled that dreadful odor once when I encountered him at the kennel, with the dogs. I smelled it again when the jacket was flung over my head, and on the man himself. He's the one who fell asleep, allowing me to escape." Lord Osborne laughed wryly, turning his ring on his finger. "I may not be able to hear as well as I might, and I am often confused in my mind. But there is nothing whatever wrong with my sense of smell—and those cigars are truly wretched."

"Charles," Lady Sheridan said, her voice taut, "it might be the man who drove me from the station. Hamilton, his name is. He's a gamekeeper, and he smells of those dreadful Indian cigars, like those Mr. Crombie smokes, back at Bishop's Keep."

"Ah, yes, Hamilton," Lord Sheridan said. "We'll find him, then. Meanwhile, Eddy, I'm afraid I must ask you, and Flora as well, to stay in this room for a few more hours. I'm sorry it's so uncomfortable, but it's secret and can be secured. I need to locate both Memsdorff and Hamilton. There seems to be another German agent involved as well—who, I cannot yet say for certain, although you may have given me a clue. You're not safe until all are found."

"And after that, what?" Lord Osborne rested his chin in his hand, his expression that of a condemned man. "I suppose my father will expect me to continue living here, as I have been?" He sighed. "I'm comfortable and well taken care of, and I suppose I should be grateful for that. But one would like to see a bit more of the world, from time to time. One would like—"

"I'm not sure you can stay here, Eddy," Lord Sheridan broke in. "The difficulty, of course, is that it is known in Germany that you are alive and living at Glamis, and there's nothing to stop unscrupulous men from using that knowledge. If we could think of a way to persuade them to—"

Lord Osborne snapped open his gold case and took out another cigarette. His laugh was bitter. "I've already died once. I don't suppose I should object to dying again." He opened the packet of matches and struck one. "What did you have in mind?"

"I'm afraid I can't answer that question just now." Lord Sheridan pushed his chair back and stood up. "It would be a good idea for all of us to get some sleep, if we can. Unless I miss my guess, tomorrow will be a very difficult day."

CHAPTER TWENTY-NINE

Friday, 16 August 1901

Any razors or scissors to grind?
Or anything else in the tinker's line?
Any old pots or kettles to mend?

> Tinker's traditional rhyme
> quoted in *Lark Rise to Candleford*
> Flora Thompson

A spy's photograph in the hands of his enemy rather spoils his
game, I should think.

> Kate Sheridan in
> *Death at Rottingdean*
> Robin Paige

Charles was already dressed and gone when Kate was wakened the next morning by a light knock on the door. Gladys came in with a stack of towels and a pitcher of hot water, placing them beside the wash basin. Then she stepped to the windows and opened the curtains to display an iridescent dawn that filled the room with morning light. In a moment, she was back with a linen-covered tea tray, which she placed on the table beside the bed.

"Lovely day," she said brightly. She poured a cup of fragrant tea and set it on the saucer. "Flora was supposed tae bring yer ladyship's tea," she added, her coppery eyebrows asking an implicit question. "But she dinna coom tae work this mornin'. Mrs. Leslie's throwin' a fit, and we're all verra worrit aboot her."

"Oh, you mustn't worry," Kate remarked, with a guileless smile. She plumped up her pillow against the head of the bed, and took the cup Gladys offered her. "I'm sure she'll put in an appearance, or let Mrs. Leslie know where she's gone."

Gladys looked provoked. "Do ye require help with dressin'?" she asked, eyeing the wardrobe where Kate's things were hung. "Shall I get somethin' out for yer ladyship tae wear this mornin'?"

"No, thank you," Kate said. In some ways, she had managed to conform to British habits, but she had never been able to allow herself to be dressed by another woman. "I can manage for myself."

Gladys nodded and flounced out of the room, her curiosity unsatisfied on all counts.

Kate added sugar and lemon and sat back against the pillow, gratefully sipping hot, fragrant tea from the delicate porcelain cup. The night had been long and eventful and very tiring, but thanks to Beryl Bardwell's curiosity—would they ever have discovered Flora's and Eddy's hiding place if Beryl hadn't insisted on going ghost-hunting?—a large part of the mystery seemed to be solved. Prince Eddy was unharmed and his whereabouts known; Flora had been found and had answered all Charles's questions; and the men who had killed Hilda MacDonald and kidnapped Prince Eddy had been identified with at least some certainty—all but their German contact, of course. All that was left was for Charles to find the men he was seeking and tell Toria what had transpired, so that the Princess could report to King Edward that Eddy was safe. She smiled to herself. Once that was done, Charles could send his troops back to London, and the two of them could start for Bishop's Keep. With any luck, they'd be home in two or three days. Home, where there was so much to be done, so many interesting projects waiting. Home, where she would see dear Patrick, who would most likely be there when they arrived.

Kate sat for a moment, thinking, her hands wrapped around the steaming cup. But her thoughts were not with home. She was reflecting on all that had happened during the night, all she had heard, all she had learned. Prince Eddy had confirmed much of what Toria had told her earlier about the circumstances of his exile. But he had revealed far more, for Kate had heard the bitterness in his voice when he described himself as "the one shut away for the blackest of all Royal sins: for being an embarrassment." Prince Albert Victor had obviously not gone willingly into exile, as Toria described it, but reluctantly and under duress. He had lived at Glamis for nearly a decade with the burden of his unhappiness, while his brother George, soon to be invested as the Prince of Wales, took his place as the eldest son. And if Eddy was unhappy, how must George feel? Must he not bear a burden of guilt, equal to that of Eddy's bitterness? And what of King Edward and Queen Alexandra? Was it true that they rarely thought of their son, or did they mourn his loss whenever the family gathered and his seat was empty? She shook her head. It was sad that Eddy and Toria had been forced by the accident of their birth to live lives that were not of their choosing. It was a tragedy.

But many people in this world seemed condemned by an accident of birth, Kate reminded herself as she got out of

bed and splashed water on her face. And yet they rose above
those challenges and hereditary handicaps to fashion useful
and more or less happy lives. She stripped off her gown and
pulled on her stockings and underthings and a fresh white
blouse and gray serge skirt, and twisted her hair into a loose
knot at the back of her head, drawing it back from her face
with a pair of silver combs. Eddy seemed to believe that he
could not escape his inheritance, but perhaps that was true
only as long as he was treated as aristocracy, as he was here
at Glamis. If he could go to a place where he was not known
and get a fresh start, he might be able to put his disappoint-
ments and losses behind him and build a new life, a *useful*
life. And if Toria could insist on following her own heart's
desires instead of merely serving her mother's wishes, perhaps she could have the home and family she wanted. And
Flora too—there could be a new life for her, away from the
sadness of her mother's murder. A happy ending for all
three.

But Kate knew that happy endings, the stuff of romance,
were hard to come by in the real world, where the best that
could be achieved was the amelioration of pain and the es-
tablishment of a kind of balance between good and evil.
Prince Eddy had been waited on and catered to all through
his life, and learning to do things for himself would likely
prove impossible. Toria had never opposed her mother, and
it would be difficult for her to find the strength to do so
now. Of the three, Flora would be most likely to succeed,
Kate suspected. She had the strength, the resilience, and the
independent spirit that would allow her to shape her own
destiny. She could set her own goals, create her own plans,
without having to worry about what others thought about
her choices.

Kate gave herself one last glance in the mirror, tucked

up a few loose curls, and straightened the collar of her blouse. Her camera and notebook sat on the table beside the door, and she picked both of them up as she left the room. If she and Charles were departing in a day or two, it would be a good idea to make as many notes and take as many photographs as possible, so that she and Beryl could remember what they had seen here. Beryl was still determined to write a Gothic tale set in this spectacular castle, the home of ghosts and monsters and long-dead queens. Kate smiled to herself, thinking about Lady Elizabeth of Glamis, the sweet little baby she had met the day before. Glamis was the home of future queens, too, if the gypsy fortune-teller was to be believed.

With the smile still on her lips, her camera around her neck, and her notebook in her hand, Kate walked down the hallway and stood at the window at the far end. It gave her a second-floor view of a bustling and busy scene: the working area of the castle, where the many self-sustaining components of the estate were all brought together in a harmonious, closely-knit whole. Off to the right lay the kitchen garden with its tidy rows of vegetables and berries, a woman in a bonnet and shawl picking gooseberries from a row of green bushes, while a girl with a hoe dug at the fresh earth. Beyond that was the chicken yard, where a large flock of brightly-plumaged birds scratched in the dirt, and still farther the dairy, where the rich milk from the estate's cows—grazing in the grassy meadows along the Dene Water—was made into butter and cheese for the castle kitchen. Directly in front of her were the carriage houses, stables, exercise yards, and kennels, all freshly-painted and neatly-kept. In the graveled yard, a boy was washing the spokes of a red-wheeled carriage with a long-handled brush, while another boy was leading a handsome brown horse out of the stable to a small forge where a farrier was already at work, shoeing another horse. Some distance away stood an impressive collection of glass houses, some quite large—fruit houses, perhaps—others smaller. Kate took special note of them, intending to ask the gardener to take her through them before she left Glamis. Much closer, between the castle and the kitchen garden, stood several large stacks of wood, and an old man with an ax was splitting fireplace kindling on a chopping block.

Kate raised her camera. Even a Gothic novel needed a few realistic details, and this industrious scene seemed to give a different kind of importance to the castle, tying it to the productivity of the land, connecting it with work and with the life of the workers. It seemed, somehow, a much more satisfying importance.

She pushed the casement window open, snapped one photograph, and advanced the film to take another. As she lifted the camera, though, a man came into the yard, carrying something over his shoulder. He was tall, with dark, ragged hair that brushed his collar, in contrast to the neatly-trimmed hair of the boys and men working in the yard. He wore old trousers, a stained leather jerkin, a dirty red neckerchief, and a brown felt hat that was decorated with colored beads and a feather. As he came closer, Kate could see that he was a handsome fellow, and that the thing he had slung over his shoulder was a tinker's pig.

Kate lowered her camera, frowning. It wasn't unusual for an itinerant tinker to seek work at country houses along his way, to knock at the servants' entrance and inquire whether there were any pots to be mended or knives to be sharpened. But how had he got past the sentries? And was this the same tinker who had visited Flora yesterday? The one—Taiso, Flora had called him—who had asked after Herman Memsdorff, and offered to take Flora and her "uncle" to Perth? The hair on the back of Kate's neck began to prickle, and a growing apprehension made her suck in her breath and hold it as the tinker came closer.

For his part, the man seemed to be quite nonchalant, his lips pursed as if he were whistling, making with a confident and jaunty grace for a door just beneath Kate's window. A few steps from the door, he paused, shifted his pig from one shoulder to the other, and took off his hat, wiping his forehead with a dirty sleeve.

Until that moment, Kate had been unsure of what to do. But as the man stood there, his hat in his hand, she leaned forward. "Taiso?" she asked, in a bright, gay voice. "Are you Taiso the tinker?"

Hearing his name, the man looked up, and Kate saw that he had quite extraordinary eyes, pale blue, so pale as to be almost glacial, and—oddly, for a gypsy—a narrow patrician face and a pinched nose. With a sudden shiver, she recalled another man with those same unforgettable eyes, icy blue eyes, cold as a frozen lake, and she remembered with a chilling clarity the last time she had seen him. It was on a beach in the south of England, near Rottingdean. Then, too, she had had a camera in her hands and she had taken his photograph. His name was Count Ludwig von Hauptmann, and he was a German spy.

The man still looked up, wary now, and suspicious. "Aye, I'm Taiso," he growled, and then seemed to recollect himself, for he smiled and lightened his voice. "Any razors or scissors to grind? Anything in the tinker's line?"

"You'll have to knock at the door and ask," Kate said. "I'm only a guest here. But I should very much like to take your photograph, if you will forgive my impertinence." She leaned over the window sill to get a better angle and, before he could object, quickly snapped the shutter. "Thank you, Taiso," she added in a satisfied tone. "That will do very well, I think."

And with that, she turned away from the window and hurried off to find Charles.

CHAPTER THIRTY

I have no desire to make mysteries, but it is impossible at the moment of action to enter into long and complex explanations.

Sherlock Holmes, in
"The Adventure of the Dancing Men"
Sir Arthur Conan Doyle

Charles knew he was going to have a busy morning. He needed to get to the ice house, which seemed to offer at least the possibility of some physical evidence that might have been discarded by Eddy's captors. But the ice house could wait until he had attended to more pressing matters of command, which had to be settled before others could get on with their jobs.

Charles hunched over the Ordnance Survey map that Kirk-Smythe had spread on a table in the castle library, along with the hand-written reports from the checkpoints forwarded by Colonel Paddington, none especially noteworthy. At Charles's request, Angus Duff had come to the library, and the two of them had drafted a description of Hamilton. Charles had added a description of Memsdorff, as well, based on details offered by Flora. Duff had carried these to Colonel Paddington, with Charles's written order to forward them to the troops.

Before he began his work, Charles had ordered quite a large breakfast to be sent to the library. It had arrived just now on three trays, almost enough to feed, Kirk-Smythe had said in surprise, an entire company of soldiers.

"It's not all for us," Charles said, forking a pair of sausages out of the chafing dish and thinking that Eddy would enjoy the hot food. While they ate, he related the events of the night before, and the story Eddy had told of his abduction and escape.

"So the Prince was in the castle all the time," Kirk-Smythe said, shaking his head in amazement. He pushed his empty plate away and poured another cup of coffee.

"Not all the time," Charles reminded him. "Flora smuggled him in the night before Kate and I arrived."

Kirk-Smythe nodded. "Well, then, what's next?"

"Organizing a careful search for Hamilton and Memsdorff, who seem to have been the ones who kidnapped the Prince. And we have this German spy to think about." Charles paused. "Flora said that a tinker named Taiso came to her cottage yesterday and asked for Memsdorff by name. We ought to go up to Roundyhill and—"

He was interrupted by a knock on the study door. A young private in field kit stepped into the room, clicked his heels, and saluted smartly. He was breathing hard. "Beg pardon, sir. Sergeant Adams sent me with an urgent dispatch from the checkpoint south of the village, on the Dundee Road." He handed Charles a folded note.

As he opened it, Charles remarked, "You've pedaled all the way, I take it. What do you think of the bicycle?"

"Haven't used one much lately, I'm afraid, sir." The private grinned ruefully. "This model takes a bit of getting used to, if you want to stay out of the ditch. But it's better than double time."

Charles read the note twice and looked up. To Kirk-Smythe, he said, "At daybreak, a pair of boys found the body of a man, facedown in the shallow water along the shore of the millpond. The sentries at the southern checkpoint fished out the corpse and placed it under guard." He turned to the young trooper, who was now breathing more easily.

"You saw the body, Private?"

"Yes, sir. In the water all night, if you ask me."

"Can you describe him?"

"Thin, blond hair. The man from the castle who was with us said his name was Hamilton. He was a gamekeeper here on the estate."

"Hamilton!" Kirk-Smythe exclaimed.

"Ah," Charles said regretfully. Finding a dead Hamilton was much less profitable than finding a live one, for the dead man could tell them nothing—which might be the reason for his death. He considered the situation for a moment, then said, "Private, tell your sergeant that the body is to be brought here to be examined by the coroner. He should avoid attention in the village by taking the long way round. We don't want a public commotion over this."

The trooper nodded. "Yes, sir."

"Cover the body, and allow no one to get a look at it," Charles went on. "And tell your sergeant that this order applies particularly to the local constable. If you encounter him and he causes any difficulty, he is to be taken into custody."

The trooper registered surprise. "Arrest the constable, sir?"

Charles sighed. "I'm afraid so. Now, be on your way, Private. And hurry."

"Yes, sir." The private saluted, executed a smart about-face, and opened the door to leave, only to collide with a breathless Kate, her camera in her hand.

"Charles," she cried, flying across the room, "I've just taken the most remarkable photograph!"

"How nice, my dear." Charles went to the desk to scribble a note to the coroner, asking him to come immediately to the castle. He put it into an envelope and handed it to Kirk-Smythe. "Have this delivered to Dr. Ogilvy, Andrew, on the double. We want him here when the body arrives."

As Kirk-Smythe stepped to the door to give the note to the soldier outside, Charles went back to the table and picked up his coffee. "Do help yourself to some breakfast," he said to Kate over the rim of his cup. "There's more than enough, and the sausages are quite good." He gave her a sober look. "And you might be interested to know that the soldier you ran into was the bearer of bad news. Hamilton's body was found in the millpond this morning."

"I'm sure that's very important," Kate said urgently, "but so is the photograph I've just taken." She stamped one foot, brandishing her camera. "Will you put down that coffee and *listen* to me, Charles Sheridan?"

Charles put down his cup. "I'm listening, my dear," he said mildly. Now that he looked at his wife, he saw the expression that meant that she felt she had important information. "What's all this commotion about a photograph?"

"It's not a commotion," Kate said, indignant. "Do you remember the German we met on the beach at Rottingdean? The spy who was trying to smuggle arms into the country? He's *here,* Charles, disguised as a tinker. He responded when I called the name Taiso, so he must be the same tinker who went to Flora's house yesterday, asking after Memsdorff. And I've just taken his picture!"

"You're talking about . . . Hauptmann?" Charles slowly put down his cup. If that was the man they were dealing with, they might never catch him. He was creative, bold, and fearless.

Kirk-Smythe gave a low whistle. "Count Ludwig von Hauptmann? Well, I don't suppose I should be surprised."

"You've heard of him, then, Andrew?" Charles asked.

"Heard of him?" Andrew laughed shortly. "We spend half our time keeping track of him. The man is not only a master of disguise, but he seems to have the ability to be in two places at once. Three, sometimes."

Charles turned back to Kate, frowning. "Are you sure it was Hauptmann, Kate?"

"I'm not likely to forget those eyes," Kate said grimly. She put her camera on the table. "And I have his photograph. I can set up my darkroom and have it developed and in your hands within the hour, so you can see for yourself."

"A tinker, eh?" Charles muttered, shaking his head. "An ingenious disguise. It gets him into the village, where he can make contact with Memsdorff and Hamilton, and into the castle, as well. I wonder what other disguises he's using." To Andrew, he said, "The last time we encountered this man, he was a diplomat, a photographer, and an antiquarian—and very good at all three. He seems to follow Sherlock Holmes's rule: the best way of successfully acting a part is to be it." He paused, remembering what had occurred at Rottingdean in '97. "I wonder . . ."

"Wonder what?" Kirk-Smythe prompted.

"Hamilton is dead," Charles replied, "and Memsdorff hasn't been seen since the night before last. Do you remember, Kate, what happened to the subordinate who threatened his Rottingdean operation?"

Kate made a face. "He shot him."

"Exactly." Charles poured a cup of coffee and handed it to Kate. "Andrew, our man has a history of dealing with those who fail him in a most effective and severe manner. He may be behind Hamilton's death."

"This fellow Hamilton," Kirk-Smythe said. "If he was one of the kidnappers—" He stopped, pursing his lips thoughtfully. "Yesterday, I was out with one of the search parties. He was one of the group, helping to guide us to various outbuildings. But I had the odd feeling that he was trying to divert our attention. To lead us away from something."

"What direction were you headed?"

"We were moving south, along a stream. He told the group that there was nothing to be gained by going further in that direction. At his suggestion, we crossed the stream and turned east, out of the woods, toward the farms."

"South, along a stream," Kate said, putting down her cup. "Isn't that where Flora said the ice house is located?"

"Right," Charles said, feeling that he was dealing with too many competing priorities, all of which had to be met at one time. "Kate, would you develop that photograph, please? It's important for me to have it as soon as possible."

"I will, but what—"

He shook his head firmly. "There's no time to explain now, Kate. Andrew, I'd like you to stay here. When Hamilton's body arrives, place it under armed guard, in this room. No one but you and Dr. Ogilvy should see it. Ask the doctor to determine the cause and time of death as nearly as he can."

"Of course," Kirk-Smythe said, "but where are you—"

"I can't linger, Andrew. Time is of the essence. I'll take

one of the guards with me and send him back for you, if my suspicions prove correct."

"Charles," Kate demanded, "where *are* you going?"

Charles was halfway to the door already. "To the ice house," he flung back over his shoulder.

CHAPTER THIRTY-ONE

Alfred Gilbert, a pupil of Boehm and a friend of Princess Louise, Duchess of Argyll, was commissioned to design and execute the funeral monument of Prince Albert Victor (to be placed in the Memorial Chapel, Windsor Castle). This grandiose conception—which included a recumbent figure with a head of Mexican onyx lying on a high table tomb surrounded by ivory weepers—was never, owing to Gilbert's dilatory habits and disorderly life, completed.

Queen Mary: 1867–1953
James Pope-Hennessy

The breakfast room was a pleasant, sunny room with windows that looked out across the rose garden. A sideboard filled with chafing dishes kept eggs, kippers, sausage, bacon, and toast hot for several hours, as some guests preferred to breakfast early and others late. Kate was late, for it was nearly eleven. But coffee still steamed in a heated urn, as did hot water for tea, and the center of the table was arranged with silver dishes of jams and marmalade, plates of butter, pitchers of sweet cream, crystal bowls of fresh fruit, and vases of hothouse flowers, their rich scent, like funeral flowers, mixing incongruously with the odors of hot sausages and bacon.

Still mulling over her unexpected encounter with the tinker, the conversation with Charles and Kirk-Smythe, and her subsequent work in her portable developing laboratory, Kate helped herself to a bowl of melon, several pieces of hot buttered toast, and a cup of tea. Now that she had actually seen the photograph, which was drying in the bathroom in her suite, she knew beyond doubt that Taiso and Hauptmann were the same, and that the German must be Firefly's contact, the man who had master-minded the plot to kidnap Prince Eddy. He must have come to the castle in search of his escaped prey.

Of course, the Prince was safe now, she reminded herself with relief, as she took her plate and cup to the table, and she needn't worry. But things might have turned out very differently. If she and Charles had not discovered Flora and Eddy in their hiding place, they would certainly have gone to the gypsy camp before dawn that morning and paid Taiso to take them to Perth. Of course, they wouldn't have ended up there, Kate knew. Hauptmann would have taken Prince Eddy to Germany, and Flora would likely have been murdered, for she knew too much, and it would have been dangerous to let her live. The thought of it turned her cold. It had been a near thing, a very near thing, indeed.

Kate had just begun to eat her melon when the door opened and Toria came in, followed closely by a footman. The Princess was wearing a tight-bodiced mulberry-colored dress that was fashionably cut and expensively trimmed but took neither her figure nor her complexion into account. She looked as if she had not slept well, and the unkind sunlight revealed the unmistakeable traces of encroaching middle age: the parenthetical wrinkles on either side of the mouth, the slight bruising under the eyes, the crepy skin of the neck.

"Good morning, Your Highness," Kate said, and added the conventional remark, "I hope you have had a restful night."

"I did not sleep well at all," Toria replied heavily, as the footman pulled out her chair to seat her. "Coffee and toast," she said. "Nothing else." She gave a dismissive wave of her hand. "And then you may leave."

Kate made another conventional remark or two as the footman served the Princess, then left the room.

When the door closed, Toria leaned forward. "Has there been any word of my brother?" she asked. "At dinner last night, Lord Sheridan seemed to suggest that something might be known by this morning." She picked up her cup and took a drink of coffee. "And even if there is no news, I suppose I should telegraph the King and let him know that the men are still searching."

Kate, suddenly realizing that she and Charles had not discussed what or how much Toria should be told about the unfolding events, was not quite sure how to answer the Princess's question. There was no reason to believe that Charles would not want her to disclose the fact that Eddy was at this moment safe and sound in the castle, or that one of his kidnappers had been found dead. But the whole thing was a delicate business, and without knowing exactly what she should say, Kate was reluctant to say anything at all. She was enormously relieved, then, when the door opened again, and Charles himself came in and greeted them. He shot a quick, questioning glance at Kate.

She smiled. "Here's Lord Sheridan now. He'll give you the latest news. Charles, Her Highness was just asking for word of the Prince." Charles nodded briefly, and she bent to her melon, glad to have been spared the task of deciding what to say.

Toria replaced her cup on its saucer. "Good morning, Lord Sheridan," she said. "Well? Have you found him yet?"

Charles hesitated for a moment, as if he were making up his mind to something, and then sat down next to the Princess. "Yes, Your Highness," he said. His face was somber, his voice grave. "I'm afraid we have." He put his hand over hers. "I wish there were some easier way to tell you this, but I fear there is not. Your brother is dead."

"Oh, dear God!" Toria gave a shrill little cry, and her face went white.

Kate dropped her fork and stared at Charles, her eyes widening. "Dead?" she gasped incredulously. "But he can't be! He—"

Letting go the Princess's hand, Charles turned to look full at Kate, and she saw the warning in his eyes. *Stop,* it cautioned. *Say nothing more.* But he only said, very softly, "I know it's hard to believe, Kate. But you and the Princess must both be brave."

Toria's eyes were dark. "How did it . . . how did it happen?" She swallowed hard, and then again, as if she were trying to choke down a bitter draught of medicine. "Was it an accident?" And then, in a calmer voice, "Did he fall from a horse?"

Charles put his fingers to his temples, as if to press away the pain. "He died in a fire," he said.

Kate stared at him, trying to see his face, to read the truth behind his eyes. "A fire?" she whispered disbelievingly.

Toria's face went still. She was holding herself rigid, as if she were afraid of making a sudden movement. "A *fire*?" she echoed, but there was no disbelief, only a kind of dull acceptance in her voice. Her lips parted twice before she was able to clear her throat and say, finally, "I see. Did he . . . I suppose he set it himself, then. Like the fires at Sandringham."

"At this point, I'm afraid the cause can't be determined with any degree of confidence," Charles replied, and Kate knew from the absolute bleakness of his tone how wretched he must feel about this turn of events. "His body was found at the back of the ice house. It's like a cave, dug into the stream bank and lined with ashlar bricks. There was no ice, and it was full of the straw in which the ice had been packed. He was sleeping there, apparently. Somehow, the straw caught fire. He couldn't . . . get out."

Toria's voice was low and so taut that it seemed to vibrate, and her face was shuttered so that no feeling could be read. "That business of the woman's murder . . . Has it been resolved?"

Kate, still trying breathlessly to cope with the idea that Eddy was dead, wondered at this apparently abrupt change of subject. But Charles appeared to understand the association and was prepared to respond to whatever question lay hidden beneath. When he spoke, his voice was comforting.

"I received a report this morning that the body of one of the gamekeepers has been found at the edge of the millpond. He was drowned." He gave Kate the smallest of warning glances. "A suicide note was found in his coat pocket, confessing to Hilda MacDonald's murder. He apparently killed himself out of remorse."

Toria seemed to sag with relief. "Then my brother had nothing to do with her death?"

Charles's answer was emphatic. "Nothing at all, Your Highness," he said. "You have my word on it."

Toria pushed her chair back and stood, working to control her face. "I need to see him," she said in a thin, mechanical voice, void of all feeling. "I must be sure that it's Eddy. My father will want to know that he is really—"

Charles took her hand again. "No, Toria," he said firmly. "I'm sorry, but I can't let you do that. He was badly burnt. He's not—" He shook his head as if to clear an appalling memory. "Your father would not want you to see him as he is. You must trust me on this, and remember him as he was."

Toria seemed to flinch. She pulled in an uneven breath and puffed it out. "If he's burned so badly, how can you be sure that he is really . . ." She sat back down in her chair and tried again. "That it is really Eddy who died."

"Dr. Ogilvy has identified him. And there is this." Charles reached into his pocket and took out a folded piece of paper. He opened it to reveal an ornately-fashioned gold ring, stained with soot. "This was on his finger."

Kate leaned forward to see, then turned her eyes away. It was the ring Prince Eddy had been wearing the night before.

Toria picked up the heavy ring and turned it in her hand. "It's his," she said. "I gave it to him for his twenty-first birthday. He was very proud of it." She handed it back to Charles. "Put it back on his finger. He should be buried with it." Her glance sharpened, and her voice became hard. "Buried here," she said, with emphasis. "At Glamis. I should like you to see to it, Lord Sheridan. And no ceremony, please. My father . . . the family would not wish it."

"As you say, Your Highness," Charles replied. He rewrapped the ring and put it in his pocket. "And how should his grave be marked?"

"His death is already commemorated," she said. She lifted her chin. "Prince Eddy's tomb is in the Memorial Chapel at Windsor Castle. It was designed by Sir Alfred Gilbert."

"Dear Toria," Kate whispered, not knowing quite what to say but feeling she had to say something. "I'm so sorry. So *very* sorry."

As if reminded to do his duty, Charles stood and bowed from the waist. "Please accept my condolences as well, Your Royal Highness," he said formally. "We are all saddened by this loss."

"Don't be." Toria turned her head away. "It's for the best, really. I'm sure my brother's life was not entirely as he would have wished it to be."

Kate stared at her. Was this all the grief Toria could manage? Or had she shed her tears a decade ago, at Prince Eddy's sham funeral at Sandringham? Or was she thinking, perhaps with relief, that the family was finally safe from the threat of disclosure? *I must not be too quick to judge,* Kate thought. *It's probably only natural for her to feel some release. The situation must have been nearly unendurable.*

Toria picked up her cup and sipped her coffee. "I suppose I should leave as soon as possible for Hamburg. I can hardly put this news into a telegram, and my father will want to know."

"I think that is best," Charles said. "The King will feel better, hearing the truth from you."

Toria nodded. After a moment, she said, in the same tone she had used to dismiss the footman, "I'm sure you must have things to see to, Lord Sheridan."

"Indeed," Charles murmured. He rose and went to the door.

Kate stood up. "Excuse me, please," she said to the Princess. "I'll be right back."

Out in the hall, Kate had to pick up her skirts and run to catch up with Charles, who was walking with fast and angry strides toward the stair.

"Charles," she cried, "wait!"

He turned at the head of the stair, his face dark. "She is her father's daughter." His voice rasped with the serrated edge of his anger. "I don't suppose I could have expected anything else from her."

Kate stood, searching his face for the truth. "But Eddy isn't really dead, is he? After all he has been through, it would be unbearable if he were to—"

Charles smiled. "Bless you for caring, my dearest." He put both hands on her shoulders and lowered his cheek to hers. "No, Kate," he whispered. "He is not dead."

CHAPTER THIRTY-TWO

I cannot tell how the truth may be;
I say the tale as 'twas said to me.

Lay of the Last Minstrel
Sir Walter Scott

It was getting on to eight in the evening as the ballad collector, leaning on his cane, came into the Glamis Inn pub, made his way to the bar, and signaled to Thomas Collpit for a glass of ale. The atmosphere was thick with the richly-mingled odors of whiskey, hot beef pie, and tobacco, and tense with hushed, urgent bursts of animated conversation.

One foot propped on the brass rail, his expression impassive, the old man kept his back to the room. But his alert blue eyes watched the reflections in the dusty mirror over the bar, and his ears were tuned to the huddle of men at his right elbow, who were discussing the village's three recent deaths, two of which had been reported only that day.

"It's lucky Hamilton left a suicide note," the joiner said, shaking his head gloomily. "Without it, we'd wudna got tae th' truth. I saw him on his way home frae th' pub last night, an' he was drunk as a lord." He raised his voice, turning to glance at the ballad collector. "Right, Mr. Donovan? Ye were with him; ye saw him." The ballad collector nodded, and the joiner continued. "Drunk as he was, he could easily hae slipped off th' dam an' drowned, accidental-like, an' none 'ud be th' wiser."

"Aye," the green-grocer agreed. He took a drink of his whiskey. "Odd, though, wudna ye say? Why d'ye s'pose Hamilton wud want tae kill our Hilda? She was a lovely woman." He set his glass back on the bar, and his voice hardened. "Tae tell truth, I'd half an eye on that woman sin' my own wife died last spring. If I'd hae known that Doug Hamilton slit her pretty throat, I wud hae slit his, by all that's holy." He gulped a swallow of ale. "I hope his soul rots in hell for what he did tae her."

"But that note's a puzzle tae me," the post-master put in. "I've known Hamilton for nigh on three years now, an' I never knew the fellow tae send a single letter. I always thought th' man cudna write."

"Maybe he dinna hae anything worth writing about 'til now," the joiner remarked. "I sart'nly wudna want tae gae into eternity wi' a killin' on my conscience."

"Ye think a few words on a paper 'll absolve him of Hilda's murder?" the post-master asked hotly.

The joiner's answer was lost in a flurry of louder voices at the other end of the bar, and the ballad collector turned his attention to the trio discussing the man who had died in the ice house on the Glamis estate.

"Lord Osborne, his name was," said the first man, in response to a question. "The one who went missing frae the castle."

"Drank himself tae a stupor an' tipped his lantern on the straw," said the second, adding wisely, "It's happened afore, mostly in stables, an' it'll happen again. Where there's straw an' lanterns, there'll be fire."

The first man shook his head. "Set himself afire on purpose, I heard. He was mad, ye know. Mad as a hatter. He's the one they say fancied himself tae be th' Bonnie Prince. Up at th' castle, they kept him off tae himself, in chains, I heard. He was always locked up, fer fear he'd do harm tae others." He shook his head again. "Ten years he lived locked away frae th' world. If th' poor chap wasna mad tae begin with, living that way 'ud drive him mad, for sartin."

"Likely 'twas him that murdered poor Hilda, then," remarked a third in a cheerful tone, pushing his glass across the bar for a refill. "She and Flora served him."

"No," said the first. " 'Twas Doug Hamilton killed our Hilda. Hae'n't ye heard? He confessed in a note afore he drowned himself."

There was a silence, punctuated by the shouts of the men throwing darts at the board in the back of the room, as the three men pondered this information.

"But ye hae tae admit, it's all verra curious," said the second finally. "Hilda wi' her throat cut, the gentl'man she served burnt tae cinders in a heap o' hay, and Doug Hamilton pitchin' himself intae the millpond. And now Flora an' her cousin's gone missing, too."

"Nae, nae," said the first, who seemed to know the most about this strange set of circumstances. "Flora an' her cousin hae gone tae th' south of England, where Hilda's sister lives."

"How'd you come tae know that?" asked the third curiously.

"Maggie Wollie's my aunt," the first replied. "She does the laundry up tae th' castle." He gave a broad wink. "She knows all aboot what goes on there."

"Aye, that she would," said the third with a leer. "Them that washes th' gentry's bed sheets always knows th' truth." This was followed by general laughter.

The ballad collector signaled for another ale. On some points, of course, he knew far more than any of these loquacious and uninformed villagers. For instance, he knew that Douglas Hamilton had not committed suicide, for it was he who had knocked the man unconscious and pushed him off the narrow dam to drown in the millpond.

On yet other points, however, the collector had to acknowledge that he was totally confounded. What was this business about a suicide note confessing to the murder of Hilda? Hamilton had been in no fit state to write a note, and he himself had written none, although he had thought later that it might have been a good idea. And where had Flora taken herself off to, and with whom? It was hardly Memsdorff, since Hamilton had confirmed that he was dead—although it was entirely possible that Hamilton had lied about that, just as he had lied about knowing the whereabouts of Lord Osborne.

But the most important question of all concerned the identity of the man who had been found burned to death in the ice house. Was it really Lord Osborne—Prince Eddy, that is? He himself had seen Princess Toria leaving the castle this afternoon, presumably for Hamburg, where King Edward was staying. If her brother were still lost, or if there was evidence that he was alive, she would surely not have left. Unfortunately, he had no proof that Eddy was dead, certainly none that would satisfy Holstein, back at the Wilhelmstrasse. Holstein was a stickler for the truth, and for proof of it.

Feeling increasingly uncomfortable, the collector frowned at his reflection in the dim and fly-speckled mirror, hung with photographs of the old Queen and the new King. Before he could determine what to do next, he had somehow to sift the truth out of these tales, for even if he did nothing more with regard to the Prince, he still needed to make his report to Holstein. If the situation could not somehow be salvaged, the report would be most unsatisfactory, for at bottom Holstein could draw only one conclusion: that he, Count Ludwig von Hauptmann, had failed once again. Failed when success seemed so assured. Failed when it was evident that only an intolerable carelessness in execution— or the most inconceivably wretched luck—could have sabotaged his scheme. But as far as he was concerned, the reason for failure most likely lay elsewhere. It was the fault of one interfering man: Lord Charles Sheridan.

The ballad collector plunged his hand into his pocket, paid for his ale, and lifted his glass, his glance going again to the mirror. He did not like to think of Sheridan, because at this point, there was very little he could do about the man, except to stay out of his way. Adding to his discomfort was the feeling, impossible to shake, that he was constantly being watched. It had begun that morning, when he had gone to the castle in the guise of Taiso, looking for Flora, to learn why she and her "uncle" had not come to his caravan, as he had expected. He had been about to knock at the door when a woman at the window above had called his name, and then had had the audacity to take his photograph. From that moment on, wherever he went in the village and on the road, and even in the gypsy camp at Roundyhill, eyes had seemed to follow him. He had become so wary that he found himself whirling around every few minutes, with the expectation of seeing the man who must be on his trail.

But surely it was only his nerves, which he had to admit were frayed. If Sheridan had found him out, he'd no doubt have had him arrested. Yet he had seen nothing at all of the man, and the local constable was sitting over there in the corner, morosely nursing a private whiskey at a table by himself, preoccupied with private worries. If he judged correctly, the constable was as confused as everyone else and probably a great deal more frustrated—and well might be, for word around the village had it that the poor fellow had hoped to marry Flora.

At that moment, the door swung open, and conversation died as the men craned their necks to see who had come in. Glancing quickly into the mirror, the ballad collector saw a small man whom he recognized as the village doctor, elbowing his way through the crowd until he reached the bar where the collector stood.

"A long day?" Thomas Collpit remarked sympathetically. When the doctor nodded, he reached for a bottle and poured a double Scotch, pushing it across the bar to the doctor.

Dr. Ogilvy tossed it back. "Ah," he said with satisfaction, wiping his mouth. "Thank ye, Thomas. You're a good man."

At the doctor's words, there was an onslaught of questions from all sides.

"What really happened tae Hamilton?" one cried.

Another shouted, "Is't true that Doug Hamilton killed our Hilda?"

"Who was it died i' th' ice house?" a third wanted to know.

The doctor held up his hands as if to ward off an assault. When silence returned, he took his filled pipe out of his pocket and lit it. His pipe in one hand, his whiskey in the other, he looked around the room, glancing from face to face as if to verify the identity of each. At the last, he glanced at the collector, inclined his head in an implicit greeting, then spoke.

"I won't keep ye from your drinkin'," he said somberly, "but I do hae a brief word or twae tae share with ye, regarding what's happened this week." He pulled on his pipe, the smoke curling over his head. "I'm sure ye all know that my work as both doctor and coroner requires that I exercise a large measure of discretion, and I hope ye feel that, over the years, I've done my best tae keep your confidences."

The joiner, who seemed to regard himself as a spokesman for the other villagers, raised his glass. "Aye, Dr. Ogilvy," he cried, "ye've stood by us well, in gude times an' bad." A murmur of general agreement rippled through the crowd, amplified by several loud ayes, and one "Ye're our man!"

"Thank you," the doctor said. "Of course, if I am tae keep yer secrets, there are some I mun keep from ye, an' ye wudna hae it diff'rent, I'm sure. However, I will try to answer yer questions as well as I can. What has occurred i' th' past few days seems tae have been a series o' most unfortunate incidents. It appears that Douglas Hamilton murdered Hilda MacDonald, for reasons we dinna understand, an' probably never will. However, Hamilton has taken himself out of th' reach of th' law by drowning himself i' th' millpond, leavin' behind a suicide note confessin' his guilt."

"That accounts for Hilda an' Hamilton," the joiner remarked judiciously. "What aboot th' chap i' th' ice house?"

The doctor drew on his pipe for a moment before he answered, his tone grown even more somber. "Some of ye know that Hilda had in her care at th' castle an unfortunate gentleman, Lord Osborne, who was mentally unbalanced. He appears tae hae been afflicted with pyromania."

"Pyro-what?" asked the green-grocer in a puzzled tone.

"He went round settin' fires," the joiner told him, low.

The green-grocer, not quite trusting his friend, looked to the doctor for confirmation.

"Right," the doctor agreed. "In Hilda's absence, this poor fellow wandered off an' somehow managed tae set fire tae th' straw i' th' ice house on the estate. He was apparently confused by th' smoke, and became trapped and died in the fire. His body is tae be returned tae his relations in London." He paused. "So there ye hae it, men, th' whole sad story. A murder, a suicide, and a most unfortunate accident."

"But where do th' troops come into this?" the post-master asked.

The collector looked up, catching the swift tightening of the doctor's lips. But it was gone in an instant, and the doctor smiled. "The troops?" he replied. "Why, they dinna figure in it at a', far as I can see. They were here on routine maneuvers—somethin' tae do with the use of bicycles for reconnaissance, I believe." He paused. "It's my understandin', though, that in view of a' that's happened, the maneuvers are bein' concluded, an' the troops'll leave tomorrow. Lord Sheridan has asked me tae apologize tae ye for any inconvenience ye've suffered. An' now, if you don't mind, I've had a long day. Even my pipe seems tae hae gone out." He applied a match to it.

"Thank ye, doctor," the joiner said. "Ye've answered our questions." He glanced around the room. "We're all satisfied, aren't we, boys?" There was scattered muted grumbling, but for the most part, the villagers appeared to agree with the joiner—all but the constable, that is. He had come up to the bar and was facing the doctor.

"I'm not satisfied," the constable said, his jaw working. He leaned close and spoke low. "What's become of Flora? Where is she?"

The doctor put a sympathetic hand on the younger man's shoulder, and compassion was evident in his voice.

"Flora was so distressed o'er her mother's death, Oliver,

that she needed an immediate change o' scene. Otherwise, I feared a complete breakdown."

"A breakdown!" The constable was incredulous. "Flora?" The collector shared the constable's disbelief. Flora had not seemed anywhere close to a breakdown when he had talked to her yesterday in her cottage. She had seemed, in fact, to be quite a strong and determined young woman.

But the doctor was insistent. "Aye, a breakdown." He softened his tone. "Perhaps ye dinna know Flora as well as ye think, Oliver. She's gone wi' her cousin Herman tae Edinburgh. I saw them off myself, this afternoon. They plan tae go tae Bavaria tae visit her mother's people."

With *Herman*? The collector felt his pulse flicker, and he frowned to himself. Hamilton must have lied after all, in an attempt to get all the money for himself. Memsdorff could have crossed over to the other side and gone to work for Sheridan. Agents could not always be trusted, no matter how well they were paid. And if Firefly caused his aunt's death, perhaps he had suffered such guilt that he could not bring himself to carry out their plan. The collector frowned. But there was that suicide note to account for, which—

"But Flora hasna yet buried her mother," the constable protested, still trying to assimilate this new information. "And what aboot her testimony at th' inquest?"

The doctor turned, held out his empty glass, and Thomas Collpit obliged. "Lord Sheridan an' I took Flora's testimony afore she left," he said equably, returning to the constable. " 'Tis our opinion that we shouldna disclose its details, or the other evidence Lord Sheridan has gathered, tae keep frae damagin' the reputations of innocent persons. An' we couldna see that disclosure wud serve the interests of justice."

The constable looked nonplussed. "But there must be an

inquest!" he replied heatedly. " 'Tis required by law. What's more, I've been left out o' this investigation. I mun demand—"

"Dinna demand, Oliver," the doctor said in mild reproof. "As it turned out, this inquiry was a matter for military law."

"Milit'ry law!" the constable exclaimed. "On what grounds, for pity's sake?"

Indeed, on what grounds? the collector echoed internally, both surprised and discomfited. *On grounds of espionage? How much of the truth could Sheridan possibly have discovered in the short time he had been here, and how? Or had Firefly betrayed their plan very early in the game?* In that case, perhaps *he* was now the object of Sheridan's attention. The collector was not a man given to unwarranted worry, but the thought was not a pleasant one.

The doctor went on as if the constable had not spoken. "Sin' Lord Sheridan is in command o' th' troops currently stationed on th' estate, he took on the investigation. I examined his orders an' am satisfied that he acted within his authority. Further, being privy tae th' details o' his investigation, I am prepared, in my official capacity as coroner, tae support his actions." He raised his eyes and looked straight at the constable. "O' course, Oliver, if ye're not satisfied wi' my explanation, ye're free tae take up the matter with yer chief superintendent. I should tell ye, though, that McNaughton has already approved Lord Sheridan's taking on the inquiry."

The collector finished his drink and turned away. The doctor's explanation might convince the constable, but it did not convince him. The fact that Sheridan had appeared on the scene confirmed his fear that the operation had been exposed. Clearly, someone at the highest level knew about the events of the past few days and wanted them hidden from public view. But who? And how much of the truth was known? His eyes went to the King's photograph next to the mirror. King Edward, whom the Kaiser had once called "that great deceiver"? Surely not, but—

"I doubt I'll ever get at the truth o' the matter," the constable said bitterly. With a shrug that suggested utter defeat, he turned to the bar. "I'll hae another whiskey, Thomas. A double."

CHAPTER THIRTY-THREE

Gloucester: All ports I'll bar; the villain shall not 'scape . . .
besides, his picture I will send far and near, that all the king-
dom may have due note of him.

King Lear, II, i
William Shakespeare

Five minutes later, the ballad collector was on his way up the deserted street, and, since there was no one to see that he had lost his limp, was walking fast. It was nearly nine now, but the way ahead was silvered, for the sky was cloudless and the moon that had been so elusive the night before shone brightly enough to illuminate his path. He had gone past the tobacconist shop and was approaching the green-grocery, when a man stepped out of the shadows and spoke to him.

"Good evening, Herr Hauptmann. I see that our paths have crossed again. May I accompany you back to the camp at Roundyhill?"

The collector felt as if he had sustained an electric shock. He turned to face a man as tall as he, with strong features, a brown beard, and shadowed eyes. Although he hadn't seen him since '97, his was not a face he was likely to forget or fail to recognize. It was the face of Lord Charles Sheridan.

Damn. But there was nothing for it but to brass it out. The collector set his jaw and, with all the composure he could muster, attempted a denial. "You have mistaken me, sir. I don't believe I have had the pleasure of making your acquaintance."

"Don't you remember?" Sheridan's smile was pleasant, as if they were indeed merely renewing a casual association. "The last time we saw one another was several years ago on the south coast, near Rottingdean. You lost your luggage in a storm that night, as I recall, for it was found washed up on the beach a day or two later, along with pieces of your skiff. But you obviously caught your ship and came through all right."

Hauptmann managed a rueful chuckle. That night had been one of the more unpleasant of his life, and he did not like to be reminded of it. "Ah, yes, indeed," he said, abandoning the pretense of forgetfulness. "Rather a trying experience, that. The seas were higher than I anticipated, and I was fortunate to escape drowning." He swung his cane as they walked, making an effort at jauntiness. "A surprise to see you, Sheridan. What brings you to Scotland? A bit of a grouse hunt?"

"The same thing that has brought you, I should think," Sheridan replied. "A hunt, but not for grouse." He paused and added, reassuringly, "Not to worry, Hauptmann, I shan't have you arrested. That would be deuced embarrassing for both sides, wouldn't it?"

Hauptmann gave an abrupt, ironic laugh. "Good of you, Sheridan. What do you want of me?"

"Oh, just an opportunity to say good-bye before you leave." There was a smile in Sheridan's voice. "And I thought perhaps you might like to ask me a question or two."

Hauptmann let the silence lengthen. At last he gave voice to his most pressing uncertainty. "Was it Lord Osborne who died in the ice house fire?"

"Without a doubt," Sheridan replied promptly. "Of course, the body was badly burnt. But he was positively identified by the doctor. His sister also recognized the gold ring on his finger as one she had given him. She is carrying the sad news to the family." He slid Hauptmann a sideways glance. "You knew, of course, that the Princess was here."

"Yes," Hauptmann admitted. "I saw her come and watched her leave, late this afternoon." He reflected for a moment and then said, rather diffidently. "I don't suppose you would be willing to tell me what has become of Herman Memsdorff."

"Firefly?" Sheridan pushed his lips in and out. "I was told that he is returning to Bavaria, with his cousin Flora. I think both of them were rather unhappy about the death of her mother. An unpleasant bit of business, for all concerned."

"I . . . see," Hauptmann said slowly. "Am I to suppose, then, that you won him over to your side?"

"To our side?" Sheridan's eyebrows were astonished. "Why, whatever makes you think of such a thing?"

Hauptmann sighed. "If you had, I don't suppose you would be willing to tell me."

"No more than you would tell me that you were responsible for the drowning of Douglas Hamilton," Sheridan agreed.

Hauptmann's smile was thin. "Just so. I am willing to assert, however, that I most definitely did *not* write his suicide note."

"I did not believe you had," Sheridan said with a little shrug. He smiled. "Any other questions?" When Hauptmann did not immediately answer, he went on. "I thought perhaps you might be wondering what gave you away."

Was the man a mind-reader? "Yes, rather," Hauptmann acknowledged. Now that they were discussing the matter, he might as well try to learn what had caused the plan to fail, so he could take steps to prevent such a thing from happening in future. "Did Firefly betray me? Or did you deduce it from some other source?"

Sheridan made a face, appearing somewhat embarrassed. "Actually, it was my wife."

"Your wife!"

"You remember her then, do you?"

Hauptmann grimaced. "The lady who took my photograph on the beach at Rottingdean." He stopped abruptly. "Damn! She was the woman who took my picture this morning!"

"I do apologize," Sheridan said regretfully. "She is a bit . . . impulsive, I fear." He reached into his jacket pocket and took out a photo. "She asked me to give this to you, with her compliments. And to remind you of that passage from the second act of *Lear*. 'His picture I will send far and near, that all the kingdom may have due note of him.'" He paused. "In fact, I think our Secret Service folk will be able to put Lady Sheridan's photograph to good use. It is something for you to consider, Hauptmann, the next time you plan a little job in England."

Hauptmann pocketed the photo. "Your wife," he said dryly, "is quite a remarkable woman."

"She is. And I am a lucky man." Sheridan stopped and put out his hand. "I don't believe that I shall walk all the way to Roundyhill with you after all, so I'll say good night here."

Hauptmann shook the proferred hand. The grip was firm

and decisive, like the man. "I suppose," he said wryly, "that things have turned out for the best."

"I suppose," Sheridan agreed. "It's too bad that Prince Eddy is dead, of course, but if you'd got him, he would have proven as great an embarrassment to the Kaiser as he was to the Royal Family. He was, after all, the Kaiser's first cousin."

"And the Kaiser is quite as mad as the Prince," Hauptmann said reflectively. Yes, things had turned out for the best, although he would now have to account to Holstein for his failure.

"You will probably want to delay your departure until dawn," Sheridan said. "By then, I'll have withdrawn the troops who are cordoning off the area. You're headed to the coast, to Arbroath, I assume, and your ship."

"Yes, right." Hauptmann sighed again, wishing that Firefly had not been quite so forthcoming. "Well, then, good night. And good-bye."

Sheridan turned and struck off in the direction of the castle. When he had disappeared from sight, Hauptmann went on his way. If he got off at dawn, he could be at the coast by sunset. He would not have to keep the ship waiting.

CHAPTER THIRTY-FOUR

Saturday, 17 August 1901

O, what a tangled web we weave
When first we practice to deceive.

Marmion
Sir Walter Scott

Charles pulled on the reins. The horse stopped, and the swaying lantern hung at one side of the gig cast shifting shadows on the Dundee Road. While he had anticipated the encounter, he was still startled by the dark shapes that materialized out of the chilly mist and darkness, Enfield rifles at port arms. He felt Kate stiffen beside him on the seat, as they heard the distinctive sounds of cartridges being chambered and locked and the command, "Halt! Who goes there?"

Charles took a deep breath. "Brigadier Lord Sheridan." He turned and called over his shoulder, to the driver of the gig behind him. "Hold up, Andrew."

Another command, from the direction of the guard post. "Step down and advance to be recognized!"

Charles handed the reins to Kate and climbed down from the gig. He took several steps toward the figures, one of them holding up a lantern and turning up the wick. The flickering light pushed back the darkness as a young corporal studied Charles's face.

"Blimey!" he exclaimed. "What's your lordship doin' on the road at this God-forsaken hour?"

"It will be getting light soon," Charles observed mildly. "Any traffic to or from Dundee during the night?"

"Not since we relieved the last watch." The corporal nodded toward Charles's gig and the other, indistinctly outlined in the swirling mist. " 'Cept for the two o' you, o'course."

"For the record, Corporal, you haven't seen anything on this watch—and that includes both of these vehicles and their passengers." Charles waited for the young man to grasp his meaning. "Do you understand?"

"Yes, sir. I am to report no traffic on our watch." The corporal stood to attention, his eyes averted, as Charles beckoned, and the second gig drove slowly past, with Kirk-Smythe at the reins and two cloaked passengers in the seat behind him. It halted some distance down the road.

"Very good, Corporal," Charles said. Smiling, he put his hands into his coat pockets. "I expect you'll be happy to know that you're going back to London in the morning."

"Yes, sir," the corporal replied. "Don't s'pose there's much point in guarding the roads now that Lord Osborne's dead. Pity, that. Him burnin' up and all."

"Yes, a pity. But accidents happen, and things don't always turn out as they're planned. You've all done your duty splendidly, though. And the bicycles have certainly proved themselves." That was a by-product of this mission, at least according to Paddington, who was planning to report that bicycles would decidedly enhance infantry mobility. Charles stepped back out of the circle of lantern light. "Stand fast, Corporal. I'll just be a minute."

Kirk-Smythe was dressed in civilian clothes and wearing his tan mackintosh and wool cap. "All clear?" he asked in a low voice.

"All clear," Charles said. He held out his hand, and Kirk-Smythe leaned down to clasp it. "This is where we part, Andrew. The three of you should have no trouble making the early train to Glasgow. From there you can easily get a boat northward, to Skye."

From the rear of the gig, Prince Eddy spoke. "Thank you, Charles," he said in a muffled voice. "You'll tell my father, won't you, that I was forced to go on account of the Germans? I shouldn't want him to think that I was deliberately disobeying him by leaving Glamis."

"I'll tell him," Charles promised. "No doubt you'll be hearing from him soon."

"Oh, no doubt," the Prince said with heavy sarcasm. "Although I rather think Papa would prefer to believe Toria's account of things." His laugh was bitter. "I am the only member of the family who has died twice, who has his own funeral monument, and yet refuses to be buried. He won't know how to cope with the idea that I am still alive." He laughed again, sadly now. "I don't know how to cope with it either, come to that."

Charles did not quite know how to answer, and turned instead to the second passenger. The hood of her cloak had fallen back, and her dark hair curled damply around her rosy cheeks. "I trust you will have a safe journey, Flora. Captain Kirk-Smythe will take good care of you."

"Thank you, m'lord," Flora said, and in her clear voice Charles could hear her eagerness to be gone. He didn't wonder at it. There was little left at Glamis to hold her here, unless she cared more than she seemed to for Constable

Graham. A new life waited ahead, on the Isle of Skye or wherever her journey took her.

Charles turned back to Kirk-Smythe. "Safe passage, Andrew. Contact me when you're back in London."

"I will," Kirk-Smythe replied. He hesitated, then lowered his voice, speaking almost in a whisper. "I can't say, Sheridan, that I'm entirely comfortable with the idea of letting Hauptmann slip away. We'll surely see more of the fellow."

"I don't doubt it," Charles agreed. "But we needed someone to carry the tale back to the Wilhelmstrasse. And better the spy we know than the spy we don't." He stepped back and raised his hand. "The sun will be up shortly. Best be on your way."

Kirk-Smythe nodded, lifted the reins, and they were gone, into the misty pre-dawn dark.

Back at the guard post, the corporal snapped to attention and saluted without a word. Charles touched his cap and climbed into the gig, where Kate was waiting.

As Charles settled himself beside her, Kate pulled on the right rein and chirruped to the horse, so that they began to turn in a circle, heading back to the castle by the way they had come. Driving, they were silent, the only sound the clip-clop of the horse's hoofs, muffled by the road dust. Then Charles chuckled.

"Something's funny?" Kate asked. She herself had thought the moment sad, saying good-bye to Flora and Prince Eddy, knowing that she and Charles would probably never see them again.

"Not funny, perhaps," Charles replied. "It still seems odd, being saluted again—and for the last time, I hope. My second term of military service is about to come to an end."

His voice became mildly ironic. "No more distinguished than the first, I should say."

Kate glanced at him. The light from the swaying lantern, shadowing his forehead and cheek, made him look younger than his forty-one years, and more boyish. And yet no trick of light or time could alter or obscure the wit in that face, or its intelligence. He turned, catching her watching him, and smiled, lifting his hand to tuck a stray curl under her wool cloche.

She returned the smile. "So it's almost over?"

"I'm afraid not, my dear," he replied ruefully. " 'The Great Game', as our friend Kipling calls it, will never be over. Not while England is of any account in the community of nations."

She thought about that for a moment. With an increasingly competitive Germany across the North Sea, with the world seeming to shape itself away from the secure past of Queen Victoria and toward an insecure future that held both titanic opportunity and enormous peril, the Great Game might take on an even greater importance. She shivered at the thought, for she did not like to imagine Charles as a spy, or involved in any sort of espionage. But she had to acknowledge that she could not keep him from doing what he felt he must.

"What time will you be leaving for Hamburg?" she asked.

"On the ten-fifteen train," Charles replied, with a sigh that told her that he was not anxious to go. "Andrew has sent a coded telegram through Whitehall, letting the King know that Eddy is alive and well and that he should disregard the tale that Toria will tell him when she arrives. When I get there, I'll give him the whole story, including the German espionage business and my reasons for sending

Eddy off to Skye. He can decide what—if anything—he wants to tell the rest of the Royals."

Kate knew that Charles had debated with himself about the wisdom of dispatching Eddy to Skye. But the Mac-Donalds' letter to Hilda had extended an open invitation to visit whenever it was convenient. And Kate had pointed out that not only was Flora anxious to see her grandparents, but that island might offer a greater security for Eddy. He had agreed.

Kate reached down to tuck the lap robe over her feet. It might be August, but they were driving into the wind. "Do you think the King will allow Toria and the rest of the family to go on believing that Eddy is dead?"

"It would be far safer, in my opinion," Charles replied. "The more people who know that the Prince is alive and where he is living, the greater the opportunity for discovery. And since Toria and George are the only members of the family to have visited Eddy in the last several years, the others will not be likely to miss him." His voice was nearly expressionless, but Kate shared the moral judgment she knew he was feeling. Was it an innate characteristic of royalty to discount the value of human feeling, or did this particular Royal Family have a special skill in this regard?

They were passing through the silent village, all the inhabitants still asleep and the houses dark, except for the baker's house and the bakery behind it, where the lights were burning and the morning's bread was already in the ovens. To the east, the sky was growing light, and dawn was beginning to break.

"I certainly hope that Hauptmann accepted the story of Eddy's death," Kate remarked as they came up to the checkpoint at the castle gate. "If he didn't, the Germans are likely to try again."

Charles lifted his hand to the guard as they passed. "I'm confident that he did, Kate, and that he accepted the idea that Firefly betrayed him." He paused as they followed the road's turning into the dark wood. "Even if he suspects the truth, he may decide that it's better to report that Prince Eddy died in that fire. Given Eddy's history, it's certainly a credible story. And it will cover Hauptmann's failure here, so he won't have to own up to the fact that his own little game was discovered." He turned and smiled at her, the amusement glinting in his eyes. "And he certainly won't mention that photograph you took of him. If the Wilhelm-strasse knew of it, his value as a spy would be compromised, even destroyed."

Somewhere in the woods, an owl called softly. Kate was silent for a moment. "Hilda's death was a tragedy," she said at last, "but if she hadn't surprised Memsdorff and Hamilton, their plan might well have succeeded. They would have returned, snatched Eddy, and handed him over to Hauptmann."

"That's right," Charles agreed, "although that probably doesn't console Flora."

Kate was silent for a moment, the reins loose in her gloved hands. "I wish I could look into the future and see what lies ahead for Flora and Eddy."

"I'm sure they will both be all right on Skye—for a time, at least," Charles said. "Flora will be well looked after, certainly. The King values loyalty, and when he fully understands the situation, he will reward her handsomely." He chuckled dryly. "Eddy isn't likely to be left in her care for very long, however. Even though he's no longer in the succession, the Crown is bound to look with disfavor on his involvement with women below his station. And he is, after all, still married to Annie Crook. The poor creature was alive, the last I heard of her, in one of the London work-houses, not fit for even unskilled labor."

Kate felt a darkening sadness. "So what *will* become of Eddy?"

"After Skye?" Charles sighed heavily. "He'll be well looked after, in a different way. Another castle, probably even more remote than Glamis. Another family of keepers, perhaps less hospitable and more restrictive than the Strath-mores. I doubt that his future will be any happier than his past."

Kate gave a little laugh, and Charles glanced at her. "Now, it's your turn. What have I said that's funny?"

"Oh, I was just wondering," she replied carelessly. "What would you do if someone actually asked to see that suicide note Hamilton is supposed to have left?"

Charles smiled. "You're not charging me with manufac-turing evidence, are you? That's a criminal offense, Kate."

"Well . . ." Kate said, with an arch of her eyebrows. "Did you?"

Charles gave a little shrug. "I'm afraid I did. It wasn't hard, and I'm not likely to be found out, since no one has ever seen a sample of his handwriting. I printed it out on an envelope that was directed to him, which I found in his room. The coroner now has the envelope in his possession—just in case someone asks to inspect it."

"Then Hamilton really didn't kill Hilda?"

"Or himself. Hauptmann took care of Hamilton, I be-lieve, although I can't prove it. But I can prove that Ham-ilton killed Memsdorff."

Kate smiled. "You seem very sure of that, m'lord."

"I am. I discovered a thirty-two-caliber revolver in Ham-ilton's room, with his fingerprints on it. In the ice house, I found Herman Memsdorff dead of a gunshot wound in the chest, with powder burns that suggested that the muzzle was in contact with the victim when the gun was fired. I extracted the fatal bullet—also a thirty-two-caliber. When I test-fired a bullet and examined it under Dr. Ogilvy's microscope, I was able to determine that it had identical lands and grooves as that of the bullet recovered from the body. My guess is that the two men fell into a quarrel, and that Hamilton shot Memsdorff, either deliberately or accidentally. I'm also guessing that it happened shortly after Eddy escaped from the ice house, and it was that shot he heard."

"If Hamilton didn't kill Hilda," Kate said quietly, "then it must have been Memsdorff—her nephew." Somehow, that made the murder seem even more horrific to her. She was glad that Flora was able to resist the idea so adamantly. It would do her no good to know the truth.

"It was Memsdorff who killed Hilda, all right," Charles said. "I found a folding knife in his pocket. There was blood residue between the blade and the knife case. If Dr. Landsteiner could analyze the residue and compare it to Hilda's blood, I'm sure he would tell us that they are both of the same type."

Kate laughed shortly. "That wouldn't mean much in a court of law—or the fingerprint evidence, either. A jury wouldn't know what to make of either one."

They came out of the woods and into the wide, green park. Ahead of them rose the ancient castle, its turrets silhouetted against the starry western sky, its mullioned windows reflecting the first rosy hints of the eastern dawn, ribbons of fog twisting and curling around its walls. The clock in the tower struck five. Somewhere in the distance, a rooster crowed, and off to the left, they could hear the rustling and cooing of pigeons in the dovecot at the edge of the park.

Charles rested his arm across the back of the seat, behind Kate. "Fortunately," he said, "this case will never go to a jury."

"And a good thing, too," Kate replied, frowning. "You'd never be able to explain why you set fire to the straw in the ice house, with Herman Memsdorff's corpse still inside." She lifted the reins, and the horse stepped faster. "What in the world would you have done if Toria had insisted on seeing her brother's dead body? She would have known immediately that it was not Eddy who had died, wouldn't she?"

Charles turned on the seat to face her. "How could she insist?" he asked with an innocent expression. "We all know that Eddy is buried in the Memorial Chapel at Windsor Castle, under a piece of massive marble statuary erected to commemorate his death."

Kate laughed shortly. "I hope the King will approve of what you've done here."

"If he doesn't," Charles replied, "perhaps he won't send us on any more of these absurd adventures." He shook his head. "Sometimes one wonders," he said soberly.

"Wonders what?"

"What would happen if the people knew the truth behind the myths and illusions of the Crown." He sighed. "Doesn't bear thinking about, I suppose."

"No, it doesn't," Kate said. She looked up at the gilded turrets of Glamis Castle. "Especially on such a beautiful morning."

AUTHORS' NOTE

So long as poetry, romance, religion, have a place in Scottish life and character, the Castle of dim memories, of secrets and haunting shadows, crowned with the beauty and dignity of years, will win men's hearts by a mysterious fascination, and stir them to their very depths.

Reverend John Stirton

The role of Glamis Castle in Scottish history is a fascinating one. The castle is justly famous, not only for its remarkable physical beauty of architecture and setting, but because it is peopled with famous phantoms. Some are the ghosts of historic personages: Macbeth; Mary, Queen of Scots; the Old Pretenders (James VIII and III); Bonnie Prince Charlie; Daniel Defoe; Thomas Gray; Sir Walter Scott. Others are more illusory: the Monster of Glamis, the Gray Lady, Earl Beardie, and various wraiths who flit through the halls at night. It is also the ancestral home of the much-loved Queen Mother Elizabeth, whom you met as little Lady Elizabeth of Glamis in this book. She is 101 years old at this writing, and (true to the gypsy's prophesy), Queen and mother of a Queen.

There is no concrete evidence, however, that Glamis Castle was ever the residence of an exiled Prince Albert Victor—and no evidence, either, that Prince Eddy lived past the official date of his death in 1892. It is true that news of Eddy's death was sudden, unexpected, and fortuitous, and that it was the subject of much rejoicing among those who saw him as entirely unfit for monarchy. It is also true that there have been others who have speculated that Eddy lived into the 1930s. What's more, a fictitious death and exile could have been easily stage-managed by Eddy's father, Bertie, the Prince of Wales, who (according to Kinley Roby, in *The King, the Press, and the People*) had long since "learned to keep before the public an image that corresponded as closely as he could make it to the myth of the ideal prince." Bertie's own scandalous shenanigans had taught him valuable lessons in deceiving the public, so the deceptions we have imagined here would not have been especially challenging. And if Eddy had lived, and if his cousin Willie had got wind of it, there is no doubt that the Kaiser would have used the information to undermine the authority of his uncle-King, whom he hated.

At this point in our series, we are entering a period in which the relationship between Britain and Germany becomes increasingly vexed by questions of political alliance, of economic rivalry, and of military dominance. International tensions have already begun to mar the tranquility of England's "splendid isolation," while domestic tensions—Home Rule for Ireland, women's rights, workers' rights, the plight of the urban poor—have already seriously disturbed the English peace. It is true that there were German spies in England in these years, and while Ludwig von Hauptmann is fictional, he had many real counterparts. About the time of this book, Erskine Childers was writing the first great spy novel, *Riddle of the Sands*, and a cloud of invasion novels and plays shadowed the literary horizon. The Brits were nervous, as well they might be, for their experience in the Boer War had been sobering and the Apocalypse of 1914–1917 was not far off.

But Glamis Castle, which has stood since the fourteenth century, would be untouched, and untouched it yet remains.

Bill and Susan Albert
Bertram, TX
December 2001

REFERENCES

Here are a few books that we found helpful in creating *Death at Glamis*. Other background works may be found in the references to earlier books in this series, particularly in *Death at Whitechapel*. If you have comments or questions, you may write to Bill and Susan Albert, PO Box 1616, Bertram, TX 78605, or E-mail us at china@tstar.net. You may also wish to visit our web site, http://www.mysterypartners.com, where you will find additional information about Glamis Castle, the family of King Edward and Queen Alexandra, and Bonnie Prince Charlie and the Forty-five.

Battiscombe, Georgina. *Queen Alexandra*, Houghton Mifflin, Boston, 1969.

Blaircowrie: Ordnance Survey of Scotland, Sheet 56, Southampton: Ordnance Survey, 1897.

Bruce, J. Collingwood. *The Hand-book of the Roman Wall*, London: Longmans, Green & Co., 1907.

Day, James Wentworth. *The Queen Mother's Family Story*, London: Robert Hale, 1967.

Deacon, Richard. *A History of the British Secret Service*, New York: Taplinger Publishing Co., 1969.

Duff, David. *Elizabeth of Glamis: The Story of the Queen Mother*, London: Magnum Books, 1977.

Harrison, Michael. *Clarence: Was He Jack the Ripper?* New York: Drake Publishers, Inc., 1972.

Massie, Robert K. *Dreadnought: Britain, Germany, and the Coming of the Great War*, New York: Random House, 1991.

Nicoll, A. R. *Glamis: A Village History*, Glamis: Glamis Publishing Group, 2000.

Shade, Harry Gordon. *Glamis Castle*, London: The Society of Antiquities of London Co., 2000.

Simpson, Colin; Lewis Chester; and David Leitch. *The Cleveland Street Affair*, Boston: Little, Brown and Company, 1976.